SOWING SECRETS

Trisha Ashley was born in St Helens, Lancashire, and gave up her fascinating but time-consuming hobbies of house-moving and divorce a few years ago in order to settle in North Wales.

For more information about Trisha please visit www.trishaashley.com.

By the same author:

A Winter's Tale
Wedding Tiers
Chocolate Wishes
Twelve Days of Christmas

TRISHA ASHLEY

Sowing Secrets

AVON

AVON
A division of HarperCollins*Publishers*
77–85 Fulham Palace Road,
London W6 8JB

www.harpercollins.co.uk

First published in Great Britain as *The Generous Gardener* by
Severn House Publishers Ltd., Surrey, 2004

This edition published in Great Britain by
HarperCollins*Publishers* 2011

3

Copyright © Trisha Ashley 2008

Trisha Ashley asserts the moral right to
be identified as the author of this work

A catalogue record for this book is
available from the British Library

ISBN-13: 978-1-84756-310-1

Set in Minion by Palimpsest Book Production Ltd,
Falkirk, Stirlingshire

Printed and bound in Great Britain by
Clays Ltd, St Ives plc

MIX
**Paper from
responsible sources**
FSC® C007454

FSC
www.fsc.org

FSC is a non-profit international organisation established to promote the
responsible management of the world's forests. Products carrying the FSC
label are independently certified to assure consumers that they come
from forests that are managed to meet the social, economic and
ecological needs of present and future generations.

Find out more about HarperCollins and the environment at
www.harpercollins.co.uk/green

I would like to thank Andrew L. Guthrie, General Manager of that glorious little paradise on earth, the Queen Elizabeth II Botanic Park, Grand Cayman, for kindly advising me on the history of rose cultivation on the island.

For Brian and Linda Long
With love

Prologue: A Seed is Sown

Lost Angel of a ruin'd Paradise!

Shelley

With a galvanic jerk Fran March opened her eyes to find herself practically nose to nose with a total stranger: a sleeping young Neptune, his lightly muscled body, carelessly disposed in sleep, green-washed by the early morning light filtering in through thin caravanette curtains.

Recoiling, she slipped from the bed, praying he wouldn't wake up, panicking as she tried to find her clothes among the clutter of a camper van that both looked and smelled like a potting shed.

This Neptune's trident was the homely gardening fork that fell over with a clatter as she struggled with the unfamiliar sliding door, almost weeping with silent frustration.

She froze as he stirred and half opened drowsy, green-flecked eyes, only to close them again and sleep on, long narrow nose pressed against the pillow, hair in improbable spirals and the darker stubble pricking out along the edge of his jaw.

The door finally opened enough to let her slip out into a world silent except for the non-judgemental birds, though, misjudging the drop, she didn't so much hit the ground running as fall to her knees in the pub car park like a penitent Pope Joan.

Altered Conceptions

'Mum, you know you've always told me that my father was a student prince who turned into a toad and hopped it when you kissed him?' Rosie asked me ominously on Boxing Day while we were watching *Who Do You Think You Are?*. Mal was safely out of the way upstairs in his study poring over his stamp collection, yearning for a Cayman Blue.

'Yes,' I agreed cautiously, the chunk of Christmas cake I had just eaten suddenly turning to stone in my stomach, though you'd think a survival instinct that sent a surge of energy to the leg muscles for a quick getaway would have been much more useful – except that Rosie had me cornered on the sofa.

She was wearing a familiarly stubborn expression, like a very serious elf maiden, all long, honey-blonde locks fronding around her slightly pointed ears and a frown above her straight brows. Her changeling green-grey eyes were fixed accusingly on mine.

'Or that other story, where you said he was Neptune disguised in human form, and he dragged you down into his sea kingdom because he'd fallen in love with you? Only you escaped, helped by friendly dolphins, and were found wandering the beach covered in seaweed next morning?'

'Mmm,' I said vaguely, though actually I was quite proud of that one – some of the details were pretty inventive, especially all the little mussel shells clapping with glee when I got away, and a desolate Neptune blowing his conch shell to summon me back every evening for a month before giving up and swimming sadly away for ever, totally conched out.

Perhaps it *was* a fishy story, at that?

My favourite was the one where her father was a gypsy king with fast flamenco fingers, cursed by an evil witch never to stay more than one night in any place. If he did, she would appear, take his Music out and shoot it. (Music was a dog.)

That one always made Rosie cry, and I had to assure her that the king never stopped more than one night in any place, because he loved Music more than anything. And so the dog lived for ever, and they were very happy travelling about in their caravan, except when he thought about the beautiful princess he had had to leave behind.

But now, seemingly, the time for fairy stories was over.

'Mum,' Rosie said sternly, 'you've never told me anything *real* about my father, and although I do know it's because you don't want to talk about it, now I'm eighteen and at university I think I have a right to know all about him, don't you?'

'Yes, darling, but there really isn't much more to tell you,' I said helplessly, because there hadn't been that many facts to embroider. He came, he went – what more could I say? 'Those stories were all variations on the truth, Rosie.'

'I've been talking about it with Granny and she says it's time you came clean, because you met my father at university in your first term and had been going out with him for two years before you got pregnant with me, so you must know all about him!'

Thank you, Ma.

'Granny is wrong: that wasn't your father,' I said shortly. 'I've never said he was.'

Mind you, I've never said he *wasn't* either, so perhaps it's not surprising that Ma, my husband and now even my daughter assumed it, and also that I never wanted to talk about it simply because he abandoned me.

And I don't want to think about him, either; why rake up old hurts?

'Well, Granny says he *must* have been, you hadn't been going out with anyone else, but when she wanted you to write and tell him you were pregnant, you refused,' she persisted.

'Because it was nothing to do with him,' I said patiently, though I suppose it was, in a way. If Tom hadn't told me it was over between us on the night of the end-of-term pub crawl and party, maybe I wouldn't have had too much to drink and ended up pregnant.

That put paid to the last year of my graphic design course, though Rosie, when she arrived was such a perfect creation that I felt I should have been allowed to submit her like a work in progress at the end of finals and get my degree anyway.

And once I set eyes on Rosie I never regretted having her, of course – except when she was giving me the third degree like now, and frowning at me as though she could extract the truth by telepathy: but only the one she wanted, a tidy truth with checkable details. A name, a face – a father.

I couldn't give her any of those things, but clearly the time had come to give her what I had; to expose the bare bones of a buried past. I knew it had to come one day.

'OK, Rosie, I'll tell you everything I remember, which isn't much – it was such a long time ago.'

I patted the sofa cushion and she plumped down, looking at me expectantly. 'This had better not be another of your fairy stories.'

'It isn't, but that doesn't mean you're going to like it any better. Granny was partly right about Tom – we did meet in my first term at university, though he was a year ahead of me. But he dumped me right at the end of my second year because he was off to Rome on an arts scholarship and didn't see me as part of his new future. It was a bit of a shock.'

That was the understatement of the year – I was devastated. He'd even given me a ring a few weeks before with 'Forever' engraved inside it, though 'For Now' would have given me more warning of his intentions.

'Poor Mum! And then you realised you were pregnant in the summer holidays?' prompted Rosie sympathetically.

'Yes, but not by Tom,' I said, quickly scotching any

6

ideas of a romantic tragedy. 'Your father was someone I met on the rebound.'

Seeing she looked totally unconvinced I elaborated. 'It was like *Brief Encounter*, but with sex. All I really remember about him now were his amazing eyes – sort of hazel with green rays round the pupils, and a lovely warm, deep, comforting voice.'

There had to have been *something* compelling about him at the time, or I wouldn't have gone off with him like that, even on the rebound and far from sober, would I?

'Come on, Mum, you can't expect me to believe that! You? A one-night stand? Per-lease!' she said scathingly. 'And after everything you've told *me* about safe sex and loving relationships?'

'Because I didn't want you to make the same mistakes I did,' I said, though I suppose if it hadn't led to pregnancy I would have conveniently forgotten the whole Midsummer Night's madness – or put a romantic gloss on it.

'Why does even Mal think it was this Tom, then?'

'He just assumed it, like Granny, since it's not an episode I ever wanted to discuss, even if it did mean I had you, darling, which I've never regretted in the slightest. And please don't bring the subject up when he's about, will you? It's all best forgotten.'

Mal is the jealous kind, so one previous lover seemed as much as he could take when we were at the true-confessions stage of our relationship. Mind you, although I didn't tell him who Rosie's father was – or wasn't – my words circled in an endless holding pattern around this perfectly obvious gaping hole in my narrative, and he never once asked the question.

Rosie had got up and was wandering restlessly about, scowling. 'But if you *are* telling the truth this time, Mum, then you can tell me *something* about my real father, can't you? You did at least know who he was? Didn't you want to tell him about me?'

She came back across the room, a paler, taller version of myself at her age, as though her father had been a ghost, which for all I could remember of him he might well have been. I mean, in eighteen years I've nearly convinced myself that there was no second party involved, so Rosie's was practically a born-again virgin birth: she's mine, all mine.

'So what was he called? Where did you meet him? What did he look like?'

'I . . . can't remember,' I said uncomfortably, but I could see I wasn't going to be allowed off the hook until I'd given her more than that. 'He was just passing through the town and we picked him up in a pub somewhere and took him on to the end-of-term party with us. We'd all had a lot to drink. He said his name was Adam, and he was a gardener, but that's about all I know about him.'

'And you expect me to believe that?' she said angrily.

'Well, *I* did. And he had an old camper van,' I added, though that's one of the details I have allowed to go fuzzy over the years . . . except that sometimes I wake up with a thumping heart in an absolute panic, thinking I'm back in the damned thing and trying to creep out before the stranger I've spent the night with wakes up.

8

(And it smelled like a potting shed, come to that, so perhaps he really was a gardener, generous with his seed. But let's leave the analogy there before I start to feel like a Gro-bag.)

'Mum, you could at least tell me the truth, and not fob me off with yet more fairy stories!' she said vehemently. 'A camper van!'

'I have, Rosie,' I said, getting up and giving her a hug, which she endured rather than returned. 'I have told you the truth, and if I knew more details I'd tell you those too. But I love you, and Granny loves you – isn't that enough?'

I didn't include Mal, fond as he is of her in his way, for the relationship's always been tinged with mutual jealousy, though things are better now that Rosie's away during term-time studying veterinary science. But she's always spent a lot of time with her granny anyway, since Mal is not a pet lover, and so most of her menageric stayed with Ma after we married, something I'm not sure she's ever quite forgiven him for.

Mal's footsteps sounded upstairs and Rosie said quickly, 'I wish I knew if you were telling me the truth this time!'

'Rosie, I'm sorry if it's not what you wanted to hear, but that's what really happened,' I assured her. (And how *did* I come to have such a bossy little cow for a daughter?) 'And by the time I knew I was pregnant there was no way to find out more – no means of tracing him. I never even knew his second name.'

'You must have talked to each other!'

'Yes, but we had both drunk an awful lot, don't

forget,' I said patiently. 'I don't remember what we talked about, but he must have been really nice or I wouldn't have gone back with him. I was only horrified next morning when I was sober, because I thought I still loved Tom.'

'But if Tom was your boyfriend, why are you so sure he's not my father?' she demanded.

On any list of twenty questions you didn't want your daughter to ask, this would come fairly high up.

'I just am . . . And although I wasn't on the pill, we always took precautions.'

'Accidents happen,' she pointed out. I hope she doesn't know this from experience, but am not about to ask her while she is interrogating me. Or even at all.

'Well they didn't,' I said firmly, though I couldn't put my hand on my heart and truthfully say that I was one hundred per cent sure that Rosie wasn't Tom's baby, because we might have got a little slapdash with the contraception towards the end of our affair . . . 'And don't think I didn't try and convince myself that you were Tom's, because I did – but I'm positive you're not.'

She changed tack with disconcerting suddenness. 'You could tell me something about this Tom Collins, though – like, why his parents called him after a drink?'

'Collin*ge*, not Collins!' I said. 'And why do you want to talk about him? It's pointless – what's past is past. We're happy *now*, aren't we? That's the important thing.'

This was rhetorical: no teenager is ever going to admit to being happy, it's not in the job description.

10

Mal came in, the tall, dark and handsome answer to any almost-maiden's prayer, except for the thunderous frown, and snapped, 'Rose, your phone's been going off every five minutes in your bedroom – can't you hear it? And why must it play such loud, irritating music?'

Rosie gave him her best 'you're speaking a dead language, you fossil' glare. 'Why didn't you tell me before?' she demanded indignantly, and dashed off.

It was probably one of the boyfriends she prefers not to tell us about, though why they have to be a deep, dark secret I don't know. Perhaps they vanish if exposed to the light of parental inspection.

I could feel the twitchings of an idea for a new cartoon coming on – or perhaps one of my Alphawoman comic strips. Something involving vampires and unsuitable boyfriends . . . But before I could pin it down Mal jerked me back into reality by demanding, '*When* did you say she was going back to university, Fran? And why does she have to be so untidy? The place is like a pigsty!'

The newborn inspiration turned its face to the wall and died; I do hate these sudden transitions from my out-of-body experiences. And 'untidy' was two abandoned magazines and a scatter of rose catalogues on the floor and an empty glass on the coffee table's otherwise pristine surface. Pigs should be so lucky.

'She takes after me and Ma: chaos comes naturally to us. And she's going back to university on the fourth, after my birthday,' I sighed. 'I *do* miss her when she's gone.'

'Well, you've got me,' he pointed out jealously.

'Not for girlie chats, though, and you're off on that six-week contract the day after Rosie leaves,' I said.

Mal is something clever with computers, so he often works away troubleshooting. I might have added that even when he *is* home he is either up in his study messing about with his stamps, or down at the marina with his boat, but I didn't want to seem to be complaining. It's not like his hobbies are gambling, binge drinking and loose women, is it?

'We'll be able to keep in touch by email now too,' I reminded him, for his surprise Christmas present to me had been the creation of the Fran March Rose Art website, which was very thoughtful of him. Rosie has promised to get me confidently surfing and emailing before she goes back to university, having much more patience with beginners than Mal, and I am to have a designated workspace under the stairs, with his old computer.

Truth to tell, I don't mind Mal's absences that much once he has actually gone, since not only do I actually like being alone, but I have lots of work to get on with out in my studio. Right now I need to finish off the illustrations for my third annual Fran March Rose Calendar, because the deadline is the end of January, and I still have December and the cover illustration to go.

And oh, the bliss of slumping into comfortable, guilt-free slovenliness! The effort of constantly maintaining the level of household standards Mal increasingly favours would be beyond me even if I tried, which

I don't, apart from token gestures, but I'd had a pre-Christmas blitz and everything still looked pretty clean. But then, *my* idea of a hygienic and tidy home is merely one where the health inspectors don't slap skull-and-crossbones Hazard stickers on the bathroom and kitchen doors on a weekly basis, while *his* is the domestic equivalent of an operating theatre.

'Do you want to go out for a walk before it gets dark?' I asked hopefully. 'We always used to go for a long hike on Boxing Day.'

'No, I think I'll watch that tall ships DVD you got me for Christmas again,' he said, and, while I was glad that my present had found favour, it occurred to me that we were leading increasingly separate lives. I expect it makes a marriage healthy not being on top of each other all the time, but I do miss the long country walks we used to take together before he got boatitis. And while nothing would induce me to get on something that can go up and down, or side to side – or even both at once – without any warning, at least it gives him a bit of fresh air and exercise when he is at home between contracts, playing doll's houses on his *petit bateau*, *Cayman Blue*, down at the marina.

Oh, well, not only have I got Mal and my beloved Rosie home and still speaking to each other, but Ma's coming down to Fairy Glen (her cottage in the village) for a few days, so we can all be together for my birthday on the third: what more could I want?

I curled up next to him on the sofa, and after a couple of minutes he noticed I was there and put his arm around me. He smelled like a million dollars, which is about what I paid for that aftershave: worth every penny.

'Fran, you're singing "I Got You Babe",' he pointed out accusingly, as though I was doing something anti-social – which perhaps, considering my voice, I was. I never know I'm doing it unless I'm out somewhere and a space clears all around me as if by magic.

'Sorry,' I said, 'I'm just feeling happy.'

And let's not forget mega relieved too: I'd managed to get through the tricky question-and-answer session with Rosie that I'd known had to come one day, and I thought it had gone quite well, considering.

Must remember to disillusion Ma too.

An Unconsidered Trifle

Although relations between them were a little strained by my birthday, Mal and Rosie still hadn't seriously fallen out with each other, which must have been a record – though I think *I* might if she carries on shooting questions at me about her father at unexpected moments, as if trying to catch me out.

The mud at the bottom of the once limpid pool of my memory has been stirred with a big stick, so that when she suddenly shoots at me, 'How tall was Adam?' up to the surface bobs the reply, 'Oh, well over six foot,' without a second's pause.

'What colour was Adam's hair?'

'Like dark clover honey.'

'What was Adam's last name?'

'No idea.'

'What colour was the camper van?'

'Blue and white.'

'What on earth were you drinking?'

'Rough scrumpy cider.'

However, I have now run out of answers so she has given up, thank goodness, and even Rosie can see that

I can hardly put an ad in the press saying, 'Did you have a one-night stand nearly twenty years ago with a slender woman of medium height, with grey eyes and long, wavy, strawberry-blonde hair? If so, please answer this ad for news that may interest you.'

Of course, had I known what the outcome would be, I would have noted Adam the gardener's full name and address at the very least. Mind you, had I known the outcome I wouldn't have done it in the first place – but then I wouldn't have had my beloved and infuriating daughter, would I?

She was now packing for her return to university the next day, and I kept missing items of clothing, like my Gap T-shirt and good leather belt. Also several pots of home-made jam and two bottles of elderflower champagne.

Ma, fresh back from her seasonal visit to Aunt Beth up in Scotland, had arrived at her cottage with the dogs and was coming round later for birthday tea, bringing the cake, Tartan Shortbread and a litre of Glenmorangie.

I crooned 'This Could Be Heaven' along with my inner Walkwoman.

'You sound amazingly cheerful for someone on her fortieth birthday,' Mal observed, tidying up the wrapping paper from the present opening and disposing of it, neatly folded, in the wastepaper basket.

At any minute he would be pointedly positioning the vacuum cleaner somewhere I'd fall over it, I could see it coming, but I'm not cleaning anything today . . . or tomorrow, or the day after, come to that. Cleaning's rightful place is as a displacement activity while you are psyching yourself up for something more interesting.

I smiled happily from under the brim of the unseasonal straw gardening hat, adorned with miniature hoes and rakes and even a tiny scarecrow, sent by my Uncle Joe in Florida. 'Of course I am! I've got everything I could possibly need right here in St Ceridwen's Well, haven't I? A handsome husband, a lovely daughter, modest success with my work – especially now I'm selling more cartoons as well as my illustrations – *and* we live in North Wales, the most beautiful place in the world. What else could I want?'

He suggested mildly, 'To lose a little weight?'

That deflated my happiness bubble a trifle, as you can imagine . . . though thinking of trifle fortunately reminded me that I must pop out and decorate mine with whipped cream, slivered almonds and hundreds and thousands.

Rosie came in, carefully carrying a tray with coffee and some of the yummy Continental biscuits covered in thick dark chocolate that had come in the hen-shaped ceramic biscuit barrel that was her present to me. This, together with microwave noodles, is about the extent of her catering skills, but still one up on Mal, who doesn't even seem able to find the kettle unaided.

She cast him an unloving look, evidently having caught his comment. 'You aren't hounding poor Mum about her weight on her *birthday*, are you? And there's nothing wrong with her – she's perfect, just like Granny. Cosy.'

'Thank you, darling,' I said to her doubtfully, 'but cosy isn't quite the image I want to project.' It sounded a bit mumsy, and though Ma isn't fat, she's pretty well rounded. Good legs, though, both of us.

'Well, *I* certainly don't want an anorexic mother, all bones and embarrassing miniskirts! You're just right – plump and curvy. No one would think you were forty, honestly,' she added anxiously.

Clearly forty was something to be dreaded, only it didn't feel like that to me. Or it hadn't until then. And of course I had noticed that I was a bit plumper, because I'd had to buy bigger jeans, though T-shirts stretch to infinity and all the tops I make myself for special occasions are quite loose caftan-style ones, so they're still fine. (The one I had on today was made from the good fragments of two tattered old silk kimonos pieced together using strips of the crochet lace that Ma endlessly produces, dyed deep smoky blue.)

'When I first met your mother at the standing stones up in the woods above the glen, she was so slender she could have been a fairy,' Mal said, smiling reminiscently, and Rosie made a rude retching noise.

'Well, nobody loves a fairy when she's forty,' I said briskly, hurt by all this sudden harping on about how I used to look.

'*I* do,' Mal said with one of his sudden and rather devastating smiles, and for him this was the equivalent of declaring his affections in skywriting, so I was deeply touched, even when he added, 'Though you'd probably feel healthier for getting a few pounds off, Fran. Perhaps you need more exercise.'

'She gets lots of exercise gardening,' Rosie pointed out, which I do, because it is my passion, though only *selective* gardening; soon after I conceived Rosie, I also conceived a passion for all things rose. Very strange. But Rosie should just be grateful it wasn't lupins or gladioli. Or dahlias. Dahlia March? I don't think she'd ever have forgiven me for that one.

Most of my Christmas and birthday presents had a horticultural theme – or a hen one, for in the absence of any pets after Rosie's old dog, Tigger, died we have had to love the hens instead.

This year I also got some garden tokens and I desperately want to use them to get a Constance Spry, even though everyone says they are terrible for mildew – but where could I put it? Would it do well in a tub on the patio? And would Mal notice my roses were impinging on his bit of the garden?

There were some non-rose related presents too. My friend Nia, a potter, gave me the delicate and strange porcelain earrings (and Mickey Mouse wristwatch) I am wearing now, and Carrie at the teashop had left a pot of her own honey on the doorstep, tied up in red and white checked gingham with pinked edges and a big raffia bow. Oh, and a mosaic kit from Ma's elderly cousin Georgie, who has it fixed in her head that I am perpetually adolescent. (She could be right.)

Mal gave me a travel pack of expensive, rose-scented toiletries (although I hardly ever go anywhere), and a storage box covered in Cath Kidston floral fabric. I thought I would have that in my studio to store odds and ends in, of which I seem to have an awful lot, some already in boxes with helpful labels such as 'Useless short pieces of string', 'Bent nails' or 'Broken pieces of crockery'. I once kept used stamps too, but Mal has rather cornered that market.

His boat being laid up safely for the winter, once Mal had tidied the room to his satisfaction he took his coffee and headed back to his study and colourful collection of perforated paper, and Rosie and I settled down to play with my presents and eat a whole packet of biscuits between us.

But at the back of my mind the weight issue niggled at me like a sore tooth. I just couldn't leave it alone and resolved to ask Nia's advice next time I saw her because she's always on a diet, though I can never see any difference. Small, dark and solidly stocky is pretty well how she has always looked.

And although I am sorry she and Paul have just got divorced, I'm also selfishly happy to have her living back in the village (if you can call a handful of cottages with a teashop, Holy Well and pub a village).

The trouble with the idea of dieting is that food is such a pleasure to me, and so is cooking: my one successful domestic skill! It will be torment to create lovely meals for Mal, and Rosie when she's home, if I can't eat them too.

Still, you can't start a diet on your birthday, can you? And Mal loved me anyway, he'd actually come out and said so.

I found I was singing the words to '(If Paradise Is) Half as Nice', cheerful once again, because if getting fat was the only serpent in my Eden I was sure I had the power to resist.

Everything in the garden was coming up roses.

Inspiration later impelled me out through the darkening January afternoon, across Mal's tailored lawn (which I'm not having anything to do with, since a carpet that grows is just outdoor housework), and under the pergola to my studio among the chaos of frosted rose stems.

Well, I say 'studio', but it's more a glorified garden shed covered in a very rampant Mme Gregoire Staechelin (the hussy), where I do my artwork for greetings cards, calendars and anything else I can sell. I've rather cornered the rose market, in my own style, which is far removed from botanical illustration, but I find I'm doing more and more cartoons lately; they're taking over my head and my life, tapping into a dark vein of cynicism I hadn't realised I'd got until lately.

Recently I had an idea for a comic strip with a female superhero . . . Alphawoman! Most of the time she's the perfect wife, the sort of woman Mal has suddenly started holding up to me as ideal: she works full time for a huge salary yet is always there for her husband, cooks, cleans, effortlessly entertains, keeps perfect house and also fundraises for charity, while staying fit, slim, young, chic and beautiful. Just about my opposite in every way, in fact, so comparing me with these Women Who Have It All is about as fair as comparing a Blush Rambler with a Musk Buff Beauty: you get what it says on the label, and it isn't going to be a rose by any other name just to please you.

And really, this is *so* perverse of Mal, because that's the way his first wife, Alison, was heading when they got divorced and, reading between the lines, he couldn't handle it. The last straw seems to have been when she started earning more than he did and suggested she pop out a quick baby and he could be a house husband and look after it while she got on with her Brilliant Career in international banking.

But when *I* got a job soon after we were married, doing casual waitressing at Carrie's teashop in the village to pay for Rosie's riding lessons and stuff like that, he didn't like it in the least, though perhaps that was mostly because he considered it menial. And while he used to say I was scatty and dreamy as though they were lovable traits, *now* he says it accusingly.

Still, my Ms Alison Alphawoman is not quite invulnerable, because chocolate is her kryptonite, and when she comes into contact with it she turns into ... Blobwoman! A scatty, plump and dreamy sloven just like me, who's only good at cooking, painting and drawing cartoons (though actually I'm pretty brilliant at all those), but who manages to bail Alphawoman out of tricky situations anyway.

And come to think of it, I don't think I did a bad job as a mother either, once I got over the surprise. Parenting just seemed to be Rosie and me having fun together, all the way from mud pies to marrying Mal, when things hit a slight blip. But in the end it was Mal who had to adjust to the idea that my life was still going to revolve around Rosie much more than him.

I wanted to linger and play with my intriguingly Jekyll-and-Hyde Alphawoman, despite my shack being cold as the Arctic – working in a wooden shed never stopped Dylan Thomas, after all – and I could always put my little heater on if I got desperately chilly. But today, birthday revels called, and so too did my miniature seventy-seven-year-old dynamo of a mother.

'Fran! Fraaa-nie!' she shrilled.

I do wish she wouldn't.

Ma had brought my birthday cake, which she had covered entirely – yes, you've guessed! – in huge Gallica roses cunningly modelled in icing sugar. It was beautiful.

With her came an inevitable touch of chaos, for when Ma walks into a room, pictures tilt, cushions fall over and the smooth deep pile of the carpet is rubbed up the wrong way and studded with the sharp indentations of stiletto heels.

Ma had dumped a rather Little Red Riding Hood wicker basket decorated with straw flowers on the coffee table and now began to unpack whisky, shortbread, a small haggis, a bundle of the grubby crochet lace she makes when she's trying not to smoke and a DVD with a mistily atmospheric photograph of an overgrown bit of garden statuary on the cover.

'The haggis and the shortbread are from Beth and Lachlan,' she said. 'I won the DVD, thought you might like it.' Ma is forever entering competitions or firing off postcards to those 'the first five names out of the hat will receive . . .' things.

'What is it?' Rosie said, pouncing. '*Restoration Gardener*? That doesn't sound exciting!'

Ma shrugged. 'That's what I thought. I can't abide gardening programmes; gardens are for walking round, or sitting in with a drink, the rest's just muck and hard work.'

Reaching into a seriously pregnant handbag she began to pull out her cigarettes, then remembered she couldn't smoke in our house in the interests of family harmony, and produced some half-finished crochet instead.

'Well, are we having that cake? And what are we drinking the whisky out of, Mal?'

'I don't want whisky,' Rosie said. 'I'm going to make myself a cocktail with the kit Mum gave me for Christmas. Do you want one, Granny?'

'No, thanks, my love, I prefer my poison unadulterated.'

'You don't know what you're missing,' Rosie said, vanishing into the kitchen to brew her potion, which was not much different in appearance to the ones she used to concoct a few years ago when she was convinced she was a witch and could do spells. That was right after the phase when she thought she was a horse and wore holes in the carpet, pawing the ground.

Soon we were all mellow and full of alcohol and food ... except Mal, who was looking a trifle constrained and narrow-lipped, and clearly fighting the urge to fetch a dustpan and brush to the crumbs on the carpet.

Unfortunately there is always a little tension between

him and Ma, and when Rosie is there too I'm sure he feels they are ganging up on him – which they often are. Ma finds his ever-increasing obsession with tidiness and hygiene, and his refusal to allow her dogs in the house, definitely alien if not downright perverted – as do I, really, if I'm honest.

It's his one major flaw, and he hid it pretty well until we were married (being jaw-droppingly handsome is pretty good camouflage for anything); when he suddenly insisted that Rosie leave all her beloved pets behind with Ma, we were very nearly *un*married again pretty smartly until we reached a compromise whereby Rosie was allowed to bring Tigger. It was touch and go, especially once Mal realised that no matter how madly I loved him I would always love my daughter more.

It is tricky for a stepfather, but deep down Mal is very fond of Rosie, and though he *says* he never wanted children I know that is just because Alison insisted he got tested and he discovered he couldn't father any himself. And while I would have loved another baby, at least I don't have to worry about contraception!

We've all had to make tricky relationship adjustments, but generally we manage to get along in a civilised way, despite Mal's slow ossification into a finicky, short-fused old fossil, trying to attach as many expensive consumer items to his shell as possible using the superglue of credit.

Fortunately, I'm not a romantic; I know a relationship has to be worked on and that this is as close to Paradise as any woman can expect. (Now I come to think about it, it even has twin snakes-in-the grass in the form of our ghastly next-door neighbours, though frankly I could do without them! They certainly rank at the top of the list of people I would be least likely to take an apple from.)

As if on cue, Ma said, 'Those Weevils wished me a Happy New Year as I came in, Fran – they must have shot out the minute my engine stopped. What are they up to, twenty-four-hour surveillance?'

'It feels like it. I can't make a move outside without feeling watched,' I said ruefully.

'*Wevills* – and Owen is my friend!' Mal snapped. 'I'm more than happy to have good neighbours to keep an eye on things when I'm away.'

'They seem to be keeping an eye on things even when you're *not* away,' Ma pointed out. 'And maybe Fran doesn't want to live like a *Big Brother* contestant.'

'No I don't, and they may be nice to me when you're there, Mal, but it's totally different when you're not. They're entirely two-faced.'

'You're imagining things, Fran, they're lovely people and very popular in the village.'

'A man can smile and smile yet still be a villain,' Ma pointed out. 'Weevil by name and weevil by nature – you can't fool me. Did you like your *skean-dhu*?'

'What?' he said, thrown by this example of Ma's laterally leaping conversational gambits.

'The knife, for putting down your sock. Thought it would be handy for Swindon. You never know what they get up to down south.'

Even I wasn't sure whether she was joking, but when

Mal said he intended using it as a paperknife she looked entirely disgusted.

Later, Mal took himself off to the yacht club for a drink with Owen, the male Wevill, who inspired his boating passion and now frequently crews for him on *Cayman Blue*. He is small, bald-headed, wrinkled and unattractive, while his wife has a face like blobbed beige wax, a loose figure, and the hots for Mal.

Is it any wonder I don't like them?

Rosie volunteered to walk back up the lane to Fairy Glen with Ma so she could play with the dogs, and I gave in to temptation and went to check my website to see if anyone else had visited.

I am getting terribly proficient now I know how to get rid of all the things I inadvertently press, so I was soon able to see that I'd had thirty-six visitors to my site . . . though come to think of it, at least half of those were probably me.

Then I checked my email and found four messages, only three of which wanted me to grow my penis longer, buy Viagra or look at Hot Moms.

The fourth was from someone called bigblondsurf-dude@home and the subject line said, cheerily, 'Hi, Fran, how U doing?'

I dithered over that one, since I didn't think I knew any surfers or dudes, but then opened it, my finger ready on the delete button just in case it was a nasty.

And it *was* a nasty, as it happens: a nasty surprise.

Hi Fran,

Remember me?! Found your website – great photo! You don't look a day older than when I last saw you. I'm glad you're doing well up in North Wales. I'm teaching art and surfing down here in Cornwall, the best of both worlds, but I often come up to visit friends at a surfing school not too far from you, so I might drop in one of these days!

All the best,
Tom

Tom?

When old loves die they should stay decently interred, not try to come surfing back into your life.

I deleted him, but printed the message out first, and shoved it into the desk drawer, just in case. But if I didn't answer, surely he would assume he'd got the wrong Fran March?

And if I hadn't been so insistent on keeping my own name when I got married, it would have been the Fran Morgan Rose Art site and Tom would never have been able to launch this stealth attack on my memories.

Thank goodness Rosie hadn't been around to see it – she'd probably have been emailing him right back by now, asking probing questions about blood groups and stuff.

Up the Fairy Glen

Rosie went back to university, together with half the contents of my larder and selected items of my wardrobe, all packed into her red Volkswagen. She calls it Spawn of Beetle since it's much newer than mine, due to both Granny and Mal's mother being putty in her manipulative little hands.

I cried for ages after she'd gone, which, as you can imagine, pissed Mal off no end, but although she drives me crackers when she's home I miss her dreadfully.

'I cry when *you* go away too, Mal,' I told him, although actually that was a lie because I don't any more, I just feel sad for ten minutes or so. I expect I've got used to his frequent absences, but Rosie is (or once was) a part of me, and although my brain wants her to be off having a life and getting a career, my heart wants her right here with her mum.

So next day I tearlessly waved Mal off too, as he manoeuvred his big Jaguar with difficulty around my car, which I seemed to have parked at an angle, half in, half out of an azalea bush.

He was too preoccupied to notice Mona Wevill

casually standing on her doorstep wearing only thin silk pyjamas in the same rather distressing pinky-beige as her face, so that she looked baggily nude. Her boobs were not just heading south, but had actually passed the Equator.

She is certainly not any competition, even though I'm nowhere near as pretty as when I was younger. You know you're past it when you stop feeling indignant at workmen shouting after you and instead want to go and personally thank them for their interest.

Anyway, not only did I *not* cry as Mal's car vanished, but I actually felt relieved he wasn't going to be there to make me feel guilty about my weight, especially since I have grasped that he finds my measly few extra pounds such a big turn-off! At least now I have six weeks before he comes back to do something about it.

I went up the frosty garden to see to the hens in their neat little coop. They looked at me as if I was mad when I opened the door of their nesting box and asked them if they wanted to come out, moaning gently as they mutinously huddled down into their warm straw nests.

'Please yourselves, girls, but you'll be sorry when Mal's back and you *have* to stay in your run all day,' I told them, but they weren't interested.

Later that morning I set off for Fairy Glen to help Ma pack up too, since everyone seemed determined to leave me at once; though at least Nia should actually be coming back from spending Christmas and New Year at her parents' house any time now.

Ma, a small bohemian rhapsody layered in vaguely

ethnic garments and with her head tied up in a fringed and flowered turban, was sitting in an easy chair in a haze of cigarette smoke doing the quick crossword in yesterday's *Times*. The lacquer-red pen she held in her nicotine-gilded fingers was the exact shade of her lipstick and nail varnish, but I knew that was just a happy accident and not by intent.

Ma is a happy accident.

The two long-haired dachshunds threw themselves at me, yapping shrilly, and she waved away a cloud of smoke with a heavily beringed hand. 'That Mal gone, then?'

'Yes, first thing. And Rosie rang last night to say she'd had a good journey down,' I said, sitting on the floor so I could let Holly and Ivy climb all over me. For the next six weeks I could safely reek of old dog, or hens, or rose manure, or anything else I wanted to.

'Ma, have you ever been on a diet?'

'Diet? No – but me and a couple of friends thought about getting fit once, years ago when we all used to play tennis. We went to this meeting of the Women's League of Health and Beauty in the village hall, and there were about twenty of them there in black leotards and tights, all being trees reaching up to the sunshine. Then they had to be beautiful gazelles, bounding across the plains. You'd have thought a lion was after them.'

'So did you join in?' I asked, fascinated.

'No, we decided not to bother. I didn't think the floor was up to it, for one thing.'

Recrossing her feet, which were incongruously shod in her favourite mock-lizardskin stilettos, she said rather abruptly, 'Fran, I've been sitting here thinking about selling Fairy Glen.'

I sat back on my heels and stared at her. 'Sell the glen? Do you mean the cottage, or just the glen itself?'

'The whole thing, of course – house and grounds. I couldn't sell one without the other, could I? They go together. The thing is, I'm seventy-seven and all this driving's getting a bit much for me. And now Rosie's off at college and you're settled and happy enough with Mal – though he wouldn't be my cup of tea! – I think the time has come to sell up.'

This was a stunner! My parents bought the place long before I was born, so all my happy childhood memories were of roaming the narrow wooded glen, from the overgrown remnants of a tea garden to the ancient standing stones set in a mysterious, magical oak glade high above the little waterfall. Victorian daytrippers had gone in droves to visit fairy glens, and this one, its natural beauty enhanced by grottos, statues and convenient flights of steps, had enjoyed a brief vogue. Long neglected, it had formed the perfect secret garden for me, Nia and Rhodri (the Famous Three) to have adventures in.

The old stone cottage had been hideously remodelled into some kind of miniature Gothic castle, the only concessions to modernity being an electric cooker and a small bathroom. Ma's chosen style of interior décor was Moroccan magpie nest crossed with dog kennel.

'But, Ma,' I croaked, finally regaining the power of speech, 'won't you miss it?'

'Yes, of course. I've had so many happy times here, and it's where I feel closest to your father – he loved it so much. But memories are portable things; I won't lose them if I sell the Glen.'

'You could sell Marchwood instead and move here permanently,' I suggested – Marchwood being her big detached thirties house in Cheshire, near Wilmslow.

'Well, my love, I thought of that, but it's always been my main home and I'm settled there. There's my water-colour class, the bridge club and the girls: never a dull moment.'

The girls are the friends she hangs out with, a sort of Hell's Grannies chapter. Never agree to play any kind of card game with them; they'd have your last penny and the clothes off your back before you could say Old Maid.

'And then Boot does the garden and any handyman stuff, and Glenda does the cleaning, so it all runs along smoothly,' she added. 'But Fairy Glen is falling apart. It needs love and money spent on it, and I feel it's time someone else had a chance to live here and love it like I did.'

I could see the sense of what she was saying even if I hated the thought of it; and it wasn't like I would never see Ma again. I knew she wouldn't come and stay with me if Mal was home, but she would be less than two hours' drive away, so I could even pop over for the day.

No, I think what dismayed me most was the sudden realisation that she was getting old. This was the first sign she'd ever given that she wasn't going to go on for ever.

'I'm tough as old boots,' she said as if reading my mind. 'I'm not about to turn my toes up, I'm just falling back and regrouping: "downsizing" – isn't that what they call it these days? And if I do sell Fairy Glen, then I could go off on that round-the-world cruise with some of the girls, and have fun.'

God help any cruise ship with Ma and the girls on board! 'Speaking of regrouping, Ma . . .' I said, and repeated much of what I had told Rosie about her transient father, while she looked at me pretty hard and blew a whole series of smoke rings.

I got the message: she didn't really believe me either.

Much more of this and I will start to think I hallucinated Adam the gardener or have got false memory syndrome or something. But at least we all seem agreed that Tom exists . . . though I have forgotten where I put that email printout from him, so I might have imagined that. I could have *sworn* I put it in the desk drawer, but maybe it is somewhere out in the studio. Or in the pocket of the jeans currently going round and round in the washing machine. Who knows?

But since it *is* mislaid and I deleted the message, I can't possibly answer it, can I?

Back home I spent a couple of hours in my studio trying to finish my calendar designs, but not only was I totally distracted by the thought of Fairy Glen being sold, my fingers were so cold that if I'd tapped them with a pencil they would have fallen off and shattered.

I could do with a more efficient heater, or better insulation, or both.

There was a phone message from Nia when I went back to the house to thaw, so I rang her once I could grasp the receiver.

'Has he gone?' she asked conspiratorially, as though poor Mal were an ogre or Bluebeard.

'Yes, early this morning. He should be phoning me any minute to say he's arrived.'

'Oh, good – see you in the Druid's Rest around seven, then?' she suggested. 'I've got some news.'

'So have I, and I want your advice on diets – Mal thinks I'm too fat.'

'You're not fat!'

'Well, I'm certainly not slim any more – even Rosie described me as cuddly!'

'There's nothing wrong with cuddly,' Nia said decisively.

'You haven't seen me since I pigged out over Christmas,' I said ruefully. 'My spare tyre would fit a tractor.'

'It's not much more than a week since I last saw you, Fran. You can't have put that much weight on!'

'You wait and see,' I told her, because it's truly amazing the way all the calories have bypassed my digestive system and gone straight to my stomach and hips, laying up a fat store for a famine that was never going to happen . . . unless *diets* count as famine. But I wouldn't need a diet if I hadn't got fat, so if my body decides this is starvation, isn't it going to be a sort of vicious circle? Or am I hopelessly confused?

Diets *must* work, or there wouldn't be any point to people going on them, would there?

I rather gingerly checked for emails before I went out, but there were only impersonal rude ones, easily deleted from both computer and memory.

The Druid's Rest

Five years ago a retired army officer and his wife bought the Druid's Rest Hotel on the outskirts of the village and bedizened the interior with a tarty modern makeover, though they hadn't been allowed to do much more to its venerable listed and listing old carcass than add a large conservatory-style restaurant round the back.

Indoors, the only area left more or less untouched was once the back parlour of the inn, Major Forrester realising just in time that, no matter how unwelcome he made them feel, in the absence of any other pub the regulars were still going to adorn his bar. Now he tried to segregate them away in the back room where his hotel guests and the wine-and-dine set wouldn't need to mingle with them.

Mrs Forrester gave me a chilly smile as I walked through the lounge bar, since I was situated socially somewhere between stairs, like a governess. Sometimes I hung out with the lowlife in the back room, and sometimes Mal took me to dine in the restaurant like a lady.

Nia was already in the back parlour, sitting in a raised wooden box with low panelled walls before a table made from an old beer keg, in the company of a faded, jaded stuffed trout and a moth-eaten one-eyed fox. She was nursing a half of Murphy's and wearing the dazed expression of one who had spent her entire Christmas and New Year dutifully shut up in a small bungalow with two stone-deaf and TV-addicted parents.

Nia must be the pocket version of the same dark Celtic stock Mal sprang from, for they both have lovely dark blue eyes and near-black, straight, shining hair, in Nia's case hanging in a neat and rather arty bob. But whatever common ancestry they share has been well diluted over the centuries because they are totally dissimilar in every other way.

She looked up as I put my virtuous glass on the table and said, 'Call that a spare tyre? It's not even the size of a bicycle inner tube! And what on earth are you drinking?'

'Soda water – I thought I'd better start trying to cut down now, and beer is full of calories.' I sat down and squidged my midriff into a thick welt between my fingers. 'Look – if that isn't a spare tyre, I don't know what is. And when I looked at myself in the mirror this morning I didn't seem to have any cheekbones any more, but I'd gained two chins.'

'I hope you aren't going to get obsessive about your weight – you know what you're like when you get a bee in your bonnet. I haven't forgotten the time you were convinced your eyes were so far apart they were practically vanishing round the sides of your head, and everyone thought you were a freak.'

'That was years ago,' I protested . . . though maybe I *do* still look a little like Sophie Ellis Bextor.

'Or when you thought your face was asymmetrical?'

'It *is* asymmetrical.'

'Yes, well, *everyone's* face is asymmetrical to some extent, only most of us normal people don't get a thing about it.'

'You can't talk. You've been on every diet known to woman and you never looked fat to me to start with!'

'Not any more,' she said firmly. 'I reread *Fat Is a Feminist Issue* over Christmas and decided I will learn to love myself just the way I am.'

How she *is* is sort of rectangular, and she's always looked much the same, as far as I recall, though maybe she used to go in at the waist a bit more. She's always been very attractive in her own rather intense and brooding way, but the divorce seemed to have dented her self-confidence.

'What does it matter anyway?' she said now, shrugging philosophically. 'I'm not going to get Paul back even if I turn into a stick insect, because he's got a forty-year itch only a giggling twenty-something can scratch.'

She'd been running a pottery at a craft centre in mid-Wales with her husband when he suddenly fell for the young jeweller in the next workshop. He's now buying her out of the house and business in instalments, so let's hope the tourist industry stays strong in the valleys.

'But would you want him back now?' I asked curiously.

'Not really. I've already wasted nearly twenty years of my life on someone who wasn't worth it; why would I go back for a second helping?'

'Well, that's one way of looking at it,' I agreed.

Nia and I go *way* back: we played together in St Ceridwen's as children when I was staying at Fairy Glen with Ma; we rode Rhodri Gwyn-Whatmire's roan pony – which he teased me was the same colour as my strawberry-blonde hair – in turns round the paddock of the big house; and both fell in and out of love with him in our early teens over the course of one long, hot summer holiday, without denting our friendship.

We even ended up at the same college together, she studying ceramics and me graphic art, the only difference being that she did her final year and graduated and I went back home and had a baby instead. *And* she was at the fatal party where I got off with Adam the gardener, only unfortunately she was smashed at the time and has nil recall of the night, except that she had a good time.

Presumably so did I.

I firmly banished the memory and got back down to the practicalities of the here and now. 'Mal seems more inclined to love me as I *was* rather than as I *am*, so I'll have to give dieting a go, and since he's away for six weeks I should be able to lose a few pounds before he comes back. So, what sort of diet should I do? What about one of those meal-replacement things, then I wouldn't have to cook anything tempting?'

'Well, there's the Shaker diet and the Bar diet, those are easy. But I'm warning you from bitter experience that even if you lose weight on one of those, you always put it straight back on again, plus an extra bit more.'

'I wondered about that. But they must work for some people, mustn't they? I'll have to try it in the interests of my sex life, but it's a pity I can't just slide into comfortable middle age and be loved anyway. Thank God he hasn't noticed my hair yet.'

What is it with men and long hair? I mean, Mal might love mine but I was beginning to feel like Cousin Itt from *The Addams Family*, so I've had to resort to getting Carrie to lop two inches off the end whenever he is away.

The shorter it gets the curlier it goes, so all that weight must have been pulling it down. It was certainly starting to pull *me* down.

'There has to come a point when he will notice,' Nia said. 'What then?'

'I'll cross that hurdle when I come to it, preferably after I've lost my excess baggage. God, the things I do for love!'

'Wouldn't you like to borrow *Fat Is a Feminist Issue*, instead?' she offered.

'No, because I'm not doing this for me, I'm doing it for Mal. Well, I suppose I *am* doing it a bit for me, because Rosie says I look plump and cosy like Ma, and I don't feel quite ready for that.'

'You're nowhere near as plump as your mam,' Nia said. 'And at least your boobs are still in the right place. Mine are heading south, and so is my bum.'

'Now who's exaggerating? You look fine to me! If you want to talk Major Slump you should see the Weevil woman next door in her pyjamas.'

'Mona Wevill? I think I'd rather not; she looks bad enough clothed. What about this news you said you had? I've got some myself, but you start.'

'I suppose mine's a mixture of good and bad – and I'm not entirely sure which bit's which. Christmas was a bit of a roller coaster, because first of all I finally had to tell Rosie all about her real father – or everything I know, which isn't much, let's face it – and she wasn't terribly convinced. Ma's been filling her head with the idea it was Tom Collinge . . . but I *think* she believed me in the end about the itinerant gardener.'

'She'll get over it. If she asks me I'll tell her it's true,' Nia said. 'Well, true that there was an itinerant gardener, anyway, because if you don't know whether she's Tom's or not, *I* certainly don't. Was that it, or is there more?'

'More. Mal created a website for me as a surprise Christmas present,' I said, 'all about my artwork and . . . but that's not important. I can show it to you next time you're round. The thing is, I've now got an email address and Tom spotted the site and sent me an email!'

'What? You don't mean *Tom Collinge*, Rosie's probably-not father?'

'Yes! Just to say hi, and how was I, and that he's got friends up here so perhaps he might drop in some time!'

She thought about it. 'I suppose once you are on the Internet you are accessible to anyone who wants to look you up, and he sounds like he's just being friendly and maybe a bit curious. You can discourage him gently.'

'I can't discourage him at all, because I deleted the email before Rosie or Mal saw it, and I've mislaid the printout.'

'Then he'll either contact you again and you can be politely chilly, or he'll think you are a different Fran March and that will be that . . . and why are you humming "Surfin' USA"?'

'What? Oh, probably because Tom said he taught surfing.'

'Surfing?'

'Yes, sorry, I thought I'd said. He teaches art and surfing in Cornwall.'

'Are you sure? It sounds an odd mixture.'

'Almost sure . . .' I frowned. 'But it's not important, like the other thing I was going to tell you, which is *truly* shattering: Ma's decided she's getting a bit past all the driving and so she's decided to sell Fairy Glen.'

Nia froze with her glass suspended halfway to her lips, a fetching fuzz of froth adorning her upper lip.

'Sell the glen? Do you mean just the cottage, or the whole thing?'

'That's what I said, but it's the whole thing, of course.'

'But she can't! I mean, she's had it since before you were born!'

'She hasn't actually done much to it, though,' I pointed out. 'It's pretty basic, and she's left the glen to run wild. And, if she's going to sell one of her houses, she's more comfortable in Cheshire with all her friends. She's going to use some of the proceeds to go on a world cruise.'

'She could give the Glen to you!'

'But Mal and I have got a house already, a very nice house – and I'd like her to have fun with the money, go on a cruise or whatever she wants.'

'Has she really thought about this? She does realise that she can't come and stay with you and bring the dogs when Mal's home? He'd vacuum them to death.'

'I know, Rosie's old dog had so many baths she used to hide at the sound of a tap running. But Ma could come when he was away, and I could go over to visit her. I mean, I don't like the idea of this any more than you, Nia, but things have to change, I can see that.'

Nia's frown cleared a little. 'The cottage is so run-down, it's not exactly weekender material, is it? Maybe it won't sell.'

'Perhaps not, or it may not be worth much, because although there's lots of land it's mostly vertical, and the cottage is tiny really – it's the opposite of the Tardis, because the outside looks much bigger than the inside. I'm going to arrange to have it valued for her, anyway, so we will see.'

'If it won't fetch much money she might change her mind,' she said hopefully.

'You know Ma once she makes her mind up about anything . . . but I'm certainly going to miss walking in the fairy glen once it's sold.'

'Me too, and I need access to the standing stones,'

Nia agreed, looking darkly brooding (not unusual; she often does), but she didn't say why.

'What's your news?' I asked to distract her, and she scowled.

'The bad news is, my planning application for the workshop's been turned down.'

'Oh, Nia, I'm sorry!'

Nia had taken over her old home now her parents had retired to Llandudno, and since her return had been making her exquisite porcelain jewellery in the old outhouse behind the cottage, while she waited for planning permission to rebuild it as a small studio. But now the new owners of the adjoining property had put in objections to the plans.

'English weekenders!' she snarled angrily, with the sort of expression that should have told her neighbours to head for the border, fast. 'Here half a dozen times a year, contribute nothing to the village, think they own the place!'

Most fortunately, she has ceased to be – and now denies she ever was – one of the Daughters of Glendower, keeping the home fires burning in the weekenders' cottages, or it might have been a case of 'frying tonight'.

Sometimes I wonder if Fairy Glen only escaped because Ma is half Welsh and it would be terribly difficult just to burn half of a house (though it is a miracle that Ma herself has not set fire to the whole place with carelessly discarded fag ends by now).

'Have you tried *talking* to your neighbours about your plans for the pottery,' I suggested to Nia, 'as opposed to just glowering over the wall at them?'

Nia does a good Frida Kahlo glower, due to having those thick straight eyebrows that meet in the middle when she frowns. 'I mean, they might see your point of view if you explained.'

'I did speak to them. They said they didn't want to have drinks in the garden to a background thump of me wedging clay, and in any case I was a health hazard!'

'You'll have to find a workshop nearby if you can't get planning permission. I'm sure there must be somewhere.'

'Rhodri's back again,' she said, seemingly at random. 'That's the good news. And do you *know* you're singing "There's a Place for Us"?'

I hadn't, but I stopped. 'Rhodri? Have you seen him?'

'No, Carrie told me – he'd been into Teapots to buy honey and a bag of doughnuts, and stayed for coffee and a chat. His divorce is going through and his ex-wife's got the Surrey house, the London flat and seemingly most of the money. *And* she's got a rich French count in tow too. I think poor old Rhodri's number was up once he went from Lloyd's Name to Lloyd's loser.'

'Oh, no, poor Rhodri! He always was weak as water when it came to the crunch. What's he going to do? Hasn't he already lost most of his money?'

'Yes, and now he's losing most of what he's got left. But he says it's a clean-break divorce so he won't have to pay maintenance, and the daughter's sort of a model-cum-socialite engaged to someone wealthy and nearly off his hands. So now he's going to live permanently at Plas Gwyn, and Carrie says he's thinking of opening it up all season to the public instead of just summer Sundays, to make some money. And he might hire the Great Hall out for weddings and stuff like that. She said he had lots of ideas.'

'It will be lovely to have him back living in St Ceridwen's, but I don't think making money is his forte,' I said doubtfully. Rhodri had been a handsome boy, but even then an air of sweet bewilderment had lurked behind his hopeful, trusting blue eyes, and the few times we'd met since I'd been married to Mal he hadn't seemed much different.

'No, it certainly isn't. But I thought I might go up to Plas Gwyn and talk to him, now there's no chance of running into that vile, stuck-up bitch he married, because there's the whole stable wing doing nothing, and he could turn it into little craft workshops and studios as an extra tourist attraction – and rent one to *me!*'

'Brilliant!' I said, and brilliant it might prove to be for Rhodri too, for if Nia was one thing it was bossy, and if he looked pathetic enough she might just supply the backbone he needed to get Plas Gwyn off the ground as a paying proposition.

She needed some outlet for her powerful energy in addition to beating the hell out of lumps of clay, and possibly, if they pushed her too far, the neighbours. And it might even distract her from whatever strange rites I had twice caught her performing up at the ancient stones above the fairy glen, which I sincerely hoped were merely some form of Druidism or Wicca, and not something much more sinister. She can be *so* intense at times!

'Do you want another glass of delicious water?' she asked.

'I've got a better idea – I've got pizza, home-made wine and some whisky at home, so why don't we go and have a girls' night in? Maybe watch a DVD?'

'OK. Shall I give Carrie a ring and see if she wants to come round too?'

'Is that greed talking?' I said, because Carrie never comes visiting without bringing a selection of the home-made goodies she bakes for her café, Teapots.

Nia, already dialling, pulled a face at me over her mobile phone.

Sex, Lies and Videotape

It felt wonderfully decadent with the three of us curled up on the big sofa in front of the TV, the coffee table groaning under the weight of pizza, leftover birthday cake and all the pastries Carrie had brought, scattering crumbs and drinking my home-made apple wine and Carrie's mead.

Mal would have gone ballistic if he'd seen what we'd done to his immaculate living room.

We watched the news as an entrée, then Nia started going through my sparse collection of DVDs to find a film to watch as the main course.

'*Ten Things I Hate About You*?' I suggested, and the other two groaned.

'We must have seen that a dozen times!' Carrie complained.

'Yes, but it's my favourite film.'

'Well, you wouldn't let me get my favourite film,' Nia objected. She may not have a DVD player but she usually carries *Fargo* round with her like a teenager with a new CD.

'Too gory,' I objected. I wanted something lighter.

'What's this?' Nia asked, holding up an unfamiliar box.

Carrie reached over and took it. *'Restoration Gardener?'*

'I'd forgotten I had that; Ma won it, but I haven't watched it yet. It's only a short one – the highlights of some TV series.'

'I've heard of it – I think its sort of archaeology crossed with gardening. Let's have a look at that first,' Carrie suggested, 'then decide on a film.'

'OK, at least we haven't already seen it a million times,' Nia agreed, putting it in the machine.

We all replenished our plates and glasses, then started the DVD and sat back expectantly. Carrie's a keen gardener, I'm passionate about roses and Nia loves flowers generally, so hopefully there should be something there to suit us all.

To the accompaniment of a gentle ripple of Beethoven's Pastoral Symphony, the title *Restoration Gardener* wrote itself across the screen with a quill pen over some speeded-up computer-generated images of a Japanese crystal garden growing like iced mould out of bare paper.

Carrie settled back with a plate containing a custard tart, a cherry-topped coconut pyramid and two cream-filled brandy snaps (and that was just for starters). 'I do love gardening programmes – it's such a shame we can't get more channels on the TV in St Ceridwen's.'

'It's a shame we can't always see the ones we *do* allegedly get,' Nia said, scattering shards of meringue.

'The reception's so bad they should be ashamed of charging us for the TV licence, and only a masochist would bother looking in the newspaper at what's on everywhere else.'

'Do you think Gabriel Weston is his real name?' I asked, as the quill pen reappeared and wrote it with a flourish. 'It's a bit olde worlde and earthy, isn't it?'

'You don't get much more earthy and olde worlde than Bob Flowerdew,' pointed out Nia, 'and that's *his* real name.'

'Gabriel *is* his real name!' Carrie exclaimed, striking herself on the forehead with the hand holding the remains of the coconut pyramid, so that it was suddenly like being inside a snowglobe (though the custard tart would have been much, much worse). 'Am I stupid, or what? I read all about him in a magazine last time I went to the hairdresser's in Llandudno. He's usually called Gabe, though.'

'It's starting,' Nia warned, and we stopped brushing bits of coconut off each other and turned to face the screen.

Helicopter-borne, the camera homed slowly in on a small Tudor manor house sitting inoffensively among a rolling, sheep-nibbled expanse of grass, with here and there a flight of stone steps or a section of herringbone-brick pathway.

There wasn't much more garden left there than around Rhodri's mini-mansion, Plas Gwyn, I thought, taking a bite of Bakewell tart and settling back. All Rhodri's old gardener, Aled, had to do was drive round and round on his little sit-on mower and indulge his passion for clipping trees into strangely rude shapes.

'Approaching Slimbourne Manor you might think that there never was a garden here at all, or if there ever was, that all trace had vanished,' said a warm, deep voice with just the faintest, tantalising hint of a West Country burr.

A strange shiver ran down my back and I sat up and stared at the screen. I'd *definitely* heard that voice before somewhere, I was sure of it – maybe on some other gardening programme. It certainly wasn't one you'd ever forget, with a mellow tone that made you think of dark, rich honey and folded tawny velvet . . . of a pint of best bitter with the sunlight shining through it, or the dappled gold-browns of a peaty stream bed, or . . . well, you get the idea. Even if the programme was no good I could see how the audience was hooked. I was half-mesmerised myself.

'Yet, as we get closer,' the velvety voice continued, 'we start to notice clues: grand steps that once led somewhere and the remains of beautiful old brick pathways. The grass at the front of the house that looked so flat from high above, from an angle shows the bumps and hollows of a long-vanished knot garden. Slimbourne was once a jewel in a beautiful setting, and we are going to resurrect it!'

'I don't see how he can see anything there,' I said sceptically, trying to shake off the near-hypnosis of that voice. 'Perhaps he just makes it up.'

'Oh, no,' said Carrie, suddenly our instant resident expert, 'apparently he has an absolute gift for garden design, a huge knowledge of the history of old gardens *and* a degree in archaeology! And, what's more, he looked totally hunky in his photo.'

'I don't think people say "hunky" any more,' observed Nia. 'They say a man is "fit" or "well fit".'

'Then he looked well fit. More than well fit. Well fit with knobs on.'

'I should hope so,' I said, watching critically as Gabe Weston slowly approached us on the screen, escorting a tall and ancient lady dressed in mottled tweed trousers and an old cricket jumper, her long string of pearls trapped under one pendulous breast.

I jerked upright as though someone had run their finger down my spine, the half-eaten cake in one hand.

'I'm lucky in having the assistance of Lady Eleanor Arkleforth, the owner of this lovely house, who has already researched the garden thoroughly in the family archives.'

'Thank you,' Lady Arkleforth said graciously. 'I'm delighted to restore the grounds to some semblance of what they once were at last.'

'I believe you've found a plan of how the garden looked originally?' Gabe Weston prompted.

The camera finally fully focused on the gardener's highly unusual face, but I could still see it clearly even when it moved on to the garden plan, because his image seemed to have been flash-burned into my retinas.

He had a strong chin, green-flecked hazel eyes rayed at the corners where he had screwed them up in laughter or against the sun, and the sort of Grecian nose you could open letters with. Rich, darkest-honey hair spiralled tightly round his face like a wet water spaniel's.

'Are you all right, Fran?' Nia asked suddenly. 'Only you look a bit startled. Your mouth's open and you've gone awfully pale.' She looked from me to the screen, where my nemesis had now reappeared in the flesh wearing one of those archaic winged smiles full of inner amusement. 'Mind you, he *is* pretty stunning – he can dibble *my* beds any time!'

'And mine!' agreed Carrie enthusiastically.

'Of course I'm all right,' I croaked, though I was by no means certain I hadn't suddenly flipped. 'Would you really say he was good-looking? He's not exactly handsome, is he?'

But distinctive; so *very* distinctive that a face whose features I had thought safely forgotten suddenly reclaimed its place in my memory, like the last piece of a puzzle locking into place.

'Back track,' I said urgently. 'I think that's Rosie's father!'

Nia had replayed the DVD so Gabe Weston's face was frozen in mid-smile like a mysterious male Mona Lisa, and just as informative.

'It's *got* to be him – there can't be two men who look like that *and* have the same beautiful voice with a West Country accent,' I said, feeling strangely breathless. 'Unless I'm going crackers!'

'You already are crackers,' Nia said, 'but I believe you. Only I thought his name was Adam?'

'So did I.'

Carrie, who had been sitting looking totally bewildered, suddenly exclaimed, 'Rosie's father is Gabe Weston? But *I* thought it was Rhodri!'

'Rhodri? Are you insane?'

'But you were here all that summer working at Teapots, and thick as thieves with him!' she said defensively.

'We were old friends, and Nia was away most of that summer, so he was the first person I told when I realised I was pregnant – but not because he was the father!'

'Well,' Carrie said, 'it wasn't just me who got the wrong end of the stick, especially when he became Rosie's godfather! I'm sure half the village still think it.'

'They think wrong, then.'

She looked at me doubtfully. 'But are you *sure* it was Gabe Weston? And if so, how come you never told him about Rosie?'

'I'm sure – and it wasn't an affair, it was a one-night stand.'

'That doesn't sound like you, Fran!'

'I was drunk and I'd just split up with my boyfriend. All I knew about the man I slept with was that he was called Adam – which, as it turns out, was a lie – that he came from Devon and was a gardener. Even if I'd wanted to I couldn't have found him from that information.'

'And until now you had no idea who Gabe Weston was?' Carrie said. 'Well, isn't that just amazing?'

'Tragic, more like,' Nia said. Then she set Gabe into

motion and speech again and we all watched him silently, and in my case angrily, though I don't know why. He hadn't sneaked away without a word, it was me who'd done that. All he was guilty of was carelessness.

'I don't suppose he's ever given me a thought since,' I muttered bitterly.

'But what about Rosie?' Nia asked.

'What *about* Rosie?'

'You aren't going to tell her who her father is, now you know?'

I shuddered. 'Who her father *probably* is – and let's not open that can of worms. You know what Mal's like, and he's always sort of assumed Rosie's Tom's baby. We've been through all that. And if I told Rosie who it was she might try and contact him and be rebuffed, which would be terribly hurtful. Things are better left as they are.'

'And it sounds like there's an outside chance she might not be his anyway,' Carrie said helpfully. 'So it would probably come down to DNA testing, and just imagine if the father really *was* your ex-boyfriend after all!'

'Thanks for that thought, Carrie.'

'It gets even better,' Nia said. 'Tom, Fran's old boyfriend, has just emailed her and he wants to come and see her.'

'Yes, but I didn't answer, so he's probably got the message,' I said hopefully. 'After all this time I don't want either of them to pop back into my life and mess things up.'

I looked at the screen again. Gabe Weston was smiling, but then I expect he has a lot to smile about, being a successful TV personality. 'He's probably married with his own family by now,' I mused aloud. 'Even if Rosie *were* his he wouldn't want to know.'

'Divorced,' said Carrie knowledgeably. 'His only daughter lives with her mum in America, but his name's been linked with quite a few other women since.'

'I bet it has,' Nia said drily.

Carrie regarded me admiringly: 'Well, you're a dark horse, Fran! It's so romantic, just like *The French Lieutenant's Woman.*'

'I can't see where *The French Lieutenant's Woman* comes in,' Nia said critically. 'Gabe Weston looks more like Meryl Streep than Fran does.'

'And I certainly haven't been waiting for him to come back,' I objected. 'In fact, I'm going to try and forget I ever recognised him. Let's just let sleeping gardeners lie – that's seemed to work for me pretty well so far.'

'Then perhaps you should stop humming "Look What You've Done to Me"?' suggested Nia.

Mal phoned late that night after they'd gone home, and strangely enough I felt as guilty while I was talking to him as if I'd just spent the night with Adam the gardener all over again.

I would have liked to have blotted the memories out in Mal's arms, but instead I simply had to obliterate them with leftover cake and a bar of chocolate.

Cool Runnings

In the early hours of this morning I got up, found a torch that worked and went to hide the *Restoration Gardener* DVD in my studio in the box marked 'Miscellaneous'.

At that hour the oddest things seem strangely logical.

As I made my way back I saw the pallid glimmer of one of the Wevills watching me from their bedroom window, so I suppose this will go into their next report to Mal, along with my girlie night in transformed into some kind of orgy. I don't know what made them look out at that time of night because I'm almost *sure* I wasn't singing.

They must use mirrors on sticks to watch me some of the time – it's the only way they can know so much about my movements – but fortunately my rose garden and studio are on the other side of the house, bordering the lane, so once I go through the pergola they've lost me unless they have radar.

After that I was wide awake, so I made some hot chocolate, got out the mosaic kit Ma's cousin sent me for my birthday and started to transform the boring, dead-white-tiled fireplace in the sitting room. I could use some of that box of broken china in the studio too: I knew it would come in handy one day.

It was a chilly day even after the sun came up, so I took to running between the house and my studio with sandwiches and Thermos flasks, watched by the cold, bored hens.

My roses were all frozen in time like so many sleeping beauties, and glittered in the sunlight, although there were still deep-red flowers on my Danse du Feu until just before Christmas.

I felt a bit weak and trembly, as though I had received a severe shock . . . which, thinking about it, I suppose I had. But, in reality, nothing much has changed except I now know Adam's real identity, so I firmly put it out of my head while I got on with my work.

I completed the final illustration for the calendar of a dog rose trailing over one of the half-ruined Fairy Glen grottoes, then began putting the finishing touches to the cover, which is taken from my studio in its thorny bower, rendered a bit more picturesque than it really is.

It was a good day's work, and tomorrow I will be able to pack them up and send them off, together with some cartoons that I've got circulating; batches of them come and go in the post, some finding a home, some not. Two have just appeared in *Private Eye*, and three they didn't want have been taken by the *Oldie* instead. I've got one or two other projects on the back burner, but the cartoons seem to be bringing in the most cash lately – perhaps because

I'm constantly dashing them off between other things. Sheer volume.

This hit-and-miss aspect of my work drives Mal mad, since I never know how much money will be coming in, but I do religiously pay two-thirds of everything I make into our household account towards the bills. I know Mal earns a huge amount more than me – but then he *spends* a lot more than me too, on boats, cars, electrical gadgets, stamps, expensive wines and stupid stuff like that, while I pay my own car bills and support Rosie and the hens: the important things.

As the song (almost) says, the best things in life are free, though Mal certainly wouldn't agree with that – and even our basic differences in the value we put on things inspires cartoons, so waste not, want not.

I'm going to start drawing an Alphawoman comic strip tomorrow now the calendar is finished, and I must buy enough meal replacement bars and shakes to get my diet off to a good start when I go into town to post my stuff.

Nia has summoned me to a Council of War at eleven in the morning at Teapots! Since Rhodri is coming too, I only hope it is a war on debt she means, and not something involving fire and her neighbours.

It will be good to see Rhodri again, though – and lucky that Mal is still away, since he is inclined to be jealous of any time I spend with my oldest friends. At first we tried to include him, but I think our shared history made him feel an uncomfortable outsider.

Just as well he spends so much time away or I

wouldn't even have the modest social life I enjoy now.

I decided *not* to tell him about the meeting when he called from sunny Swindon to remind me to take his suit to the cleaners, pick up his migraine prescription (he only gets migraine when he drinks red wine, so the answer to that one lies in his own hands) and purchase a birthday card and present for his mother.

Why me? She hates me! I still have to call her Mrs Morgan, and she never spends a night under the roof of the double-dyed Scarlet Woman – for not only did we marry in a registry office, which doesn't count, but also I already had an illegitimate child! This makes it all the stranger that the only chink in her scales is her love for Rosie: she succumbed immediately, though don't ask me why – you'd think only a mother could love such an obstreperous little creature. But love her she does, to the point where I'm sure she's managed to forget that Rosie really isn't her granddaughter at all.

She is also convinced that Mal and his first wife would have resumed their marriage by now if not for me, since they have remained in friendly contact over the years. In fact, they will probably meet up for lunch or dinner a couple of times while he is down there on this contract, but I am not in the least jealous . . . just illogically uneasy.

Seeing Alison again seems to make him dissatisfied with our life here together in St Ceridwen's Well, although when he lived the high life in London he wanted to move to the country and chill out. But now he's *in* the country he seems to be trying to live the consumer-driven high life again, so what's that all about? He's not going to turn into a middle-aged male weathercock, is he?

And another worrying thought: we've now been married about the same length of time as his first marriage lasted, so did *I* come with built-in obsolescence? Especially with the Wevills dripping their sly insinuations about me into his ear like a pair of Iagos.

I wish I wasn't suddenly having all these worrying ideas.

And what *do* you buy a dragon for its birthday? Firelighters for damp mornings?

Inspiration! Spotted an advert in a magazine for a firm who will create a bouquet to reflect any message you want to send, together with a little booklet explaining the meanings of flowers and plants, so the recipient can have hours of harmless fun working it out.

I am trying to be subtle here, so no deadly nightshade or anything of that kind.

The dog rose, 'pleasure mixed with pain', perhaps? (Her son is the pleasure – to look at, at least – and she is the pain.)

After that, feeling rather put upon, I finally ordered a Constance Spry – 'pink old rose form ... luminous delicacy ... myrrh scented' – with my birthday garden tokens.

OK, I know that they're prone to mildew and I haven't got an inch of space left in my bit of the garden, but they are so very pretty that I'm sure Mal won't mind if I put it near the patio somewhere. The scent would be heavenly when we are sitting out, and I could train it over the trellis round the door.

I won't tell him, I'll just dig a little tiny bed for it while he's away and heel it in to see if he notices.

As I sealed the envelope with the order it occurred to me that I might be one of the last people in the country using cheques. Apart from one Switch card I don't possess a single bit of plastic, although Mal more than makes up for it: when he opens *his* wallet it unfolds like a stiffly backed patchwork quilt.

Teapots is right next to the Holy Well and smack opposite the one smallish village car park. Inside it's painted a brave, welcoming yellow, lined with shelves displaying Carrie's collection of hundreds of teapots, and with red-checked tablecloths and fresh flowers on each table.

There are no menus: she bakes breads and pastries each morning as the fancy takes her, but doesn't do hot food, because she isn't interested in poaching eggs and deep-frying chips. I admire that – she only cooks what she enjoys, the way I only do gardening involving roses. Her Welshcakes are superb.

The room was already half full, even though it was too early in the season for the coach parties who come to visit the Holy Well and Rhodri's house, Plas Gwyn. The café's popular all the year round, not just for tourists but with the locals too.

Did I say that Carrie is originally American? I tend to forget, and you can hardly tell from her accent, which I suppose must have worn off over thirty years here in St Ceridwen's. She arrived as a hippie with a rucksack, guitar and a notebook full of recipes and never left, except for closing up for a month every November and going back to visit friends and relatives in the States.

She's very popular in the village, maybe because it's seen as a sort of compliment that she has elected to live here, bringing in tourists and money. Even her attempts to speak Welsh are treated with benign tolerance, though her grasp of the language is excruciatingly formal and grammatically old-fashioned, like someone talking the most impeccable Elizabethan English. 'Prithee, wouldst thou like thy Olde Welshe Cream tea with jam or, mayhap, honey from mine own hive?' That sort of thing.

But we all love Carrie, she's so unsquashably bouncy and cheerful. (And she knows everything about everyone, having been conducting a part-time affair with the village postman, Huw, for about a quarter of a century.)

She was presiding behind the counter when I arrived, and smiled and pointed to where Rhodri and Nia were sitting at a corner table, arguing.

Nothing new there – they've always argued, but it's mostly Nia's fault; she's so prickly, and has this big chip on her shoulder about being a quarryman's daughter, while he is the lord of the manor – as if Rhodri ever cared about stuff like that.

Although we've always kept in touch, I hadn't seen Rhodri to talk to properly for absolutely ages, but as soon as I saw his pinkish face under the unruly thatch of burned-straw hair light up at the sight of me, it was as though we'd never been apart. It's the same with Nia: whenever we meet we just pick up where we left off, and that's the sign of true friendship, I think.

He sprang to his feet – he has such beautiful manners, and this lovely posh but friendly voice. 'Fran!' he said, giving me a hug and a kiss on both cheeks. 'You look wonderful!'

It was more than I could say about him; he was looking not only older but sadder, like the poor lion in *The Wizard of Oz*. He has a wide blunt nose and straight, thick fair eyebrows over his pale blue eyes, which add to the resemblance.

'Sit down, Fran,' ordered Nia bossily. 'Carrie's bringing coffee and Danish pastries over, so you don't have to order. We need to get on.'

'With what?' I asked, sitting down and thinking it was just as well I hadn't actually started the diet yet.

'Sorting out Rhodri's far-fetched plans to turn Plas Gwyn into some kind of kiddies' Camelot theme park.'

'Oh, *now*,' protested Rhodri, 'that's not fair! I never said anything like that! Just that I wanted to open the house up to the public all season – maybe even all year – and perhaps have a tearoom and gift shop to try and make a bit of money to live on. And I only *mentioned* the possibility of having a Camelot-inspired children's playground.'

'Forget it,' advised Nia. 'That's not the way you should be going. Plas Gwyn isn't a holiday camp, it's a historic gem in the middle of nowhere, and you need to attract the type of visitor who already comes to St Ceridwen's to see the Holy Well, only more of them.'

'I think Nia's probably right about that,' I agreed. 'I'm sure lots of people would come to Plas Gwyn if it was on the historic houses list, because it's so beautiful, but at the moment they can only see it at weekends in July and August, which restricts your visitor numbers a bit. But if you open it to the public all year where are you going to live?'

'In the new wing,' Rhodri said. 'It's where I spend most of my time anyway, since it's the only part with modern plumbing or anything remotely civilised.'

The new wing is mainly seventeenth century, which gives you some idea of how old the *old* part is.

'I can close the doors off on all the floors between the two wings of the house to make it private. And I thought I could take any modern furniture out of the old house and put it in the attic, where there's loads of stuff that I can use to furnish it back into period style . . . or maybe each room in a different period. I'm not sure yet.'

'Eclectic can look good too,' suggested Nia. 'It gives some idea of a family living in the house over centuries. And it's a good idea to rent out the Great Hall as a wedding venue eventually, but you need more – and turning some of the stable buildings round the courtyard into craft workshops, a gift shop and a tearoom would not only bring more people to visit, but give you some income all the year round.'

'Yes,' agreed Carrie, who had arrived with the coffee and was unashamedly listening in. 'And I can supply your tearoom with cakes and pastries and my Welsh honey – in fact, it can be an off-shoot of Teapots and then it's not competition, just extra profit!' She wandered off again, notebook in hand, to take an order.

Rhodri was looking slightly dazed. In the past the Gwyn-Whatmires had never been averse to making money, but poor Rhodri doesn't seem to have inherited the knack. 'That all sounds great – but I can't afford to do much more than any basic building work and garden clearance that's needed to start with.'

'We were just talking about the garden when you arrived, Fran,' Nia said with a sudden glower at poor Rhodri. 'I've told him about your mam wanting to sell Fairy Glen, and since it was once part of the Plas Gwyn estate I think he should buy it back and make it into an extra attraction.'

'I think fairy glens went out with the Victorian day-trippers,' I said dubiously. 'I mean, I know it was terribly popular in its day, and all credit to the Gwyn-Whatmire of the time for walling it off from the estate and flogging it, and to whoever put in the paths and grottoes and made the tea garden, but it's all gone back to wilderness now.'

'Well, I think you're wrong,' Nia said firmly. 'But you could at least make an offer for the oak woods and the standing stones up at the top of the glen, Rhodri – they're part of your heritage.'

'Yes, but Fran's right. It was all walled off with the glen and it's *part* of it now,' he objected. 'And it would cost a fortune to restore. I'm more concerned with hanging on to Plas Gwyn itself.'

'But we don't want more weekenders buying it and stopping us walking in the glen,' Nia said firmly, which is something that I hate the thought of too: it's such a special place to both of us, and seemingly *vital* to whatever Nia does up there. (This involves a robe, a strange little knapsack and a long staff and, just once, some kind of interment – but I've decided not to speculate on that one . . . too much. Now I just turn and creep away if she's there.)

'I think the glen is a burden the estate doesn't need,' Rhodri said stubbornly. 'And there's enough garden around the house to restore without it.'

'There's no garden around the house,' I said. 'It's all grass and trees. How on earth can you restore *that*, Rhodri?'

'Ah, but there *was* a garden once – and, what's more, I've written to Gabriel Weston and he's considering putting Plas Gwyn on the shortlist for his next TV restoration! What do you think of *that*?'

'Oh my God!' I said despairingly as my heart came into sudden collision with my ribcage before dropping into my boots, potted in one. 'Are *all* my vultures coming home to roost?'

'I thought you kept hens?' he said, puzzled. 'You're not keeping birds of prey now, are you, Fran?'

'You did say Gabriel Weston?' demanded Nia.

'Yes. Have you seen his series, *Restoration Gardener*?'

'Well, would you Adam-and-Eve it!' she said, turning to exchange an incredulous glance with me.

'What?' Rhodri said, puzzled.

I gathered my wits together. 'It's just that by a strange coincidence we watched a short DVD with clips of the series last night and saw him for the first time. Don't forget, Rhodri, that the TV reception is impossible here unless you've got a satellite dish.'

'You're right, I had forgotten,' he agreed. 'And you haven't got satellite?'

'No, but we don't watch much TV anyway.'

'Just endless *Buffy* DVDs,' pointed out Nia. 'You're addicted.'

'Well, Carrie's addicted to *Sex and the City*, and you don't seem to mind watching either of them when we have one of our girls' nights in.'

'No, but I haven't got a DVD player,' Nia said. '*I* haven't got time to sit about glued to the box – and neither have you,' she added pointedly to Rhodri. 'We're both divorced and broke, and had better get on with making a living.'

'What were you saying about this Gabriel Weston, Rhodri? We seem to have side-tracked,' I said innocently, 'and we don't know much about him.'

'Well, he's appeared on various things over the last few years, but now he presents this really popular show called *Restoration Gardener*. He chooses a house that once had a special garden and surveys it, researches family documents and stuff, then draws plans to recreate what was there. Then his team spends a few weeks restoring part of it, at the programme's expense. They often go back and see how the earlier ones are getting on too. It's really interesting.'

'And they might do Plas Gwyn?' I asked, impressed despite my personal disinclination to have Adam delving anywhere in my Eden.

'I don't know – I sent in photos and details and told them there were lots of family documents, and I've just heard it's being seriously considered. Though of course that's only the first step, because even if it gets on the shortlist it still has to win the TV vote-off. But it would be wonderful if it did – and even more wonderful to have garden features again at Plas Gwyn other than a lot of grass and trees!'

'There's certainly nothing much there now,' I agreed. 'Apart from the turf maze, and even that's getting hazy around the edges, because hardly anyone ever goes and walks around it these days, and Aled drives straight over it on the mower.'

'*I* walk around it,' Nia said, 'especially at certain times of the year.'

'Yes, and I still think it's unfair that you came back and were allowed to be one of the Thirteen for the May Day maze-walking, but they will only let me watch from a distance,' I said, distracted by the injustice of being excluded from participating in the local mysteries.

'The Thirteen have to be from certain local families, especially the leader, the Cadi,' Nia said firmly. 'Even Rhodri could only watch, even if he wasn't a man.'

'I think I forgot to mention the maze in the details I sent,' Rhodri said, knitting his brows like a Neanderthal sheep. 'Not that it *is* a maze at all really, just a sort of winding pathway.'

'It's a unicursal maze,' said Nia, who seems very knowledgeable about these things lately, 'and it's probably been there as long as the house, so you should look after it.'

'Right,' he said vaguely. 'And you'd be surprised how the rest of the garden's changed over the centuries. There used to be a big terrace, and there was a pond with a fountain, only Mother filled that in when I was small so I wouldn't drown.'

Rhodri's mother was mega protective, which is why he was taught at home until he finally went off to Eton or Rugby or whichever posh public school his name was down for and thenceforth only ever appeared in the school holidays.

'It would give the place a bit of publicity if they chose Plas Gwyn for a TV makeover,' Nia said. 'Contacting them was a good idea, Rhodri!'

'You needn't sound so surprised!' he objected. 'But I don't suppose they will choose us – we're a bit out of the way.'

I said nothing, torn between realising how good for Rhodri it would be if Plas Gwyn was chosen, and being appalled at the thought of Rosie's incarnated maybe-father practically on the doorstep.

'They might, but even if they do I expect this Gabe Weston only spends a couple of days actually on site filming,' she said, pointedly looking at me. 'His minions probably do the hard work.'

'Which would include me,' Rhodri agreed. 'I'll have to do a lot of the donkey work myself. Aled's not up to much – he should have retired years ago, but he just loves driving that mower around.'

'And clipping things,' Nia put in drily. 'I've never seen a pleached walk quite so pleached, the stilt hedge looks half naked, and what that bit of topiary by the front gate is I'm not going to even *try* to guess, but it looks obscene.'

'I asked,' he said gloomily. 'It's suppose to be a rocket.'

'Well, that's a relief,' I said. 'I think you should put a little sign in front of it, telling visitors.'

'If there are any visitors. I don't really think we stand much chance of winning the garden restoration because I'm sure the other properties are a lot more deserving.' Rhodri smiled his rather heartbreaking smile at me. 'But I'm glad *you're* happy and your illustrations and cartoons are so popular, Fran. Nia's been telling me all about it and how well Rosie is doing with her veterinary science course.'

'She was always mad about animals,' Nia said. 'It was a logical choice. And what about your Zoe, Rhodri, wasn't she doing some modelling?'

He nodded. 'Yes, though only in a part-time sort of way – and she's getting married soon.'

'She's a very pretty girl,' I said kindly, though she's tall and skinny with big bug eyes in a triangular face and reminds me of nothing so much as a praying mantis, but with Rhodri's sweet nature.

'I'm glad I don't have any children to complicate things,' Nia said complacently. 'My sister, Sian, is enough to cope with. She's convinced I'm swindling her out of her birthright just because I'm buying the cottage from Mam and Dad! But I'm paying a fair price and they wanted it in instalments to live on in their retirement, so it's suiting us all round – except Sian.'

'She's not married?' asked Rhodri.

'No, though she's been through men like a dose of

salts,' Nia said. 'Works for a newspaper down in Cardiff.'

While we had been talking we seemed to have demolished a plate of pastries between us, though I suddenly had a deep yearning for one of Carrie's luscious gingerbread dragons, with scales in scalloped red icing . . . I think this is what comes of deciding to diet: all I can think about now is food.

'I think we should all go up to Plas Gwyn and see what fresh ideas we can come up with on site,' suggested Nia. 'Maybe see what's stored in the attic.'

'That would take more than one afternoon,' Rhodri said, 'but we could have a quick look now.'

Rhodri wanted to pay for everything but we insisted on going thirds, and I took the money up to the till. I emerged from the teashop five minutes later rather sheepishly holding a paper bag.

Being the smallest one, I sat crammed into the back of Rhodri's impractical old Spyder sports car. 'Have to swap this for something more useful, Rhodri, like an old Land Rover,' Nia said, and he winced. I don't think she will divorce him from his car; that's one bridge too far.

Halfway up the drive we met his cousin Dottie (whose name is quite apt) riding towards us on a large bay horse with three white socks.

She halted next to the car and looked down at us disapprovingly, especially me with a half-eaten gingerbread dragon in one hand. 'Came to see you, Roddy – didn't think you'd be out gallivantin' with gels when the house is falling to rack and ruin around you. And you the last of the Gwyn-Whatmires!'

'Did you want anything in particular, Dottie?' he asked, wincing again.

'Cup of tea,' she said. 'Made it myself. Come on, Rollover!'

Fortunately she seemed to be addressing the horse, for it moved off skittishly sideways, was gathered in and trotted briskly off.

I was glad the drive was short, because I was starting to feel a bit queasy, and tossed the dragon's tail out into the bushes for the squirrels. Come to that, this last couple of weeks I've felt odder and odder. Am I coming down with something? It's that sort of brink-of-illness feeling – or maybe brink-of-overdue-period feeling? I'm so erratic, and it always makes me feel bloated and strange.

Yes, come to think of it, I'm sure that's what it is, because I'm Emotionally Weird, always a sign.

Grand Designs

Plas Gwyn is a collection of mossy, ancient grey stones that evolved haphazardly round three sides of a paved courtyard. The oldest part is the three-storeyed hall, with the solar tower poking up above the roof and Zéphirine Drouhin and the knotty trunks of old wisteria entwined around its nether regions; then there is the seventeenth-century wing where Rhodri would have his private apartments, and the stables and outbuildings of various kinds, ripe, as Nia pointed out, for conversion into studios, gift shop and refreshment room.

The cast-off furnishings of centuries were stored on the top floor of the hall, which opened right into the roof and was accessible by a twisty stair that made you wonder how they carried some of the larger pieces of redundant furniture up there – and how some of them were to be got down again.

'The thing is,' Nia said, as we finished our tour of the main house and passed through a low door and down two well-worn stone steps into what was once the kitchen, 'you need to channel the visitors around so that they *have* to exit through here into a gift shop. Then they step out into the courtyard and there will be the tearoom and the workshops in the old stables – more lovely spending opportunities! And in the summer you could put little iron tables and chairs outside here.'

'I'd need to employ people, though – there'd be wages to pay,' Rhodri pointed out gloomily.

'You already have Mrs Jones and her team of local ladies to come in and clean, and open it to the public on summer weekends,' I pointed out. 'They would probably be happy to work more hours.'

'Yes, and Carrie will staff the tearoom,' Nia agreed, 'so you would just need to find someone to run the gift shop, and, if you made it the entrance to the house as well as the exit, they could sell the tickets too.'

'He'd need signs along the drive to direct cars to a parking area,' I said. 'You could rope off that flat bit next to the paddock. And people could come to the workshops in winter even when the house wasn't open, so that would work well.'

Rhodri was looking dubious about becoming the area's major employer – in fact, apart from the hotel, pretty nearly the *only* employer – but as we went around and Nia enthused, he began to look more relaxed.

I thought it all sounded possible too, with hard work, and Rhodri would be able to keep his family home, scrape a living and still be comfortable in the new wing with the family ghost. (The Grey Lady is a quiet, benign female presence who closes the great oaken doors gently from time to time and tiptoes across the dark wooden floors so as not to disturb the living occupants.)

Rhodri is going to get some plans drawn up for the gift shop, tearoom and studios, and Nia volunteered to help him to sticker the furniture that is being consigned to the attic, the new wing or the old hall, so that strong removal men can come and change it all about.

She was having fun, I could tell by the bright colour in her cheeks and the sparkle in her eyes, so after a while I left them to it and walked off home to feed the hens and do a bit of work before driving into town.

The work didn't get done, though; instead, I drew a cartoon of Rhodri as a sort of amiable heraldic lion with the caption 'Come to Plas Gwyn for a roaring good time!'

When I checked for emails later there was one from Mal, which I'd expected, but also another blast from the past from Bigblondsurfdude, which I nearly deleted unread with the spam, except that it said 'Thanks!' and curiosity got the better of me. Just as well it did.

Hi Fran!

Thanks for your message. No, I'm not married. I was in a long-term relationship but we broke up before Christmas. Your daughter sounds great – almost made me wish I had kids! Yes, you're

right, we've got a lot of catching-up to do. Hope
to call in and see you sometime soon.
All the best,
Tom.

My *message*? For a minute I thought I really had flipped
and emailed him back . . . until the truth dawned and
I realised where my missing email printout had gone.
It comes to something when your children plot against
you.

I opened Mal's message expecting it to be a soothingly mundane list of instructions or fascinating
details of how clever he was being, but it was far
from that: more an accusation, really, though I'm
not quite sure of what. Enjoying myself in his
absence, maybe?

Apparently Owen Wevill emailed him after he and
Mona spotted an intruder in our garden the other
night, when they couldn't sleep due to the sound of
my late-night party. Of course they weren't
complaining about the noise – on the contrary, they
were glad to know I could enjoy myself while my
husband was away, and were sure that my old friend
Rhodri would do his best to keep me entertained, now
he was back living in the village!

I was livid and sent a reply off straight away.

Dear Mal,
I hadn't realised the Wevills had such over-
active imaginations – or that they were sending
you bulletins on my movements. If they had really

thought there was an intruder, surely they should have phoned the police?

Of course, what they actually saw was me going up the garden with the torch, as I thought I'd heard a fox trying to get at the hens. This was several hours after Carrie and Nia had been around for an absolute orgy of pizza eating and the riotously noisy watching of a gardening DVD. The Wevills must have ears like bats if that kept them awake.

If you want to know my day-to-day movements while you're away, all you have to do is ask, they're not secret.

Fran.

I didn't deign to mention the Rhodri insinuations. I'm not protesting my innocence to my own husband like some damned Desdemona. He ought to know me better by now.

Mind you, by now he should also have realised that the Wevills are conducting an undercover hate campaign against me and jumped to my defence, but he takes them entirely at face value. So when Mona fawns and drools over him like a sex-mad boxer bitch she is just being 'friendly', and since Owen shares his passion for boats (indeed, was the one who infected him with the mania) he can do no wrong.

Before the Wevills arrived on the scene my only significant competition for Mal's attention was his stamp collection, and at least that kept him in the house. But messing about in his boat and going down to the yacht club now occupies all the time we used to spend doing family things together, like walking and going to the zoo. (Rosie was addicted to the zoo – we had to go every Sunday for *years*.)

I was still seething about the email when Rosie rang. She's been phoning me on a nightly basis since she went back, crying into the receiver about her assignment marks, which were not as brilliant as she thought they should be, although they sounded fine to me. This anguish is all mixed up with her dilemma over whether to dump her present nameless boyfriend *now*, in the hope that the boy she really fancies will ask her out, or whether that would be cruel while he is working hard for his finals.

When I could get a word in I said sternly, 'Rosie, did you take an email from Tom Collinge when you were home, and reply to it in my name?'

There was a gasp. 'Oh God, Mum – I'm sorry! I was just curious, and I didn't think you'd reply to him yourself. I meant to keep checking so I could delete the answer before you saw it.'

'Is that supposed to make it all right? And even though you know my password, don't you think my mail is private?'

'Yes, and I wouldn't have opened any of the others, really I wouldn't! And I only told Tom you had one daughter and were married, and asked him whether *he* was, that's all!'

Then she started crying again, so I ended up assuring her I wasn't really cross and she mustn't worry about her marks, and suggested a way to finish with her boyfriend so they stayed friends – and I felt like a wrung-out dishcloth after I put the phone down.

While each call like this leaves me totally on edge and overwrought, it seems to have a totally different effect on Rosie; whenever I ring back worriedly an hour or two later to check that she hasn't locked herself in her room with a bottle of pills and the breadknife, it's always to be told by one of her flatmates that she has just left in high spirits for a party and isn't expected back for hours.

And what's with all these ball dresses she seems to need? When I was at college I could fit the entirety of my belongings in a rucksack and one holdall, and I'm not sure I even knew what a ball dress was. Even now, ninety per cent of my clothing consists of jeans, T-shirts and home-made patchwork tops – it's economical and saves all that worry about what to wear every morning. I only need to get dressed up to go out with Mal. But Rosie seems to alternate between wearing a collection of paint-stained hankies held together in unexpected places by large plastic curtain rings, and off-the-peg but hideously expensive Princess Bride creations. I don't think there's a Schizophrenic Student Barbie yet, is there? There should be, there's a gap in the market.

Still, maternal guilt combined with a love that is positively painful always makes me scrape together enough for the next dress, even though I suspect that Mal's mother has already subbed up the wherewithal for several without telling me.

Mrs Morgan often phones me, asking how Rosie's

work is going, and whether she's eating properly and only going out with nice boys – though how I am supposed to know any of this when she is a couple of hundred miles away and never gives me any details, I can't imagine.

I asked Carrie to pop in later if she isn't too tired, and help me put a new password on my email, since she did a Computing for Small Businesses nightclass last year, so is pretty good at that kind of thing.

I heard her exchanging jolly greetings with the Wevills when she arrived – she couldn't have missed them, since they were on the drive filling my wheelie bin up with their rubbish.

Dragging her indoors, I told her what they were like to me when there was no one else around, but she was frankly incredulous.

'But they're so nice! Don't you think perhaps they are just trying too hard to be friendly, Fran? I mean, they often come into Teapots, and they seem very genuine people.'

'That's just it, Carrie – they *are* nice to everyone, except to me when I'm alone,' I said, but I'm sure she thinks I'm getting paranoid.

I might have started to think so myself if Ma hadn't taken a dislike to them on first sight; and Nia can detect insincerity at a glance, so all their attempts to smarm all over her met with curt rebuffs even before she realised what poison they were trying to spread about me – in the nicest possible way, by telling people *they* didn't believe such-and-such a rumour.

'Well, if you say so, Fran,' Carrie said doubtfully.

'Ask Nia, if you don't believe me.'

'Of course I believe you,' she said hastily. 'Oh, and I've collected some more info about Gabe Weston, if you'd like to see it sometime.'

'Oh, have you?' I said with vague interest, but I don't think she was really fooled.

After she'd gone I went out, removed the Wevills' bags of stinking rubbish and lobbed them back over the fence into their front garden where their two cats instantly started to close in on them. Although no one ever sees the Wevills doing anything antisocial to *me*, I'll bet my bottom dollar everyone in the village will know what I've done by tomorrow – and I used to be such a nice person.

The new password I put on my computer was 'trust'.

This is the first day of the Shaker diet, though it would take a concrete mixer rather than a quick whisk to make that strange powder homogenise with any liquid except, possibly, rubbing alcohol.

It certainly didn't satisfy my hunger, fill my stomach or titillate my taste buds, so what is the point of it unless it is simply meant as a kind of self-inflicted punishment for being gross?

Already craving real food I went up to the studio, where the only edible temptation was the sack of Happyhen mix (which I was pretty sure I could resist – for the first few days at least), and began roughing out some Alphawoman comic strips. Then I started a card design based on the hens, who are all big fluffy brown ones like in a children's picture book. Photos of them in various exciting poses line my walls together with hundreds of snaps of roses.

When I checked my website later lots of people had been looking at it, so it's not just me with the rose mania. Perhaps if I had good-quality prints done of some of my pictures I could sell them through the site. Limited editions, all numbered – and they'd be easy to post . . .

I'll ask Carrie what she thinks about it – if I ask Mal, he will only blind me with technology and put me off the idea.

Oh, and I finally replied to Tom's email, but more to occupy my hands than anything, since typing and eating simultaneously can seriously clog up your keys.

Dear Tom,

Nice to hear from you, and glad everything is going well for you. Yes, I'm happily married and love living here, but since I'm terribly busy, what with my family commitments and work, perhaps we could postpone having a reunion? I'll let you know when I have a bit more free time.

All the best,

Fran

That should hold him . . . for ever?

I am doing loads of work to distract me from my gnawing hunger, though in between I pore over the soft porn of cookbooks, salivating. Oooh, crème caramel! Aaah, *tarte aux cerises*!

Which somehow reminds me of the afternoon I took the *Restoration Gardener* DVD out of the miscellaneous box and started guiltily watching it with the curtains in the sitting room shut tight, which must have made the Wevills frantic with curiosity.

They have started parking halfway across my drive like they did last time Mal was away, making it very difficult for me to get my car in and out; however, they prefer that to parking on their own narrow drive because it means they get to stare in the front of the house whenever they get in their car.

They only do this when Mal isn't here, of course. And how do they know he's away? Because he tells them – and gives them permission to do it, so they don't have to keep moving one of their cars to get the other out!

After my sharp email to Mal he didn't communicate with me at all for two days, which was probably just as well since I was seething, and then suddenly he rang me as if nothing had happened. I might have thought he hadn't got my reply except that I could spot the Weevil-shaped hole in the dry biscuit of his conversation. I expect they have put a whole new spin on my daily round of giddy dissipation: walking in the fairy glen, going up to Plas Gwyn to help Nia whitewash her studio and see what new finds she and Rhodri have made in the attic, coffee (and sometimes a hand with the washing-up – old habits die hard) at Carrie's, or down to the Druid's Rest in the early evening for a wicked glass of diet tonic.

Now Mal phones me every couple of days, though

there was a time when he would call me every night when he was away; and even though he is the other side of London he would still have driven back for the weekend at least once. And I'm sure he forgets who he's talking to half the time, since he tends to address me in computer-speak monologues that slide effortlessly in through one ear and out the other.

I have barely touched on the fringes of understanding the Internet, though if the day ever dawns when I have to start submitting my artwork by computer I expect I will manage it: when I need to know something, *that's* the time to learn it, otherwise I'd just be cluttering up my brain cells with a lot of useless information.

Since he doesn't ask me anything about myself I haven't mentioned that my hair has mysteriously got two inches shorter and shows a distressing tendency to go into ringlets, I've planted a rose in his part of the garden and half-covered the fireplace in pottery shards and mosaic tiles.

The only personal thing he let fall is that he has seen a bit of Alison, his first wife. What I want to know is, *which* bit?

This morning I let three lots of estate agents into Fairy Glen to value it for Ma, and they didn't seem to know quite what to make of it.

The bright colours and sparkling, cluttered rooms stunned them speechless, as did the very basic amenities, even though it does have a bathroom and a kitchen of sorts. And none of them explored the garden further than the flattish area around the cottage, not having come equipped for hiking.

They scribbled in their notepads, scratched their heads, then valued it at about ten times what I thought it was worth, even though the glen is pretty useless for anything much except enjoying (and I must take lots more photos of it in case it is lost to me as inspiration – or at least in its present, magically neglected, form).

Of course, Nia might be right and no one will buy it, though then Ma couldn't afford her cruise, which would be a shame. Dad left her quite comfortably off, but I don't think she could get right round the world without augmenting her cash flow.

When I phoned her with the valuations she was absolutely amazed, but decided she would go with the highest one from sheer hopeful greed, though she *still* wouldn't sell it, even at the asking price, if she didn't like the person who made the offer!

Later I went to the Druid's Rest, since Carrie wanted to show us the fruits of her research into the Life and Times of Gabe Weston before Rhodri got there, and secretly I am sure that Nia was as keen to see what she had turned up as I was.

Mona Wevill was sitting in her car in front of my house smoking when I went out, and she stared at me deadpan as I skirted round the bonnet and headed into the village. Creepy, or what?

Nia and Carrie were in the back parlour with the stuffed trout, two halves of Murphy's and an open packet of dry-roasted peanuts between them.

'Hi, Carrie. Hi, Nia – how's it going up at Plas Gwyn?'

'Fine, except I wish Dottie would stop trying to stable her horse in my workshop. I've left her a perfectly good loose box at the end of the wing, but she can't seem to grasp the concept of change. She *does* realise Rhodri's doing his best to maintain the place, though, in her own dim way, and she's trying to help.'

'I went up there yesterday,' Carrie said, 'and planned how I wanted the tearoom set out, once we get permission.'

'And reminded us that we hadn't thought of toilets for the visitors,' Nia sighed. 'Another thing to fit in somewhere.'

'You'll get there,' Carrie said encouragingly. 'Anyway, aren't you both just *dying* to see what I've got on Gabriel Weston?' And she dumped a big carrier bag of stuff on the tabletop.

Not only had she scoured her contacts, the Internet and the magazine racks of the nearest town for further information on Gabriel Weston, she'd even gone to the length of buying his book!

Restoration Gardener looked just the sort of thing I would like if I weren't horribly and unreasonably prejudiced against the author, who smiled enigmatically at me from his book jacket photo.

'You know, the more I look at his face, the more I wonder if I've totally flipped and become one of those women who *imagine* they are having a relationship with someone famous,' I confessed, picking it up to study it more closely. 'Maybe it was just someone who looked a bit like him? I mean, he can't be unique, can he?'

'He looks pretty unique to me,' Carrie said, scrutinising his picture with the eyes of a connoisseur. Then she riffled through the heap. 'I got most of this off the Net. There's lots about a paternity claim case, back when he'd just started making a name for himself on TV.'

'What? A *paternity* case?' I snatched up the first sheet that came to hand and started reading, and so did Nia. After a bit I looked up. 'It wasn't his baby after all!'

'No,' agreed Carrie, 'but there must have been something in it, because his wife divorced him – see, read that one there.'

'Reputation Restored! TV gardener cleared in paternity claim row . . . but too late to save marriage.'

'Perhaps she simply wasn't the "stand by your man" type?'

Nia was frowning over a magazine article. 'Or maybe she wanted to divorce him anyway? It says here that she went to America and remarried.'

Carrie fished out a copy of *Surprise!* magazine: 'Yes, and she's just divorced and remarried again – for the third time, I think. This one's a plastic surgeon.'

'Once Gabe Weston started being a familiar face on the telly he'd probably have had lots of opportunities to play around,' Nia said cynically. 'I suspect all men would if they got the chance.'

'Not *all* of them!' Carrie protested defensively.

'Ignore Nia, she's jaundiced on the subject,' I told her. 'Your Huw would never dream of being unfaithful to you.'

'He'd better not,' Carrie said. 'And actually, maybe we're wrong about this guy, because once I'd waded through all the information I sort of got to like him. Listen to this one:

Gabe Weston lives quietly these days in his small London mews house near Marble Arch, a strange place to find a gardener, although he is said to be looking for a country property.

Part of his charm is his everyday unpretentious nature. He is a deeply private man despite his many TV appearances. You won't find out from him about his tragic family history: the older brother killed in Northern Ireland, the widowed, alcoholic father who reduced the family to poverty. Strictly off limits too is the failure of his marriage: his ex-wife, the former Tamsyn Kane, recently remarried for the third time, lives in America with their only daughter, Stella.

'So the poor man seems to have had a difficult childhood, but he still got to university and he's made a name for himself with this archaeological gardening thing.'

'He doesn't seem to have ever been the wild party type,' Nia admitted, 'though there are a couple of kiss-and-tell-type articles.'

'Some people will do anything for money,' Carrie commented. 'He seems to be living pretty quietly these days, but there was some gossip that his wife was pregnant when they got married, which was more of a big deal back then, I suppose.'

'When?' I demanded suddenly.

'When what?' Nia said, puzzled.

'When did they get married?'

Carrie pounced on a cutting. 'I'm just working it out . . . the daughter must be nearly eighteen now.'

'About a year younger than Rosie,' I said, thinking that Gabe Weston seemed to have put it about a bit, making me just a member of a not-so-unique club.

'She was the daughter of his first major client – some garden down in Cornwall or somewhere. They filmed a documentary about it, and that started his TV career off.'

I frowned. 'You know, that may be where he said he was going when I met up with him – so he didn't waste much time, did he?'

'Me Mellors, you Lady Constance?' Nia asked.

'She must have liked a bit of rough,' I said tartly, feeling full of a smouldering rage that was quite unreasonable in the circumstances.

'Was he?' Carrie asked interestedly.

I shrugged. 'He looked like it – you know, grubby jeans and a T-shirt, five o'clock shadow.'

'He certainly didn't come across like a bit of rough in that DVD,' Nia said. 'Lady Whoosit could hardly take her eyes off him, and she must have been seventy if she was a day!'

'I didn't say he wasn't attractive – he must have been, because he certainly didn't make me go back to his van and have his wicked way with me. I really fancied him. I may have been practically legless, but I do remember that much.'

Nia and I sat and worked our way through the rest of the stuff, which mostly repeated hearsay and old news, and soon we could all have won *Mastermind* on the public domain knowledge about Gabe Weston's life. I'd have failed on the general knowledge, though, unless it was about roses.

At some point Carrie must have put a half of bitter in front of me and I'd drunk most of it before I realised what I was doing, I was so involved in trying to find the man among the myths and extract the minotaur from the maze of misinformation. Actually, though, if he wasn't exactly coming out smelling of roses, he certainly was far from a monster.

'Well, what do you think?' Carrie asked eventually.

'I think your intelligence-gathering resources are impressive, and you are secretly a mole for the CIA,' I said.

'Did you see the *second* paternity claim?' Nia said. 'That must have knocked him for six, even though the poor woman was delusional and he'd never as much as met her.'

'Yes, but it did sound like he'd been having an affair with that woman in the *first* paternity case, even if the baby turned out not to be his, so he doesn't come out of this entirely white as the driven snow, does he?' I shuddered. 'Just imagine if I'd suddenly discovered who he was and popped out of the woodwork with a paternity claim too! But he doesn't know about Rosie, and he never is going to know about Rosie – and nor is the press, so that's that!'

'Yes, but what if Plas Gwyn does get chosen for the

programme?' Nia asked. 'Don't you think he might recognise you?'

I pondered. 'I don't think so, do you? One night, one woman among many – probably one in every place he stopped! And I've altered a lot after all these years. I think women change much more than men do.'

They looked at me consideringly.

'He can't have met many girls with long hair the colour of faded candyfloss,' Nia said.

'But even my hair is much less strawberry and more just dark blonde now that I'm older, and it's a whole lot shorter.'

'I still don't think you do look much different from how you used to,' Nia said obstinately. 'Your face is a bit plumper, but still heart-shaped –'

'A fatty little heart.'

She gave me a repressive look. 'And now you regularly have your eyelashes dyed you don't have that startled-rabbit look you used to have when you forgot to put your mascara on, but that's about all that's changed.'

The eyelash tint is my one beauty extravagance, but very effective. I have smallish, neat features otherwise, nothing remarkable.

'You have very lovely big grey eyes,' Carrie said kindly.

'With lovely big crow's feet. No, I can't believe I'm so memorable he will recognise me, but if Plas Gwyn wins the makeover, I'll make sure I've got my head covered at all times and wear dark glasses, OK?'

'The whole village will think Mal's been beating you up,' Nia objected.

'They certainly will. Well, this is really fascinating,' Carrie said, 'but I'll have to go. Shall I leave all the stuff for you to have another look through?'

'No, thanks,' I said, bundling it back into its bag, 'I think I've got it all by heart.' Then I hesitated. 'Perhaps I could borrow the book for a couple of days, though?'

'OK,' she agreed, 'if I can have the DVD in exchange?'

She went off home – she gets up early most mornings to bake – and later Rhodri came in. Even though he was wearing cord trousers and a battered lumberjack shirt, the landlord fawned over him like he was royalty; he simply can't understand why the local gentry should want to hang out in the back parlour with us peasants.

His old jacket smelled foul; I don't know what they do to them, but on rainy days the entire waxed Barbour jacket brigade stink like wet tents whole flocks have lambed in.

Up the Garden Path

I have been dipping into Carrie's book, and Gabe Weston sounds more like a psychic gardener than a restoration one to me. Cop a load of this:

> Old gardens, no matter how big or small, from the overgrown parterres of the great estates to the seemingly aimless dips and hollows of long-vanished cottage gardens, all have a history. The ghost of what once was still lingers on the air like the faint fragrance of old potpourri.

He seems to be able to dowse for long-buried garden features like other people can find water with a bit of twig, although he seems happy to use modern technology like geophysical surveying too.

> Walking over what was once a garden I can feel the resonances of time as though I were a human echo-finder tuned to every nuance of the old pathways, walls, trees and even the more transient plantings of the past.

Can this be true? Or is it just how they sell the series? Not, of course, that he wouldn't be a big success without an angle like that, because any even *halfway* decent man who can talk gardening is terribly seductive, and he is much more than that.

Ma came down for the weekend and we did a bit of sorting out and cleaning ready for any viewings, while the dogs contributed a fresh silting of hair, and Ivy sicked up half a rubber ball on the Chinese rug.

I frantically felt her little fat furry stomach for signs of the other half blocking something vital, while she wriggled ecstatically and tried to lick my face, but then Ma found Holly chewing it behind the sofa.

After that excitement I flicked a feather duster over the magpie litter of Ma's sitting room, where every surface is encrusted with shells, pebbles, sea-washed glass, bits of mirror and those plastic things they used to put in cereal packets. Ma sat in her favourite chair in the window, smoking and crocheting simultaneously.

'You look a bit peaky, my love,' she commented when I started to flag.

'I do feel a bit off lately – but I've been dieting, so that probably isn't helping.' In fact, pottering about the studio playing with my ideas and wandering the garden looking for something to prune followed by a trio of hopeful hens is about all I've got the energy for lately.

'Dieting's unhealthy, Fran. I hope you're eating a balanced diet.'

'I've tried those meal-replacement things – they're supposed to have all the vitamins and minerals you need. But I only survived a week on the Shaker diet before going totally off the rails.'

'Shaker?'

'Yes, though I don't know if it's called that because it's all milkshakes, or for the way it makes you shaky after the second day – or even because it's dead simple. But after a week I found myself in the kitchen at two in the morning eating a big slab of that disgusting chocolate cake topping, and I realised my mouth had got totally out of control.'

'I'm not surprised!'

'So then I tried diet bars, but that was just as bad ... all I could think about was food! Bacon and eggs, fish and chips eaten from newspaper on the harbour front at Conwy, those fresh shrimps we used to get at Parkgate when I was a little girl ...' I sighed. 'Oh, yum! I'm starting to feel ravenous all over again.'

'I'll take you to the Druid's Rest for a bar meal, Frannie. You need feeding up.'

'I don't know about feeding up, but it's clear that a starve-binge cycle isn't going to make me thinner,' I said, and she certainly didn't have to twist my arm to get me to eat real food at the pub.

I'm going to have to think about this dieting business a bit more unless Mal can just learn to love me the way I am, as I love him, fossicky little ways, undiscriminating friendships and expensive habits included. Do I *have* to keep young and beautiful? Why can't I be plump, middle-aged and beautiful?

Come to that, why aren't the women's magazines full of articles on 'The Beauty of the Wrinkle and How to Enhance Them'? Or 'How to Successfully Put on Weight in Middle Age', instead of featuring those Petra Pans of the celebrity circuit who are holding time at bay with applications of ground-up sea slugs at a hundred pounds a dab?

Nia says *she* hasn't put on any weight since she read *Fat Is a Feminist Issue* and stopped worrying about it; in fact, she has lost a bit, but I think that is partly because of all the work she is doing with Rhodri trans-forming Plas Gwyn. She seems to have more or less taken charge of the renovations and innovations (*and* of Rhodri), so it's just as well it's a *very* bijou stately home and not a Chatsworth.

They have now furnished each of the rooms in a particular period, with furniture and hangings that had languished unseen for years – out with the new and in with the old! Workmen are busily putting new electric wiring into the craft studios and plastering the soon-to-be gift shop and tearoom.

I took Ma up there to see how they were getting on before she went home again, and Rhodri gave us tea and chunks of Caerphilly cheese on limp crackers and told her all about Gabe Weston (which *I* hadn't mentioned since I wasn't sure my face wouldn't give something away) and the trunkful of family documents he had found in the attic.

'I haven't had time to go through them yet, but there might even be a plan of the garden, or at least some lists of plants or something,' he said hopefully.

'That's the sort of thing they like on *Restoration Gardener*.' He picked up his own well-thumbed copy of the accompanying book and read out: '"All kinds of family documents can offer clues to vanished gardens, from detailed plans and planting lists to chatty family letters. Even a passing mention might be the one missing piece that will make the picture clear."'

'Most of the top ones appear to be old household accounts and linen lists,' Nia said, 'but goodness knows what's at the bottom. They seem to have been tipping paperwork into it for centuries.'

'There's bound to be *something* interesting in there,' Rhodri agreed optimistically.

While Rhodri is much better at using his hands than his head, he's pretty knowledgeable about antiques and the history of his house, so when he has time he will be compiling a guide that he can sell to visitors.

I gave him that cartoon I drew of him and he loved it so much he is going to have it on lots of items in his gift shop, from postcards to mugs and tea towels: the Lion of Plas Gwyn! And he is not quite such a sad lion any more, for he has cheered up no end now Nia has taken him in hand. Some men just *love* to be bossed around.

Once I became aware of Gabe Weston's existence I seemed to see or hear mentions of him everywhere, as though my ears and eyes had tuned into his frequency. And I even bought another copy of the book so I could give Carrie's back, because I found the workings of his mind strangely fascinating, especially combined with what I've already learned of his history. As he says on page 56, 'It is amazing what can be grafted on to tough native rootstock.'

And the more I stared at his author photo, the more doubtful I was that he could be Rosie's father: I couldn't see the least resemblance. Could I have got it wrong, and it was really Tom after all? But she doesn't look in the least like *him*, either!

I still didn't want Gabe Weston anywhere near St Ceridwen's Well, but as time passed I started to think nothing would come of it – until the day Rhodri heard that Gabe was about to tour the six properties on the long list in order to decide which three would go forward for the TV vote-off.

Rhodri was terribly excited about it – think of the publicity if Plas Gwyn were featured! – but unfortunately he will be in London doing his Father of the Bride stuff when the Great Gardener turns up, and so has had to delegate the honour of showing him the estate to his cousin Dottie as Token Family Member. Nia will be around too, in case Dottie totally blows it, since she has not only got a screw loose but a whole bolt, a gasket and several vital rivets.

And I know I ought to lie low that day, but I am *terribly* tempted to go up and spy on him! I have this burning curiosity to see him in the flesh, and this could be the only opportunity I ever get. I could watch him in perfect safety from Nia's workshop, because he's bound to park out front in the paved courtyard.

Dare I?

* * *

Fairy Glen is about to go into the property papers and this morning I heard hammering from up the lane, which turned out to be the estate agents putting up a 'For Sale' sign. This seemed pointless since the lane peters out into a farm track beyond the glen and no one uses the old rear drive to Plas Gwyn, so there is virtually no passing traffic except Ma and tractors.

I went up there to give it a quick vacuum through, but was so exhausted I gave up halfway. I can't imagine what's the matter with me lately; my legs feel as if someone sneaked in and filled them with lead. Wonder if I've got that ME thingummy? I hope not, I haven't got time to do an Elizabeth Barrett Browning on a chaise longue – especially without a large and devoted family to run about after me.

I'm juggling cartoons, card designs and the first illustration for next year's rose calendar as it is, not to mention Alphawoman – *and* Mal is back on Friday, so I've got my own house to scrape back to hygienic bedrock. So much has been happening that the time has just flown by – and soon no more nights out at the pub until he goes off again!

Do most married women lead a double life like a secret agent? But, come to think of it, now the Wevills are reporting my movements he knows *exactly* what I am doing while he is away, so my cover is blown. *Yes, I admit it! I do have vestiges of a social life – I see my friends! I even – gasp! – go to the pub sometimes or hang out in the village teashop! Is there no end to this woman's depravity?*

Mal's only going to be home until Monday, then he

100

has to go off to Manchester for a few days, which means I will have to launder half his wardrobe over the first weekend we have together in six weeks.

I spent Valentine's Day having a cleaning blitz, attacking it with all the savagery of one who had not received a card from her supposedly loving spouse, and though I did finally get a bouquet by Interflora in the late afternoon it might as well have had 'Suddenly realised at the last minute!' written on the gift tag. He knows I hate scentless, senseless flower-shop roses too: give me the blowsy, velvety real thing any time.

Nia got a Valentine's card, which she said was just Rhodri being silly although I could tell she was pleased. His writing is big and loopy, like him, so pretty unmistakable.

I felt a bit fed up, to tell the truth, so I would have gone out except that Carrie was off somewhere for a romantic dinner with her aged lover, Rhodri was spending the evening sifting through the papers in the trunk in search of garden titbits to entice Gabe Weston with, and Nia had to go to a meeting – though she didn't say what of.

So I ended up finishing the mosaic on the fireplace, which looks great, and watching old Buffy DVDs.

Oh, *bite me*, Angel!

Rhodri has gone off to London bearing the wedding gift Nia and I clubbed together to buy for the rich and happy couple: a beautifully carved Welsh lovespoon. Bet Zoe hadn't got one of those on her list.

He was in such a froth of nerves worrying over his

role at the wedding, plus what sort of impression Dottie was going to make on Gabriel Weston, that we were quite glad to finally wave him off.

'I think he's got a stone up his exhaust,' Nia said critically, listening to the Spyder's receding rattle.

'And a loose marble or two,' I agreed, 'though not as many as Dottie. Do you think she *will* cock everything up tomorrow?'

'Not if I can help it: I'm going to hang around and make sure she tells him all the interesting stuff, even if she can't get the hang of who I am or what I'm doing there.'

'She'll probably think you're a loyal retainer.'

'She already thinks I'm a groom now I've started intercepting her at my workshop door and taking Rollover to his new loose box myself, and she seems to be warming to me. Rollover's warming to me too, but he has very big feet and he's not careful where he puts them.'

'Well, save me any manure for my roses,' I said. 'Just say the word, and I'll be up there with a shovel and a bag. Oh, and did I tell you I've got people coming to view Fairy Glen tomorrow? Two lots, at twelve and one. Gabriel Weston should have come and gone by then, shouldn't he?'

'If he manages to find St Ceridwen's in the first place. Are you still plotting to hide in my studio dressed like Michelle of the French Resistance, just so you can get a sneaky look at him?'

'I don't think I can resist it – and if he doesn't pick the garden then it will be the only chance I ever get to see him, won't it? But it'll be from afar, so you'll still have to tell me if you think Rosie looks like him at all.'

'She doesn't look like his photograph, that's for sure,' Nia said. 'Mind you, she doesn't look even remotely like Tom either, apart from being blondish.'

'I've always said she was a changeling – she's never looked like anyone I've ever met. Maybe I created her all on my own, like a frog? *Is* it frogs that can do it themselves if they have to, or something else?'

'You're nearly as barmy as Dottie,' Nia observed. 'And I wouldn't show the viewers round the cottage tomorrow singing "There Are Fairies at the Bottom of My Garden", either, unless they're the sort you want to put off.'

Before leaving the house next morning for Plas Gwyn I put on the dark wraparound sunglasses I picked up at a charity shop and then tied on a headscarf with the ends knotted round my neck in a very *Dolce Vita* way, as though someone might be going to whisk me away to the Italian Riviera in an open sports car at any moment and show me a good time.

Although heaven forbid, because Gabe Weston's already shown me one of those (even if the sports car was actually a camper van and the Riviera a pub car park), and it certainly made me realise I was not cut out to be the proverbial good time had by all.

With my hair and eyes hidden I looked very non-descript, especially once I put on my warm hooded pink duffel coat with the rather ratty fur trim, another second-hand bargain. (Fake fur, of course, for until genetic engineering plumbs new depths, animals don't come in mauve.)

Quite sure even my nearest and dearest wouldn't recognise me, I set out for Plas Gwyn with a knot of strange excitement in the pit of my stomach and that song about being a second-hand Rose on my lips. I was feeling cheerful despite it being a wet and breezy day, until I saw the Wevills' car parked so far across my drive I would have to ask them to move it if I wanted to get mine out.

'Is that you, Fran?' called Mona from her front window as I skirted her car, but I ignored her and set out on foot. I am certainly not asking permission to use my own drive or complaining: last time she said smugly that Mal told her it was fine with him as though she were scoring points, and then Owen emailed him forgivingly about my strangely unneighbourly attitude.

Suddenly there seem to be four people in this marriage, two of them deeply devious and one consistently batting for the wrong side. Mona is clearly motivated by jealousy: of my marriage to Mal, my being younger and prettier than she (not hard) and successful with my work. But what makes Owen such an Evil Weevil?

And, for a clever man, Mal can be very stupid about people. At some point very soon I am going to have to have this out with him, because I have definitely had enough and the campaign has evidently only just started to hot up.

My mood was now much more Aretha than old-time music hall and I could hear her belting out 'Think!' in my head as I plodded up the drive to Plas Gwyn – so Mal had better think what *he's* trying to do to *me*.

'There he is,' Nia said, peering through the shifting veils of rain that coyly granted us – and presumably Gabe Weston too – unexciting glimpses of grass and strangely shaped trees.

I pushed my shades up on top of my head and watched him park his big silver Mercedes next to Dottie's steaming and battered Land Rover and get out, stretching, but there was no sign of Dottie, who had vanished into the house on her arrival a few minutes before.

'Where *is* she? She should be there to meet him!' Nia muttered, resignedly reaching for her mack.

'Quick, Nia!' I said urgently. 'He must have spotted the light and he's coming this way – head him off.'

But now the rain was coming down harder, and he sprinted across and burst in just as I flattened myself against the wall behind the door. My sunglasses slammed down hard on the bridge of my nose, making my eyes water copiously.

'Hi,' he said to Nia, shaking rain off his hair in all directions like a dog. 'What a day! I'm Gabriel Weston. Are you . . . ?'

'You're looking for Dottie Gwyn-Whatmire,' Nia said with a polite smile that warmed on contact with his. 'I think she went into the hall – perhaps I'd better come across and show you?'

'Thank you, that would be —' He stopped suddenly, having spotted me spreadeagled like a scared refugee against the wall. Possibly, going by the rather tortured sketches Nia had stuck to the walls, he assumed at first glimpse that I was some kind of strange art form.

I straightened up slowly and shuffled my feet, sneaking a quick monochrome look at him. 'H-hi!'

'This is Fran March, a local artist, and I'm Nia Thomas; we're both friends of Rhodri Gwyn-Whatmire,' Nia explained, 'and this is my studio.'

'Well, I didn't mean to startle you both,' he said kindly, 'but your light was the only sign of life.'

My tongue was stuck to the roof of my mouth, but he probably just assumed I was star-struck. I turned my dark glasses beseechingly in Nia's direction and she stopped smiling at him and said briskly, 'Come on then, and we'll find Dottie. I must warn you, though, that she is just a *little* bit eccentric.'

He didn't know the half of it.

Without in the least intending to follow them my feet simply carried me across the courtyard in their wake, so I was right behind as they pushed the huge dark wooden door open and stepped inside, though I had to shove the sunglasses down my nose far enough to peer over the top before I could make anything out in the Stygian gloom.

Dottie Gwyn-Whatmire was flitting up and down the large stone-flagged hall, wringing her red-knuckled hands like a skinny wraith of Lady Macbeth, but one incongruously attired in tight corduroy jodhpurs and waxed jacket. Her face drooped sadly at the jowls, and wisps of hair the colour of wet hay showed under a drover's hat. It was clearly not one of her good days.

Gabriel Weston moved towards her holding his hand out, but barely had time to say: 'Hello, are you Miss Gwyn –' before she turned on him like a fury.

'There are *no* conveniences!' she hissed fiercely, fixing him with pale, sunken eyes. 'Only garderobes in the outer wall. You wouldn't like it. The children would fall down and wash into the cesspit and drown – every last one. Your wife wouldn't like it. The Grey Lady wouldn't like it.'

He stood his ground. 'I haven't got a wife *or* little children.'

She sidled up like a nervous horse, eyeing him suspiciously. 'No wife?'

'No. Who's the Grey Lady?'

She ignored that, becoming suddenly more expansive. 'No *wife*! Then the house is too big for you! They should have told you – Rhodri should have explained. It's not a weekend cottage, you know, it's the birthright of the Gwyn-Whatmires!'

'Miss Gwyn-Whatmire,' he said patiently, 'I'm not here to buy the house, but because I present a TV programme on garden restoration, and we're thinking of featuring Plas Gwyn in our next series. Didn't your cousin tell you?'

'A TV programme?'

'*Restoration Gardener*. You might have seen it?' he asked hopefully. 'I'm Gabriel Weston.'

'No, no, no!' She shook her head violently, backing away again. 'Never seen it. Don't know it. Never watch it. *Horse of the Year Show*'s the only thing worth seeing and I *go* to that. No TV even: get up, work, go to bed, that's my motto.'

'Is it? I mean, jolly good,' he said heartily, and I felt pretty certain he'd never used the word 'jolly' before in his life. 'Well, let me explain why I'm here: if we choose the property to feature in the programme we draw up plans for the garden restoration and actually recreate part of what was once here, at our own expense.'

She took another look at him and stopped wringing her hands, which was a relief. 'Do the work and *pay* us?' she queried, like he was the mad one. 'You're a *gardener*, did you say?'

'That's right.'

'Mad, quite mad, poor man!' she muttered. 'Well, then, come along, garden's this way.' She set off past us at a brisk trot out of the door and cantered across the courtyard into the driving rain.

He turned and stared at us, his eyes wide so you could see all the splotchy green rays round the irises . . . which belatedly made me realise I still had the sunglasses on the end of my nose and hastily shove them back up.

Nia shrugged. 'I did warn you she was a bit eccentric.'

He hesitated. 'Rhodri Gwyn-Whatmire . . . ?'

'Oh, he's not like his cousin at all,' Nia said firmly, 'if that's what you were going to ask. Go on, or she'll be back to see where you've got to. I'll catch up with you.'

'Right,' he said, and followed in Dottie's wake.

'What are you *doing*?' Nia hissed at me as soon as he was out of earshot. 'I thought you were going to keep a low profile.'

'I was,' I said, finally getting my voice back, 'but clearly he has no idea who I am, so it's safe enough.'

'Not surprising: even your mam wouldn't recognise you in that get-up.'

'I thought I looked pretty good, actually,' I said, stumbling over a tree root, 'though I can't see a thing in these shades.'

'You look twice as conspicuous as usual and the sunglasses are useless as a disguise if you keep looking over the top of them, Fran!'

'Shh! They'll hear us,' I warned as we caught up.

Dottie warmed to Gabe once she'd decided he wasn't trying to buy the house, even remembering the packet of photocopied documents Rhodri'd given her to pass to him after Nia prompted her. They were somewhat crumpled and had that strange damp tents-and-sheep smell from being stuffed in the pocket of her waxed jacket.

We all surreptitiously watched Gabe Weston stride up and down with the rain darkening his hair and turning it into tight coils, then finally stand deep in thought like a particularly nice bit of garden statuary, though fully clothed.

'Seen enough?' Dottie enquired finally, waking him out of his reverie.

'Enough to know Plas Gwyn has a special magic of its own,' he agreed. 'Spirit of place, it's sometimes called.'

'Is it? Only it's bloody wet, and I've got work to do.'

'Thank you then, Miss Gwyn-Whatmire, you've been very helpful. Perhaps I could just walk around the grounds a little more? You don't need to stay.'

She gave him a suspicious glare, as if he might be planning to steal something, though unless he had a penchant for rude topiary and a large lorry it was hard to see exactly what. 'Well, s'pose so,' she conceded reluctantly. 'Mind you leave by the back way this time: cheek of tradesmen these days, parking bold as brass in the courtyard!'

'I'll do that,' he said meekly, and with another mistrustful look she finally headed off for her Land Rover.

'Extraordinary!' he muttered.

'Well, we'll leave you to it as well,' Nia said. 'I'll be in my workshop, if you want to know anything else. Come on, Fran.'

I couldn't resist one quick backward look over my shoulder, and found him staring after us, but then he almost instantly turned his back and walked off, so I expect he was just thinking of the garden.

'I think Dottie's blown it. What do you think?' Nia muttered furiously as we headed off into a wet wind. 'I *told* Rhodri that even Rollover would make a better job of it!'

'It was a bit hard to gauge what he was thinking – but I'd say Plas Gwyn has worked its mojo on him, Dottie or no Dottie.'

'God, I hope so! We need the publicity and even if we don't win the makeover, being shortlisted and on the TV would be a huge help.'

I noted the royal 'we'. I also suddenly noted the time. 'It's five to twelve, Nia – I've got to run!' And I pelted off down the rear drive towards Fairy Glen.

Thriller

By the time I got to Fairy Glen I was soaked and breathless, and all the *dolce* had gone right out of my *vita*.

I also had Kylie Minogue singing 'Can't Get You Out of My Head' on my inner Walkwoman, to which even Dolly Parton would have been preferable, and I'd just like to say to whoever up there is dishing out all this punishment: 'Enough, already!'

Fortunately the first viewers were so late that I had plenty of time to unlock everything and adjust my wet headscarf before they rolled up in a huge gleaming off-road vehicle with two small and horribly lively children.

I could see right away that they were *not* going to suit the Glen, even before Mr Woods started smiling with silent condescension at everything I said. Then he went round tapping the walls and furniture as though he were trying to raise ghosts, while his wife seemed unable to believe that the kitchen really *was* the kitchen, and there wasn't another one hidden away somewhere.

'No, this is it,' I assured her. 'Look – cooker, kettle, even a Belfast sink – and they're terribly trendy these days, aren't they?'

Mrs Woods, who combined a cultivated and erratic lisp with the breathless delivery of a tiny tot, looked doubtful but asked me where the water came from.

'The tap – see, there it is over the sink,' I said encouragingly, turning it on and off to demonstrate.

'No, I meant is it spwing or mains?'

'Mains. Haven't you read the leaflet?'

'Oh, no, we saw the advewt in the paper and just booked to see it wif one at a mawina, where we could keep the boat too.'

'Well, we are *miles* away from the sea here,' I lied, for actually it's hardly any drive to get down to where Mal keeps *Cayman Blue*, if you know the little back roads.

Mr Woods opened every cupboard door in a frankly nosy way, finding nothing more offensive than tins of game soup, cockieleekie and baked beans, then finally straightened and fixed me with an accusing eye. 'This place isn't even *habitable*! It needs totally gutting and replastering. Plumbing, wiring, new kitchen, bathroom, an extension –'

'Chwome kitchen,' put in his wife firmly.

'The garden's a wasteland and it would cost a fortune to have the glen landscaped,' he finished.

'Landscaped?' I began, when Mrs Woods suddenly broke in anxiously.

'Whewe awe the childwen, Mike? Oh my God!' And she rushed out shouting, 'Bwidget! Fweddie!'

'They won't come to any harm out there, *I* never did,' I assured Mr Woods, though actually he wasn't making any move to rush out after his wife. 'Mind you, it's got more overgrown with every year.'

She came back with the two mutinous and slightly grubby children and looked at me accusingly. 'Thewe's a well! They might have fallen down and dwownd!'

'Not unless you can drown in hard concrete! It was blocked off years ago, and first of all you'd have to prise the padlock off the cover to get at it . . .'

I turned as the children shuffled their feet guiltily. 'They haven't . . . ?'

'It must have wusted,' she said quickly. 'Well, Mikey, I think we'd better get on and see the uffer house, hadn't we? Fank you, Mith . . . ?'

'March.'

'Mith March. And I hope your hair soon gwows back after the chemothewapy,' she added mysteriously as she left.

Chemotherapy?

I looked at myself in the mirror. I wasn't that pale and wan, was I? The rather barbaric and clashing colours of the silk scarf did make me look a bit washed out, but it was the only one of Ma's I could find.

Maybe I should have put a bit of lipstick on. It was too late now, though, because not only was I sure that the only lipstick I might find in Ma's room would be in Siren Scarlet, but the next viewer was on the doorstep.

He was a pleasant-seeming youngish man who whizzed round competently with a clipboard making notes, and it became more and more apparent from what he let drop that he was some kind of property developer, until eventually I came right out and accused him of it.

'Yes, I *am* looking for development potential – and there's a lot of land with this cottage.'

114

'But it's almost vertical and heavily wooded – you'd need to be a Frank Lloyd Wright to get anything built on that, even if you got planning permission – which you won't,' I assured him vehemently.

'You'd be surprised where you can get permission to build these days,' he said good-naturedly, 'though you're right about the glen. It's steeper than I thought.'

He turned and looked back towards the cottage. 'But there's enough flat land around here to get two houses on, with a slice of the glen at the back for a garden each, even if I wasn't allowed to demolish the cottage itself.'

'Demolish the *cottage*?'

'Well, it is a bit of any eyesore, isn't it?'

'It's wonderful,' I said hotly. 'It's – it's Victorian Gothic!'

'It's that all right, but it needs a fortune spending on it to make it anything like a saleable proposition, so I don't know what those estate agents were about to price it so high. I'll be making an offer, probably – but a reasonable one!'

'It'll be pointless,' I assured him coldly. 'My mother will only sell to someone wanting to live here and love the property as she has done. As we *both* have.'

He smiled again as though he knew something about human cupidity I didn't, and took himself off, and I went back in to close and lock the windows and back door. When I came back out a big familiar silver car was pulling up outside, and I hastily pulled my sunglasses back down and twitched my headscarf forward.

Like magic, Kylie vanished from my head to be replaced by Janis Joplin entreating the Lord to give her a Mercedes

Benz, and I crooned resignedly along as the door opened and a tall man with a head of hair like a badly knotted silk carpet got out and started towards me.

There was a feeling of doomed inevitability about it all. You know that Michael Jackson video where all those ghastly zombie things are slowly and inexorably closing in on him? Well, I was starting to get the same feeling. I even looked over my shoulder to see if Tom Collinge was also sneaking up on me from the woods, trailing tattered bandages of grubby reminiscence behind him.

'Hello again,' Gabe Weston said warmly, smiling in a reassuring sort of way as though he thought I might become hysterical at any minute, or ask for his autograph or something.

'Hello,' I said unenthusiastically, though my heart was flip-flopping about like a dying fish. 'Are you lost? You should have turned left out of the drive to get back into the village.'

'I know, but I caught sight of your "For Sale" sign and stopped on impulse! Are you the owner?'

'No,' I said, taking an involuntary step back.

He smiled again, crinkling up the skin around his eyes in a way that probably drove his legion of female fans wild.

'No. No . . . I'm . . .' I cleared my throat and tried again. 'My mother owns it. I've just been showing people around.'

'Have you? Then could you possibly let me have a quick look too? Only I've been searching for a country property for ages and it looks interesting.'

I closed the door behind me and took out my keys.

'Sorry, I'm afraid it's by appointment through the estate agents only,' I said firmly.

'Yes, but I'm here now, and you know who I am, so it's not like you would be showing a dodgy stranger around, is it?' he said persuasively.

'No,' I snapped, resisting the lure of that deep, velvet-soft voice. 'But Fairy Glen can't possibly be what you're looking for.'

'Fairy Glen? Unusual name.'

'Not really, because it *was* one – there are still the remains of a tea garden out the back, and bits of statuary and grottoes and stuff up the glen.'

'I know all about fairy glens, I just wasn't expecting to find one here, in such an out-of-the-way place.'

'No, well, it's hugely overgrown and the cottage is tiny with *very* basic amenities. I'm sure it's not worth your while looking at it.'

'On the contrary, you've whetted my appetite Mrs . . . March, was it?'

'Yes.'

'And if you were kind enough to let me have a quick look now, I'd be able to tell for myself whether it was totally unsuitable, wouldn't I? Then I wouldn't waste your time and mine by making an official appointment and driving all the way back up from London especially.'

'But I'm sure it's not what you're looking for!' I protested again, last ditch.

'How do you know what I'm looking for?' He raised one eyebrow enquiringly.

'I don't, I just assumed that a tiny, run-down, barely modernised cottage with a couple of acres of nearly vertical undergrowth several hours' drive from London isn't what you really had in mind.'

'So you think I'm just a time waster?'

'It's not an impulse purchase,' I said severely.

'*Please?*' he said winningly. It might have been even more winning if I wasn't seeing everything in shades of deepest black and grey again.

I hesitated, then turned and opened the door, sensing rather than hearing him following me into the dark hallway. He moved quietly for such a big man.

'You know, I keep thinking there's something very familiar about you! Have we met?' he said suddenly from right behind me.

'Met? No, I – yah!' Totally missing the step down, I plummeted forward with a yelp, only to be jerked back upright by strong hands at the last minute. My shades flew off and ricocheted off the wooden hallstand, and I was certainly glad *I* hadn't, since it is one of those spiky carved ones of a bear in a tree: prongs all over the place. I'd have had more holes than a colander.

'Careful,' he said, setting me upright before picking up my glasses. 'I'm afraid these are broken and – excuse me – but do you really *need* them in midwinter?'

'Conjunctivitis. My eyes are sensitive to light,' I said quickly. Brilliant – hand the girl a coconut.

'Well, there's none in here and precious little outside now the rain is closing in again.'

He was looking at me curiously, but I avoided his gaze. 'Perhaps we'd better press on, then, Mr Weston,' I suggested. 'The electricity often cuts off in a storm too, and the daylight will be going before long.'

I'd have liked to have added that the plague still visited St Ceridwen's Well on a twice-yearly basis, and how we all hoped the chronic dysentery would clear up once we had mains water, because the stuff we got from the well was so full of nematodes we had to chew every mouthful; but I remembered Rhodri and his hopes for Plas Gwyn just in time.

Tucking an escaped strand of pinkish hair into my scarf I whisked him through Fairy Glen like Dottie on speed.

'Sitting room. Kitchen – sinks, tap, table. Bathroom – toilet and bath.'

'Interesting colour scheme,' he commented, deadpan.

'Decayed Elastoplast-pink bathroom suites were the height of fashion in the fifties when my parents put this one in,' I said stiffly.

'Yes, but most people wouldn't have complemented it with mauve, magenta and gold décor – or a disco ball.'

'Possibly not. Shall we get on? Stairs . . . mind your head . . . Two bedrooms, both *minute* . . .'

'The girlie pink one was yours?'

'A long time ago.' I closed the door firmly and led the way up two steps. 'Boxroom in the turret with views of the glen.'

Here I paused for breath and he joined me at the window, slightly too close for comfort since I was backed into the embrasure with nowhere to go but vertically down should the slightly rotted frame give.

'And the glen comes with the house?' He glanced down at me and smiled. 'I'd be master of all I surveyed?'

'Well, yes, but you can't do anything with it: it's too steep to build on.'

'No one in their right mind would want to build on somewhere with a wild beauty of its own – but I see there's some flattish land around the cottage.'

'There used to be a sort of rose arbour and tea garden behind the house. There still are roses in the glen but they've gone wild, though I think the *Hemisphaerica* was pretty wild to start with and it seems to love it here.'

'Does it?' he murmured absently, transferring his gaze from the vista to my face. 'You know, you really *do* look familiar – I thought so up at the house. Are you *sure* we haven't met before?'

'Certain,' I said positively, trying to edge away around the wall, but he took another step closer. 'I probably just remind you of someone. Don't you find that happens more and more as you get older?'

'I suppose it does.' He frowned down at me as I shifted uneasily, then suddenly put out his hand and pushed my scarf back. Half-dry hair exploded round my head; I probably looked like a mutant pink dandelion clock.

'What on earth are you doing?' I demanded, trying to pull the scarf back up again.

'It's ...' he screwed his eyes up in an effort of memory, 'Mary? No, Maddie, that's it!'

'Sorry, my name's Fran,' I said icily. 'Now, if you've seen *quite* enough ...'

But he remained there, big, solid and entirely immovable, one eyebrow raised quizzically. 'I've seen enough to know I'm not mistaken: huge eyes the colour of wood smoke and *that* hair! It may have been one hell of a long time ago, but I'm *sure* you said your name was Maddie. Well, well!'

'And you told me you were called Adam!' I snapped angrily, then went scarlet.

'Did I? Must have been wishful thinking – I've never liked Gabriel much. So . . . ?' He looked consideringly at me. 'Didn't we . . . ?'

'Yes, but years and years ago,' I said hastily. 'I'd forgotten all about it until I saw a *Restoration Gardener* DVD recently and realised who you were.'

'Oh? I'd sort of forgotten about you too, but now it's coming back to me . . . or some of it, anyway! Didn't we get loaded and go to bed in my van?'

'Look, I would much rather *not* talk about it, if you don't mind!' I said stiffly. 'It was a *very* long time ago, and totally out of character, so I'd be grateful if you forgot all about it again.'

'Well, that's a novelty at least,' he said, grinning. 'Women I've never even clapped eyes on have sold stories to the papers saying they've had affairs with me, yet you want me to pretend I never met you.'

'Yes, of course I do!' I said angrily. 'Maybe you think I should be grateful you remembered me, but it's not like it's something I'd want to boast about, is it? I have a family now and obviously my husband doesn't know anything about you so –'

'OK, I get the idea, Mrs Fran March: *I* won't tell if *you* don't.' He leaned forward so close that one damp curl touched my face, and whispered thrillingly, 'Fear not, fair maiden, your secret is safe with me! How many years ago was it?'

'Too many to count – over twenty, at least,' I said firmly.

'It's all coming back to me – and it was quite a night!'

I pushed past him rudely and he followed after me.

'Sorry, Maddie –'

'Fran!'

'Sorry, Fran!' His voice still sounded annoyingly amused. 'I wouldn't dream of doing any kiss-and-tell stuff. I've been the victim of that sort of thing myself. Besides, it wasn't such a big deal, was it?'

'No,' I said shortly and perhaps with unflattering emphasis. 'No, it wasn't!'

I was having another 'Thriller' moment, what with him almost silently following me through the Gothic gloom, so I stopped to let him pass me on the landing.

His face looked unfathomably serious, as though he was trying to work out if he'd been insulted or not. He paused uncertainly. 'Right – so, let's just start again like we first met up at Plas Gwyn. And much though I'd like to stay and talk to you some more, I've got to get off back to London right now.'

'And *I* need to get home,' I said pointedly. 'I've got work to do!'

'Oh? What kind of work?'

'Graphic design.'

'Interesting . . . and look, I love the cottage, so don't sell it before I come back for a longer viewing, in daylight! An official one this time, with an appointment.'

'That's entirely up to my mother, but it has only just gone on the market.' I followed him back down the narrow stairs, noting how his shoulders brushed the walls on either side and his hair formed little spirals like damp silkworm cocoons all over his head. It was odd and slightly unbelievable to think that I had ever gone to bed with this man . . . and even more to imagine he had any connection with Rosie.

Oh God, *Rosie*! What if they met and he let something slip so that she guessed he was my mysterious gardener? I prayed he would go away and never come back . . . and then remembered that poor Rhodri, at least, was desperate that he did.

'Mr Weston, what did you think of Plas Gwyn?' I asked cautiously.

'I think we could be on first-name terms, Fran, don't you?' he said, looking over his shoulder at me with a wicked smile.

One good shove and all my troubles would have been over. The thought might have shown on my face, because he stopped smiling and carried on down the stairs.

'Plas Gwyn is a little gem. I'll look at the photo-copied documents and then make my mind up later, but it certainly made an impression on me.'

It was pouring again, and when he realised I intended walking he insisted on driving me home. God knows what the Wevills will make of that, but something imaginative, I'm sure, despite the tinted windows preventing them from seeing him properly.

His last words were, 'I'll be in touch – Maddie!'

I sincerely hope he isn't seriously interested in the cottage, because there are already more bloody snakes than grass in my little Eden, and the idea of him living here is too disturbing to contemplate.

And even if we *were* in agreement about forgetting our one little bit of shared history, I suspect he wouldn't be able to resist teasing me about it whenever we met.

I had a horrible feeling my mother would adore him.

Saturday Night and Sunday Morning

'And *then* he insisted on dropping me home on his way back to London, because it was raining so hard,' I told Nia on the phone later. 'And the Wevills' car was back on their own drive: it's odd how it almost never seems to be blocking mine whenever anyone else is around, isn't it? Uncanny.'

'Maybe they have second sight,' she suggested. 'If I hadn't seen it there myself, perhaps I'd think you were imagining it too.'

'I bet they saw me with Gabe Weston, though since his car has tinted windows they won't have known who he was, unless news of his visit has got out.'

'I don't think it has yet: you, Carrie, Rhodri and me are the only ones who know.'

'And Dottie,' I reminded her. 'If she hadn't told Gabe to leave by the tradesmen's entrance he wouldn't have spotted Fairy Glen and rumbled me.'

'Well, it didn't turn out so bad, did it? If he managed to see through that disguise then you clearly made a lasting impression on him, which must be sort of flattering.'

'I suppose so . . . but he seemed to find it amusing that I wanted to keep it quiet that we'd ever met before!'

'That's not surprising when you think of those newspaper articles about him, not to mention the paternity-claim stuff! Someone desperately trying to pretend she'd never met him in her life was probably a refreshing change, and he did promise he would keep it secret, didn't he?'

'Yes, and I'm pretty sure he meant it, only he couldn't resist teasing me about it. And I sort of inadvertently cast a slur on his performance in bed too . . .'

'You did? I thought you said you couldn't remember much about that night.'

'Um . . . just bits,' I said, shifting uncomfortably. 'And I did say "inadvertently": I didn't mean it the way it came out.'

'Oh, well, then all you have to do is send him a postcard with "By the way, your performance in bed left a lasting impression on me too", she said helpfully.

'I don't think so, he might ask me what kind. Nia, when we were talking it was really hard to believe that I'd once slept with him! He was sort of familiar and unfamiliar at the same time. What did you think of him?'

'Tall, attractive, strong, a voice that could charm the birds off the trees, those fascinating greeny-hazel eyes, the cleft in his chin, the way his mouth goes up at one corner when he smiles –'

'I could see that myself,' I interrupted. 'And he's

already charmed this bird off her tree once. I meant, what did you make of the man himself?'

'Oh, I liked him. He came back and talked to me this morning after you'd gone, and he certainly knows a lot about old houses and garden design. I told him all about the renovations and Rhodri's plans for Plas Gwyn, and he seemed really interested. Fingers crossed we make the shortlist!'

'Yes,' I sighed. 'And at least if he does I've got the worst over with now, haven't I? I'd only have to concentrate on forgetting we've got a little slice of shared past when other people are around – especially Mal.' I looked up and caught sight of the clock. 'I'd better go and see how the dinner is doing – Mal's arriving back any minute so I'm cooking something special. What are you doing tonight?'

'I'm going up to have supper with Rhodri,' she said, slightly self-consciously. 'We're still going through papers trying to find interesting stuff about the garden.'

Long experience of Nia's touchy, oversensitive nature has taught me when and when not to tease her, so with great self-restraint I merely wished her good luck and put the phone down.

Even after ten years I still get a little flutter of excitement when my darkly handsome husband arrives home, anticipating that sweep-you-off-your-feet hug, but this time he just casually kissed my cheek instead, as though he'd been away a weekend instead of six weeks.

I was a bit disconcerted, but supposed he was tired

after the long drive. He wasn't to know I was feeling especially in need of love and reassurance after the double whammy of the resurgent Bigblondsurfdude and Gabe Weston – and heaven forbid he ever finds out about either of them!

Unlike his namesake, clearly Gabriel is no angel, but I don't think he *will* tell anyone we once knew each other in the biblical sense if I don't; and I'm hoping Tom has got the message that I don't really want to see him again, though I may be rating his intellectual abilities slightly too highly.

I wonder if he's worn as well as Gabe. He must still be pretty fit if he's surfing.

Mal usually brings me little gifts when he's been away, but this time all he gave me were two bags of dirty laundry, folded and colour-coded, and lots of enthusiastic praise for some IT manager he'd been working with called Sarah. Then he added the bonus ball of an extensive update on his ex-wife's brilliant career and high-flying prospects, so I began to feel completely peed off; but the good news is she's been head-hunted by some firm abroad and by now will have left the country!

Oh, happy day.

I might have been a little over-enthusiastic about that news until he started going on and on about how much she would be earning, and how slim, toned and smart she was looking.

I immediately felt fat and frumpy – and some-what miffed again – so I hardly let him sit down before inflicting on him all the minutiae of *my* daily existence, which normally I don't since his eyes glaze over much like Rosie's used to do at the thirtieth repetition of Neptune the Fishy Father.

I told him about Ma's plans to sell Fairy Glen (which elicited a faint interest as to what she was going to do with the proceeds until I said she was going to blow it all on a cruise), Rosie's assignment marks and Nia's failure to get planning permission for her pottery. By the time I had got on to Rhodri's plans for Plas Gwyn Mal had blanked out, though usually any mention of my seeing Rhodri gets the jealous fires raging.

Piqued, I rambled on to even thinner ice, describing how Rhodri'd contacted Gabe Weston, presenter of the *Restoration Gardener* TV programme . . . and after that I might also have mentioned the hens, my latest cartoons and what I had for breakfast that morning.

In fact, I told him about everything except what was most on my mind – much like the time I *didn't* tell him who Rosie's father was when I had the opportunity. All my sins of omission seem to be on the same subject, but had he been paying close attention on either occasion he would surely have noticed my evasions.

Clearly none of my abridged budget of news was of any interest to him whatsoever, and he didn't even attempt to make a polite show of it, like I do when he waffles on about boats, android wonder women, or Cayman Blue stamps with exciting misprinted bits.

The give and take of married life seemed to be suddenly all give, and I was the one doing it.

129

'Have you been cutting your hair?' he asked, abruptly breaking into my monologue and taking some notice of me at last, but unfortunately the wrong sort.

'Oh, Carrie trimmed the ends, but it seems to have made it go curlier this time, so it looks much shorter,' I said casually, and he stared at me suspiciously; but it's *my* hair, I shouldn't have to resort to these subterfuges and evasions.

When he spotted my mosaic fireplace he said it looked like something out of a cheap makeover programme, which it doesn't: it's *terribly* Charles Rennie Mackintosh. Then he gathered up all his post and went upstairs, and I started to wish I hadn't bothered cooking his favourite dinner of roast duck cooked the Delia way, with crunchy brown potatoes roasted in the fat, to be followed by mango mousse, especially since I'd had to go all the way to the supermarket in Llandudno for the ingredients. Mangoes don't grow on trees up the Welsh valleys.

He couldn't find fault with the dinner, but instead complained that the wine I'd bought was the wrong one.

'But it's Chilean Chardonnay,' I pointed out. 'It's what you often have!'

'Yes, but the wrong *year*, Fran.'

'It seems just fine to me,' I said, taking another sip – though actually anything would taste good after those ghastly diet bars and shakes, and the flavour of the melt-in-the-mouth duck had been almost orgasmically wonderful.

'Yes, well, you think your home-made wine tastes

"just fine" too,' he pointed out before lapsing into a fit of the sulks that probably lasted until his bedtime, but by then I'd left him to it and was fast asleep.

Mal seemed to wake up in a better mood, so perhaps he really was just tired from the journey home last night.

I stuffed the first load of his washing in the machine before breakfast, then suggested we go out for a walk somewhere. 'Betws-y-Coed? We could take a picnic and flasks and –'

The phone rang and I picked it up impatiently. 'Hello?'

'I want to speak to Mal,' said an odiously familiar voice. 'Put him on, will you?'

'We're just going out,' I said tersely. 'Sorry.'

'Who is that?' asked Mal, taking the phone as I was about to slam it down.

'Owen Weevil.'

'*Wevill*, Fran!' he snapped, his hand over the receiver, but the name had slipped out quite unintentionally. I must have caught it from Ma.

'Hi, Owen! No, nothing decided . . . Yes, love a sail if you feel like crewing . . . Pick you up in half an hour?'

When he rang off he caught my eye and said defensively, 'I *deserve* a bit of fresh air after six weeks in Swindon, don't I?'

'A walk would give you fresh air, and I thought you might like to spend some time with me!'

'There's nothing to stop you coming with us,' he

said, even though he knows I get seasick looking at pictures of boats. Besides, I wasn't going anywhere with Owen tagging along when Mal always refuses to go anywhere with my friends, who are at least all recognisably human.

'No, thanks. I don't suppose you'll be back until late, and don't forget I've got all your laundry to do. I presume you will be wanting to wear clothes next week?'

'There's no need to be sarcastic, and I *won't* be too late, because it goes dark early. You don't need to pack any lunch, either, because Mona's doing that.'

'I wasn't going to, anyway,' I told him coldly. 'If you're going to be out all day I might walk up to Plas Gwyn and see Nia. She spends most of her time up there setting her pottery up and helping Rhodri with the house.'

'*You've* been spending a lot of time up there too, I hear – *and* in the pub, with Rhodri.'

'And Nia and Carrie – didn't our friendly neighbourhood spies tell you that?'

'Come on, Fran!' he said. 'The Wevills aren't spying on you.'

'Yes they are – and while I remember, I'd be grateful if you'd stop telling them they can park on our drive when you are away. I couldn't even get my car out the other day!'

'That's ridiculous, Fran! You're being silly and neurotic about two perfectly nice people.'

'Neurotic? I am *not* neurotic!'

'Then let's invite them to join us for dinner at the Druid's Rest tonight.'

'No!' I said explosively. 'I am *not* socialising with them, haven't you got that yet? And why can't it just be you and me any more?'

He sighed long-sufferingly. 'OK, if you want to be so unreasonable! I just thought it would be an opportunity for you to get to know each other and iron out the misunderstandings.'

'I already know them more than I want to – and I haven't seen you for six weeks, Mal, so don't you think it's natural for me to want to spend some time with you? Don't *you* want to be with *me*?'

'Of course I do, Fran. Look, perhaps you're right,' he said soothingly. 'Book an early table for two at the pub and we'll talk later – must go and get ready, look at the time!'

Mona always makes them cheese and pickle sandwiches using the malty bread Mal hates: I hope they both choke on them.

Up at Plas Gwyn a camera crew had turned up and was filming the exterior of the house and gardens. I could see Rhodri hovering around them – like an anxious father keen that his offspring should show itself off at its best – but, thankfully, no sign of Gabriel Weston.

I found Nia hiding out in her workshop. 'You didn't tell me about the filming,' I said, joining her at the window so we could watch what was happening. 'Is this a positive sign?'

She turned a glowing face towards me. 'Yes – it means we're definitely on the long list, one step closer!

When Gabe Weston went through those documents Rhodri copied for him and spotted the one about the turf maze he was on the phone right away – apparently mazes are a *major* passion, so that clinched it. I don't know what else he found but he said it was all very interesting.'

'He hasn't come down again himself, has he?' I asked nervously.

'No, he doesn't need to for these shots and he's too busy at the moment, but he said he hoped to pop down soon for another look around and to discuss things with Rhodri. I would have told you the news last night, but I didn't want to disturb you with Mal just back.'

'There's nothing much to disturb – he's out on the boat with the Weevil as we speak and I was a bit mad about it. But he *is* taking me out to dinner at the Druid's Rest tonight.'

'Kiss and make up,' Nia said vaguely, still glued to the window, her mind clearly on other things. 'The best thing is that Gabe told Rhodri that at the end of the last of his present TV series he was going to show all six of the long-listed gardens before announcing the three for the vote-off, so Plas Gwyn will get on TV whatever happens.'

'That's great,' I said. 'If only we could get the *Restoration Gardener* programmes, we could watch it!'

'Rhodri's having a satellite dish put up specially.'

'Won't he need some kind of planning permission to put a dish on a listed building?'

'Not if he hides it in the wisteria,' she said optimistically, then stiffened. 'Oh, no, it's Dottie! She will probably order the camera crew off the premises, or beat them up with her riding crop or something. I'd better try and head her off.' And away she darted.

I cravenly left her to it – heading Dottie off was a near impossibility at the best of times – and made my way home. I needed all the time I could get to render myself beautiful ready for this evening.

Being a Saturday night, the Druid's Rest could only give us a table at six, when they started serving, on the strict understanding we would have eaten and gone by the time the next customers arrived – but when there is only one local restaurant you can't argue about it.

The big glass dining room with its divisions of rampant silk tropical plants was almost empty at that time. Mrs Forrester came out in person to smarm all over Mal – but then he did look rather delectable after his day's sailing, all rosy cheeks and sparkling dark eyes and in a much better temper.

'We don't often see you in the restaurant,' she said rather pointedly to me.

'No, I know my place is below the salt in the back parlour,' I said cheerily. 'But my lord and master is kindly treating me tonight.'

Mal gave me a repressive look. 'I'll have the Welsh lamb,' he decided, which was no surprise: he always does.

I dithered, and then went for grilled trout and a salad, which I thought might be good for me *and* slimming, and she slapped the menus together and bustled off.

In the interests of marital *entente* I encouraged Mal to describe his day's exciting sailing on *Cayman Blue*, and some stamp he'd bid for on the Internet, and how clever he'd been down in Swindon; then he asked me how Rosie was getting on, which just goes to show that he hadn't heard a word I said when he got home.

'She's fine. She's got a new boyfriend called Colum.'

'Colum? What kind of a name is that?'

'I think it's rather nice,' I said mildly. 'I expect he'd think your name was pretty weird.'

'Maldwyn's a perfectly good old Welsh name,' he said slightly stiffly, but he was soon mellowing over a bottle of wine that cost about as much as I spend on petrol in a month.

It was all going swimmingly (apart from Mrs Forrester briefly appearing to harry us into finishing our main course quickly), when something made me look up.

There in the doorway to the lounge stood Tom Collinge, Bigblondsurfdude personified: the ceiling lights bounced off his shock of sun-streaked golden hair, his eyes were more azure than a summer sky and his skin tanned right down inside the open V of his fleecy blue sweatshirt. He gave you the feeling that if the lights were off he'd glow in the dark.

It was like a vision – but one I didn't want. I hunched down in my seat, hoping he wouldn't spot me. Our corner *was* quite dark, and there were all those plants too . . .

136

'You're humming,' Mal said critically. 'The Mamas and the Papas, "California Dreamin'", if my memory serves me right.'

'Sorry,' I apologised, leaning towards him so that his body partially screened me from the door. 'I was just thinking how nice it is when we are alone together like this and –'

'Fran!' Tom's voice said, practically in my ear, and I jerked upright, spilling the last of my wine down my one decent dress.

'It *is* you – I can't believe it! What a stroke of luck – I only came in here to see if anyone knew where you lived.' He swooped down, grinning, and kissed me on the cheek. 'And just as pretty as ever!'

'Oh, you – you startled me!' I exclaimed, dabbing distractedly at my dress with the napkin, which was the totally useless non-absorbent linen kind.

'And this must be your husband,' he said, turning to Mal in a friendly fashion, which was certainly not the way Mal was looking at him.

'Yes, Mal Morgan,' I said hastily. 'And Mal, this is ... is ...' But the words stuck in my throat, as well they might under the circumstances.

Tom said helpfully, 'Fran's probably told you about me: I'm her old flame, Tom Collinge – like the drink, but with a g. Silly, I know, but it's my real name, and at least I wasn't christened Gimlet or Long Slow Scre—'

At this point Mal rose suddenly to his feet and socked him one on the jaw.

Surprised? I thought I'd never be able to shut my

mouth again – and it wasn't just that ancient joke about the drink. But if the blow was a shock to me, who'd never seen Mal do anything quite so rugged, it was even more of a shock to poor old Tom. He reeled away, stunned more by surprise than anything, I think, and, almost falling over a chair, hung on to the back and stared incredulously at Mal.

'What the hell was *that* for?' he demanded aggrievedly. 'Are you so jealous you can't even shake hands with your wife's ex-boyfriend?'

It was fortunate that Mrs Forrester had by now succeeded in chivvying everyone else out of the room, except one old couple who were watching us with glazed surprise.

Mal sat down again, looking rather pleased with himself. 'You mean the ex-boyfriend who got Fran pregnant and then vanished off abroad?' he said, though not without a look round to see if anyone was in earshot.

'What?' Tom said blankly.

'Now, Mal,' I began nervously. 'I never said –'

'Let *me* deal with this, Fran,' Mal snapped.

Tom turned wide, stunned blue eyes on me: 'You were *pregnant*? But –'

'Fran told me how you dumped her when you got an art scholarship abroad. She only discovered she was pregnant after you'd gone.'

Tom paled under his tan. 'Yes – but I didn't know! And, Fran, you knew my parents' address, you could have found me if you'd wanted to.'

'I didn't want to,' I said flatly.

'*And* I wrote to you after a few months because I missed you, and you never replied!'

'I know,' I agreed. 'So it's not Tom's fault, Mal. Let's just drop it and –'

'What do you mean, it isn't his fault?' Mal snapped. 'Don't you think he had a responsibility to you? To make sure you were all right?'

'You mean I'm a *father*?' Tom suddenly demanded as illumination finally dawned – but then he never was Mensa material.

'And do you mean you never even *tried* to get in touch with him, to tell him you were pregnant?' Mal said incredulously as the penny dropped a second later. He *is* Mensa material but his brains had clearly packed up for the night. 'You never told him about Rosie?'

Tom turned, wide-eyed: 'Is that –'

'My daughter,' I said.

'Oh?' I could have sworn he was starting to look pleased. 'So, how old is she?'

'Nearly nineteen,' I said reluctantly. 'She's at university studying to be a vet.'

I could see him doing a bit of painful mental arithmetic, then he turned the chair round and sat in it, one wary eye on Mal. 'Don't think I want to butt in at this late date, Fran, but don't you think you should have told me about her, even if you didn't want me in your life any more?'

'No, because it wasn't anything to do with you.' I was starting to feel desperately cornered and they were now both looking accusingly at me.

'What do you mean?' they said in unison.

'The baby wasn't Tom's – I don't *think*,' I said honestly. 'I'm ninety-nine per cent sure it wasn't, anyway.'

There was a small, incredulous silence.

'But *I* was your first serious boyfriend,' Tom pointed out, as though I might have forgotten. 'You never went out with anyone else!'

'Yes, but you finished with me,' I said tartly.

'Only in the very last week of term! And you were always Little Miss Prissy, not the kind to jump into bed with the next available man!'

'Well, I did. I found someone else.'

'But you've let me think it was Tom all these years,' Mal said, looking at me as though I were a stranger, chance met and slightly unsavoury.

'No I haven't, I just didn't discuss Rosie's father at all. You drew your own conclusions.'

'Isn't that the same thing?' he said. 'If it's true, then you've been less than honest with me!'

'Who?' demanded Tom abruptly, furrowing his brow. '*Who* was the father?'

'Wouldn't you like to know!' I said, glaring at him, and for a minute we were back to our student days, when bicker and make up was the pattern of our life together. 'But it's none of your business!'

'So you say – but I'm not sure I believe you!'

'And I think it's certainly *my* business, Fran, don't you?' Mal said coldly. 'I thought we had been frank with each other, and now I find you've lied to me about something as important as this!'

'I haven't lied –'

'Look,' Tom interrupted, hastily rising to his feet, 'I'll leave you to it, you don't want a third party at a time like this. I'm sorry to have stirred everything up, but I had absolutely no idea . . . and now I don't know *what* to think!'

Mal got up too. 'Well, sorry I hit you,' he said magnanimously, shaking hands with him. 'Clearly you were as in the dark as I was . . . and God knows what the truth of the matter is! What puzzles me is how you knew where Fran lived?'

'Oh, I came across her website and got in touch, thought it might be nice to pop in and catch up with old times – just in a friendly sort of way,' he added cautiously.

'Right. And all this was clearly as complete a shock to you as it was to me.'

'Yes,' agreed Tom, preparing to make his escape. 'You've said it! Well, great to see you again, Fran, and – er – keep in touch!' he said, and left, though not without a last doubtful and puzzled glance over his shoulder.

Mal sat back and levelled an accusing stare at me, arms crossed. 'I'm not sure I've got to the bottom of this affair yet,' he had begun ominously, when fortunately Mrs Forrester marched in and informed us we would have to have our dessert and coffee, if we wanted them, in the bar.

'No, that's fine, thanks – we'll have the bill and go home,' Mal said, summoning up a social smile.

He didn't say a word all the way there and then went straight in and picked up the big photo of Rosie

I keep on the mantelpiece and studied it as if he had never seen her before.

Presumably he was trying to trace some resemblance to Tom in her features and failing – I've done it myself.

'Rosie's blonde,' he remarked, as though I might not have noticed. 'But *much* darker.'

'*I'm* blonde, Ma was blonde . . . even Dad was fair-haired,' I said snappily. 'Look, Mal, after Tom dumped me I went to an end-of-term party, got drunk, met another man and ended up pregnant with Rosie. I was quite sure she wasn't Tom's, that's why I didn't tell him.'

'You didn't tell me either.'

'You didn't ask, and it was so long before I met you it didn't seem important. After all, you didn't give me a list of all the women you ever slept with, did you? You just told me about Alison, and I told you about Tom.'

'So who *are* you saying is Rosie's father?'

'I'm not,' I said firmly. 'It was a one-night stand and I only ever knew his first name – and, before you ask, it wasn't something I made a habit of! It was only the once, which hardly qualifies me for Super Slut status. I've already told Rosie all about it.'

He was still looking at me as if I was a stranger, shaking his head in disbelief. 'I really don't know you at all, do I? And I don't know if you are telling the truth now, or whether you made the story up because you didn't want to let Tom know he had a daughter . . . or maybe because the real father was someone else entirely. Someone you want to *protect*.'

And then I saw he was looking at the photo on the

other side of the mantelpiece, of me and Rhodri and Nia aged about fourteen with our arms round each other, laughing into the sun.

'You surely can't think I had a thing going with Rhodri!'

'I don't know what I think any more. I'm going to bed!' he snapped, and slammed out of the room.

Clearly his illusions are now shattered, though it is not like I have confessed to multiple bigamy or an affair since we've been married – or really anything at all that is his business.

When I went upstairs he had his back firmly turned towards me and disgust oozing from every pore.

Sunday morning I seemed to have been sent to Coventry, so I went up to the studio simply to get out of the atmosphere and sat there reading *Restoration Gardener*, feeling prickly and defensive.

I found a whole section on roses.

Historic rose gardens can be easily recreated or restocked, since many of the ancient varieties of rose are still obtainable, although the topsoil must first be dug out and replaced with fresh earth to prevent rose sickness. Roses can also be used to infill the intricate convolutions of the knot garden with its low, clipped box hedges; utilised to soften later anachronistic garden features, grown over arbours and up pergolas ... in fact, the uses of the rose are as infinite as the number of varieties!

I bet he'd like to see my Omar Khayyam.

I went back to the house to cook our big Sunday lunch as usual, since I thought it might soften Mal up a bit, but we ate it in silence so I wished I hadn't bothered. After that I was in two minds whether to iron the shirts he would need to pack for tomorrow, but in the end I slammed the iron over them a few times, producing creases in strange places, then hung them up in the wardrobe.

Mal was holed up in his study with his stamps by the time I'd finished, so I went back to the studio and drew an Alphawoman comic strip with a blacker than usual storyline, because I had long stopped feeling upset and apologetic and started feeling angry.

Then he took the wind right out of my sails by coming up to the studio, which he practically *never* does, and saying he'd been thinking it all over and he could see that he was partly to blame for the situation because he had never asked me who Rosie's father was!

'Were you telling the truth about it being a total stranger?'

'Yes, of course,' I said firmly (which was true ... sort of). 'Mal ... do you still love me?' That just sort of slipped out – I hadn't meant to sound needy.

'I suppose so, but it's all been a shock,' he said, looking handsome, noble and tragic (but sounding like Eeyore), and I noticed that he didn't ask me whether *I* still loved *him*.

He'd forgive me, I knew he would, he just needed a little time.

But will *I* forgive him for *needing* him to forgive me, that's the question?

Cayman Blue

Monday morning I woke up feeling more positive, sure Mal would soon see reason and realise my past didn't make any difference to what we had now, except in so far as it had shaped me into the woman he fell in love with.

I crept out of bed so as not to wake him and went out with a coat over my dressing gown and wellies to let the hens into their run and toss them breakfast, before taking my shower.

I was standing under the warm spray softly singing 'Raindrops Keep Falling on My Head' while idly shampooing my hair when it occurred to me how very small and fragile my skull was! I mean, I could hold it in my two hands like a little round gourd, and there didn't seem enough room in there for an intellect, though since I seem to function on impulse drive I probably don't need one. Or maybe it's Improbability Drive, like that spaceship in *The Hitchhiker's Guide to the Galaxy*?

I still have more hair than wit, though at the rate Carrie's chopping off the ends the ratios could change at any minute.

'Do you think my head is abnormally small?' I asked Mal when I emerged with my hair in loosely ravelled wet curls.

He gave me a long-suffering look and finished buttoning up a crisply ironed shirt the same intense deep blue as his eyes – and I do wish he wouldn't buy linen, since he just doesn't seem to grasp that it's *supposed* to look crumpled, so there's no point at all in pressing it.

I was just thinking he wasn't going to answer, when he said very coldly, 'No, it's the rest of you that's got much bigger by comparison.'

Staring at him, his words whirled around my head like dark portents of marital doom. He'd always been inclined to be critical and fussy, and admittedly he'd had a bit of a shock over the weekend (hadn't we all?), but it was unlike him to be cruel.

Finally getting my dropped jaw back into position, using both hands, I said in a tone of sweet reason that I certainly wasn't feeling, 'Look, Mal, it was your idea I diet, and while you were away I tried two, but they simply don't work. They left me feeling starving and ill – and, what's worse, I put on weight after each one! On my birthday I was just a bit plump and curvy, but now I'm definitely a good half-stone heavier and fed up with the whole idea.'

'You lack willpower, Fran, that's all,' he said, knotting his silk tie into a tight, silver-grey nugget.

Maybe I should try that, and then the food couldn't actually slip down my throat. Or tighten *his* until he stops breathing.

'Oh, I lack willpower – is *that* all it is? Well, that's all right then,' I said sarkily, all the sweet reason going out of the window.

'*And* motivation – you used to be so slim and pretty that I was proud to be seen out with you, so couldn't you lose weight to please *me*?' he asked, smiling winningly just like the old Mal I knew and loved. But it was way too late, now that I'd spotted the monster within.

Come back, Dr Jekyll, all is forgiven.

'I thought that was what I was trying to do, Mal! I'm sure as hell not doing it for *me*,' I snapped. 'Why can't you just love me as I am, not want me back the way I was? You can't turn back the clock, and while we might both be older I don't love you any the less just because you've got one or two grey hairs and some irritating habits.'

'What irritating habits?' he demanded, looking stung. 'I don't have *any* habits!'

This was good coming from the man who spends hours putting all the ornaments in the house at exact right angles to each other, straightening the pictures and picking up imaginary specks of fluff.

'How about that hoarse cough you've got first thing in the morning, barking away like a seal in the bedroom? Sometimes I don't know whether to get the throat syrup or throw you a fish.'

'It's just a dry throat, and you're exaggerating,' he snapped. 'And speaking of annoying habits . . .'

But by now I'd tossed on a lilac velvet and lace patchwork top and jeans, and was heading hastily for the door. 'Let's not – if I don't get breakfast going now you won't have time to eat it before you set out.'

I am delighted that someone else will have the pleasure of coping with his breakfast while he is in Manchester. Although I'm an inspired cook when left to do things my own way, can I soft-boil his damned egg to his exacting taste in the mornings? Can I hell!

Still, in the interests of marital harmony I've always done my best to soothe the savage beast first thing in the morning before abandoning him for the rest of the day with almost indecent haste. So I zipped downstairs, placed his neatly folded newspaper on the breakfast table, put the egg in the pan and set the timer, brewed the tea and got out the juice – you know, all that stuff his mother used to do for him and his first wife told him to do himself, she was busy.

After we were married the realisation slowly and incredulously dawned that he thought I'd entered into an unspoken pact whereby I was to be the Angel in the House but was also allowed to be the Artist in the Shed whenever it didn't impinge on his comfort! Of course, once I'm in the shed I totally forget about the house, so short of a character transplant this was never going to happen – and he now knows I'm no angel, in or out of the house.

I found I was singing that song about a man opening a magazine to find the centrefold was the angelic girl he'd once worshipped, and bit the last word off midwarble. Whoa – inappropriate lyric alert! But suddenly all these brilliant ideas for cartoons came cascading like bright sparks of light into my mind as my subconscious picked over the dark issues lying stunned and unacknowledged at the back of my skull. My teeny, tiny, *shrinking* skull . . .

'I'd like to do a painting of the inside of one,' I decided aloud, hastily shoving bread into the toaster as Mal came in, shaved, fragrant and svelte. 'A sheep skull would do and, goodness knows, there are enough of those lying around, all bleached clean by the weather.'

'Can we *not* discuss sheep skulls over breakfast?' he said, sitting down and picking up *The Times*. 'And the egg timer pinged two minutes ago, I heard it.'

'An offence punishable by a hideous and painful death,' I said lightly, but he was carefully opening and folding back the paper.

He'd be wanting me to iron the damn thing next, I could see it coming, and you know what will happen then? Yes, I'll forget to clean the print off the iron, and headlines will be emblazoned across every shirt he owns, and serve him right too.

Well, laid back I am, but Stepford Wife I most certainly am *not* . . . which gave me the idea for yet another cartoon. What a deeply worrying (but very productive) morning this was turning out to be!

The letterbox rattled and I went to fetch the post, most of which was for Mal, as usual.

Apart from the sort of 'Dear Occupier' letter I only open if desperate for *any* correspondent, I had one other, from a magazine I submitted some cartoons to so long ago I'd nearly forgotten they had them.

Dear Ms March,

Thank you for your most recent batch of cartoons. We particularly liked your 'Famous Book Jackets Revisited' series, especially 'Ms Crusoe builds a washing machine' (very Heath Robinson!) and would like to see more of these, and perhaps make them a regular feature of the magazine . . .

'I've sold some more cartoons, Mal,' I said, looking up. 'About classic book jackets – and they might make it a regular feature! Great, isn't it? I'm doing really well!'

'Umph?' he said absently, while opening a large envelope and extracting glossy, expensive sheets of paper; but then he's never taken a real interest in my artwork and considers my studio the realm of Mess and Disorder, where I reign as Queen of Chaos.

Probably just as well since he would certainly not be amused by my cartoons should he take a good look at them. What funny bone he used to have seems to have atrophied, apart from what passes for levity among men after a drink too many at the yacht club following a Sunday spent scraping the barnacles off their bottoms, or whatever it is they get up to down there.

I realised I'd spent too long dreaming at the kitchen table when the toast exploded half singed from the toaster. Not only was trying to scrape the burned bits into the sink behind Mal's back without making a noise a lost cause in itself, but by now his egg had been sitting going rubbery for ages, though it still looked much more inviting than my breakfast of grapefruit and coffee.

Suddenly I felt self-conscious eating anything in front of him after that nasty dig, not to mention the insinuation that I now look such a dog he doesn't want to be seen out with me. And, thinking back, the last time he literally swept me off my feet he had to put me down again, because he felt a twinge in his back, so I must be so much fatter than I realised – positively gross! But that still didn't excuse him being so nasty about it.

Mal removed the top of his egg and peered into it as though it might contain the answer to Life, the Universe and Everything, although we already know the answer, post-Douglas Adams, is forty-two. 'How many minutes?' he demanded sternly.

'Four exactly,' I assured him. 'But I think it's Dolly's, and she always lays eggs much bigger than Shania or even Sheryl, so that might make a difference.'

With a long-suffering sigh he abandoned his unsatisfactory breakfast and became absorbed in reading the last of his mail. One dark eyebrow was raised and a touch of colour tinted his high cheekbones, signs of excitement I certainly hadn't managed to induce in him for a long, long time . . . since before Christmas, in fact, now I came to think of it. Oh dear, how happy and uncomplicated life seemed then, with the Wevills only starting to claw at the edges of our happiness and no resurgent old lovers!

Mal was now smiling, so I presumed he had received a really good job offer – but then, being a sort of free-lance virus-busting, problem-solving IT expert speaking several languages, most of them computer, he is much in demand.

'Good news?' I prompted.

'What?' He looked up and slowly focused on me. 'Oh, yes. I've got an interview at the end of the week for a six-month contract in Grand Cayman! I'll have to go down to Swindon for the day.'

'Where's Grand Cayman?' I asked, puzzled – geography never was my strong point.

'The Caribbean, Fran, that string of islands the other side of the Atlantic just before you get to America?'

'Oh, right. But did you say six *months*?' I stared at him. 'You're never away for that long.'

'Not usually, no, but when I heard about it I thought it was too great an opportunity to miss, *and* somewhere I've always wanted to go.'

'What do you mean, when you heard about it?'

'Someone told me about it in Swindon, so I applied.'

'You might have told me rather than doing it behind my back, Mal,' I said angrily.

'I didn't mention it because I really didn't think I'd get an interview, but I've told you now, haven't I?'

'But you should have discussed it with me before you applied. Six months is a hell of a long time to be away!' A thought struck me. 'I suppose for a contract that long, I'll be able to come too?'

He was shaking his head. 'I'm afraid not – it's a single man's contract, it won't pay for two people's travel and expenses, though you could probably come out for a couple of weeks' holiday if we can get a cheap flight.'

'Gee, thanks!'

'There's no need to be sarcastic. I'd take this contract

even if we didn't need the money – which we do – and perhaps a bit of space between us would be a good thing at the moment.'

'Yes, but not *six months*' space!'

And if he wasn't so increasingly addicted to expensive hobbies, fine wines, new cars and all the other trappings of a consumer-driven lifestyle, we could manage just fine!

'I'd rather live on less money and have you here,' I said forlornly, but he wasn't listening again. His eyes had gone all remote and that excited colour was back in his cheeks.

'I might even come across a Cayman Blue out there in the Caribbean,' he said dreamily, and I got up and left the kitchen by the back door, which I slammed, and made my way blinded by tears towards my shed, watched by a trio of hens.

Clearly, the Paradise train has been seriously derailed.

Faint sounds of life came from beyond the stone wall as the village awoke to prepare for another day of work and visitors to St Ceridwen's Holy Well and Teapots, as good a reason to detour from the main road as any, and after a while I heard the angry snarl of Mal's Jaguar leaving for Manchester.

He hadn't bothered coming out to say goodbye before he went, but perhaps while he was away this week he would realise just how much he would miss me if he took such a long contract. And with things a bit rocky between us, I don't think being apart for six months *is* a good idea. We should work through this together like all the other rough patches in our marriage.

Yes, once he's actually had a chance to think about it, even if he gets the contract he will turn it down and our life will resume its normal course. He'll probably say something like: 'Fran, darling, I realised I couldn't bear to leave you for so long after all! And it doesn't matter *who* Rosie's father is – I love *you*!'

And then he'll tell the Wevills to go and infest someone else's marriage and pretty soon everything will be coming up roses again.

I picked up a pencil and started to sketch, dreaming of paradise regained while softly singing 'This Could Be Heaven', now the music police was well on its way to Manchester.

Later I went round to Teapots to give Nia and Carrie a graphic description of the meeting with Tom, only to find that the whole village has already got the basics from the elderly couple who were our only audience. Current rumour has it that I've been having an affair with Tom, and Mal found out.

'They saw Mal hit him, put two and two together and made a big scandal, but of course they don't know what it was really all about,' Nia explained.

'Well, now Mal knows all about my murky past, and he doesn't like it.'

'Barely murky, one slight slip.'

'One slight slip and a *pregnancy*,' I sighed. 'It just seemed easier to let him think it was Tom's baby, like Ma did, but in retrospect I should have Revealed All while he was mellow with the first flush of love. Now he's talking about leaving me for six months and saying we need some space between us for a while!'

Nia pointed out that even some of the contracts Mal has been offered fall through, and with six months' work in the Caribbean as lure, he'd probably be killed in the stampede for the job.

'That's true, I hadn't thought of that! He was really disappointed when the one in California didn't come off. Or he might think better of it anyway once he realises what it would be like to be apart for so long, don't you think?'

'Yes,' she allowed, sounding unconvinced.

'Of *course* he will, Fran,' Carrie said comfortingly. 'Naturally, the news about Rosie was a shock to him, but you never actually lied to him, did you?'

'No, I just didn't talk about it at all. Let us hope that he never discovers who Rosie's father really is . . . though probably he'd think I was imagining it or something. Both he and Tom seemed to be harbouring doubts about my mysterious stranger, and Mal's got poor Rhodri lined up as first reserve father!'

'Well, half the village already suspect that anyway – the *stupid* half. I think he's being totally unreasonable about something that happened years before you met, and he should get over it and stop being such a plonker,' Nia said incisively.

'I thought he was getting over it on Sunday afternoon, but then he woke up in a foul mood this morning.'

I told them what he'd said about my weight and

not being proud to be seen out with me any more. 'And it was as though the mask of the man I loved slipped for a minute and this horrible monster looked out of his eyes! Do you think it was a temporary aberration or do all men have a touch of the Jekyll and Hyde about them?'

'I think they're *all* two-faced monsters,' Nia said positively, 'and the stronger, nastier Mr Hyde takes over more and more the older they get. Look at Paul: I'd known him for years and I thought if he was one thing he was a man of honour, a man I could trust. Only that was just half the man. The other half was a lying, cheating scumbag who made a mockery of the life we'd had together.'

'Not Huw and Rhodri!' protested Carrie.

'OK, I suppose there are always one or two exceptions to the rule.'

'You don't think Mal is cheating on me, do you, Nia?' I asked suddenly.

'Only with his boat and the stamps, I should think: they're selfish pleasures but reasonably harmless, though I don't think it's a healthy sign when your husband spends more on his hobby than he does on his wife.'

'Paul didn't have a hobby, did he? Apart from growing vegetables and stuff?'

'Fishing. He used to get up at five every Sunday morning so he could listen to a live fishing programme called *Big Rods* on the radio.'

'Go on! You're making that up, they couldn't *possibly* broadcast live fishing!'

'No, it's true, I heard it once. This man with a sloweddown soporific voice was saying it was a grand day for flies and interviewing someone who caught a trout in 1962.'

I eyed her doubtfully, but she looked quite serious. And after all, they broadcast live cricket matches, don't they?

'What's Huw's secret vice, Carrie?' I asked.

'Me.'

'I'll have to watch Rhodri isn't glued to rugby matches now we've got a satellite dish. He hasn't got time to sit about watching TV; it's only supposed to be there for the *Restoration Gardener* programmes,' Nia said. 'Gabe Weston's getting to the end of the present series, so we will be on soon. Plas Gwyn was the last house to be chosen for the long list. You will both come up and watch it – and help me console Rhodri if we don't make the shortlist – won't you? Only I think his stiff upper lip has had about all it can take lately.'

'Yes, of course, we wouldn't miss it for the world,' I assured her, and Carrie said she would bring cakes and we could make a party of it, 'because whichever way it goes, it is still good publicity for Plas Gwyn – and St Ceridwen's Well.'

'Yes, the secret will be out once it's on TV,' I agreed. 'Then there's bound to be lots more visitors.'

'The news seems to be out already. You couldn't miss that huge BBC van, and I don't think Gabe Weston can go anywhere in Great Britain without being spotted by a drooling fan, from the sound of it. Anyway, Sian phoned me up yesterday, the cow,' she said unaffectionately of her sister. 'Somebody passed the rumour on that Plas Gwyn might be on the TV series – it's not only round the village now, it's around *Wales* – so she was pumping me for information. If by some miracle we actually win it, she'll be up here and all over him like a rash.'

'For the newspaper?' I said.

'Ostensibly, I suppose, but being male and having fame and money are all it takes to get Sian's interest.'

Something else was on my mind, and when I got back I called Auntie Beth, Ma's sister. She and her husband are GPs up in the Hebrides and their idea of a good time is tramping over the moors with several of the Highland terriers they breed.

She was out on a call, but I had a nice chat with Lachlan and asked him if he thought I had an abnormally small head. I mean, the more I look at myself in the mirror, the smaller it seems.

'Away with ye, lassie!' he said, or something equally Scottish in his gorgeous, rolling accent. 'You're in perfect proportion!'

This was reassuring and I am now resolved to stop obsessing about the size of my body parts. (I'll leave that to the men.)

There was no email or phone call from Mal, but there was one from Bigblondsurfdude:

Dear Fran,
    Sorry if I landed you in it, but you really *should* have told me! It was a bit of a shock. Was that

true, about another man? Or were you just saying that because you didn't want me involved with Rosie? And I'd like to meet her, anyway.

You still look just as pretty as ever – haven't changed a bit! I hope that husband of yours appreciates you.

Love, Tom

I haven't answered it yet – I can't think what to say, though it is rather balm to have Tom's compliments after what Mal said! Besides, if there is even an outside chance that Rosie might be his, doesn't he have a moral right to meet her? I'll have to think about that one.

I was still undecided what to do for the best when I spoke to her that evening.

Practically all the everyday village news I would usually give her was now so peppered with the comings and goings of old lovers that I felt I was tiptoeing through a conversational minefield.

'Are you all right, Mum?' she asked eventually. 'You sound a bit peculiar. Distracted.'

'Now you come to ask, I have felt a bit off colour for a few weeks now,' I agreed hastily. 'Perhaps I ought to go and have a chat with the doctor and get a tonic or something.'

She might know a good diet too, because it looks like an integral part of making up with Mal is going to be based on my ability to render myself down to the dimensions of a tapeworm.

'If you're just going to sing "Keep Young and Beautiful" at me, I'm off!' Rosie said, disgusted.

Less than half an hour later she was back on the phone. 'Mum, I've just had a really weird email from Mal.'

'From Mal?' I echoed blankly. 'I didn't know he emailed you.'

'He doesn't usually; he wanted to tell me all about Tom Collinge turning up, which seemed to have sort of slipped your mind?' she said sarcastically.

'Oh God!' I said. 'Rosie, I *was* going to tell you, I was just trying to work out how to put it.'

'No wonder you sounded distracted earlier, Mum! Anyway, Mal told me what you said to them both about my father being a stranger and that neither of them believed you, and how deeply hurt he was about it all – what a wuss! I said you'd already told me, and *then* he said he was sure my real father was Uncle Rhodri! He's mad.'

She insisted I gave her my version of the Highlights of the Night, then said, 'So you really *were* telling me the truth about my father being a stranger?'

'Yes.'

'And you really *don't* know who he is?'

'He was a total stranger before that night,' I said truthfully.

But maybe there was some new element in my voice because she said suspiciously: 'Why do I have a feeling you are holding out on me?'

'I can't imagine,' I said briskly. 'I've told you the truth, and I know it's not what you really want to hear, but that's it. I really don't for one minute think that Tom is your father, but short of a DNA test we will never know. He – he said he would like to meet you anyway.'

'Did he?'

She sounded pleased, and I was about to warn her about building castles in the air – or fathers out of surfers – when I thought better of it. She might still be a little girl to me, but she was grown-up enough to make her own decisions.

'You'd better tell Granny before she visits and hears the village version in the teashop,' she said sensibly, so I did.

And, actually, it didn't turn out too difficult. Ma may harbour doubts about my passing lover too, but certainly never mistook Rhodri's affection for me as anything other than brotherly.

Dear Tom,

Thanks for your email. Sorry everything was such a mix-up and Mal got the wrong end of the stick and hit you.

Actually, it wasn't me who emailed you in the first place but my daughter, Rosie, in a fit of curiosity after coming across that first note you sent me after finding my website. I didn't know she'd done it until she forgot to intercept your reply.

Do believe me when I say that had I really thought there was any chance that you were Rosie's father, I would have told you about her, but I'm certain she's not.

Rosie knows this, and now I've had to tell her all about the scene in the pub too, but I've left it up to her if she wants to contact you. I'm trusting you on this one, Tom – if she does write, please be kind, but don't give her any false illusions that you are her father.

Had it not been for the circumstances, it would have been good to see you again! You look very fit and tanned – the surfing life down in Cornwall must suit you. Please don't contact me again, though, since all this has upset my husband and made things very difficult.

All the best,

Fran

I have the greatest sympathy for Pandora now, for once the lid is off the box of ghastly delights it simply won't jam back on again no matter how you try. All my efforts are merely damage-limitation exercises, and I have a horrible feeling that my lies and evasions are going to beget even more lies and evasions until the whole thing snowballs unstoppably downhill, crushing me into a fairly extensive grease spot on the way.

It's been a few days now, and if Rosie *has* emailed Tom then she is not telling me about it. It is odd and strangely unsettling to think that this substratum of communication might be going on without my knowledge.

I think what I'm feeling is jealousy. Rosie has just

been mine for so long, I don't really want to share her. (And she used to feel the same: before Mal she managed to get rid of every boyfriend I ever had, and if she'd been on the spot when I met him she might have managed to put him off too.) I'm also afraid she will somehow get hurt, but Tom was always quite kind except for suddenly ditching me in a callous-young-man kind of way, so I expect he will be nice to her even if she puts him through a third-degree interrogation on his entire life, which, knowing Rosie, is very, very likely.

Mal's never emailed or phoned her before, so what got into him? Was it just pique, or did he really think she ought to know? I suspect the former – he's never done much in the fatherly input line. In fact, Rhodri's been more of a father figure to her than Mal has, even though he hasn't been around much. He takes the godfather bit seriously: never misses her birthday or Christmas, and always loves to see her, or hear what she's up to.

Perhaps that's why Mal's suspicions fell on him. Or maybe the Wevills tapped into the old village rumour supply and passed the idea on.

I knew Mal's grievances were still festering away because I didn't hear from him until the next day, and by the time he rang I'd convinced myself that there would be so many candidates for a contract in the Caribbean that he wouldn't get it.

'Fran?' he said, sounding tired. 'I've had the interview – been there all day because they narrowed it down to just three of us and we had to wait for them to decide. It's been a long day.'

'Well, never mind, Mal. I'm sure another contract will come up soon, a more suitable one, and –'

'But I *got* it!' he broke in. 'They offered the job to me – providing I can be out there by the end of the month.'

'By the end of *this* month? But that's impossible, Mal, it's too soon – and so far away!'

'I thought you might be pleased,' he said sulkily. 'There was a lot of competition and the money's more than generous. It's not as though I'm doing it just for me either – it's for both of us: when I get back we can put the past behind us and make a fresh start.'

'I'd rather have you home – we can work things out a lot better if you are on the same side of the damned globe! *Please*, Mal, don't take it.'

'Too late: I have,' he snapped, and put the phone down.

He came back home rather sullen and defensive, and Ma telling him to his face that he shouldn't even *think* of leaving me alone for weeks at a time like he did, let alone for six months, didn't help.

However, he has now done one of his quick Jekyll-and-Hyde switches and is trying a charm offensive to win me round to the idea. This is not going to happen, because even without the recent hiccup in our relationship, having your darkly gorgeous husband going off on his own to spend six months on a tropical island with goodness-knows-what temptations is not a thought to gladden a wife's heart.

Mal is so good-looking that when he walks into a room other women tend to sit up and point in his direction like hunting hounds (or boxer bitches in Mona Wevill's case), and it's just a pity they can't tell from looking at him that this is a man who likes his pyjamas ironed with creases down the trouser legs and who can throw a wobbler of epic proportions if his breakfast egg is not exactly to his liking.

Nor am I deceived by his gestures of forgiveness, since I really haven't done anything to be forgiven *for*. I can see that he still harbours doubts about whether I am telling him the truth . . . and now even whether I have been faithful to him since we married! Apparently the Wevills have helpfully assured him that they absolutely *refuse* to listen to any gossip about me and other men, and they are sure there is nothing in it!

Since Mal seemed to lose sexual interest in me long before all this, due to my metamorphosis into Blobwoman, all his sudden gestures of affection are not actually leading into the bedroom. I'd be getting worried about this if I felt more in the mood, but not only am I still off colour but I'm now having strange abdominal pangs, so I have finally made that appointment for Thursday with my doctor.

I was lucky – normally unless you are screaming with agony down the phone they won't give you one for three weeks, probably hoping you will either give up or die before then, thus reducing the number of people in the waiting room.

In addition to my being a hormonal disaster area,

the cramping pains are getting a bit much. Could it be my appendix after all? Peritonitis can be a killer! Where, exactly, *is* my appendix?

Misconceptions

It was *not* my appendix.

Last night – was it only last night? – I had such severe stomach cramps and haemorrhaging that I was rushed here to the hospital by ambulance, not even knowing I was pregnant until they broke the news to me later that I had lost the baby.

It's so hard to take in – difficult to believe that I'd had something so precious and lost it without knowing. I was only about three months gone, so you wouldn't think a being so newly formed and tiny could stage such a spectacularly awful exit.

When I married Mal I accepted that there weren't going to be any more children – only now I suddenly realise how desperately I wanted that baby. They only let Mal in briefly after it was all over, and I was pretty out of it by then, but he probably feels the same way. I don't know what I'm going to say to him, because I feel so guilty, wondering if it was something I did, like cleaning Ma's house, or hefting that big heavy bag of hen food about.

* * *

I've just annoyed the doctors by refusing to have someone else's blood pumped into my veins to replace the half-gallon or so I lost – but it could have been round *anyone*; it's not like they tell you where they got it.

They have put me on a saline drip instead, which will water down the bit of blood I've got left to a pretty translucent pink, and also give my tear ducts a bit of ammunition, since I can't seem to stop crying even though I haven't got the strength to sob. I should think my iron count is about nil, and I feel like a burst balloon.

One of the doctors – I think he was a trainee, because he looked about eight – took a few minutes to tell me that about one in five pregnancies end in miscarriage, and it was just my bad luck I was the one. He also kindly assured me that it didn't mean I would lose the next, and there was nothing to stop me trying again as soon as I had more opacity than a glass of water and a discernible red blood cell count.

Try again? When Alison went broody and strong-armed Mal into having that sperm count apparently it took half an hour for each one to doggy-paddle languidly past the microscope, and half of *those* were going in circles. But I suppose into every generation of sperm a swimmer is born. And if it could happen once, it *could* happen again ... couldn't it?

When Mal came back to visit me, bringing my spongebag and other necessities, he was very quiet and sat down next to the bed with barely a word. He looked dark under the eyes from lack of sleep and not only was his dark hair ruffled, but his shaving had evidently been a pretty hit-and-miss affair, proof to anyone who knew him as well as I did that he was unusually upset.

'Mal, I – I'm terribly sorry!' I said painfully, reaching a hand out to him, though it was quite an effort to raise it from the bed. 'I know you *said* you didn't want children because you thought you couldn't have any, and now it seems you can, and I've lost it and –'

'But, Fran,' he interrupted, looking startled, 'I wasn't just saying that: I never *have* wanted children! If I'd realised it was possible, I'd have been more careful – had a vasectomy, even.' He took my limp hand in his and squeezed it. 'No, it's me who should be sorry that you've had to go through this, darling.'

Tears welled up again. 'I know you're just being kind, Mal. And the miscarriage *was* horrible, but the doctor says it was sheer bad luck and I'll probably be all right next time. So I told him about your sperm count being so low and he said they can do things about that these days –'

'You're not serious, Fran?' he said incredulously, paling. 'I thought if there was one thing we agreed on it was that we didn't want any children! I mean, apart from the complications you could get at your age, think what it would do to our *lifestyle*!'

While we stared at each other aghast (but for different reasons), he suddenly and magically regained all his poise and colour, like a chameleon in recovery.

'*Poor* Fran!' he said kindly. 'You aren't in a fit state to think logically about anything just now, are you?

170

But I do understand how you're feeling, and we'll discuss it later, when you're better.'

I nodded, since he seemed to be expecting some kind of response, but my throat was too choked with tears to speak, even if I'd known what to say. But, after all, I'd married him knowing it meant I wouldn't have any more children, even if I hadn't realised before today that he actually didn't want any – so I expect I will eventually settle back into my previous mindset, preferably before I have drowned the entire village in a Niobe of tears.

But who'd have thought my Achilles would turn out to be such a heel?

I hardly slept last night, what with everything circling my mind on an endless loop, but at least they have now taken the drip away and my head doesn't spin when I sit up.

Irrationally, I'm finding it hard to forgive Mal for not wanting the baby, as if he had somehow caused its loss: that's about as sensible as blaming the heavy sacks of Happyhen I carried from the car boot.

He has just been in to visit me again, still in Dr Jekyll Nice Guy mode, bearing a large card and a bouquet and being almost insufferably kind and forgiving. But now I've regained one or two of my faculties I've come to the conclusion that a lot of the kindness stems from guilt; he even held my hand when I cried, something he usually finds so hideously embarrassing that it makes him cross.

Then he started talking about our future as if the

baby were the merest unfortunate blip on the even line of our lives together.

'I've been thinking things over while you've been in here, Fran, and things are going to change. For one thing, I've realised what a financial hole I've got into – and I'm going to sort it out! For a start, I'm going to sell the car before I go out to Grand Cayman.'

'Go to Grand Cayman?' I echoed blankly, for without really thinking it through I'd sort of assumed that he would turn the job down now. 'But, Mal, it's the week after next!'

'I know, but I accepted the job and I can't let them down – and the doctor assures me you will be as right as rain in a few days.'

'But, *Mal* . . .' I said again, but my voice was sounding a bit whiny so I shut up.

He took my pale hand in his and squeezed it, but I just let it lie limp: it didn't feel like it belonged to me anyway.

'Look, I wouldn't leave you at a time like this if I didn't have to, but I'm doing it for us. With what they are paying me I can clear off any outstanding loans and we can make a fresh start when I get back. I might remortgage the house at a lower rate too, and I'm even thinking about selling *Cayman Blue* and buying a smaller, one-man boat!'

'Couldn't you do all that anyway, so you didn't have to go, Mal?'

'I'm thinking about what is best for our future, that's all,' he said, shifting uncomfortably and avoiding eye contact. 'You can come out for two or three weeks once

I'm settled, darling, and I'll make everything up to you: it'll be the holiday of a lifetime. Grand Cayman's a tropical paradise, with coral beaches and palm trees.'

He sounded like a travel brochure.

'It would cost a lot of money for me to go out there, you said so before,' I whispered from behind the sheet of invisible glass that seemed to have come down between the world and me. It didn't seem important, anyway, because no prize was big enough to fill the aching void within me. When all the colour has leached away from your world, even tropical islands lose their magic. Someone was droning out an old blues song like a dirge, but it took me a few minutes to realise it was me.

'It's nice to hear you singing again – you must be feeling better!' Mal smiled, relieved.

'That's not what you usually say,' I pointed out weakly.

'Well, I'm saying it now – and it won't cost much for the air fare out to the Caribbean if we pick the right month, and it'll be like a second honeymoon. Don't worry about coping while I am away, either, because I'll transfer money into our joint household account every month just as usual, and I can negotiate the remortgage over the Internet. And,' he added, as though it was an extra and very lavish present, 'I know you don't like credit cards, but you need something for emergencies, so I'm getting you a gilt credit card on my account. It'll come in handy for the holiday too.'

'A credit card? But, Mal, I really don't want one!' I

objected automatically, because the thought frightens me. I mean, if I don't have the money in the bank then I don't spend it: that seems to work OK for me.

'You never know what might come up, or what you'll need for the holiday – it's going to be hot, for a start, and you'll need cool clothes. Look, I've brought you these.' And he laid a bundle of Cayman Island brochures and a guidebook on my bed.

I lose a baby and he's so pleased he vows to sell his toys and gives me a credit card with a huge spending limit and the promise of an exotic holiday? Or is it all just guilt for leaving me alone at a time like this?

'Grand Cayman is a tropical paradise,' he said dreamily, looking at the cover on one of the brochures.

'We *had* Paradise,' I whispered, but he didn't seem to hear me. Proust got it right when he said the true paradises are the ones you have lost . . . and it was a long time since Mal had looked at *me* like that. Hot tears were rolling down my face again, but he was now gazing inwards at some wonderful vision.

'Palm trees, coral beaches, lagoons . . . lots of sailing. I'll show you the website when we get back home.'

'I want my mother,' I said weakly, childishly, but I don't think he heard me, he'd gone into the Cayman blue again.

Maybe he did hear me after all, for the next day Ma turned up bright and early and took practical measures to improve my surroundings, if not my state of mind.

By using a sort of cheerful persistence she soon had

174

me arrayed in white broderie anglaise with pink satin ribbon threaded through, all very girlie Victoriana, but, sickeningly, the sort of thing that actually suits me. There was a matching dressing gown and fluffy pink mules.

'As soon as Mal finally told me what had happened, I rushed out and got them. If only I'd known, I'd have been here sooner, my little Frannie,' she said affectionately, busily tidying the contents of my bedside cupboard and arranging a randomly selected bunch of flowers she had brought in an ugly vase so that it acquired an unexpected air of bizarre charm, like herself.

'There,' she said with satisfaction, 'I told the girl in the flower shop I wanted one each of everything pink, and see how well it came out!'

Once she had managed to infuse the clinical ambience with a hint of home she sat back, crossed her surprisingly slim ankles, folded her hands over her little fat stomach and said: 'That Mal behaving himself? Apart from not telling anyone what was going on until last night, that is?'

'Oh, yes,' I said, tears coming to my eyes – but they seem to do that every five minutes at the moment, anyway. 'That big card and the bouquet are from him.'

'Huh!' she said, unimpressed. 'Well, clearly there's more to him than I thought, so you can try for another baby when you're well again, can't you?'

'Oh, no, I don't think so ... I mean, this wasn't planned and I'm getting on a bit.'

'Rubbish.'

'No, you know I never intended having more children – Mal doesn't really want any. Besides, Rosie's enough for me,' I said firmly. If I keep saying it enough, maybe I will believe it.

'He's a waste of space, that Mal, I've said so all along. If he hadn't made you go on all these diets you probably wouldn't be anaemic now.'

'I don't think that's anything to do with it, Ma. And Mal just doesn't like fat women . . .'

I tailed off, looking at my plump but strangely attractive mother, thinking that if it weren't for Mal, looking at the blueprint of what I might become wouldn't bother me. Then suddenly I wondered what blueprint Rosie was following: she's a changeling princess and might become *anything*.

And I'd barely even thought about how she would be feeling about all this. What sort of mother *was* I? A tear squeezed painfully out and trickled down my face onto the pillow.

'Let it out, my love,' Ma said, handing me a tissue. 'Better out than in.'

She ferreted about in her huge, bulging handbag and produced a scrap of paper. 'Now, I've left a message on your Uncle Joe's answering machine, but he hasn't replied yet, so it's probably night over there, isn't it? I expect we'll hear from him later. And Auntie Beth says if you want to have a holiday in the Hebrides to recover you are very welcome, and Lachlan would drive down and take you back up there with him. She's writing. I'll phone Rosie up later and break the news to her myself, and I'm going to stay at Fairy Glen and look after you until you are better, because I'm not going home until I see some roses in your cheeks.'

'Yes but –'

'I've got the dogs with me, and Boot is going to feed the cats and Oz.'

Oz is the tortoise (Tortoz) and Boot is Vernon Bootridge, her gardener/handyman. Theoretically she has him three mornings a week, but actually he seems to have more or less taken up residence in the potting shed, a huge run-to-seed Mellors of a man. An unfortunate penchant for gardeners seems to run in the family.

'I'm supposed to be showing people round Fairy Glen . . . tomorrow? Or the next day? I've lost count.'

'Don't you worry your head about it, my love. I'll ring the estate agent on my mobile and sort it out.'

'And the hens – can you make sure the hens are all right? Mal is probably feeding them, but he won't be *nice* to them.'

She patted my hand. 'Don't worry, I'll take care of everything. And it's just as well you've got your old ma, because that Mal said he's still going off jaunting to the Caribbean, leaving you on your own at the end of next week.'

'It's work, Ma, and he's already accepted it,' I said, weakly defensive. 'I'm going out later for a holiday.'

'He should take you with him if he's going for so long. He can't act like a single man just when it suits him.'

I closed my eyes. Did she think I wasn't worried, my handsome, restless husband on the loose in another Eden?

Grapes of Wrath

After Ma had gone I must have dozed off, for when I woke up the light was indefinably different in my corner of the little ward, with its swaying, snot-coloured chintz curtains.

Mal's mother was sitting on the very edge of the vinyl visitor's chair with her clasp handbag dead centre on her bony lap and her dark eyes fixed on my face.

'You've committed a great sin, and this is your punishment,' she whispered when she saw I was awake, leaning over the bed in a wave of menthol and euca-lyptus. 'In the eyes of God you are living with a married man – but I'm sorry for your loss,' she added perfunc-torily, though with a tiny flicker of genuine emotion. 'And this is no time to rake up old sins, especially with Mal off abroad soon and you weak as a kitten.'

'Ma's going to stay at Fairy Glen and look after things until I'm better,' I said quickly, in case she was going to let Christian charity move her to look after me on my sickbed. 'And I'm going out to see Mal.'

'Well, Frances, he knows my opinion on your marriage, but even so I can't condone his leaving you alone for so long. But he has been consumed by greed, avarice and lust and doesn't listen to my advice.'

'*Lust?*' I said, startled.

'The burning lust for earthly possessions.' She primmed up her coldly righteous little prune of a face.

'Oh . . . right. Yes, he does seem to want every new hi-tech gadget that comes on the market, and he's always buying things for the boat, but he's promised to change.'

'What of Rosie?'

'He doesn't buy her anything at all.'

'No, Frances, I meant has she been told that you are in hospital?'

'Ma is ringing her up and trying to persuade her not to come home until the end of term. Although I'd love to see her, I don't want to interrupt her studies, and I'm all right really.'

I lay back again and closed my eyes, hoping when I opened them that I would find Mrs M. had been a horrible dream.

But after a short inward struggle I opened them and managed to say, 'It was kind of you to come, Mrs Morgan. I really appreciate it.'

'*Kindness* doesn't enter into it, Frances. I hope I am a Christian!' she said, and, handing me a small booklet called 'Roads to Redemption' and a damp bag of hard green grapes, she hauled herself upright and tottered off in her sensible glacé leather shoes.

Nia only came in once, but that was a big concession since she hates hospitals. She was carrying a potted miniature pink rose and a box of Liquorice Allsorts, and trailed Rhodri behind her like a grateful stray who had unexpectedly latched on to a good owner and couldn't believe his luck; if he'd had a tail he'd have wagged it.

Although I was glad to see his familiar face, it meant I couldn't do more than exchange a few hasty private words with Nia when we sent him away to buy chocolate. But she has never been the maternal type, so although sympathetic she was also down to earth, pointing out that had I had the baby I would have become one of those exhausted geriatric mothers who totter dazedly through the daily treadmill with glazed, hopeless eyes, their clothes covered in food stains and baby vomit and their hair unbrushed.

'You're not Superwoman material, Fran. Remember all those broken nights when you had Rosie? Think what that would be like *now*, when you're twenty years older!'

'That's true, I hadn't thought of that,' I admitted. 'I'm horribly ratty and drained if I don't get a full night's sleep – and could you imagine Mal getting up in the middle of the night to feed a baby, even if he happened to be home?'

'No,' she said positively, and changed the subject to one that was clearly occupying most of her mind: her last-ditch attempt to persuade poor Rhodri to make an offer for Fairy Glen. She sees the 'For Sale' board as a Sword of Damocles poised to part it for ever from the rest of the Plas Gwyn estate and, more importantly, prevent her from doing whatever it is she does up at the standing stones.

'Now your ma's down for a bit he could at least go and discuss it with her,' she said obstinately.

'But he's struggling to find the money to get Plas Gwyn up and running as it is,' I pointed out. 'Look how hard he's working, doing all the unskilled stuff. *I'd* love him to buy it too, but I can see it's impossible, even if Ma let him have the glen separately and sold the cottage to someone else. And I'm going to miss being able to go there for inspiration as much as you will.'

'I don't think so,' she said, with one of her fierce frowns, and it is true that I don't perhaps use the standing stones in the way she does, but clearly she had come up against the rock of one of Rhodri's occasional fits of obstinacy.

She frowned. 'Tonight at eight it's the last of the present series of *Restoration Gardener* and if Plas Gwyn does get shortlisted we will have a huge amount more visitors so I'm sure Rhodri *could* buy the glen. It would be an investment.'

'Oh, Nia, I'd entirely forgotten the programme was tonight!'

'Well, it's hardly surprising, is it? Don't worry, we will record it for you and I'll let you know immediately if Plas Gwyn gets through to the next stage. I'm feeling a bit more optimistic because Gabe Weston seems so keen on it – did I tell you that he rang up and – no, that's right, Rhodri only heard on Monday, so I never got the chance. He found one or two interesting things in the documents Rhodri sent him that he'd like to check out, and also he's dying to look at

181

the maze, so –' she looked at her watch – 'he should be turning up at Plas Gwyn any time now.'

'Now? Today? But, Nia, if he's coming back, what on earth is Rhodri doing here? He should be there to meet him this time!'

And I really, *really* didn't like the thought of Gabe Weston invading my Eden again . . .

'It's all right, he's delegated Dottie to hold the fort again, but just until he gets back.'

'But she's crackers! She nearly blew it last time.'

'She'll be all right – and we got on the long-list, didn't we? Gabe Weston chose that and he gets to pick the final three properties for the vote-off too, so you never know.'

'Rhodri should be up there going all out to persuade him, not down here!'

She shrugged. 'He insisted he'd rather come and visit you, and you know what he's like once he actually makes his mind up about something.'

'He's so sweet, but I wouldn't have minded, and they are letting me go home tomorrow so he could see me any time.'

'Mal doesn't exactly make him welcome, Fran! I think he'd rather see you here.'

'Yes, I suppose now Mal's got the crazy idea that Rhodri might be Rosie's father, it's best they don't meet.'

Rhodri came back carrying the unwanted chocolate and looking large, chunky, wholesome and masculine. The women in the other beds on the ward fell silent as he passed them, only to resume what they were saying after he'd passed.

'I've told her about the Weston man coming again,' Nia said. 'And about you still refusing to buy the glen!'

He opened his light-blue eyes wide. 'But, Nia, I can't! You know how I'm fixed financially, especially after Zoe's wedding, but you can walk all over the rest of the estate any time you like, including the maze.'

'I already do, but I also need access to those oak woods and the falls, and especially the standing stones,' Nia said obstinately.

'Why?' asked Rhodri curiously, the sixty-four-thousand-dollar question.

'Don't ask,' I said faintly, closing my eyes. I only hope she isn't performing anything involving sacrifice, or Rhodri could be doing an Aslan any time now.

'I'm a Druid, that's all,' Nia said shortly. 'There's no big mystery about it.'

'*Are* you?' Rhodri said with mild interest. 'Poetry and folk music and stuff?'

'You inbred chinless wonder!' Nia said scathingly. 'You can hardly think I go up there to skip round the stones while reciting rhyming couplets!'

'Well, that's more or less what you do at the May Day ceremony at the maze with the others, isn't it?' he pointed out reasonably, grinning. 'I've got a bird's-eye view from my bedroom window.'

'Oh?' Her brow furrowed, so she looked pretty fierce. 'You can't see the standing stones from there, can you?'

'Not really, even in winter when there are no leaves on the oak trees the canopy of branches is pretty dense. Why, you're not doing all that nude dancing by the light of the moon thing, are you?' he asked interestedly.

'Rhodri, I'm a Druid, not some New Age hippie-dippy witch!'

Just as well, the way she was looking at him. 'I think it's really interesting, Nia, but let's talk about it another time,' I said weakly.

'You're getting tired,' Rhodri said kindly. 'Perhaps we'd better go.'

They bickered off down the corridor together, Nia addressing him as 'my Lord High and Mighty', something she only does when cross with him, or remembering her socialist working-class roots or whatever, so clearly she was still miffed about the folk music bit.

Left alone, I lay there feeling uncomfortable just knowing that Gabe Weston was in the village.

'Mr Gwyn-Whatmire just asked me if we could put the *Restoration Gardener* programme on the ward TV tonight. It's so exciting to have somewhere local on!' one of the nurses said, stopping by my bed. 'And that Gabe Weston is *gorgeous*!'

'Isn't he just,' I murmured weakly. 'But I'm sure everyone else would rather watch a soap.'

'Oh, no, they'll all be glued to it, you'll see. And you should eat that chocolate,' she added. 'Full of iron, it is.'

So I did, even though I wasn't hungry: I couldn't lie about there for ever like a dying duck.

I don't know what Rhodri thought I would do with the magazines he'd brought me: an old American *Vogue*, *Fly-Fishers Monthly* and *Your Stately Home*, but it was a kind thought . . . and even that made me burst into tears again.

If there'd been a drought I could have hired myself out as a sprinkler.

True to her word the nurse wheeled the TV into a central position at the end of the small ward and switched on *Restoration Gardener*, so that all those of us in a reasonably sentient condition could watch.

In fact, when Gabe came on, one or two of the patients I'd thought totally out of it suddenly stirred and showed signs of life too. He certainly scrubbed up well: for the programme he was wearing a leather jacket over what looked like one of those supersoft cashmere jumpers, but he still gave the impression he knew which end of a spade was which.

He also looked very familiar now, which was odd – but no odder than everything else happening to me lately, especially this feeling I was experiencing that I was levitating above my bed with my air-filled head bobbing about like a balloon.

'Welcome to *Restoration Gardener*,' he said, in his seductively deep furry voice, 'the last of the series featuring the Old Mill, where the millrace and water gardens are now nearing completion. But just before we go there, I'm going to show you the six wonderful gardens, each worthy of restoration, that I've chosen my final three from – and amazingly difficult it was too!'

With spaced-out detachment I watched as he showed us brief vignettes of each one of them, Plas Gwyn being the very last. The house looked lovely, even with Dottie bobbing about in the background like a demented scarecrow, and there were some artfully lit shots of the maze showing the bumps and hollows of the pattern.

'Plas Gwyn in North Wales is an ancient house in a lovely setting, with a unique unicursal maze . . .' he was saying. 'I'll tell you later which will go through to next week's vote-off, when *you* get to choose our new restoration project! For now, though, let's go down to Hampshire and see how the Old Mill is getting along . . .'

The arrow-head smile that accompanied this seemed to be directed straight at me, bringing me back down to earth – or my hospital bed – with a bump. I couldn't tell you much about the Old Mill because while it was on I was too busy coping with an emotional seesaw of wanting him to shortlist Plas Gwyn for Rhodri's sake, yet fearing anything that might bring him one step closer to St Ceridwen's Well and into my (and Rosie's!) orbit.

'That's all from the Old Mill, though we will pop back in the next series to see how the project has developed,' Gabe said finally. 'Next week's programme will be the last in the present season, but don't forget to tune in and choose the winner of the next makeover. The three who have made it through are . . .'

He paused tantalisingly, then said, 'Edge Cottage in Devon with its walled apothecary garden, the fascinating grottoes and topiary of Wisham Hall in Gloucestershire and, finally – Plas Gwyn in North Wales with its unique ancient maze.'

He looked full at the camera. 'I know which one is

my favourite – now you get ready to tell me yours!'
And with a final smile he vanished from the screen to
be replaced by the credits.

'There,' the nurse said, 'isn't that wonderful? That
will have made you feel so much better, Mrs March,
knowing that your friend's house is on the shortlist!
Wouldn't it be wonderful if it won?'

'Yes,' I said, a trifle hollowly. 'Absolutely wonderful!'

I tottered down to the phone later and called Nia and
Rhodri, who were both wild with excitement, and then
Carrie. After that, worn out with making enthusiastic
and congratulatory noises about something that could
well prove to be the oil slick on the, so far, fairly placid
sea of my life, I thankfully climbed back into bed again.

Apart from the occasional coachload of tourists
nothing much happens in St Ceridwen's Well (though
I suppose that is all about to change), so next day when
I arrived home from hospital several of my neighbours
were hanging about outside their houses in a casual
sort of way, ready to wave and call greetings. That was
nice, but I could have done without the Wevills
standing watching me from their doorstep, wreathed
in more wholesome toothy smiles than an Osmond
convention.

After the heat of the hospital it felt very cold to me
as Mal assisted me from the car, and I'd looked in the
unforgiving hospital washroom mirror, so I knew it
was my turn to look like a 'Thriller' zombie, all ashen
face and dark-socketed eyes.

I tottered on rubber legs towards the house, turning to give my watchers a rather Queen Mother salute before I went in, and just at that moment a familiar big silver Mercedes glided to a stop. The tinted window noiselessly slid down and for one interminable minute I gazed into a pair of concerned green-rayed hazel eyes. Then the window slid back up and the car moved almost silently on.

It was disconcertingly like a slow-motion scene from a Mafia film, but without the machine guns; I even had Hendrix in my head singing 'Hey Joe' as the soundtrack.

'Nosy bastard!' Mal muttered, putting his arm round my waist and trying to hurry me over a doorstep that seemed to have suddenly grown to the size of the north face of the Eiger. 'Looks like that TV gardener man – heard he was staying at the Druid's Rest last night.'

I didn't say anything – in my present condition I was just grateful that I hadn't hallucinated the little scene. In the house everything seemed unsettlingly unfamiliar, and even more clinical than the hospital. Mal's way of showing his love, regret, and possibly guilt, had been to render the house sterile.

Ma returned from showing two more lots of people around the cottage, bearing *coq au vin* and a bottle of good red wine to build me up.

She found me weeping with frustration because I hadn't got enough strength left to tear up the Wevills' get-well card, but did it for me without comment, repelled Mona when she had the nerve to turn up at the door with a plate of Welshcakes like curling stones, and banished me off to bed.

'Mona and Owen are good friends of mine,' Mal was protesting as I went. 'It was generous of Mona to offer to help, despite the unreasonable way Fran has taken against them.'

'They may be *your* friends, but they're not Fran's,' Ma said. 'I could tell at a glance that that Mona's a two-faced cow with her eye on you, despite all her smiling ways, and anyone with shiftier eyes than her husband I've yet to see! Anyway, if Fran doesn't want them in her house, that should be enough for you.'

'*My* house too, don't forget,' began Mal, but that's all I heard before I shut the bedroom door. Normally I try to pour oil on troubled waters, but just then I didn't care if the waves engulfed the whole of St Ceridwen's Well.

I felt much better by next day, which was just as well, because it was pretty exhausting, despite entertaining *en négligé* from the sitting-room sofa.

Rosie phoned me at some length, and I had to dissuade her from driving all the way home to 'look after' me. It was all pretty fraught, I can tell you, because the selfish part of me wanted her there with me, while the rest knew it was better that she finished her term and came home at Easter.

'Really, darling, I'm fine, just a bit anaemic, and Granny's giving me lots of nourishing food so I'll soon be over that.'

'But I could help and cheer you up,' she insisted,

'and soon you're going to be all on your own when Mal goes away! How *could* he leave you like that?'

'He accepted the contract, Rosie, and it's very well paid so really he's doing it for all of us,' I said, though somehow it didn't sound quite as convincing when I, rather than Mal, said that sort of thing, probably because he was the one who'd been consistently outspending our income.

Mind you, if by some miracle Plas Gwyn does win *Restoration Gardener*, Mal being away for so long could prove a blessing in disguise, since at least I wouldn't give myself away in front of him or be presenting him with yet another man to be jealous of.

'As soon as I'm well I'm going out there for a holiday, Rosie, so it's all right, really – and I've got Carrie and Nia and Rhodri here even when Ma's not at the cottage, so I'm not going to be alone.'

Eventually I persuaded her to wait until the Easter holidays. And I must say, I've always loved being alone in my studio working, so even though I would have loved to see her I was actually starting to feel overly surrounded by people cooped up like this, and ready for a bit of solitude.

After lunch Carrie popped in with some of her Welshcakes, which are on a totally different culinary plain to Mona Wevill's, and a warm and fragrant bara brith. She told Mal right to his face that he should be ashamed of himself even *thinking* of going off and leaving me alone for six months after I'd gone through such a trauma! He was coldly polite when she was there, but afterwards I ended up having to assure him that I didn't mind a bit and understood why he had to do it, and the sincerity factor was probably distinctly lacking.

Aunt Beth had already phoned last night to offer me a Highland terrier puppy when Morag next whelps, but she had forgotten Mal's dog phobia. She wanted me to put Mal on the phone so she could give him a piece of her mind, as did Uncle Joe when he called from Miami, but I didn't, because it isn't going to do anything except make him angry that all my family and friends seem to be united in condemning his trip into the blue.

Nia, when she paid a visit later in the afternoon, said it was because they didn't understand the nature of the clever, tricky, brooding dark Celt, not being Welsh themselves, but I reminded her that Ma is half Welsh, which is why she didn't burn our holiday house down back in the seventies when she was being a Daughter of Glendower and keeping the home fires burning for the English holiday-home invaders.

'I was *never* a Daughter of Glendower,' she said firmly.

'And don't you mean Mal is a *selfish* dark Celt? It's only making him cross because he knows he really shouldn't leave me for six months, particularly now. But at least if Plas Gwyn is chosen for the restoration, Gabe Weston should have been, filmed and gone before he gets back, shouldn't he? If he doesn't seduce Ma into selling him Fairy Glen, that is.'

'You mean he's seen it again?' Nia demanded. 'I know he stayed at the Druid's Rest overnight because he wanted to spend the whole day at Plas Gwyn, but he didn't mention the cottage. Mind you, he didn't even hint that we were on the shortlist either!'

'Yes, I thought I'd hallucinated him driving past and staring at me when I was coming home from hospital yesterday, but actually he was the Miss Patten Ma was showing round the Glen.'

'*Miss Patten?*'

'His PA, apparently, he got her to book the viewing. He told Ma Fairy Glen was totally unlike what he was looking for, but had a strange attraction for him. He seems to have a strange attraction for Ma too: she said he was a lovely man. She's going to make all her friends phone up and vote for Plas Gwyn next week.'

'He *does* seem very genuine,' Nia said a trifle self-consciously. 'I met him again when I went back up to the house with Rhodri. He's really enthusiastic about the maze.'

'I know.' I reached for my rather well-worn copy of *Restoration Gardener*. 'It says here: "I suppose all gardeners have a passion for some particular aspect of their profession, and with me it is a fascination with the history and development of the maze, from its earliest beginnings as a ritual pathway cut from turf or stone, to the later high-hedged puzzle labyrinths."'

'Amazing – you hardly had to look at the words!' Nia said pointedly, and I flushed slightly and hastily put the book down again. 'But at least it means if they do the restoration he will take care to keep the turf maze as it should be.'

'Perhaps he's enthusiastic about all ancient

monuments, and that's the attraction of Fairy Glen,' I suggested.

'You don't think he *really* might buy it, do you?'

'Ma said he isn't looking for a holiday cottage, but somewhere to live. He'd keep his London place on as well, though. And they seem to have got on like a house on fire,' I added gloomily. 'Ma, of course, mentioned what happened to me, and he said he was very sorry and hoped I felt much better soon, or something. And she told him about my rose garden.'

'So did I,' Nia said guiltily. 'It just sort of slipped out.'

'Well, it's not one of my guiltier secrets.'

'Where's your mam now?'

'Showing yet more people around Fairy Glen. I'm starting to think we should charge for viewing, because I suspect at least half of them come just out of curiosity.'

'I hope so. You'll just have to put anyone unsuitable off when you are well enough to show the cottage again.'

'That's what I thought I'd done with Gabe Weston!'

'Well, we need an artist or craftsman to buy it, someone like us.'

'I suppose he might not do much to the glen, and let us walk there anyway,' I suggested hopefully. The glade and the standing stones had always been my place for being quiet, my refuge, and I longed for the moment when I could go up there again and feel some kind of healing begin.

And it was where I first set eyes on Mal, striding up out of the misty trees like a Celtic prince, as I was sitting contemplating life on the fallen slab. He'd been a great walker then – it used to be one of the things we all did together, with Rosie circling round us in her little green frog wellies like a jealous sheepdog.

It's strange how life changes: it all seems just the blink of an eye ago.

'Why should Gabriel Weston send you flowers?' Mal demanded, practically tossing a hand-tied and beautiful bouquet of roses into my lap next morning. 'You hardly know the man.'

'Oh, aren't they *lovely*!' I exclaimed, softly stroking the velvety petals and breathing in the heavenly scent. 'No, of course we've barely met, but I expect Ma told him all about my miscarriage while she was showing him round the house – you know what she's like.'

'Only too well, but I would rather she didn't retail our personal affairs to every chance-met stranger.'

Before I could point out that Gabe was hardly a chance-met stranger I spotted an Interflora van drawing up by the gate. 'I think there may be another bouquet on its way, Mal.'

I sincerely hoped that this one was from someone innocuous, like Aunt Beth; but unfortunately the arrangement of blooms set in a square glass vase full of what looked like frogspawn came with an off-beat get-well message from Tom.

Mal read it over my shoulder: '"Hey, Fran, get back up on that board, there's a big one coming!"'

'What does he mean by that? And you can't tell me your mother told *him* about the miscarriage as well,' he snapped.

'No, I think it must have been Rosie.'

'Rosie? Why on earth should it be Rosie?'

'Well, *you* were the one who emailed to tell her all about Tom turning up in the first place, so it's hardly surprising if they are now in touch,' I pointed out, but it still didn't stop my Celtic prince getting into a right royal huff.

My hand still does not really seem connected to my head, so it is just as well I have several batches of cartoons doing the rounds already, and had already dispatched samples of the Alphawoman strip on its merry way.

Although I have been back home almost a week now I still feel light-headed and tired all the time due to the anaemia, and sort of anti-climactic and depressed, which I expect is a combination of losing the baby and Mal's imminent departure.

An endless loop of that old 'MacArthur Park' song about leaving a cake out in the rain and losing the recipe plays inside my head and sometimes breaks out in doleful snatches, but Mal doesn't complain, even about that.

Apart from the huff over the bouquets, he has on the whole been quite patient and sweet since I got home, even with everyone being disapproving towards him, and Ma constantly around making large quantities of nourishing food and reducing our kitchen to a slightly flour-dusted state of homely chaos.

Usually he's really annoyed with me when I'm ill, because he's so useless at looking after himself, but all my get-up-and-go has got up and gone, and he's *still* being nice to me. While I expect a lot of this is due to guilt over both his attitude to the baby and his imminent departure, not *all*, surely?

He's even asked the Wevills not to use our drive while he is away, so I hope they will just leave me alone, apart, perhaps, from reporting my movements.

He paints a beautiful picture of my having the holiday of a lifetime out there in the Caribbean with him, and our turning a new page on our life together . . . or something. He can actually have a very poetic turn of phrase sometimes, though when you try to analyse it later without the dark blue, long-lashed eyes, the handsome face and enticing tinge of a Welsh accent to go with it, it doesn't sound quite as impressive.

He's trying to involve me in his plans by showing me all the information, which *does* make it look like a different kind of paradise from the one I already thought we'd got. Hopefully, without snakes or vultures.

Dear Fran,

I know you didn't want me to contact you again, but ever since I saw you I keep thinking about you, especially now – I'm really sorry about the baby.

Of course I wouldn't do anything to hurt you, or Rosie, so don't worry about that, just concentrate on getting well.

Love, Tom

Dear Tom,

Thank you for the lovely flowers and message. It was very kind and thoughtful of you.

I'm feeling much better already, and will soon be back to normal, which is just as well since I have lots of work I should be getting on with!

Fran

I just answered the door to find Dottie on the step, with Rollover breathing down the back of her neck.

'Visit of condolence – heard you'd slipped your foal,' she said, and thrust a jar of calf's foot jelly at me.

Then she mounted Rollover, clicked through her teeth and rode off.

The jelly looked vile – her housekeeper (or maybe that should just be 'keeper'?) makes it for these lady-of-the-manor occasions.

Dottie's heart is in the right place, I'm just not sure where her brain is.

'The whole village seems to be going *Restoration Gardener* mad. I don't know what's got into the place,' Mal grumbled. 'All I wanted was a quiet pint at the Druid's Rest and it's all done up with posters saying "Vote for Plas Gwyn!" In fact, every window in St Ceridwen's Well seems to have one, and there's bunting across the high street.'

I glanced guiltily at the small poster in our front window, which he hadn't yet spotted – Carrie had breezed by earlier and stuck it there. 'Well, if they do win it tomorrow, it will be a great thing for the village.

Lots more visitors equals more jobs at the castle, more customers for the café and gift shop – more everything all round. And even if they don't, this next programme should still put St Ceridwen's on the map.'

'Yes, and house prices will probably rocket!' he said, looking more cheerful, though I don't know why since we are here for ever, so the house going up in value has no relevance at all. 'But I knew you would be as garden restoration mad as the rest of them so I thought we could go down to the pub tomorrow night for an hour and watch it there, if you feel up to it,' he said generously. 'They're having a special night. The place will be packed out but we can go early enough to find a seat and a bar snack before the rush starts.'

'That's a lovely idea, Mal,' I said, though really I would have much preferred to have watched it up at the hall with Carrie, Nia and Rhodri, and I didn't much feel like going out at all yet, come to that. 'And perhaps Ma could come too?'

'Come where?' Ma said, her gaily-turbaned head appearing round the door suddenly like a benign genie.

'The pub, for the *Restoration Gardener* programme and celebrations – or commiserations,' I explained. 'It's the vote tomorrow night.'

'Wild horses wouldn't keep me away,' she said, 'but if you are going, Fran, I'll drive you there and back.'

'It's not that far,' Mal said. 'Time she started to get out and about again.'

'Yes, I'm fine really, Ma – I just feel a bit light-headed and far away.'

'I'll drive,' she said firmly.

'Do you think the dogs would like calf's foot jelly? There's a jar in the fridge.'

'I'm sure they would love it – what a treat!' she said, so at least Dottie's offering would not be entirely wasted.

We arrived at the pub just early enough to bag a big corner table with a good view of the giant TV screen, which was just as well, because in the end Nia, Rhodri and Carrie decided to come down too, closely followed by the rest of the village.

Ma beckoned them over as soon as she spotted them, and though Mal was his usual slightly stiff and tight-lipped self at first, he soon thawed out when Rhodri, who was practically incoherent with nerves, began pressing drinks on him. After a couple of stiff whiskies I'm sure he had forgotten his daft suspicions about me and Rhodri – or even that he didn't like gardening – for he cheered just as loudly as everyone else when the programme started.

'Welcome to a special edition of *Restoration Gardener*,' Gabe Weston said, 'where you vote for the garden *you* want us to feature in our next series.'

Then he showed pictures of the three contenders with the numbers to call and declared the voting lines opened. After that, you could hardly hear the commentary for the sound of clicking mobile phones.

The first two properties ('Boo! Rubbish! Throw them out!' shouted the partisan crowd) seemed to have an awful lot going for them, as far as I could see: there already were garden features, overgrown or partly hidden though they might be.

Then they got to Plas Gwyn ('Winner – winner – winner!' everyone chanted) and there was nothing much except grass and lewdly clipped topiary – until clever camera angles and a commentary by Gabe brought out the hidden shapes of what had once been there, so that you could see it appearing out of thin air before your eyes.

And when he got to the maze he made it sound so fascinating that you felt it would be an absolute crime not to restore such 'a national treasure' . . . though actually it was unclear whether he was referring to the maze or to Dottie, who had appeared suddenly through a gap in the hedge looking like a perambulating hay tarpaulin and could be faintly heard ordering the camera crew to 'Clear orf!'.

'Oh God, she's blown it!' Rhodri said, clutching his fair head in his hands despairingly.

'No, I think she might have just clinched it – look,' Nia said.

In the background Dottie could still be heard shouting, 'Hey you – gardening feller!' before she was faded out and the camera panned to Gabe's face, smiling.

'For the chance to restore Plas Gwyn – and meet more of the Gwyn-Whatmire family – please phone . . .' he said, giving the details, and it might have been just me, but he seemed to be much more enthusiastic and persuasive about Plas Gwyn than the other two.

'So, that's all three properties,' Gabe said. 'All worthy of restoration; all, in their own way, capable of being stunningly recreated to their former glories. Now, the lines are about to close, and while the votes are being counted I will let the owner of the Old Mill, our latest project, tell you what winning the restoration has meant to him and his family.'

At the Druid's Rest you could hardly hear yourself speak for the sound of voices demanding drinks, but the second Gabe came back on screen again, an envelope in his hand, the whole room fell silent.

'The votes have now been counted, and I'm about to open this envelope and find out which property you think should be the winner . . .' He pulled out a card and looked up: 'And I can tell you now that the winner is . . .'

There was a theatrical pause and I heard an anguished groan from Rhodri.

'The winner is Plas Gwyn in North Wales!'

The place erupted into noise so that the end of the programme was drowned out, but by then Rhodri was embracing everyone within reach, beaming, and Ma was bouncing up and down like a clockwork monkey, clapping her hands and screeching: 'Yes! *Yes!*'

Nia was looking stunned. I nudged her. 'You've done it – you've won!'

'Yes, congratulations,' Mal shouted across the table.

'I can hardly take it in,' she said, then made a sudden lunge for Rhodri, whose lips were forming the words 'The drinks are on me!', luckily unheard in the din.

'Shut up, you idiot,' she said, pulling him down. 'You can't afford grand gestures and, anyway, everyone will buy you drinks now until they run out of your ears!'

Which they did, but by then I was safely tucked up at home in bed, exhausted, but filled with a strange mixture of excitement and happiness for Rhodri's sake that we had been chosen and nervousness that for the next few months I could meet Gabe Weston around any corner – though if Ma does sell Fairy Glen to him in the end I might just have to get used to coming face to face with my murky past all the time.

Restoration fever died down slightly and Ma finally returned home to Cheshire, though whether that was to be tactful so that Mal and I could have a last couple of days alone together, or because she was missing all her chums, I don't know.

She left me a large supply of bottled Guinness, someone having told her that it was full of iron, and also a sack of dried apricots, ditto.

Nia has promised her she will keep an eye on me, though how she will do that while working in her new pottery, having just moved her kiln and everything up there, and simultaneously orchestrating Rhodri's grandiose schemes, is anyone's guess.

Besides, I don't need keeping an eye on since I'm getting better by the day and will soon be back to normal, especially once I lose this feeling that everyone is very far away behind a sheet of thick glass.

The hens were glad to see me again instead of the muttering old madwoman in the paisley-patterned wellies. Ma'd been going on about Shania making good broth instead of eating her head off and laying nothing, until finally I burst into tears and said I couldn't possibly eat one of the girls, it would be cannibalism, so Shania had probably felt a sense of threat.

It looked like Mal was sincere about clearing his debts and starting afresh, because he sold his car!

Unfortunately, this meant that he was reduced to driving my old Beetle around for the last few days, and he didn't like it. (I didn't like it either – I'm possessive about the poor old thing.)

'What on earth is that smell coming out of the heater?' he demanded the first time he used it.

'I spilled a cup of McDonald's cappuccino down the air vent last time I was over at the supermarket, shopping,' I explained. 'The whole car smelled lovely for about a week, and then it seemed to go off.'

'It smells like vomit. I've got you an air freshener.' He didn't offer to buy me a newer car, but I am fond of my old one anyway.

Mal was busy with last-minute preparations, like laying up his boat for the duration. I expect he still has a huge loan on *Cayman Blue*, but there is no sign of him selling that yet, and Owen Wevill is going to keep an eye on it for him while he is away. Mal has packed all the papers regarding the mortgage to go with him; it is in his name, since he bought the house before we met, and I suggested the remortgage would be a good time to put the house in joint names. I know it doesn't matter really, since what is mine is his and vice versa, it's just this feeling that I'd like *my* name on the deeds to the home I love too.

Mal has also invested a lot of energy in rendering

the house spick and span after Invasion of Ma, *I* clearly not yet being up to anything other than a little desultory dusting even were I remotely interested. This early spring clean might have to last for six months, the way I feel now.

He is still being affectionate and understanding . . . only now I sense that a slightly critical note has begun to creep in, as though he thinks I am malingering and should be back to normal, especially when he said he knew how I felt (which I'm very sure he doesn't), but I was to concentrate on getting fit and well while he was away and back to the old Fran that he loved.

The thin, much younger one, I think he meant. I just wish he'd drop this constant harping on my becoming 'the Fran he fell in love with', as though his love were conditional. Even if I lose some weight by the time I go out there – which I fully intend to do, only I feel too tired just yet to even *think* about it – I am glad to say that I will not revert to the thin, dreamy and trusting thirty-year-old single mother, still living at home, that he married.

I've got more chance of turning into a fairy.

Bigger Things

'That nice Gabriel Weston has offered me the full asking price for Fairy Glen!' Ma told me when she called on Mother's Day to thank me for my card. 'But I told him I would only sell it to him if you agree too, my love, since you are as fond of it as I am and, what's more, will be living practically on the doorstep.'

'But, Ma –' I began to protest automatically.

'You just think about it, Frannie, because he absolutely loves the cottage and wants to make it his home, and he *is* a gardener so he would look after the glen.'

'Yes, but he might just be *saying* that. He probably wants to knock the cottage down and build a huge house and landscape all the magic out of the place,' I said stubbornly.

'I don't think so, Fran – and I don't know what you've got against him! In fact, I thought you'd be all for it, another gardener, especially since he told me you'd been very nice to him, and he felt like you were old friends already.'

I bet he did – and if he's going to make a habit of

that kind of remark I'd *much* rather he lived some-where else!'

'He seems genuine to me, Fran – but there, it's up to him to persuade you differently if he really wants it.'

'He did send me a lovely bouquet, with a kind message,' I admitted reluctantly. 'And so did Tom Collinge. I thought he must have found out from Rosie.'

'Yes, Rosie told me she's been emailing him,' Ma said cautiously. 'And he's going to visit her, I think.'

I sighed. 'I can't stop them even though I'm not happy about it, though with a bit of luck the whole thing will peter out of its own accord eventually when they see they're not alike in the least. This isn't a fairy tale where a fairy scientist waves a magic DNA result and declares them father and daughter, and they live happily ever after.'

'If you say so,' Ma said doubtfully. 'What about Mal? All those heavy hints about poor Rhodri got terribly wearing, although I can see why he doesn't quite believe in your Mysterious Stranger story, Frannie, when you didn't tell anyone about it until this year!'

'No one asked,' I said shortly. 'No, Mal still thinks I am holding something back – probably that it was Rhodri, but that it was just a brief, mistaken fling.'

(Come to think about it, I *am* holding something back! But then, should I suddenly start claiming that Gabe is Rosie's father, everyone would *really* think I had gone mad, wouldn't they? It's much more un-believable than any of my other stories!)

'He accepts now that what happened before I knew

him isn't really important, it's what we have *together* that matters, and I would never be unfaithful to him. He was always a bit jealous, but he didn't really suspect me of anything before the Wevills moved in and started putting ideas into his head.'

'Those Weevils are slow poison,' she agreed. 'Where were they living before, did you say?'

'Some small village in mid-Wales . . .' I racked my brains and produced the name.

'Never heard of it.'

'Neither had I, but it does exist. I don't know why they moved here after Owen retired early because of his Mystery Illness, and it doesn't seem to stop him doing anything he wants to. Mona does nothing except insinuate herself into the WI, which according to Carrie has suddenly become a battlefield. I'd bet any money that when the dust clears she will be seen modestly accepting the chairwoman's seat.'

'You're probably right,' Ma agreed. 'Still, at least if Gabriel buys the Glen you will have *one* nice neighbour.'

'Neighbour as in several hundred yards away up the lane?'

'Close enough – *and* he's a cash buyer,' she said pensively. 'I could be booking that cruise in no time!'

'I'll see what he says,' I conceded reluctantly, since it would be like having a gently ticking bomb permanently on the doorstep. As far as he is concerned I expect the novelty of constantly running into an ex-lover who most definitely *doesn't* want to kiss and tell would add spice to his otherwise humdrum country existence,

but if he had the least idea about Rosie he would probably be looking for a property on a remote Scottish
island instead.

After this I expected every phone call to be Gabe
Weston trying to persuade me that he was the right
buyer for Fairy Glen, so it was sort of anti-climactic
when there was a huge silence instead. I am in hope
that he has thought better of the idea.

Mal is a whirlwind of activity, organising things for
his trip, and has already dispatched a couple of boxes
of belongings freight, ready for when he gets an apartment: sheets and pots and pans, CDs and gadgets. I
expect I will be constantly missing things in the kitchen
after he's gone, but at the moment I can't raise much
interest.

He has locked his stamps away with instructions
that in case of fire or hurricane I am to rescue them
first, but I am much more likely to be sitting on the
coop with the hens watching them go up in smoke
while clapping my hands in girlish glee. I'm not risking
my life for some scraps of printed paper.

Because he said I wasn't up to the drive yet, he
booked a costly taxi all the way to Manchester airport
to catch his very early connecting flight to Gatwick.
(The Wevills couldn't take him, since Mona was having
one of her Strange Turns, though how she could be
any stranger than she is is anyone's guess.)

I haven't actually driven anywhere since I came out
of hospital, so I was glad about the taxi but guilty that
I was so selfishly lost in my own woes I hadn't even

thought about how poor Mal was going to get himself and all his bags to the airport.

We said our goodbyes at home in the cold, dark early hours, and I still found it unbelievable that not only was he really going off and leaving me for six whole months but, however much he tried to conceal it, was happy and excited about it! It's not that he didn't do and say all the right things before he left – he did – but the fact that he could just walk away from me and jump into the taxi and go was deeply hurtful.

I think maybe I was expecting a last-minute reprieve.

His face and suit glimmered palely inside the darkness of the taxi (and my God, was I glad *I* wouldn't be the one having to launder that linen suit at the other end), he waved his arm, and then he was gone.

Just after he vanished the Wevills' front door flew open and out shot Mona in her beige silk pyjamas, waving a weak torch: *Honey, I Blew Up the Gloworm*, coming soon to a cinema near you.

'Gone, gone!' she wailed.

'"And never called me Mother",' I finished for her, since we seemed to be in Victorian melodrama mode.

Owen materialised out of the darkness behind her and silently dragged her back into the hall, slamming the door like a pistol shot.

I expect I will get the blame for waking the entire village up.

Our house felt totally empty and cold, and in their neat run behind the cottage even the hens seemed to be moaning in sympathy, although the sharp wail of a peacock would sum up much better how I felt at that moment. Bereft. Deserted. Not Wanted On Voyage.

I felt everything settle like a huge burden of responsibility on my shoulders, even though all the cottage outgoings including the mortgage are arranged on standing orders from our joint household account, so I need to cope with nothing except emergencies. And Mal's going to phone me every other day, and email me in between, he says.

After a while I found he'd left me a little note propped against the kettle, together with some more computer printouts about the delights of Grand Cayman and my new gilt credit card . . . or should that be the guilt card, in my case, given my hang-up over credit?

The note mysteriously directed me to look on the desk in his study, where I found three gift-wrapped presents, which I carried down to the kitchen to open, though not without difficulty, since one was quite large and heavy. They contained the following items:

1) A gleaming chrome fruit and vegetable juicer.
2) A copy of a detox diet.
3) A return aeroplane ticket to Grand Cayman, dated late May, standard class.

Why do I get the feeling there is a causal relationship between these three objects?

Have conditions been attached? And a nice ring would have been more of a spur, since he has never got round to giving me one – but preferably not an eternity one, since a ring with any sort of time limit like that 'Forever' one Tom gave me seems to be an invitation to disaster.

And since I'm probably still anaemic and need to build my strength up, won't this make dieting a little difficult?

What liquidises well with Guinness? Apricots?

The dead hours between night and day should be banned. I don't think I've ever felt so bleakly depressed in my entire life.

Just noticed that one of the printouts Mal left me was all about how Grand Cayman was 'the premier place to celebrate your nuptials'.

But since I've already been nupted (dreary registry office ceremony though it was), I thought it had got in by error until I read the bit where they said it was also the perfect place to renew your vows. Nupted revisited? Is that what Mal meant by my holiday there being a second honeymoon? He was pretty insistent that I buy something special to wear.

How secretive – but romantic – of Mal! It makes me feel more hopeful about our future together. (And the advert on the same page for Colombian emerald engagement rings was pretty interesting too.)

I won't mention it – though I may just hint about the emeralds . . .

Rhodri and Nia called in to cheer me up, Rhodri bearing six bottles of champagne, which apparently also contains iron. He suggested I mix it with Guinness, but not in the liquidiser.

'Rhodri is so kind,' I said when he went off to the kitchen to find glasses.

'Too kind and trusting – anybody could take advantage of him,' Nia said. 'Absolutely nothing would get done up at Plas Gwyn if I didn't take a hand, because tradesmen would swindle him, and he'd let the studios to just *anyone* instead of good-quality craftspeople who will be able to pay the rent!'

There is something to be said for a malleable husband. Wouldn't it be lovely if he and Nia got together once they are over their divorces? Of course, she would have to stop referring to him as 'you chinless wonder' and 'Lord High and Mighty', but these are probably only from long habit and don't really reflect how she feels about him now. And he is *not* chinless – he's got a perfectly good one.

On the other hand, if he carries on making weak Druid jokes like he was today, which were of the 'a Bard in the hand is worth two in the bush' variety, he may not live that long.

Rhodri, of course, thinks Gabe Weston buying Fairy Glen would be brilliant, and can't quite understand my lack of enthusiasm.

'Perhaps you'll feel differently when he's talked to you about it,' he suggested. 'He's really a very nice man.'

'*If* he talks to me about it. He hasn't contacted me yet,' I pointed out, 'so he's probably thought better of it. He can't *really* think it would be convenient to live here when his work takes him all over the country, can he?'

'It hasn't stopped him driving up here whenever the

212

fancy takes him, has it?' Nia pointed out. 'That sort of huge car probably just about drives itself.'

'They're coming to film the preliminary scenes at Easter,' Rhodri said. 'Perhaps he's simply waiting until then? He's going to show me the plans he's drawn up then too . . . or did he say he was going to come back and discuss them with me *before* that? I've forgotten.'

'He'll probably email you,' Nia said. 'He must be very busy.'

When they left, Mona Wevill just *happened* to be on her drive, polishing her car very, very slowly and looking about as normal as she ever does. She rushed to the fence eagerly, calling, 'Oh, Mr Gwyn-Whatmire, isn't it wonderful news about the *Restoration Gardener* programme! I'm so –'

Rhodri, the soul of politeness, seemed transfixed by a smile that exposed more teeth than a crocodile's, but Nia dragged him off with the threat that if he didn't get into his car and drive, *she* would. That did it. Nia's driving is of the 'treat 'em rough' school and he wasn't about to abandon his beloved Spyder to that sort of treatment.

Mona looked at me as they drove off, and her eager expression closed tightly into bitter resentment as though I had scored points in some game we were playing.

I wish I had a copy of the rules and/or an impartial referee.

She made a basic tactical mistake in ignoring Nia, though she would have been unlikely to have fooled her even if she'd sucked up to her from the day they moved here, because Nia is just naturally suspicious of everyone; it's the way she's made.

Although it seemed days until Mal phoned me from Grand Cayman to say he had arrived, I expect that was due to my permanent confusion as to whether he had been flying backwards in time and was going to land yesterday, or forwards, and it would be tomorrow . . . or something. Anyway, he'd had a good flight and was staying in a hotel until he found a suitable apartment.

He said he was missing me already, but he didn't talk for long, and I could hear office noises in the background so I suppose he had to get straight down to work.

How odd to think of him so far away, *and* I forgot to thank him for the presents, which were kindly meant, even if not quite what I might have chosen myself – except the plane ticket, I suppose, since that is the only way I will get to see him for the next six months.

Strangely enough, while at the time his departure felt like some kind of ultimate abandonment, it has proved to be the usual case of 'out of sight, out of mind', probably because it's so hard to take in the length of time before he comes back, and the enormous distance between us.

I'm more concerned with trying to fight off this dark cloud of depression hanging over my head and threatening to descend. Nothing really seems to matter any more except Rosie, and my maternal worrying over her has intensified to the point where I'm fighting the urge to rush down and check that she's safe and well all the time, something she certainly wouldn't appreciate. It's also unnecessary, since she has been amassing huge mobile phone bills checking up on *me* since the miscarriage.

She's now cautiously started mentioning that Tom has emailed her and visited, and says he is a fun person. It's pretty clear that Tom has never quite got any older, and one day very soon Rosie will mentally outgrow him, but meanwhile I can see the attraction – and he has promised to teach her to surf at some point!

On the subject of whether she still thinks he's her father, she is tactfully silent – or maybe they don't discuss it. They could find out once and for all, of course: the truth is out there somewhere. But then, the truth might not be what either of them wants.

Oh, well, I expect it will all sort itself out over time. I can't seem to raise enough energy to care that much at the moment, so long as Rosie doesn't get hurt.

At least now I'm back at work in my studio in its nest of thorns, guarded from the immaculate conception of Mal's lawn by a trellis fence completely covered in a demented, ever-expanding Kiftsgate, and once I lose myself in my work I feel happy again for a while.

Will my arms and legs be less rubbery by rose-feeding time? I can't ask Ma to stagger round with a full watering can of Up-She-Roses at her age, although I dare say Nia would if I asked her. But I don't want to be a weak and wimpy drain on my friends, who have already been doing my shopping and, in Carrie's case, supplying me with home-baked goodies.

I am certainly eating well: too well. Losing the baby left a big empty space inside me that I have been attempting, unavailingly, to fill with chocolate among other more nutritious things, so surely I should be feeling better by now . . .

Got a funny little sketch in the post from Tom today, of him standing on a surfboard while painting at an easel, captioned 'Catching the big wave!'

Maybe he missed his vocation as a cartoonist. His painting style used to be rather precise and dead photographic realism. I didn't know he had this kind of thing in him.

I've just weighed myself for the first time since the miscarriage and discovered that I am nearly two stone over my ideal weight! This may not sound gross to you, but bear in mind that I am only five-four in my bare feet, and slightly built.

Mind you, if you stretched me a few inches I'd be just right, so perhaps there's a new dieting angle no one's thought of yet. The Stretch? Get out your rack and I'll be your first customer, since clearly I am the sugarplum rather than the fairy Mal yearns for.

I really need to lose some weight before my second honeymoon in the Caribbean (not that I had a first one anywhere), but, to tell the truth, the idea sounds terribly unreal somehow, despite all Mal's enthusiasm. He loves it there, has moved into a beachfront apartment, been sailing with someone from the office, and boasts of the searingly high temperatures as though I will find the prospect of being barbecued irresistible.

Suddenly I feel a bit better, and the cloud, while still hovering, has lifted slightly.

An alternative women's magazine, *Skint Old Northern Woman*, has taken my Alphawoman comic strip too, which has given me quite a boost, and also, now the weather is milder, I'm spending a lot of time communing with the hens, doing studies of them in various mediums. I expect there are lots of hen lovers out there, so maybe I could get some card designs or something out of them. While the Fran March Hen Calendar doesn't have quite the same cachet to it as my rose one, maybe someone would be interested in it.

The other good news is that the doctor confirmed yesterday that my iron count was so much better I shouldn't stand near magnets, but she still didn't think I should start dieting just yet.

She is very friendly and, despite nearing the end of my allotted five-minute appointment, I suddenly found myself pouring out to her how the miscarriage had made me realise I really wanted another baby, and about Mal's horrified reaction. She said men often felt like that because they feared they would no longer be the centre of attention, so their noses were well out of joint, and I told her he had always been jealous of Rosie.

Then we had a good long discussion on this book we'd both read by Margaret Forster called *Good Wives*, about how women had to choose between putting their husbands first or their children, and, historically, it seemed to have been expected that the husband would be in pole position, even if it tore their wives to bits to have to leave their children for years while they followed their lord and master wherever their fancy took them.

Of course there are some women who are so in love with their husband they put them first anyway, but although I am mad about Mal, I'd *die* for Rosie, so clearly I am not one of them. The doctor said she had the hots for her husband to the extent that she'd sell her offspring to the gypsies if he asked her to, but she was just joking. I *think*.

When I eventually came out, everyone in the packed waiting room gave me dirty looks.

Another little sketch from Tom, this time of me reclining in a nest of thorns like a bosomy, date-expired Sleeping Beauty, and a figure on a surfboard riding a big wave that seemed to be about to crash down on the sleeping princess's head. I expect Freud would have a field day with it.

Mal mentioned the diet in last night's email, and I assured him that the very second my blood count was normal I'd be juicing like mad and doing the detox thing, though it sounds like living hell to me. A physical scourging to go with the mental one over the baby.

I *have* read the book now, though – with amazement! Surely this diet wasn't meant for humans. Maybe I should try it on the hens first. But no, I couldn't do that, when they always seem pleased to see me, all running up their coop whenever they spot me and then, as is the way of something with a brain the size of a *petit pois*, all running away again in a fright.

There's been a fox about, so I've just been letting them out for an hour or so before dusk. They scratch about the garden companionably while I potter round pruning my precious rose bushes, before taking themselves to bed in warm straw. We seem to be on a mental par.

OK, I've drunk all the Guinness and champagne, and eaten my way through the food parcels Ma left in my freezer, so my iron count has to be totally restored. I'm just tired out by every little thing because I'm unfit – and so fat that I look as if someone has stuck a super bicycle pump up an orifice and inflated me.

It's no use Carrie and Nia assuring me I'm not gross when my mirror tells me I'm nearly spherical. No more excuses: I *must* diet.

Once my legs were up to the climb I was drawn irresistibly back to Fairy Glen: I'd missed the solitude and the soothingly hypnotic sound of the water falling, and somehow knew that the process of grieving wouldn't be complete until I'd spent some time there.

I got up to the waterfall and rested for quite a while on my favourite rock, then slowly made my way up the more overgrown path to the oak glade and sat on a fallen stone watching a finger of sunshine work its way towards the orange and yellow lichened surface.

Then I opened my mind to let all the black thoughts flood in: I grieved for the baby I nearly had, and for the way I was naturally losing some part of Rosie too, as she grew older and lived an increasingly separate life. I'd like to have her back with me – but I know she should be out there getting a life, not home with her mum.

I mourned too for the way Mal and I had moved further apart in more ways than the physical one, so that even if the wound healed over the scar would always remain.

I even howled over the good times with Nia and Rhodri here in the glen, though short of amnesia there is no way you can lose a happy childhood: it's with you for ever.

It was a damn good wallow and I wept floods until I felt empty and sort of cleansed. The black cloud was lifting and receding, letting the light touch me again, and I was conscious once more of the rustling of small creatures and the birdsong.

With a sigh I blinked and found I was now literally sitting in a golden circle of sunshine: spotlit as if to say, 'Fran March, that's enough of that! Now get on with the rest of your life. It's what you make it.'

So, maybe things won't ever be quite the same again, but when Mal and I renew our vows on Grand Cayman it will be a symbol that we are ready to reforge our relationship into something even better and stronger when he comes home.

Tom and Rosie's contact will dwindle naturally into a casual friendship once the novelty wears off, and

Gabriel Weston will make his programme and then be gone back out of my life like a passing comet; soon there will be nothing to disturb our lives again; no more old secrets waiting to pounce.

And as if on cue the bushes rustled and Gabe walked out of the trees into a patch of dappled sunshine and stopped dead at the sight of me, much as Mal had the first time we met – only here was no darkly handsome Celtic prince, but a man who seemed to blend and be one with his surroundings, woodland wild.

All Cried Out

Actually, it was a bit eerie for a minute: he blended in so well I thought I'd conjured up some mythical forest being like the Green Man or Herne the Hunter, but then I saw that he was just as taken aback to find me perched on the stone slab.

'Fran?'

'No, it's Tilly the two-ton tooth fairy,' I said rather waspishly, angry at being caught out tear-sodden and with reddened eyes like a wet rodent. 'I wasn't expecting to see you – especially up here!'

'Well, *I* wasn't expecting to see *you*, either – but I prefer my fairies substantial,' he said, grinning. He walked out from the darkness of the trees and turned into a mere mortal, though the greens and browns of his clothes still fitted the general ambience a whole lot better than my pink duffel coat. Instead of wearing prosaic wellies like me he had on beautiful dark chestnut leather cowboy boots darkened by the damp grass, which should have made him look affected, but actually suited him.

He got a better look at my face and the grin faded.

'Sorry, I didn't mean to intrude on a private moment.'

'You're not, I've had it,' I said shortly. 'I was about to go.'

'Were you?' He came and perched on the other end of the slab, half-facing me. I bet it felt cold through his cord jeans, because his thick forest-green fleece didn't reach below his hips ... assuming he had any. He could have turned into pure snake for all I know.

'Don't rush off, then, because I wanted to talk to you. Ever since your mother told me I couldn't buy the cottage unless you agreed to it, I've been trying to think how to persuade you – and then I thought I'd just jump into the car and talk to you face to face. I suppose I should have warned you I was coming, but I *am* a creature of impulse.'

'Lucky you found me, then.'

'I tried your house first, and I was going to go back later, because your neighbour said you'd gone out.' He grimaced.

'Let me guess: she was a blobby, beige woman who was all over you like treacle?'

'Got it in one. She recognised me, said she was all alone and pressingly invited me in for coffee and to show me her garden.'

'Everyone in the village recognises you after that last *Restoration Gardener* programme – and she hasn't got a garden, just paving and the odd pot, and even those she buys ready-planted from the garden centre and kills almost instantly.'

'I wasn't staying to see, so I thought I'd take a walk up the glen, since I only got to the waterfall last time, but if I'd known you'd come here for a bit of peace and quiet I wouldn't have intruded.'

'That's all right, I really was about to leave – I've been here for ages.' I looked around and sighed. 'I *needed* to come here, and this is the first time I've felt well enough to face the climb.'

'I'm very sorry about the baby,' he said sincerely.

Although I'd thought I was all cried out, tears pricked the back of my eyes again. 'Thank you – and for the lovely roses. That was kind.'

He smiled. 'I *am* kind! When I was passing the day you got home from hospital I meant to speak to you – only your husband gave me such an evil glare and you looked so ill that I thought better of it and drove off!'

'He thought you were a nosy stranger. He . . . tends to be a bit jealous too.'

'Well, just don't make me out to be some kind of ogre because we once spent a night together! If you let me buy the cottage I'll promise to officially forget all about it, so you see, I'm no threat at all to you.'

'*Officially* forget?'

'*You* may have been struck by handy amnesia, but *I* remember it as quite a night, *Maddie*! I never quite forgot you, though I suppose since you are the only woman ever to run out on me like that, you would tend to stick in my memory,' he added honestly.

I winced. 'So you were only pretending you didn't recognise me at first.'

'I wasn't certain it was you, but then it all came back to me. And, Fran, although I had to go on down to

Cornwall that day or I'd have lost my chance of my first big garden restoration project, the first opportunity I got I drove back up and searched for you.'

'You *did*?'

I must have sounded slightly incredulous, as he grinned and added, 'Believe it or not, it's the truth. But, of course, no one knew of Maddie with the big blue-grey eyes and strawberry-blonde hair, and we were into the summer holidays so all the students were away and . . .' he shrugged, 'that was that. As a matter of interest, why did you leave so abruptly? And what on earth were we drinking that night?'

'Scrumpy cider – someone had flagons of the stuff, and it was pretty rough. I had way too much of it, and . . . well, you were sort of on the rebound because my boyfriend had just dumped me. But next morning I woke up in your van with a splitting headache and a stranger, which is not something I made a habit of. And I thought I was still in love with Tom and it was all a bit . . . well, anyway, I just wanted to get away,' I said honestly.

'You did that all right. Vanished without trace,' he said pensively. 'But I still think it's a pity you ran off, because we might have had something going there if you'd given it a chance. There was that classic "eyes meeting across a crowded room" moment at the party – and I recall a certain chemistry between us.'

'*I* don't,' I said decisively, though actually I was experiencing another just then and it was an effort to look away. 'I expect you're mixing me up with someone else.'

225

'No, I'm not. I even bought a framed book print a few years later simply because it reminded me of your big sad eyes! It was from that fairy story about the sealwoman going back to the sea when her human lover betrayed her trust – you know that one?'

I nodded, trying not to look flattered.

'I admit I couldn't remember what you actually looked like until I saw you again, but then I knew you right away. You were a happy memory, Maddie. A lingering taste on the tongue ...'

He smiled again, his eyes wrinkling up around the corners, and I went pink and looked away hastily, feeling oddly breathless. 'I wish you wouldn't call me that!'

'All right,' he said equably. 'If you tell me honestly whether you've ever thought of me since.'

'No, never,' I said shortly and *totally* untruthfully. I have trouble admitting to *myself* that I crept back to the car park in search of him later that day (think 'moth' and 'flame'), only to find the van long gone.

'It was so out of character that I decided to put it right out of my head. By the end of that week I was here to spend the summer living at Fairy Glen and working for Carrie at the teashop.'

I looked around the sunlit glade. 'I first met my husband, Mal, right here on this spot, just after he bought the house we live in now.'

'And so promptly forgot all about *me*?'

I let his assumption that I'd met up with Mal that very summer slide. 'More or less,' I agreed.

'So, when did you know I was Adam?'

'Only a few weeks ago when I saw a DVD of

Restoration Gardener; but then I thought I might be imagining the resemblance since I'd more or less forgotten what you looked like.'

'And now fate has thrown us together again – in a platonic sort of way, of course. It's a small world.'

'I think it's imploding,' I muttered.

But I don't think he caught it because he just hitched himself up on the stone a bit more and said, 'Didn't you say your husband was jealous? So what's he doing going off and leaving you alone for months, *and* at a time like this?'

'How on earth do you know that?' I demanded, startled. My God, I only hoped he couldn't read minds as well as find lost gardens!

'Your mother,' he said predictably.

It wouldn't surprise me if she'd also shown him that pull-out concertina folder of photos of me from age nought to now that she keeps in her handbag, my school report cards and the china pig I won at a funfair when I was eight.

'Not that it's any business of yours, but he'd already agreed to do this contract and we need the money. It's only six months anyway, and I'm perfectly well again.'

'Are you? You look a bit pale.'

'I was anaemic, but I'm nearly better. I just need to get fit and lose a bit of weight.'

'You look about right to me,' he said consideringly, though most of me was enveloped in duffel coat and wellies so there wasn't much to go on. 'Curvy – which is how it should be. Who wants to go to bed with a bag of bones?'

I assumed this was rhetorical, but I could have replied, truthfully, 'My husband does!'

'I'd just concentrate on getting fit again. And you have a daughter already, don't you? That must be a consolation.'

'Yes, Rosie – she's lovely,' I agreed. 'She's at university, studying to be a vet.'

'Must be a clever girl.'

I looked at him sharply, but clearly the date of our encounter hadn't stayed in his head the way it had stayed in mine, and he hadn't the slightest suspicion that Rosie might be his.

Come to that, even this close up I couldn't see any resemblance between them, so maybe she *is* a changeling. Or perhaps I really did that frog thing – is it parthenogenesis? – and created her all on my own.

I found our gazes had locked again but I couldn't drag my eyes away until he blinked. It's not chemistry, it's hypnotism, I'm convinced of it.

'I have a daughter too – nearly eighteen,' he confided.

'Yes, I remember reading that. Carrie – at the teashop – looked you up on the Internet when she knew you might be doing a programme here.'

'I didn't think I was that fascinating.'

'You're not. It's just that nothing ever happens in St Ceridwen's Well so you're a seven-day wonder,' I said dampeningly. 'But you were telling me about your daughter?'

'Stella. She went to live in America with her mother when we divorced, and I haven't seen her since. I tried, but she didn't want anything to do with me, and it was all very difficult. I still send letters and presents, but she never replies.'

'I'm sorry,' I said sympathetically. 'It must be terrible not seeing her grow up.'

He sighed, then looked up. 'Do you understand teenage girls?'

'Having been one myself helps,' I said drily, 'and my Rosie's not twenty yet.'

'Stella sent me a text message a couple of weeks ago, out of the blue. All it said was "how r u dad?"'

'Just that?'

'Just that, after what – seven years? – of unbroken silence. It was so weird! I mean, she was a little girl last time I spoke to her, so I felt as though an alien being was trying to make first contact with me. Do you know what I mean?'

'Only too well, but all girls mutate into strange life forms when they become teenagers,' I assured him.

'But sending me a *text* message?'

'Texting is their first language and comes as easily as thought to them. Easier. What did you do? Text her back?'

He looked sideways at me and smiled crookedly. 'I'm a dinosaur – I'd never texted, so I had to find the instructions first. Then I sent her a cautious one back – I was afraid of saying the wrong thing.'

'And she replied?'

'Yes, and I've had a few more short text messages since, and now one or two emails as well. Informative stuff like, "Mum just got back from honeymoon *again* and I hate Hardy."'

'Who's Hardy?'

'Her new stepfather.'

'What, as in "Kiss me, Hardy"?' I asked, interested.

'Apparently. Unless she calls him by his last name.'

'Weird,' I said. 'But I think the messages mean she's reaching out to you, Gabriel. Now she's older she probably realises there can be two sides to every story, and because you carried on sending her letters and presents she must know that you never stopped loving her.'

He looked at me with rather touching hope. 'Do you really think so? I was never sure whether Tamsyn – my ex-wife – was passing them on or not.'

'*Is* she that spiteful?'

'Probably not, though the divorce was a bit acrimonious. It was partly my fault, I suppose. I left her alone in London when I was off shooting new series . . . too much free time and too much temptation. Then when I found out she'd been unfaithful –' he shrugged – 'I indulged in a bit of tit for tat with her best friend! Ex-best friend. Big mistake.' He looked at me. 'Do you know all about the paternity case and the divorce?'

'Yes. When Carrie goes into something she makes a thorough job of it,' I admitted.

'Oh,' he said sombrely. 'Then you know about that other poor woman too – the delusional one?'

'Yes, but that's all it was, wasn't it?'

'Yes, but the dirt stuck anyway. And then it seemed whenever I went out with anyone else I'd find it all raked up in the newspapers and magazines, so it's no wonder Stella didn't want anything to do with me.'

'But the scandalous bits all seemed to be old stuff,

nothing recent,' I pointed out. 'You're the blue-eyed boy of the TV screen now, and the recent articles all said how quietly you lived and things like that.'

'I do live quietly, but then, I was never much of a party animal to start with.' He shrugged again. 'Perceptions change, but I thought if I moved to the country, made a fresh start, Stella might even come and visit when she's over here.'

'Does she come over?'

'To see her grandparents in Cornwall – and *they* won't have told her anything good about me. But she's going to start university over here this autumn.'

'Then I think she's definitely trying to build bridges and she does want to see you again.'

'I hope so. I've certainly no intention of stirring up any new scandals that might make her change her mind – not that I ever wanted to stir any up in the first place.' He looked at me. 'You know, I haven't really talked about all this to anyone before . . . sorry to unload on you.'

'That's OK. I suppose we hold a secret or two about each other now, so we're safe. I don't want any hint of what we did to reach my husband's ears, and you certainly don't want your daughter to hear even a raked-up old scandal.'

'We could even get to be friends,' he suggested. 'If you agree to let me buy the Glen, that is!'

I stood up a bit shakily. My bottom was both cold and numb, and I'd had a good thick layer between me and the stone. I only hoped Gabe's extremities were not frostbitten – but in a detached and entirely altruistic sort of way, of course.

'Back to the purpose of the visit?'

'The place draws me like a magnet,' he agreed.

'Not to mention the maze?'

'You heard about that?' He laughed. 'I have a passion for them. That's the first thing that's going to be restored.' He put his hand under my elbow as I slipped on the damp earth, and kept it there while we scrambled back down the overgrown paths to the cottage.

I felt so shaky I probably would only have made it back down on my bottom so I didn't protest.

'If I'm not going to let the cat out of the bag about our previous short but sweet encounter, is there any other reason why you don't want me to have the cottage?' he asked.

'Of course not!' I said quickly.

Liar, liar, your bum's on fire! said a helpful voice in my head.

'*If* you are the right man for the Glen. Ma said you like the cottage as it is?'

'I love all its grotesque little baroque flourishes,' he declared.

'And its inconveniences?'

'Well, maybe not *all* of those. I would hope to do a sympathetic extension eventually, and maybe update the facilities a bit. But I do like your ma's style. It's cosy and a little eccentric.'

That's one way of describing it. 'But isn't it too far from London? It must take you hours to get here.'

'I don't actually have to be in London that much, though I do go off all over the place from time to time filming follow-up visits to gardens and other engagements.'

'TV celeb stuff,' I suggested.

'Well, yes. I can only get out of doing so much of it. I'll probably keep a *pied-à-terre* with office space for my PA in London, but I'll spend most of my time here. This would be home,' he added gravely. 'Somewhere to return to, a place where I can put down roots.'

'And the glen itself – what would you do to that?'

'Nothing that would make it any less magical,' he said quickly. 'Restore the paths and steps, and maybe tidy up the grottoes and arbours a bit, but I wouldn't touch the trees and the stones at the top, even if I could – they're bound to be protected. And you and your friend could walk there any time you wanted – or in Nia's case, dance.'

'Did Ma tell you about Nia being a Druid? I didn't think she knew!' I said, startled.

'No, Rhodri let it out. He gave me the impression that if I even *thought* about touching the oak grove or the standing stones, Nia would sacrifice me on one of them.' He looked at his watch. 'I'm going up to Plas Gwyn now. I want to go over the provisional plans for the restoration with him, and make sure he understands what's happening when we start preliminary filming at Easter – the opening scenes. But first I'm going to take you home.'

'Oh, I'm quite all right now,' I protested hastily. 'I –'

But he didn't listen to any protest, just whisked me

into his admittedly comfortable car and took me home. The Wevills' curtains were twitching like a poltergeist with a fit was in them, but it must have been Mona because Owen was out pretending to polish the brass numbers on his gate.

Coming home with Gabe is getting to be a habit – and since they now know his car, the Wevills will be scandal-mongering like anything before their cat can lick its ear.

'So, what about it?' Gabe said as he pulled up.

'What about *what*?' I said. I'd been sleepily daydreaming in the warmth, enveloped in the scent of expensive leather and whatever light but compelling aftershave he was wearing. Or maybe he just exudes an attractive scent like a flower sends out signals?

'The Glen – can I buy it?' he said patiently.

I hesitated. 'Look, it must be clear that I don't want it to be sold at all, but if it has to be . . .'

I stared at him, brows knitted as I contemplated the possible consequences, and he stared back. I had time to count all the bright green rays around his pupils, and *he* blinked first.

'Yes, I suppose so,' I said finally, and scrambled out. 'Thanks for the lift – 'bye.'

The car moved off, and as I turned I caught Owen watching us out of the corner of his eyes like a ventriloquist's dummy. I couldn't see the hidden camera or tape recorder. He turned his back and started rubbing as though the genie of the gatepost might appear and grant him two stone balls and a pineapple.

'A murrain on all your cattle, and may your number

nine drop off,' I murmured in passing, and a sudden breeze whisked his yellow duster from his loosened grasp and hooked it on to his TV aerial like a dingy pennant.

The moment I stepped indoors a wave of exhaustion hit me, and I lay on the sofa with the whole scene replaying over and over in my head. Finally I fell into a half-doze where images of dappled leaves, green-rayed hazel eyes and warm brown skin danced about like reflections on water.

Posted

I woke from my doze with a feeling of impending doom that wasn't entirely due to the dream I'd just had, in which I'd been forlornly looking down at an iridescent oil stain on the pub car park where a camper van had once stood. Its rainbow had held no promise of a speedy return.

The part of my brain not occupied with projecting unwelcome memories onto my inner eyelids had been tossing over the facts while I slept, and now presented me with the conclusion that if Gabe Weston actually came to live in St Ceridwen's there was a high risk that he would get to know that I'd had Rosie years before I met Mal. (Father unknown, candidates various, but popular opinion awarding the cherry to Rhodri.)

Surely he would then eventually suspect that she might be his ... or was the whole thing only blindingly obvious to *me*? And what would he do if he did find out ... and then *Mal* found out that he found out? Or Rosie? Well, the complications seem endless.

My God, what if the *press* ever found out?

Feeling a need to run this past Nia I left a message

on her mobile asking her to meet me at the pub later – and her actually getting a mobile phone, something she's always been against, is a sure sign that she is seldom going back to her cottage to pick up her messages these days! Is there something she isn't telling even me, her oldest friend?

While I slept, the post had come. (Huw daily performs languid concentric circles around the village on his bicycle, so the mail can arrive any time.) There was yet another sketch from Tom, this time of a rose with a flattering representation of me in its heart-shaped centre. I think it was meant to be a Damask, but clearly a rose is just a rose to him.

No written message, but when I checked for emails he'd sent me one to the effect that as he rode a big, creamy wave in today he was thinking of me.

Oh dear. I rather feel as though a big wave is trying to overturn *me* when all I'm trying to do is paddle my own canoe to safety.

Elvis was helpfully singing 'Return to Sender' in my head, but there doesn't seem to be a computer button that sends messages back with the words 'thanks, but no thanks'. And he knows I live here, so I can't return the sketch.

Maybe Nia can suggest a way of cooling him off – unless I'm flattering myself, and he's just being kind. I'll take his little missives with me, anyway, and show her if I get the chance. It will be the first time I've been to the pub since I came back from the hospital, apart from my brief appearance on *Restoration Gardener* night, though I have been round to Teapots a couple of times to exercise my legs and see Carrie.

Life is slowly getting back to normal. Well, normal apart from my husband being on the other side of the world, the probable father of my only child moving into the village at any second, and my ex-boyfriend bombarding me with romantic messages while ingratiating himself with my daughter in the mistaken belief he is her father.

I suddenly wondered if Gabriel might just be staying at the hotel tonight. But even if he is, we should be safe enough in the back bar in the early evening, when any halfway decent TV celebrity ought to be stuffing his face in the restaurant or hitting the bright lights of Llandudno.

Before the light went, I fed the hens and then shut them up for the night. The garden was peaceful, just the sighing of the breeze through the bushes and the grating of rose stems against wood . . .

In fact, there was something very odd about the way the Mermaid and Golden Showers hung loosely from the trellis I'd nailed along the top of the fence dividing our garden from the Wevills', and I walked across to have a closer look.

Since they moved in I'm used to finding rose prunings from their side tossed over into our garden, but this time they have gone one better. They must have put their secateurs right through the holes in the trellis and snipped through every stem within reach, so the top branches hung there swaying, amputated from the roots.

I am sure I would have noticed if they'd done it this morning when I let the hens out, so perhaps they did it while I was out. Though God knows why – unless Mona had a fit of pique after being rebuffed by Gabriel.

I felt certain they were watching me, even though I couldn't see them for the tears blurring my eyes, so I made a very rude gesture towards their house.

Tomorrow I would have to pull all the dying stems out and prune the bushes properly, though I'm not sure they haven't served a death sentence on my poor Mermaid, who was doing so well after a very slow start.

And although they are entitled to cut back any of my plants that grow over into their garden, isn't cutting them on *my* side illegal?

I drove to the Druid's Rest since my legs were still a bit trembly from climbing up the glen, but halfway I stopped and tossed the air freshener Mal had hung from the rear-view mirror into a roadside litter bin. Whatever that aroma was supposed to be, the fading smell of vomit from the heater was infinitely preferable.

Huw and Carrie were already there in a dark corner when I walked in – but unusually they seemed to be arguing instead of all lovey-dovey.

'What's up with Carrie?' I asked Nia, joining her at our usual table.

'Hasn't she told you? Huw had a poison-pen letter saying she was seeing someone else!'

'That's ridiculous!'

'Yes, but these things are sort of insidious – they

plant nasty ideas in people's minds. There are a few going round lately, apparently, though not everyone is admitting to it.' She looked a bit self-conscious.

'Nia! Have *you* had one?' I demanded, wide-eyed.

'No, Rhodri. I was there in his office when he opened it, and he's so transparent I knew something was up and made him show me.'

'So what did it say?'

She went slightly pink but said off-handedly, 'Oh, something about my setting my cap at him – so old-fashioned – and he'd better watch out, and perhaps he'd better find out why my last husband got rid of me so fast.'

'I don't call nearly twenty years fast,' I objected.

'No, it was quite ridiculous, and Rhodri said he'd *like* it if I set my . . . well, anyway, we just laughed it off,' she said hastily.

I didn't press her: things seemed to be going quite nicely without any intervention from me, and with a bit of luck she would shortly lose the last vestiges of her 'you lord of the manor, me peasant' hang-up, which is totally outdated, and then there would be no bar to True Love.

Do Druids have weddings?

'I wonder who the poison-pen writer is? And why haven't *I* had one? I mean, everyone knows I had an illegitimate baby, and then what with Tom turning up and that scene in the restaurant you'd think I'd be a prime candidate!'

'Yes, but maybe *other* people are getting them about *you*?' she suggested, which was a bit disconcerting.

'There has been an odd sort of atmosphere around the village lately,' I said thoughtfully. 'And old Miss Griffiths didn't answer me when I spoke to her the other day, but I assumed she was just going deaf. Do you think –'

'Don't get paranoid. As you say, your misdoings are all old news, so raking them up again wouldn't shock anyone.'

'I wouldn't be too sure about that,' I said, and described (suitably edited) my conversation with Gabe Weston. 'I don't want him hearing any rumours that might make him speculate about who Rosie's dad is!'

'Even if he's living here, I don't suppose he'll hear any local gossip,' she said reassuringly. 'But did he *really* say he wouldn't touch the standing stones and oak grove if he bought the Glen?'

Nia's priorities are clearly in a different order to my own.

'Yes, apparently Ma had told him we both loved to go there, and it was a special place for us.'

I tactfully refrained from informing her that he also knew about the Druid thing, since she seems a bit secretive about it. 'He doesn't want to do anything radical to the rest of the glen, or the cottage either. In fact, he was being so horribly understanding I ran out of reasons not to let him buy it – only now I'm afraid that if he's actually living here and finds out that Rosie isn't Mal's, eventually he might suspect that she's his daughter.'

'Oh, I don't think so, from what you say,' she said optimistically. 'He doesn't seem to know exactly how long it's been since the night you met, does he? So unless something does put it into his head, you should be safe enough. I mean, even if he *does* hear the village gossip, the palm is likely to go to poor old Rhodri.'

'I suppose so – and, Nia, you've never even thought for a minute that it actually *was* Rhodri, have you?'

'No, stupid. He's as transparent as a jellyfish – how could he keep a secret like that? Every time he looked at you or Rosie it would be written across his face. He loves you like a brother, and Rosie like an uncle.'

I was tempted to ask her how he felt about her, but decided not to: I don't want to make her go defensive and scupper a promising romance.

'Where is Rhodri tonight? Is he coming down?'

'He *is* down – I should have warned you that Gabe is staying over until tomorrow. They went to talk to some gardening firm – the programme hires local labour as well as the regular team they bring with them. Of course, after they finish filming you either have to pay for any help or do it yourself. In our case we'll have to carry on alone, plus students in the summer and –'

'What do you mean, he's down? Down *where*?' I cut in.

'Here, in the restaurant, having dinner. They invited me too, but you know how I feel about eating over-priced fancy food with old lemon-face serving it out as though she would like to see me washing the dishes and sweeping the floor instead.'

I relaxed slightly. 'Oh, well, I'll be long gone by the time they finish, and I don't suppose he would come in here anyway.'

'Why don't you want to meet him? I thought now you'd had it all out you might not mind so much, and he's very nice.'

'He is nice,' I admitted, 'and he was really kind about the baby. But even so, Nia, when you've shared one night of . . . shared one night with a total stranger, you don't automatically feel relaxed and happy meeting him in social situations years later. Especially when you've got a great big secret you really, really don't want him to know.'

'I think you're going to have to harden yourself to it, then,' she said drily. 'Here he comes with Rhodri.'

Over a Barrel

It says something for their social standing and/or celebrity status that Mrs Forrester had let them dine in the restaurant at all, since Rhodri looked like a rather down-at-heel lumberjack and Gabe was still wearing the cords and sweatshirt (but not the cowboy boots) he'd had on earlier. I strongly suspect they had been placed in the darkest corner and the candle on their table hastily extinguished.

'Fran!' Rhodri gave me a great bear hug and kissed me affectionately as usual. 'Wonderful to see you out and about! Gabe's been telling me he met you earlier and that he's going to buy the Glen – great news!'

Gabe watched our embrace with interest, then awarded me a polite kiss on one cheek. He smelled rather enticingly of sun-dried cotton and lawn mowings. 'So long as Fran hasn't changed her mind in the interval.'

'No . . .' I began. 'Not quite. I just –'

'Good, because I've already phoned your mother, and she says she's delighted.'

'You have? She is?' I blinked. He hadn't hung around

long enough for me to have much time for second thoughts!

'Yes. It should go through very quickly, since I don't have to sell my house first – two or three weeks at the most should do it. She's going to phone you later.'

'Right,' I said, slightly dazedly.

'And she's driving across tomorrow morning to talk it over, so I'm staying here tonight.'

'She is?' I parroted, starting to feel punch-drunk.

'Yes, and she's also kindly suggested I move in whenever I want to, rather than stay here in the hotel when I start filming at Easter.'

'She did?'

Ever had the feeling that the ground has been cut right away from under your feet? I sat down again since my legs had folded, rather than because I'd intended to.

'Of course, I told her I could only do that if you agreed too,' he said with a look of limpid innocence that didn't fool me one bit.

'Well, that calls for a celebration, doesn't it?' Rhodri said, happily unaware of any undercurrents and taking my agreement for granted. 'Let's have a bottle of champagne!'

'You can't afford champagne. You need all your money for the restoration,' Nia said firmly. 'It had better be Murphy's all round.'

'I'll get them,' offered Gabriel, getting up. 'In fact, I'll get champagne if you really want it, though I'm not too keen on the stuff myself.'

'Let's stick to beer,' Nia said, 'and not get delusions

of grandeur. If you want to push the boat out you could get a couple of packets of crisps, though – Fran and I haven't eaten yet.'

I watched as two giggling women who had been watching him avidly from the corner suddenly leaped to their feet and intercepted him. *And* noted his delightful smile as he wrote his name across their proffered paper napkins – and across their hearts too, going by the adoring expression on their faces.

The locals, who had been watching him just as keenly if less overtly, at least left him alone – for the moment.

'I'm glad you're here, Fran,' Rhodri said, ' because we've got the designs for Plas Gwyn and I wanted you to see them.'

He pulled some papers out of a cardboard tube and opened them out. The corners kept trying to spring back until we pinned them down with bottles and ashtrays.

Gabe returned. 'She's bringing them out.'

'You're honoured!' Nia said admiringly. 'What it is to be famous!'

He grinned at her and sat down next to me, so close our knees brushed – which is admittedly difficult to avoid when you're sitting on a semi-circular seat around a barrel. Leaning over the plans he smoothed them out with long, slightly spatulate fingers.

'I don't know how much sense these are going to make to you,' he said. 'This top one gives some idea of how I hope the garden will look when it's finished, and if we put this overlay over the top you can see how it relates to all the earlier garden features we've got evidence for.'

'It looks a bit complicated because of the overlapping,' Rhodri explained. 'Every generation seems to have added something, and then most of it was simply turfed over in the eighteenth century when landscape gardens were in vogue, and has stayed that way ever since.'

Nia and I stared at him, amazed: he was really getting into this, but I suppose it was just an extension of his keen interest in his house.

'Most gardens evolve through several different styles according to fashion,' agreed Gabe. 'Sometimes the whole lot is swept away and a new scheme replaces it; sometimes it's piecemeal – which is what happened at Plas Gwyn.'

'But there doesn't seem to be a garden at all,' I objected. 'Just grass and trees.'

'That's mostly what a landscape garden is – a carefully arranged vista of grass, trees and water. At the front of the house it stretched right down to the river; they just remodelled what was there. Some of the garden features dotted about, like statues and arches, were left over from previous schemes.'

'And Aled's artistic trees,' put in Nia helpfully. 'Though I don't suppose for a minute that they were originally meant to be those shapes.'

'There's the ha-ha too,' Rhodri said. 'The one that stops the cattle from Home Farm getting on to the grounds.'

I pored over the map, trying to make sense of the

two layers. 'So are you going to restore the landscape garden at the front of the house?'

We were interrupted by the approach of Mrs Forrester with a laden tray. Rhodri stood up and took it from her politely, but she didn't give him even the ghost of her usual simper: this time her smiles were all for Gabe.

There was nowhere to put it on the table, so we took our drinks and lined them up on the shelf along the back of the seat. Gabe's arm brushed the back of my head as he pushed his glass along, and I was suddenly very conscious of his closeness. I would have moved my knees away by now, if there had been anywhere to move them *to*. Getting up and sitting next to Rhodri would be tantamount to admitting I found Gabe's proximity disturbing.

If he's going to make a habit of joining us we are going to have to sit at a proper table, one with lots of space between the chairs.

He turned and looked down at me, his eyes crinkling up at the corners in the way they did when he was amused by something – and if he can read me like he can read gardens, then I'm sunk.

'The long-term plan does include restoring the landscape garden, of course, but most of that will be left to Rhodri,' he said. 'The programme will mainly concentrate on other areas – and there was a mass of information in those documents Rhodri found.'

'Yes, even a scale drawing of the maze, so it can be restored to its original size – it was nearly twenty-five feet across!' Nia said enthusiastically. 'The paths at the edge that have almost vanished will be recut, and the yew hedge around it only needs trimming so it looks less like a row of enormous breasts.'

'This area between the house and the maze should be a Dutch garden with lots of topiary,' Gabe's finger traced the path down, 'with a fountain here, where that statue is.'

'It is – the statue is actually the top of it. Mother filled it in,' Rhodri said, 'but we can dig it out again.'

'The wilderness on this side can be thinned and restocked at a later date,' Nia put in. 'This stretch of grass will be for parking cars, so it just needs roping off and some signs putting up.'

'And the knot garden that was once right here in front of the courtyard is going to be put back – but with lavender and not box,' Rhodri said.

'I hate box, it smells of pee,' remarked Nia.

'I thought that was privet?' I said.

'No, box stinks too.'

'Lavender certainly smells better,' Gabe agreed. 'Though the effect isn't quite as neat.' He pulled out one of the other sheets and put it on top. 'This is a larger-scale plan to the north-east, with the steps down to the pleached walk. Luckily they're still there, under the soil and turf.'

'How do you know?' I asked, surprised. 'Have you been digging?'

'No,' he said, 'some things I just *do* know. I'd put money on it.'

'I'd forgotten you were the psychic gardener!' I muttered.

'Gabe's simply more in tune with nature than most people,' Nia said approvingly. 'But we could all be like that, if we wanted to be.'

'Oh, I don't know,' Rhodri said vaguely. 'Isn't it a bit like dowsing for water? Either you've got the knack or you haven't. But here's something that will really interest you, Fran!' He put his finger on the lawned north-east terrace with its low stone balustrading. 'This was a rose garden in the early 1800s.'

'It was? And they *removed* it? Why on earth would anyone rip out a rose garden, for goodness' sake!'

'I don't know, but that's one of the first restoration projects,' Nia assured me. 'And the maze, of course.'

'Yes, and then reconnecting all the isolated garden features like the pleached walk and the fountain and the arch to the river will be great fun, like joining dots up and finding a picture,' enthused Rhodri.

'It all sounds like a lot of hard work. Presumably the programme only do a small part of it?' I said to Gabe.

'Oh, we're here for four weeks, and it's surprising how much we get done in the time. The maze and the rose garden are the main projects, with a bit of work here and there on the other stuff where something is being excavated, like old steps or walls – anything that makes good TV. After that, we leave Rhodri with the plans and he carries on – but we do return regularly and update the viewers on what's happening, and give advice on the ongoing restoration.'

'But *now* I'll have you practically living on the doorstep, my own resident expert,' Rhodri said happily.

Being a TV gardener must be like being a doctor,

in that everyone you meet wants you to diagnose their problems, free.

'I wonder what sort of roses they would have had in Regency Wales?' I mused, staring at the plan. 'Apart from the obvious ancient ones, like Rosa Mundi, which they used to grow as a herb.'

'There are only one or two mentions of particular varieties in Rhodri's documents, but it will be easy enough to find out what was available at the time,' Gabe said. 'And I suggested to Rhodri that he could plant a modern rose garden below it, so that one terrace leads down to another.' He frowned. 'I feel there should be some more steps – and maybe a water feature – right *here*.'

'I think that may be the stone sarcophagus the cows drink out of down at the Home Farm,' Rhodri said apologetically. 'Apparently my grandmother took against it when she came here as a bride, and had it removed. A stone gryphon spouted water into it, but I've no idea where that went.'

'Well, the cows don't have to drink out of a stone coffin,' Nia said firmly. 'We'll have that back and find them something else. An old bath, perhaps.'

'You'll have to go and see Fran's rose garden, Gabe, to see what does well around here,' Rhodri suggested.

'So everyone keeps telling me – and I will, if she'll invite me.'

'There isn't a lot to see just now,' I said hastily. 'Later, perhaps.'

'I'd like to see it, whatever the season. What roses have you got?'

'What *hasn't* she got?' Nia sighed.

'Nia, there are thousands of wonderful roses out there, and I have room for only a fraction of a fraction of them!' I turned back to Gabe. 'There's no particular type of rose that I like better than any other, so it's a complete hotchpotch of varieties. I've even got an Omar Khayyam,' I added proudly. 'I know there are more spectacular pink Damasks, but it's so romantic, knowing it came from the original one found growing on the poet's grave!'

'Do you believe that?' He looked down at me, eyebrow raised.

'Of course! Don't you?'

'As much as I believe in the existence of Tilly the two-ton tooth fairy,' he said gravely, and the other two gave him rather startled looks. 'Go on – what else have you got?'

'I've just bought a Constance Spry – they're so beautiful – and I've got a Kiftsgate and a Madame Gregoire Staechelin, and a Gloria Mundi, of course, and an absolutely *enchanting* Mermaid . . .' I stopped suddenly, remembering what had happened to the poor thing. 'But you don't want to hear me going on about them!'

'I could listen to you going on about roses all night,' he said, in a voice like molten honey. 'I find it *terribly* seductive!'

I could feel myself going pink and looked away hastily, only to meet Rhodri's slightly puzzled eyes instead.

'Will you come up and help me with ideas for the Plas Gwyn rose gardens?'

252

'I'm sure you have more than enough of your own,' I said stiffly.

'I'm always happy to have a fresh eye on things . . . and a pleasure shared with a fellow enthusiast is a pleasure more than doubled, don't you think?'

'You could get in the picture when they start filming, too,' Rhodri suggested. 'They like to include local characters and they're even roping Dottie in to ride across the scenery at one point, though I've told them she doesn't take direction very well. Or even at all,' he added honestly.

'She's a true eccentric – she was a big hit on the programme and people want to see more of her,' Gabe said.

'But not me – I'd hate that,' I said firmly. 'I will come up and help when I can, but there is no way I want to be on the telly.'

'I'll have to warn them to keep the cameras off you, then,' Gabe said, amused. 'It's usually the other way round – loads of local people trying to get in the frame, and fans of the programme too, when they know we are here.'

Fans of Gabriel Weston, more like!

'It would be good publicity for your work, though, Fran!' Nia pointed out. 'They're going to feature me in my studio, aren't they, Gabe?'

'Yes, and any other craftworkers you've got installed by then. We'll show the interior of the house too. It all adds interest to the programme.'

'We're going to officially open Plas Gwyn to the public at Easter, don't forget, Fran,' Nia reminded me, 'just after the preliminary shooting for *Restoration Gardener*. The whole place is going to be a work in progress for years, but we need the punters to start flowing in to give us a bit of cash to keep going.'

Back to the royal 'we' again, I noticed. The Spyder would probably soon be sporting a 'Nia 'n' Roddy' windscreen sticker – it was very promising.

'But we're only going to open the house at weekends until summer,' Rhodri explained. 'By then we hope the gift shop and tearoom will be finished. The plan is to have people buy their tickets to see the house *in* the gift shop and have to enter and leave the house through it – but they can just come and look at the craft shops for free. Nia thought of that one – she's so clever and practical!' He beamed at her fondly and she went faintly pink.

'You're not going to have much privacy, Rhodri.'

'Ah, but this paved terrace behind the new wing, where I'll be living, is going to be roped off – maybe hedged and trellised later to provide a bit of personal space.'

'I'm still thinking about that one,' agreed Gabe.

'My workshop is functional now, and a couple of the others will have moved in by Easter, when we open with the Grand Easter Egg Hunt. I've already done the leaflets – and you're going to help me hide the eggs, Fran, really early that morning,' Nia told me in her usual bossy way.

'I am?'

'And me,' Gabe said. 'I'm doing the official opening, so I may as well make myself useful!'

'What if it's raining?'

'We'll just have to put them in plastic bags or something – don't be a wet blanket!'

'OK,' I conceded. 'Well, that should get things going!'

'Is Rosie coming home for Easter?' Rhodri asked. 'She could help too.'

'Only for a couple of days and then she's going to Ma's: her local vet's going to give her a week's work experience. I'm not sure what she's doing after that.'

'Well, tell her if she's at a loose end over the summer I'll give her a job up at Plas Gwyn,' he said kindly. 'We'll probably take on a few students.'

'Once word about the filming gets out, we should have hordes of people here to watch,' Nia said. 'Perhaps we should have "Help the Restoration" donation boxes dotted about.'

'It wouldn't hurt,' agreed Rhodri.

'Won't you mind crowds of people watching you?' I asked Gabe. It sounded like my idea of hell.

'No, we're used to it. We'll cordon off where we're working for safety, of course – they can only watch us from a distance.'

'I don't suppose *you'll* be spending much time on site anyway; only when they're filming.'

'Then you suppose wrong! I thought you'd seen the programme,' he said, giving me a surprised and indignant look. 'I'm a gardener, not an actor, so I don't suddenly spring into action when there's a camera on me; I work all the time.'

'Actually, he works harder than anyone,' Rhodri said

admiringly. 'He built a dry-stone wall himself in the last series!'

'That's the fun bit, my reward for doing the camera thing,' Gabe said. 'I like getting my hands dirty.'

'Oh?' I said, thoughtfully looking at his strong, long-fingered hands again. Come to think of it, they didn't look as though he had a daily manicure – or even a yearly one.

'Of course, I'll have to go off and do a day's shooting at earlier projects from time to time. But even after the programmes are made, when I'm living here, it will be hard to resist the temptation to come and muck in.'

'And I don't think *I* could stay away if you were planting a rose garden,' I admitted ruefully. 'Though I suppose it will give me lots of new varieties to paint once they're established, so in the long term I would be helping my work!'

'This is all going to be such fun,' Rhodri said happily, and I could see that suddenly the Famous Three had become Four. He raised his beer glass: 'Here's to success!'

Since I was suddenly feeling tired again, even though all the lovely calories in my glass of beer and two packets of crisps had made me much less shaky, I took myself off, leaving them hunched over the plans like three conspirators.

Carrie had already gone, leaving Huw sitting morosely in the corner over a pint of bitter, which did not look promising. I must ask her what's happening.

They have been together such a long time it would be a pity if they parted simply because of some malicious rumour-mongering.

I was glad to get home, but instead of having something to eat and an early night, which was what I had intended, I ended up talking on the phone for hours. My ear was hot by the time I'd finished.

Ma was first, to say she had spoken to 'dear Gabriel' again (she must have his mobile phone number, unless they have established telepathic links) and was glad to hear that already he felt we were old friends and he was looking forward to seeing my rose garden!

She really did tell him he could use the cottage whenever he wanted while he was working at Plas Gwyn until the sale went through, which I think is pretty rash of her, because what if it turns out he is bankrupt, or she changes her mind or something?

When I pointed this out she said, 'Don't be silly, my love. He's such a nice young man. Do you know, he says that he would love me to carry on using the cottage whenever I like, even after he has bought it! He's all alone in the world, no family at all.'

He didn't mention *that* part of it, and neither can I see him in the role of Little Orphan Annie.

'You can't call him a young man, Ma – he's older than I am, so he must be in his forties. And you can't shack up with strange men!'

'He's not strange, and he's only forty-three, I asked. That's practically a boy to me,' she said stubbornly, 'and you know I'm *never* wrong about people!'

I wouldn't exactly say that, but prudence kept me

quiet, especially on the subject of divorce, paternity claims and estranged family on the other side of the Atlantic. And is this love? Should I be worried? Does Gabe Weston have a sort of generic attraction for female members of the March family?

Ma hopes to arrive before lunch tomorrow to talk things over with Gabe. And I suppose we will have to sort out the contents of the cottage fairly soon – not a job I am looking forward to.

Gabriel Weston appears to be insinuating himself into my life here without any apparent effort at all, and even Nia seems to have fallen under his spell. Maybe she sees him as a sort of honorary Druid.

I'd hardly put the phone down after talking to Ma when it rang again and Rosie aggrievedly demanded to know where I'd been, like an anxious mother (somebody else's – mine was never anxious since she always assumed I would be fine).

'The pub, with Nia, Rhodri and that *Restoration Gardener* man, Gabriel Weston,' I told her, and then added that Ma had definitely agreed to sell Fairy Glen to him.

'I suppose it's quite exciting for you, having him coming to live in the village,' she said kindly. 'How old is he? And is he good-looking?'

'Early forties, and he's not handsome the way Mal is,' I said, 'though I suppose he's attractive in his way . . . charismatic. He has lots of fans – some of them were drooling over him in the pub tonight.'

'How *is* Mal?' she asked, losing interest in geriatric gardeners.

'Fine – he loves it out there. You know his idea of heaven is to bask in the sunshine like a lizard, preferably on the deck of a boat. He's got an apartment with a swimming pool and maid service, but he says they're all like that on Grand Cayman,' I added doubtfully.

'Granny says she's going out to visit him too, because he's lost in the joys of Mammon and needs to be shown the hard path back to righteousness ... or, at least, something like that.'

I was astonished. 'That's the first I've heard it! Are you sure, because Mal hasn't mentioned it?' It was hard to conjure up a vision of Mrs M. on a Caribbean island.

'Yes, certain, but I think she's only just decided. She doesn't expect to enjoy herself, she said, but it was her duty to go. I wish she thought it was her duty to take me with her!'

'I wish you could go too, darling. How is the course going?'

'OK,' she said uninformatively. 'I'm coming home on Friday with all my stuff – and then, Mum, I hope you don't mind, but on Saturday morning, very, very early, Tom's picking me up and taking me over to the Lleyn Peninsula to learn to surf!'

'Oh,' I said. 'I mean, well, that *will* be fun, won't it? But won't the water be terribly cold?'

'Wetsuits. I'll be able to borrow one. Then I'm back on Sunday to pick my car up and go over to Gran's.'

'If you want to watch them shooting the opening scenes of *Restoration Gardener*, you'll have to take a day off,' I said. 'I expect half the village will be watching.'

'I probably won't bother. I'm only working that week, after all, and it's good experience: the practice does livestock as well as domestic pets.'

'How's Colum?'

'Who?'

'Your boyfriend.'

'Oh, *him*,' she said dismissively. 'He's all right. He's a bit jealous of Tom, actually, even though I've told him . . . well, I've told him he's stupid.'

'Right,' I agreed.

'Tom's old enough to be my father, even if he *isn't* – and he's a lot of fun.'

'He always was,' I said reflectively. 'It used to get a bit wearing sometimes, all that nonstop boyish high spirits.'

'Well, it makes a change from Mal,' she said shortly, which is true: the last thing you could accuse him of is an excess of *joie de vivre*. 'Tom says he's been thinking about you a lot since he saw you again, and he never forgot you, which is romantic, isn't it?'

'It might be, if he hadn't dumped me in the first place.'

'Yes, but he said he realised it was a mistake almost immediately. You could have got back together again.'

'No, we couldn't,' I said patiently. 'Even if I hadn't discovered I was pregnant with you, darling, I was over him by the time he wrote to me to try and make up.'

'He's still pretty good-looking, isn't he?' she persisted. 'You wouldn't think he was forty! The surfing must keep him fit.'

'I expect so, for a geriatric,' I agreed slightly tartly.

'But I can't say I really noticed at the Druid's Rest – other things were on my mind.'

'He was really sorry about that, but he'd like to meet you just for a chat sometime – and he says Mal must be absolutely out of his mind to go away for six months leaving you all alone!'

'You know Mal had to take this contract, Rosie, and I'll soon be seeing him. And it appears I'll soon be seeing Tom too, if he's picking you up on Saturday.'

'He always drives up overnight, so it will be really, really early. You might not be at your best then, Mum.'

'I'm sure he'll survive the experience,' I said drily. It might even do him good to see me freshly risen from my bed, since methinks she is plugging Tom's charms just a little too much. Wonder what she's told him about Mal.

After that, I unplugged the phone and went to bed. Chances were that Mal would be trying to phone me later, possibly already regaled with Wevill-borne tales of my driving around and visiting pubs with TV celebrities, but to hell with it, I was beyond exhausted.

This time I dreamed that Gabe was offering me a rose, but I couldn't quite make out what kind, since I kept snatching my hand back at the last minute.

Maybe it had thorns.

Stemmed

I woke up really early and checked my emails, finding one from Mal saying my phone line was out of order when he tried to ring me last night, and he would try again today. How he thinks I'll be able to read his email if my phone line is *really* out of order, I don't know, though the way emails come down phone lines and TV gets plucked out of thin air by the aerial never ceases to amaze me. Certainly it seems much more magical and unlikely than Gabriel's claim to be able to sense lost garden features.

Bigblondsurfdude had also been emailing again.

> Dear Fran,
> 　　Rosie's probably told you I'm taking her surfing next weekend – don't suppose you want to come too? You'd love it, surfing's great fun, and we could spend some time together, catching up. Looking forward to seeing you soon anyway.
> 　　Love, Tom

Is he completely insane? Even were it summer I would

still not be up for encasing myself in rubber and throwing myself gaily into the briny deep. And, also, what sort of catching up does he have in mind? Am I reading too much into his little communications?

It is ironic that I would positively welcome the same ambiguity in Mal's, since they have become increasingly short, terse and businesslike, except when he is enthusing over any of his major interests, of which clearly I am not one.

Dear Tom,
    Thanks, but no thanks – watersports aren't my thing. I hope you and Rosie have lots of fun, though, and I expect I will see you briefly when you pick her up, if my eyes will open far enough at that time of the morning.
    Fran

I was out in the garden the moment it was light enough to see what I was doing, pulling out the decapitated rose stems from along the trellis and pruning the ends properly. I was wearing one of my best smoky blue patchwork tops and the crochet edging kept getting caught up, which didn't make the job any easier. I can't think what got into me to put it on this morning instead of a sensible T-shirt.

It was a long fence, and I wasn't halfway along it and tiring fast, when I heard the squeak of the side gate.

'Good morning! Can I come in?' called Gabe, standing on the patio with his hands in the pockets of his jeans and the light breeze tossing his knotted tangle of hair about like a slightly nonplussed invisible hairdresser. He was wearing the kind of old jumper that would have gone straight into the rag bag at the church jumble sale: pre-owned is one thing, pre-holed another.

'You *are* in,' I said resignedly, sinking down on to the edge of the wheelbarrow to rest my trembling legs. 'How did you know where I was?'

'Rhodri told me you were usually to be found working in your studio in the back garden, but left the side gate unlocked for friends. I didn't want to disturb you if you were busy, but I've got the morning free until your mother arrives, and I'd love to see your roses, so I thought –'

He stopped, having got near enough to take in the significance of what I was doing. 'That's a fairly radical way to prune climbing roses!'

'*I* know that,' I interrupted brusquely, 'but my neighbours don't seem to. I found it like this yesterday.'

'Your *neighbours* did this?'

'If you don't believe me, just look where I haven't trimmed yet: they've stuck their secateurs through the holes in the trellis all the way along and cut through everything they could reach.'

'I didn't say I didn't believe you,' he said, examining the butchered stems, 'and the evidence bears you out. But why would your neighbours do such a thing?'

I shrugged. 'They're both weird, and they seem to have it in for me, although I haven't done anything to provoke them. This is the worst thing yet. I'm not sure my poor Mermaid will ever recover, and it took so long to get it established.'

'Well, I wouldn't advise hacking a Mermaid down, but it looks pretty healthy, so there's a good chance it will recover. I hope so – it's one of my favourites too. What's the one you've already pruned?'

'Golden Showers. I'm not so worried about that: it barely touched the ground before it was off like a rocket, so it should be all right.'

I wiped a tired hand across my forehead, which had damp wisps of hair clinging to it. 'I'd better get on.'

'You're shattered – look, let me do it. It would be a pity to snag that pretty top on the thorns too. It's exactly the same woodsmoke colour as your eyes.'

'Oh, this old thing doesn't matter,' I said, going slightly pink.

He held out his hand for the secateurs, but I still hesitated.

'Don't you trust me with your roses?' he said, grinning.

'Yes, of course – you must have pruned more of them than I have.' I handed them over, but still watched him critically as he began to snip, quickly and neatly.

'So,' he said, his back turned, 'what else have your weird neighbours done?'

I sighed. 'It's more a case of what they *haven't* done. They've spread rumours about me by telling people that they *don't* believe in some story they've just invented . . . and they – they watch me all the time.'

I paused. 'It never sounds very much when I try and describe it because it's all such petty stuff, but since they moved here about eighteen months ago they seem to have been slowly building up a sort of harassment campaign against me, and I've no idea why.'

'Does your husband know about this?'

'No – it's pointless telling him, because he'd just think I was exaggerating things. They're totally different when he's there – they're different when most other people are around. He even goes sailing with Owen Wevill, they're *friends*. If they hadn't been nasty to me once or twice when Nia was around I might even have started to think I was getting paranoid! Oh, and Ma can't stand them either.'

He looked over his shoulder and smiled at me. 'Well, not only do I have the greatest respect for your mother's judgement, but I've seen the proof myself now, and I certainly don't think you'd damage your roses when you thought hard about letting even me near them!'

He was carefully working his way along, but was still much faster than I was, so I got up and started to gather the clippings together in one big heap.

'Does Nia have a thing going with Rhodri?' he suddenly asked, to my surprise.

'I hope so, but Nia's a very private person, and she'll tell me when she wants to.'

'But the three of you are really old friends?'

'Yes, we've been friends as long as I can remember. Rhodri and Nia have both got divorced recently, but I'm hoping when they get over that they will realise they are just so right for each other.'

'He's a brave man. Your friend Nia frightens me to death!'

266

'I can't believe that! And, anyway, she's got lots of backbone, which Rhodri needs, and *he's* got a sweet, affectionate, loyal nature –'

'Like a dog?' he suggested blandly, but I ignored him.

'Which is what *she* needs after her ex, Paul, dumped her like that for someone much younger. They both deserve a little happiness.'

'And do *you* deserve a little happiness?' He turned and looked at me again, the April sunshine catching golden glints in his dark honey hair.

'Me?' I said, surprised. 'But I've already got my lovely garden, and my work and Rosie, so this is as close to paradise as life gets. Especially when my husband is home,' I added firmly.

'He can't see it quite the same way, to leave it – and you – for six months?'

'He's always gone away on contracts. It just happens that this one is slightly longer than usual,' I said defensively. 'I'm flying out there soon, and we're going to renew our wedding vows and have a second honeymoon.'

Now, what on earth made me blurt that out?

'Very romantic,' Gabe said drily, and turned back to the clipping.

'Have you heard any more from your daughter?' I asked, changing the subject.

'An email, just general chit-chat. I've told her about Fairy Glen. I thought it might – well, I thought she might find the idea fascinating. I'm going to email her some pictures of the cottage with the little turret.'

267

'I don't see how she could resist that,' I agreed.

I made some tea (Earl Grey in rose-spattered Royal Albert mugs), and brought it out to find he'd finished pruning and was now stuffing all the debris into the old fertiliser sacks I'd left on the grass ready.

'What are you going to do with these?'

'Put them by the gate and feed them into the wheelie bin over the next couple of weeks until they've all gone.' I sipped my tea, watching him and thinking that I quite liked this sort of gardening, where someone else did the hard work. Ma has a point.

The three brown hens, treading delicately, finally ventured out of their run onto the lawn and, making 'oh-er!' noises, began to scratch around with one eye on us.

'Thank you for helping me,' I said. 'I'm not very fit yet, and I was getting tired. It's terribly frustrating: I feel I should be completely back to normal by now, and then my arms and legs go all rubbery on me!'

'Don't be too hard on yourself: you've been through a really bad time and should still be taking it easy. I'm just glad I showed up this morning – but when I'm around, all you need to do is ask if you want me to help you with anything.'

'You're very kind!' I said, tears pricking my eyes, because I'm still prone to crying at the slightest provocation.

'Look on me as an old friend,' he said, grinning. 'Not as old as Rhodri and Nia, but perhaps a little more *intimate*.'

'I do wish you wouldn't say that kind of thing!' I

snapped, the tears popping straight back into the ducts again.

He widened his eyes in hurt innocence. 'What kind of thing?'

'You know.' I got up. 'Come on, I'll show you the rest of the garden – but there's nothing much to see. Sometimes I have roses practically all winter, but it's been a bit colder than usual this year.'

The hens followed after us under the arch, but at a safe distance in case we suddenly turned into psycho chicken-murderers.

It was so lovely to have a fellow enthusiast there that after a bit I forgot who I was talking to and ended up telling him about my artwork too, and taking him into the studio to show him my latest Fran March Rose Calendar designs.

'And this is a painting I did of the Mermaid in bloom last year. I do hope it will recover, it's one of my favourites!'

'It'll be fine, trust me. When you work to a schedule like mine you find yourself pruning and planting everything at the wrong season, just because it fits in with the filming schedule. We'll probably be planting the roses in the Regency garden in late May.'

'Will they be all right?'

'Well, they'll be container-grown, but I've found they usually settle, though sometimes it's as well to remove any buds the first year so they can concentrate on making strong roots. I don't expect it to look very spectacular for a couple of years, but then that goes for a lot of the restoration gardening. It doesn't happen overnight.'

269

'I looked up some of the roses you could have found in a Regency garden,' I said, picking up a list, 'and most of them still appear in specialist rose nursery catalogues. Some are the older roses that have been around for ever, like the Alba – Cuisse de Nymph would be nice, don't you think?'

'Very,' he said gravely. 'When you can get it. Go on, what else?'

'*Banksiae* for climbers . . . China roses, like Old Blush . . . cabbage roses – the Centifolia. Oh, and I wondered whether you'd considered infilling the knot garden with Petite de Hollande. I think it would look very pretty.'

'I'll make a note of it.'

'Then there are Damasks, and Gallicas – Rosa Mundi, of course – Moss roses . . .' I stopped for breath. 'I expect you've already thought of most of those.'

'I have started making a list and sourcing them,' he admitted. 'But perhaps you could bring your list up to Plas Gwyn next time I'm down and we'll go over the terrace again and compare notes. You might have some ideas for the newer rose garden below too.'

I was quite flattered even though I was sure he didn't really need my help – but there was no way I could resist the lure of talking roses. 'OK,' I agreed. 'When are you thinking of coming back?'

'A couple of days before Easter, when we shoot the opening scenes, and I'll stay on to open Plas Gwyn and help with the Easter egg hunt. I'm looking forward to that.'

He was now wandering around looking at all the stuff

I'd got pinned to the walls, including cuttings of my cartoons, which might as well have been wallpaper last time Mal was up here for all the notice he took of them.

'I love your sense of humour!' he said, grinning.

'It's a bit black, generally.' I looked down at a half-finished Alphawoman strip. 'And sometimes feminist.'

He leaned over my shoulder to see. 'You do comic strips too? Are they published?'

'This is my very first one, and an alternative women's magazine has taken it as a regular feature.'

'What's it called?' he said, reading the captions. 'I'll subscribe!'

'*Skint Old Northern Woman*, and you can't possibly subscribe – it's not your kind of thing at all!'

'I don't see why not. Clearly I ought to be exploring my feminine side.'

I gave him a look of disbelief and he laughed. 'Well, I can see you are dying to get back to work, so will I see you later at Fairy Glen to give the sale the royal seal of approval?'

'It's all up to Ma, but I'll pop over later if she wants me to.'

After he left I went back to the comic strip feeling rather revived: must have been all the invigorating rose talk. I mean, talking about roses to the hens gets my juices going, never mind someone who actually *responds*.

I'd left Alison Alphawoman crisply informing her tiny daughter that she couldn't possibly produce an angel costume overnight for the school nativity play, she had work to do and it wasn't *scheduled*.

In the next frames she's opening the kitchen cupboard to get a bar of chocolate as a consolation prize for her weeping offspring, and then we see her smeared round the mouth with chocolate and metamorphosing into – tara! – Blobwoman.

I began to draw the final picture where she's sitting in the school hall as Alphawoman again, and someone is asking her how she managed to make such a wonderful costume when she is so busy. 'Something just came over me,' she says. 'Must dash – I've got a meeting.'

Oh, Alphawoman, if I could only transform myself into you, I would be Mal's idea of perfection!

Mother Makes Three

'Where were you last night?' Mal demanded, when he finally managed to reach me just before I set off for Fairy Glen.

This was keen, since if my sums are correct it must have been the crack of dawn over on Grand Cayman.

'At the pub,' I said shortly, since there is no point in hedging when your neighbours are reporting your every move to your absent spouse. Anyway, it's not like I have any guilty secrets – or any *more* guilty secrets. 'I was looking at the plans for restoring Plas Gwyn's gardens with Nia and Rhodri – and Gabriel Weston.'

'Oh? You seem to be getting quite friendly with him!'

'If friendly is showing him around Fairy Glen, and accepting a couple of lifts home from him, then yes, we are bosom buddies.'

'Apparently he visits the house too!'

'He visited the garden this morning,' I corrected him. 'He wanted to see my roses, because it helps to see what kind already thrive in the area. But my, my, how quickly news travels!'

'I didn't mean to sound suspicious, Fran. It's just that he suddenly appears to be around all the time.'

'He's going to be around even more. Ma's definitely agreed to sell Fairy Glen to him.'

'She has? I thought she didn't want to sell it as a second home.'

'She doesn't – he intends living here. She's finalising things with him today.'

There was a short but expensive silence. 'Well, I suppose it's a good thing, because once it's known that celebrities are buying into the area the value of all the houses including ours will go up even more.'

'So you keep saying, but I'm not sure that *is* a good thing – and immaterial in our case, because we'll never sell our lovely cottage, will we?'

'I don't know. I didn't envisage living in a rural backwater for ever when I bought it.'

'You *didn't*? That's not what you said when we first met! You said we would live happily ever after in St Ceridwen's!'

'Well, we have, haven't we?' he said snappily. 'But things change and we might want to move on some-time.'

I held the receiver away and looked at it as if it had bitten me. It made a quacking noise, so I put it back to my ear in time to hear Mal say, 'So, does this TV gardener have any family? And how old is he?'

'He's divorced, and in his early forties. Older than me, younger than you,' I said callously, since Mal approaching the big five-oh is sore point. I don't know why he's worried. Men are allowed to have grey hair and wrinkles, and he's always going to be handsome, because it's in his bones. 'And the only thing we have in common is an interest in roses, so don't start imagining anything.'

'Of course not – I was just interested. I *trust* you, darling.'

'And I trust you, too – which is just as well when we are apart for so long!'

'Yes, but you'll soon be coming out for your holiday, and you're going to love it here. It's a wonderful place.'

'It sounds a very expensive place, what with swimming pools and maids!'

'No, it's just a different lifestyle, and I'm still economising: I've made up my mind to sell *Cayman Blue*!'

'You really have?' I said, amazed.

'Yes, I've told Owen to look for a buyer for me – put some adverts in the boat mags.'

'But you love sailing.'

'Yes, and I've managed to get some in here, because I know lots of people with boats. But I overstretched myself buying *Cayman Blue* – maybe Owen over-persuaded me. I'll replace it eventually with one I can sail single-handed, so I don't have to rely on getting crew before I can take it out.'

'That's great, Mal! And you can repay that loan too, once it's sold.'

'Probably make a loss on it, like the car, but at least it's a step in the right direction.'

'I think it's wonderful. If we can live according to our means, then you won't have to take so many contracts away from home, will you?'

'Well, there's still a whopping mortgage to pay, and you don't earn all that much. Still, it'll all help.'

'Did you look into remortgaging the house?' I asked.

'Not yet. I've been too busy. But I will,' he promised.

'Oh, well, I suppose this separation will have been worth it in the end, but I do miss you, Mal.'

'How's the diet?'

'Oh . . . coming along,' I said vaguely. 'I had to wait for my blood count to be normal first, of course.'

'But you're better again now?'

'Oh, yes, just a bit unfit,' I assured him, because I am physically OK again really, though losing a baby even in the early stages is not something you are ever likely to forget entirely.

'Good. Mother was asking about you the other day. She's going to come out to Grand Cayman for a holiday too.'

'Yes, she told Rosie, but it doesn't sound like her sort of thing at all!'

'Well, I am her only child, after all, and she misses me. Besides, I invited her in the first place – thought she would enjoy it and the warmth would do her rheumatism good.'

'I expect it will,' I said charitably. 'So when is she going?'

There was a short pause. 'Well, that's the thing, she just went ahead and booked her flights, and it turns out that she'll be here for part of the time you will.'

'What! But, Mal –'

'Now, Fran, just calm down! She's arriving before

you, and leaving earlier, so there's only a *little* bit of overlap.'

'But this is supposed to be our second honeymoon!'

'Yes, and we will still have almost a week alone together after Mother's gone home. But I'm working hard and can't spare the time to drive her about the island, so it's actually worked out well.'

'You mean you expect me to run her about instead?'

'I thought she would be company for you!'

'But she hates me!'

'You're being silly. Naturally she can't condone our marriage, but she's got used to the idea, and she has nothing against you personally.'

'Apart from my being a Scarlet Woman. She vowed she'd never spend a night under the same roof as me.'

'She hasn't called you that for ages, and she said she was very sorry you lost the baby. I really didn't think you'd take it like this, Fran!'

'Mal, you didn't think in the *first* place. I thought this was going to be our special holiday together and –'

'It will be, you'll see,' he said hastily. 'I've got all sorts of things planned for after Mother goes home. Have you bought some nice clothes yet, or are you waiting until you've got all the weight off?'

'Er . . . waiting,' I said evasively. 'But it sounds like a chauffeur's uniform is all I'll need!'

Even Mal could tell I wasn't happy about the situation, and he did his best to smooth me down before he rang off. But I am not smoothed, I am ruffled: there was only one holiday companion I wanted, and it wasn't his mother. He would have quite some making up to do after she'd gone.

After wandering around the house slamming doors and muttering for a while I began to calm down. I suppose it's natural he wants to see his mother, and he couldn't just leave her alone in his apartment all day, every day. And he *has* been working hard and trying to reduce our debts – working for *us*.

Perhaps I really had better get on with the diet now. I've only got until the end of May, which is not actually that far off.

OK, detox time. I'll start on Monday when Ma will have gone home again and so not be scuppering my resolution with chocolate digestive biscuits and offers of meals out.

It was another mother and son reunion up at Fairy Glen, with Ma and Gabe all cosy over a pot of tea and a plate of Jaffa Cakes in the kitchen, greedily watched by the two fat-bellied dachshunds.

Ma was smoking and crocheting simultaneously, which rather defeated the object of the exercise. I do wish she would start crocheting bedspreads or something instead of the eternal strips, since I already have enough bundles of the stuff to stretch to the moon.

Now, there's a thought: astronauts could skip up its grubby length instead of having to be tossed into space in a tin can. I expect there's a blindingly obvious reason why it wouldn't work, though, like we're turning in opposite directions and it would get into a giant knot, or something.

'We were starting to think you weren't coming, my love,' Ma said.

'Mal rang me just as I was about to leave.'

'With details of your second honeymoon, presumably,' Gabe said smoothly, like the snake in the grass he is.

'Yes, *and* to tell me his mother is coming along for part of it!' I snapped.

Ma looked surprised. 'Is she? I thought she didn't like you? And I must say,' she added, 'it doesn't seem at all tactful!'

I hooked up a brightly painted chair and sat down with a sigh. 'No, but naturally she misses him, and she'll be leaving several days before I do.'

I found I was humming 'And Mother Came Too', and clamped my lips together. Ma is entirely to blame for my eclectic repertoire of terrible songs.

'Well, my love,' she said, after shifting her cigarette to the corner of her mouth, 'we're practically signed, sealed and delivered here – and parting with Fairy Glen isn't half as painful as I expected, thanks to dear Gabriel.'

'Don't think of it as parting,' he said. 'Your room will stay just as it is, ready for you to come and go as you please.'

'That's very generous of you. *And* brave,' I added as a volcanic fallout of hot ash alighted on Ma's bundle of lace.

She brushed it absently. 'He is a generous, kind boy,' she agreed, 'and what's more, he likes the dogs. *And* the furniture.'

'The furniture?' The cottage is furnished in a mishmash of auction-room leftovers bought for a pound or two and painted in wild colours and designs.

'Yes,' Gabe agreed, 'I want to buy the furniture too, except for anything you'd like. Most of my London stuff would look out of place here.'

That wasn't a surprise – almost *anything* would look out of place here.

'Me? I . . . no, it wouldn't fit in with our house . . . but perhaps there are one or two things that would fit in my studio.'

'Anything you want, you take it, Fran,' Ma agreed, 'and then Gabriel can have what's left. I don't need it – got a houseful already.'

She raised her mug. 'Well, here's to the new owner of Fairy Glen! Now, Gabriel's going to come and stay over part of Easter, before the sale goes through; I've given him a key. Do you think you could pop in and make a bed up for him, Fran?'

'I can make my own bed,' he protested. 'There's no need for Fran to do it!'

'But I know where everything is. I'll put him in the turret, Ma.'

'I'm just grateful there isn't an oubliette,' he said blandly.

'No, the house is only *mock*-Gothic,' Ma assured him. 'And even if there were an oubliette, it would be bound to be damp. But are you sure you wouldn't like my room? It's the biggest.'

'He can sleep anywhere he likes once the sale has gone through, but meanwhile I'll make up the bed in the turret room,' I said firmly.

280

He looked at me, eyes crinkling around the corners. 'Not yours, either?'

'I haven't slept there for years, hence the girlie décor. I expect you'll want to change that when you've bought the place.'

'I don't know, roses and fairies might grow on me.' He put his cup down and got up. 'I'll have to go. I need to pick up my stuff from the hotel and get back to London. But I'll return for the Easter egg hunt and the filming – and soon I'll be back for good.'

'And I hope you'll be very happy here,' Ma said, so warmly I started to feel a bit jealous. 'I'll not be seeing you over Easter, because Rosie's going to be staying with me while she spends the week working for my vet – good practice for her – and then I'm off with the girls to Amsterdam for a long weekend.'

'What are you going to do in Amsterdam?' I asked suspiciously. 'You didn't tell *me* you were going to Amsterdam!'

'Didn't I?' she said vaguely. 'I thought I had. And I'm sure we'll find something to do. I'll bring you a nice present back.'

'Not clogs,' I said hastily.

'All right,' she agreed.

All the way home I had a horribly twee little song about mice with clogs on running through my head, one that Ma used to sing to me when I was little, even when I pleaded with her not to.

As a mother, she's got a lot to answer for.

Bedding Out

Once Ma had gone home again I started the detox diet, but after only a couple of days I felt at breaking point. Either it's much harder than the book would have me believe, or else my body is one big toxic waste dump. I suspect the latter.

My fridge is full of fruit, but I've gone right off it, especially melon, due to the inside of a ripe one looking like alien afterbirth. The juicer is getting dusty – and who invented a machine that liquidises anything in seconds, yet takes fifteen minutes to clean afterwards and won't go in the dishwasher? A man?

I don't even feel any thinner, and I've been wondering what will happen to the stretched and wobbly tops of my arms if I do lose weight. Will the skin snap back at my age, or just hang in huge flaps, enabling me to glide from tree to tree like the biggest flying fox in the world?

And now I come to examine my arms more closely in the mirror, aren't they abnormally long? Longer than other people's, certainly – practically dragging along the ground when I walk!

'Ma,' I said, next time she phoned, 'have you ever noticed anything odd about my arms?'

'Why, my love, have you got a tattoo or something?'

'No, they just seem very long, don't you think? Unnaturally long?'

'Oh, no, Frannie, I'm sure I would have noticed. And you wouldn't be so attractive to all those men if you had arms like a gorilla, would you?' She giggled.

'*Which* men?' I demanded, baffled.

'I've had a poison-pen letter, darling, and very entertaining it was too! I must have scooped it up with the junk mail at Fairy Glen and brought it back with me.'

'Yes, they've been going round the village. What did yours say?'

'It said I had a harlot for a daughter, and I should be ashamed of dressing like one at my age. Then it raked up that silly story about Rhodri being Rosie's father, and said you'd been carrying on with another man recently until Gabe Weston turned up, seemingly interested in restoring more than just a garden – only it put it a bit more crudely than that. Interestingly earthy analogies – fascinating.'

'That seems pretty comprehensive – and I'm *not*. And neither do you look like a harlot.'

'I look how I want to look,' she said nonchalantly. 'I don't care about that. But which bit are *you* not?'

'I'm not any of them,' I said. 'You know the bit about Rhodri isn't true already, I've only seen Tom once since we split up, and that was at the Druid's Rest when Mal was there. As to Gabe Weston –'

'He's a *proper* man,' she said approvingly, 'not like

283

Mr Buttoned-Down Morgan! Gabriel agrees with me that any husband who callously leaves his lovely wife alone for months at a time like this deserves to find her snapped up by another man when he gets back.'

'I'm not some kind of giant fishing fly, Ma – I'm not about to be snapped up by *anyone*!' I said hotly. 'What's more, I *love* Mal, and I fully support what he's doing.'

She ignored my hot defence. 'We also agreed that you shouldn't be trying to diet before you are totally recovered from the miscarriage, and you can tell Mal I said so. Anyway, you look fine to me.'

'I'm definitely too fat, Mal's right about that. And I'm perfectly well again now, so Gabriel Weston should keep his long nose – and his opinions – out of my business!'

'He talks a lot of sense, and he feels quite like family already.'

'Well, he's *not*. And don't you dare tell him what was in the poison-pen letter, either!'

'I bet the Weevils are writing them,' Ma said.

The suspicion had crossed my mind too.

So far as I can tell, the village has slumped back into seeming quiet, only underneath it is gently seething like a pot slowly coming to a boil. Everyone knows about the *Restoration Gardener* programme now, and that Gabe Weston is buying Fairy Glen, but the spate of poison-pen letters and unfounded rumours have stirred all sorts of other things up.

Could it be the Weevils? Since decapitating my roses

they haven't done anything horrible that I know of, but perhaps they saw Gabriel helping me to prune them back and realised they had gone a bit too far, and in front of a third party.

I had meant to go to ask Carrie how she was getting on with Huw after their argument over his poison-pen letter, but I've been so busy trying to catch up with my work (as well as rather faint from the detox) that I haven't really been anywhere. But then Nia summoned me to a meeting at Teapots early on Thursday morning, before it opened.

I wasn't sure what it was about – the reception was awful because she was up in the mountains somewhere delivering a consignment of her lovely porcelain jewellery to a gift shop – but I'm sure she said something about bagging eggs. Or maybe that was *bad* eggs?

Five minutes after arriving at Teapots, my detox diet came to a spectacular end nose down in a fresh cream horn, and that was before Nia even got there.

She arrived carrying a wicker basket of small chocolate eggs and a stack of little Cellophane packets.

'So you *did* say bagging eggs, after all. I thought I'd misheard you.'

'Me too,' Carrie said. She was lightly dusted in flour and icing sugar from her morning's baking, and both she and the café smelled delicious. 'What do you want us to do?'

'Put one egg in each bag and then seal up the ends with this little tape dispenser thing I've borrowed from the garden centre. It's just in case it rains on them.'

'They look rather pretty like that, too,' I said, admiring my handiwork.

'If you frill out the ends of the bags on all of them we'll be here for the rest of the day! I already suspect we'll be finding the damn things for months afterwards. You *can* still come up at first light on Easter Sunday to help hide them, can't you, Fran?'

'Yes, all right – providing I can eat every tenth one.'

'Have you seen how many there are? You'd be sick after the first few minutes!'

'Just joking, though the smell of chocolate is starting to get to me.'

'Do you want a cream horn, Nia?' offered Carrie. 'They've got home-made strawberry jam at the bottom. Fran, have another one, and pour yourself some coffee.'

She took one herself and we settled down to bag and eat simultaneously.

'I've got an old bath in the back of my van,' Nia said.

'Isn't that taking personal hygiene a bit far?' I commented.

'It's not for me, it's for the cows to drink out of at Home Farm so we can have the sarcophagus back,' she explained. 'And what's more, I found the stone gryphon under a trough in one of the barns!'

'Gabe will be pleased,' I said, which reminded me. 'Ma's had a poison-pen letter now, more or less accusing me of having affairs with Tom *and* Gabe Weston! And it said Ma looked like an old slapper. She found the whole thing highly amusing – you know what she's like – and said she thought one, or both, of the Wevills must be sending them. I think she's right!'

Nia looked up. 'Well, they're the obvious candidates,' she agreed.

'Oh, no, surely not, they seem so nice!' protested Carrie, troubled. 'Mona was in here only yesterday, and I can't believe she would send such a horrible letter about me to Huw!'

'Well, think about it – none of this started until they moved here. The village was quiet and pleasant but now half the inhabitants seem to be at loggerheads and open warfare has broken out at the WI!'

'Have you made up with Huw yet, Carrie?' Nia asked.

'Yes, and he's abject,' she said rather smugly. 'Of course he realised how stupid it all was once he'd got over the shock, and he keeps buying me presents to make up.'

By the time we'd refilled the basket with bagged eggs it was almost time for Carrie to open the café, and the cream horns were but a slightly queasy memory and a few crumbs on a plate.

'Do you want to come up to Home Farm and then on to Plas Gwyn with me?' asked Nia. 'It would give you a bit of fresh air. You look pale.'

'No, I'd better go and make a bed up at Fairy Glen for Gabe, because I don't know what day he's arriving.'

'Come up for tea tomorrow, then; as far as Rhodri is concerned, *every* day at half-past three everything stops for tea. And is Gabe actually moving in, or just staying temporarily?'

'Temporarily, I think, but the sale will soon be

287

through – the power of money! He wants Ma to carry on treating Fairy Glen as her holiday home: they're in love, and he and Ma are going to live together happily ever after, so the poison-pen writer picked the wrong March.'

'It's all worked out very well,' Carrie said, 'them getting on like that. You've not so much lost a cottage as gained a –'

'*Please* don't say brother,' begged Nia. 'Remember?'

'Oh, yes – though, actually, I do find it hard to – and then there was that big handsome blond man . . .' She stopped, looking embarrassed.

'You *saw* Tom?'

'Only briefly, getting out of his car,' she said regretfully.

The second cream horn was getting to me and I began to feel *really* sick.

'Anyone want the detox diet book?' I offered. 'And what am I going to try next?'

'I've got a copy of Atkins – even that can't be as extreme as detox,' suggested Carrie.

'OK, I'll give it a go,' I agreed, and she went to fetch it. It was a very ancient-looking copy, the pages loosening with age. I think *my* pages are too, so it might be the ideal book.

'Give it up,' Nia urged me.

'No way – it's only a few weeks before I go out, and Mal's expecting Svelte Me, not Thundering Great Carthorse Me. Not,' I added bitterly, 'that the holiday is going to turn out quite like I thought, because his mother's invited herself on it. He thinks it will be good because I can drive her around and look after her while he's at work!'

'He can't do that to your second honeymoon, the swine. It's – it's unfair! He owed you this holiday,' Nia exclaimed indignantly.

'And the wedding vow ceremony – so romantic,' Carrie agreed.

'Well, I presume that's still on: we've got several days to ourselves after Mrs M. goes home.' I brightened. 'Perhaps he'll take some time off work then.'

'It's probably a sign that Mrs M. accepts you're married to her son at last, if she's agreed to stay under the same roof with you,' suggested Carrie. 'I mean, if you're driving her round and everything, she can't ignore you, can she?'

'I wouldn't put it past her,' I said gloomily. 'And another thing: how can I wear a decent swimsuit when I'm practically deformed?'

'You're only a bit plump, for goodness' sake!'

'Nearly spherical, and with huge long arms like an orang-utan!'

Nia rolled her eyes and said, 'Last time it was your tiny, pea-brained head! For God's sake, stop getting fixations about the size of your body parts – there's nothing wrong with you!'

Only Carrie was sympathetic: she said it was strange the way if you looked at something long enough it started to seem odd and out of proportion, and sometimes when she was trying to spell a word the more she thought about it, the odder it looked.

This could account for some of the weirder spellings

on her menu blackboard: I'd already noticed that today's specials included 'Current Buns', 'Mades of Honour' and 'Ginger Parking'.

I made the bed up in the turret room with Rosie's old Flower Fairies bedding. Well, Gabe did say he wanted to get in touch with his feminine side.

I've had a quick look at the Atkins diet and it looks easier to follow than the detox: I can basically eat anything I want, so long as it's protein and the odd leaf. There has to be a catch somewhere.

I will officially start it on Monday, but I have transferred anything non-Atkins from my fridge and freezer to Fairy Glen's, ready, so perhaps the next TV series will be *Fat Restoration Gardener*? Can't see it, somehow.

Friday started fine, with the thought of Rosie coming home later to give me something to look forward to.

I worked all morning in the studio, and had just got back in for lunch when the doorbell rang, and there, to my complete astonishment, stood Mrs Morgan!

This was a first: she's never visited me when Mal's not here before. I probably goggled at her, for she said quite sharply, 'Well, Frances, are you going to keep me standing here in this sharp wind, or invite me in?'

There was an old Volvo saloon parked in the drive, and an elderly woman with a frizz of pepper-and-salt hair seemed to be having a picnic in the driver's seat. She gave me a severe look as she unscrewed the lid of her Thermos.

I dragged my attention back to my mother-in-law. 'Of course, do come in. But isn't that your friend outside in the car? Wouldn't you like to bring her –'

'She's not coming in: this won't take long,' she stated, and, stepping past me, inspected a chair carefully for unspecified filth before sitting on it.

'Tea?' I offered, politely baffled.

'No, thank you. I mustn't keep my friend waiting too long.' She paused, eyeing me doubtfully, but that may have been fear that I was about to explode out of my clothes like the Incredible Hulk. I *knew* I shouldn't have had the second cream horn.

'As you know, Frances, I consider your marriage bigamy in the eyes of the Lord. The bond of wedlock is for ever. However, Maldwyn *has* made a commitment to you, and therefore I cannot be happy about the ambiguity of the current situation.'

'I'm not ecstatic about it myself,' I agreed, though I wondered where the ambiguity came in. 'But it *is* only six months. I'm so glad you're coming out to Grand Cayman too,' I added, lying heroically.

'I felt it was my duty to try and instil some degree of propriety. I am deeply disappointed in Alison: when she helped Maldwyn to get this contract, she should have considered how it would look with them both living on the same island, especially when you remained at home.'

'On the *same* island?' I stared at her, what she'd just said sinking in. 'You mean *Alison* is working on Grand Cayman too?'

'Maldwyn assured me that you knew!' she said, staring at me in some astonishment.

'Knew?' I sank down on the nearest chair, my knees weak. 'Of course I didn't know! And I'm certainly not happy about it, either!'

'He definitely gave me to understand that you both knew about and condoned the situation,' she said doubtfully. 'But I told him that he should either have refused the contract or arranged to take you with him: when *we* arrive there will be three Mrs Marches on the island, which I consider open to misinterpretation and vulgar speculation.'

That will make two Mrs Marches too many, by my reckoning, but in a strange sort of way Mrs M. seemed to be taking my side.

She got up and hooked her small hard handbag over one arm. 'That's all, I think, Frances: just so long as you realise that I'm not approving your marriage to my son by my actions.'

'I understand,' I said, though quite honestly I'm not sure I'm entirely following her reasoning. 'And . . . thank you.'

'Give my love to Rosie,' she added, as though the words had been extracted from her by extreme torture, though the slight softening of her adamantine façade gave her away. 'Tell her to come and see me soon.'

Outside, her friend seemed to be asleep at the wheel, covered in crumbs, but jerked upright when Mrs M. got in and slammed the door.

I didn't wait to see them off but went straight back in to call Mal . . . *whatever* time of the day or night it was over there.

* * *

'But you knew!' he protested faintly when I finally got him on his mobile. 'I told you when she landed her job here, and then when she told me about this contract.'

'No, you didn't! I'm *certain* you didn't – and what's more, you haven't mentioned her once since you've been out there! What am I supposed to make of that?' I demanded furiously.

'Haven't I?' he said innocently. 'I'm sure I must have, because it certainly wasn't a secret I was keeping from you, Fran! And, actually, our paths have hardly crossed since I got out here – much less than they used to at home. It's not like we're working at the same place, or move in the same social circles, darling. I don't know why Mother is in such a state about it, or why you're so bothered about it, either: Alison and I are just friends now.'

Words failed me – which is just as well, because he had to go at that point. I expect I will have more to say when I've had time to think it over.

I went up to Plas Gwyn for tea, and of course poured it all out to Nia and Rhodri, who were suitably indignant on my behalf. I am feeling more and more unsettled the more I think about the whole thing, and I'm very sure he *did* keep it a secret, whatever he says!

But Mrs M. knew . . . maybe because she has always kept in touch with Alison. It sounds as though Alison has shot herself in the foot this time, though, and that despite my Scarlet Woman past I may yet rise in Mrs M.'s esteem.

Then again, I might not.

We all pigged out on buttered fruity bara brith, which Nia had bought from Teapots. These pleasures will be denied me from Monday: the butter might be OK with the Atkins diet, but not on bread.

After tea we had a walk round to see how everything is coming along. I'd already noticed some changes, like the signs along the drive directing cars to the car park, and a couple of information boards.

The planning permission is being looked on favourably, and hopefully is about to be passed, the electrics and plastering in the café and gift shops are finished, and two out of the three workshops have got tenants ready to move in – a woodworker and a weaver. Everything's nearly ready in the garden, the sarcophagus and gryphon manhandled back to their original positions, and Aled has been persuaded to trim all the trees into less lewd shapes.

Even a temporary Portaloo block has been put in the car park, screened by a hedge, until more permanent arrangements can be made.

Rhodri and Nia were like a pair of excited schoolchildren, interrupting each other all the time. Clearly they are having fun, and I tried not to feel as if they were at the start of a new and wonderful relationship, while mine was thrashing about in its death throes.

Got back to a long and placatory email from Mal. I have decided to pretend to Rosie that I knew all along about Alison being there and didn't mind in the least, or she will worry and maybe tell Tom my marriage is on the rocks and I'm up for grabs.

And on the subject of big blond surf dudes, there was another sketch in the post, a self-portrait. He was partly hidden by a large surfboard, but clearly in the rude nude. The caption was 'For surfing, strip down to the bare essentials'.

From what I remember, he was *definitely* boasting.

Go, Lovely Rose

Rosie arrived home, her car crammed to the roof with stuff, and although I was desperate to see her again – the first time since the miscarriage – we ended up crying all over each other the moment she stepped through the door.

'You won't try and get pregnant again, will you, Mum?' she implored me tearfully. 'Promise me you won't!'

'I didn't actually *try* in the first place, darling, it just happened,' I said evasively, because although mentally I've accepted that I'm not going to have another baby, part of me *would* like another little accident to happen . . .

'You're not *promising*,' my first little accident said, looking at me accusingly with those changeling grey-green eyes. 'Aren't *I* enough?'

'Yes, of course you are!' I assured her, giving her a big hug. There didn't seem to be any point in trying to explain that I would still love her just as much even if I did have another baby, since Mal has made his feelings plain.

Fortunately she was distracted at this point. 'Who is that man in the back garden?'

'He's delivering some well-rotted manure – didn't you notice the Land Rover and trailer in the lane? Gabe Weston was having a load delivered to Plas Gwyn, ready for work to start on the rose garden up there, and he asked him to drop some off for me too. The roses down the trellis between us and the Wevills have taken a bit of a hammering lately – they hacked the tops off.'

'But he seems to be doing the mulching too,' she said, looking out of the back window.

'Apparently Gabe asked him to, and he insisted.'

'But why? You're not an invalid, Mum – you said you were totally well again!'

'I am, darling. It was just a kind thought.'

'I don't see why he's sending you presents, either,' she said suspiciously.

'Rosie, it's just a kind gesture from one gardener to another. We share an interest in roses, and when he came to see mine he stayed to help me prune the Mermaid – he thinks it will recover.'

'Did you say the Wevills chopped it down? Gran's right, they *are* mad!'

She seemed satisfied, and went off to unload the car and re-sort her belongings ready for her trip with Bigblondsurfdude, while I took the Man with the Mulch a cup of tea.

It really was kind of Gabe to think of me – or perhaps he was just concerned for my roses.

I made a huge vat of spaghetti carbonara, one of Rosie's

297

favourites, and a big Pavlova for afterwards, though I had to use frozen raspberries.

While we ate Rosie put me through one of her third-degree interrogations about Mal, asking awkward questions like how could he go off and leave me just after the miscarriage if he really loved me, and whether I still loved him, which I did my best to fend off.

It wasn't easy, since I've asked myself the same things over and over again, and finding out about Alison being over there hasn't exactly helped, either.

But *of course* I do still love him – when Dr Jekyll is in the ascendancy. Let's hope Mr Hyde stays out there when he finally comes home, because I'm sure he and Alison would make a wonderful couple.

My assurances can't have rung very true for, seemingly satisfied that Mal had more or less abandoned me, she embarked on a sales pitch for Bigblondsurfdude. Apparently he talks about me all the time (must be boring for everyone), and was *just* the sort of father she wished she'd had.

'Except he's *not*,' I pointed out firmly.

'He might be,' she argued, pouring out more elderberry wine. 'In fact, he says he's sure he must be.'

'Darling, it's very nice of him to wish you were his daughter, but I've told you that it's extremely unlikely. But if you do want to prove it for certain I think I could afford one of these new paternity test things. Doesn't it cost a couple of hundred pounds? Well, I've been selling loads of cartoons lately, so –'

'Tom's already suggested it,' interrupted Rosie. 'But it was me who didn't want to in case . . . well, in case it *wasn't* him. He's such fun – not like Mal, who always treated me like something he had to put up with!'

'Now, Rosie, Mal is very fond of you, he's just not the fatherly sort and he doesn't show his feelings easily. But if you do change your mind and want to do the test, just let me know,' I offered, not entirely altruistically, because at this stage I really would like to be certain one way or another myself!

'Why did I have to be born at all?' Rosie said gloomily, and went upstairs to pack for her surfing weekend, while I cleared away and then brooded over another glass of wine.

This mother business seems to get more difficult as they grow up, not less.

When she came down again she seemed to have cheered up, and offered to make us cocktails using a bottle of absinthe she'd brought with her.

She described it as a sort of Pernod, but it must have been rather stronger because events were a little hazy after the second one. I was definitely *not* at my best when Tom rang the doorbell at some unearthly hour of the morning, fresh as a daisy after an all-night drive up from Cornwall. I opened the door half dead and with my hair in my eyes.

'Fran!' he cried, embracing me with enthusiasm, and since I needed both hands to hold my dressing gown shut it wasn't easy to fend him off.

'For goodness' sake, come in!' I said, as a light snapped on at the Wevills', sending a shaft of questing illumination into the night. They'd counted him in, and if I had anything to do with it they would count him out again almost immediately.

I left him in the sitting room while I went to wake Rosie up. She looked positively angelic asleep. Did I really want my only child to go off surfing with Tom, who was always verging on hyperactive, slightly crazy and not terribly bright?

'Why are you standing over me like Bride of Frankenstein, Mum?' asked Rosie sleepily.

'Tom's here.'

She woke up completely, looking as fresh as if she'd slept for hours. 'It doesn't seem to be five minutes since I went to sleep! Tell him I'll be right down.'

'Tell him yourself, darling – I'm going to put my warm dressing gown on. I'm freezing, and I seem to have lost the belt to this one.'

And what's more, I didn't particularly want a tête-à-tête with Tom while half-clothed, though I didn't mention that.

When I'd watched the tail lights of Tom's car disappear into the night I went back to bed, but I couldn't sleep for thinking about great waves crashing on to Rosie – *and* sharks. I'm sure someone said they'd seen a Great White somewhere off our coast recently, and I sincerely hoped it wasn't anywhere near Wales.

I had to get Gabe's number from Ma so I could thank him for his gift.

'We've made beds for each other now, which seems fair, doesn't it?' he said, his deep, golden-toned voice sounding amused, and I immediately felt a bit guilty about the Flower Fairies. 'I thought it might give the Mermaid a boost,' he added.

'If that doesn't, nothing will.' I paused, wondering what quality it was about his voice that sent shivers up and down my spine – and probably that of every other woman who heard him, too. 'I've found a couple more Regency roses, though one is 1819, which is a bit late.'

'Oh, I think we could go up to about 1820, at a push.'

'It's dark purple, which would contrast well against the lighter ones.'

'Sounds good – what's it called?'

'Rose du Roi à Fleurs Pourpres,' I said, carefully reading it out. 'And I thought of the Burgundy rose – that's a really old one, and very pretty.'

'I know that one. And how about a Spong?'

'A what?'

'Spong – small, hardy, pink, reminds me of you. Now, don't tell me you haven't come across that one?'

'Are you making it up?' I asked suspiciously.

'No, you look it up and see.'

So I did, and the Spong does exist, though I think I would rather remind him of a rose by any other name, even if it does smell sweet, since Spong is hardly music to the ears.

Tom dropped Rosie off in the middle of Sunday afternoon but didn't hang about, thank goodness, since he had to get back to the surf school again. I simply don't know how he does it, shuttling up and down the country teaching in two places (three, if you count his one-day-a-week stint teaching art in a sixth-form college).

Rosie looked glowingly healthy but exhausted, which she said was mostly due to the partying till all hours that surfers appear to go in for.

'Tom never seemed to stay still – he's a real party animal,' she said, but despairingly rather than admiringly, like the mother of an over-energetic toddler.

'He always was a bit hyperactive and full of boyish high spirits,' I agreed. 'Also, although very good-natured, not terribly bright. I don't ever recall him reading a book when we were going out together.'

'His boredom threshold *does* seem to be set a bit low,' she admitted. 'But he's a very good surf teacher!' She got up. 'I'm going to have a long soak in the bath and then pack up for Granny's.'

'You could go very early in the morning instead?' I suggested.

'No, I'll be fine after a bath and some food,' she said, surprised. 'I'm not *really* tired. Oh, and Tom's invited me and Colum to go down and surf in Cornwall next weekend – you don't mind, do you?'

'That's an awfully long way to drive,' I began anxiously.

'It's all right, Mum! Colum can do the driving. He's got a bigger car than me too.'

I looked at her sadly. I'd been *so* looking forward to seeing her, and she was hardly going to be home at all at this rate!

'Mum,' she wheedled, 'you don't think you could

just stick my dirty clothes in the machine while I'm in the bath, do you? Only there are a couple of things I'll need to take with me, and everything's a bit sandy, or salty, or both.'

Muttering darkly I loaded the washer, removed the clean clothes, put them in the dryer, and cooked a full chicken dinner – you know, all the stuff you should make them do themselves, only some strange compunction forces *you* to do instead.

My reward was the big hug she gave me before setting off for Granny's, and Ma made her phone as soon as she got there to say she'd arrived safely.

OK, this is officially the start of the Atkins diet! Rosie won't be back until Friday, so I've got no excuse to cook anything fattening – and at least on this one you can eat all you want (providing all you want is protein and a handful of leaves, of course).

Out went the fruit: the cupboard now contains more tins of fish than a Norwegian canning factory.

Work should distract me from eating too. The calendar firm who do my rose one are now extremely keen on the hen idea, and of course want it by yesterday, so I am going to visit a rare-hen breeding centre tomorrow to take photographs and do some sketches.

Another email from Mal this morning. Since I found out about Alison, he's been phoning and emailing me more often, but I still feel unsettled by the idea – and the deception. I am absolutely sure he didn't mention it to me. And while he still seems keen for me to go out there I suspect his motivation has radically changed from when he first suggested it at the hospital, and now he wants me more to look after his mother and reassure her that we're still an item.

He's going to have to reassure *me* of that too.

And why does Gabe Weston's face have a disconcerting tendency to slip into my mind whenever I think about Mal? Is it just because I'm worried about his move to Fairy Glen and the possibility of him finding out about Rosie, so he's always at the back of my mind?

Today I received a present from Mal! It was posted in England, and there was a note explaining that his friend Justin had popped in to see him in Grand Cayman and, since he was coming back to the UK for a few days on business, volunteered to send the parcel to me once he got here.

Justin is an old school friend of Mal's who has made pots of money and jets about the world doing deals and having a good time. There was a point when he seemed to think *I* might be a good time, but I swiftly disillusioned him.

The present was a little hessian sack of coffee beans, which seemed rather disappointing until I tasted it: but my God, once you've had the Jamaican Blue Mountain coffee experience, anything else is just burned acorns!

I'm telling you, this is the champagne of coffees, and I'm now redefining my concept of happiness as a new rose catalogue, the rich smell of Blue Mountain coffee and a plate of freshly baked (non-Atkins) macaroons.

I suppose Mal's idea of perfect happiness is neatness, order and good (i.e., expensive) living. Also sailing, fine wine and stamps. If he ever manages to find that elusive Cayman Blue, his cup of vintage *vino* will runneth over.

He sounds pretty happy now, so he must have found most of those elements out there already. He does still say he misses me, but doesn't specify in what way. Nor does he say it very often or with any great conviction.

It's odd how he keeps telling *me* how high the cost of living over there is, and that most foodstuffs are flown in from America, but in the next breath mentions some fancy French-sounding restaurant he's been to the night before. It doesn't sound like he is exactly stinting himself, does it?

Today being Friday I phoned Ma up to tell her to behave herself in Amsterdam, but fat chance.

Rosie had already left for the vet's surgery, but Ma said she was setting off home at four, so would be back in the early evening.

I expect it will be another fast turnaround of washing, ironing and repacking before she vanishes off with the unknown Colum to Cornwall. And of course I am happy that she is off enjoying herself and having all these lovely opportunities, but by the time she returns from Cornwall it will practically be the start of term again.

I'll just have to get used to this: after all, I want my daughter to have a life, don't I? It would be much more worrying if she never did anything and was still living at home with her mum at thirty-six.

Today's the day they're going to shoot the opening scenes of *Restoration Gardener* too, but I didn't know Gabriel had arrived until the gate squeaked while I was mixing the first watering can of Up-She-Roses of the year, and there he was.

Despite the name, there's never anything particularly angelic about his appearance, and it's going to be disconcerting if he keeps popping by like this all the time when he lives here. Do I want to be that matey? And what are the Wevills going to make of it?

He said he'd just dropped in to thank me for the food parcels and the long-life milk I'd left at Fairy Glen, and I told him it was mostly overflow stuff that didn't fit in with my diet.

Then he insisted on carrying the heavy cans up to the rose garden for me, although I told him I could do it myself and pointed out that he would be late at Plas Gwyn.

'It won't take long – and then you could come up to the house with me and watch, though it won't be terribly exciting.'

'Oh, I'm not coming,' I said quickly. 'I've got loads of work to do ... and, besides, I'm still in my old gardening clothes.'

'You look fine to me, and since you're not going to be in the film it doesn't matter, does it? I expect it will all be over in a couple of hours. We don't shoot it in sequence. The scene where I approach in a helicopter is going to be shot later in the morning, and we're going to do the bit introducing the house and Rhodri first. I thought you might like to see that.'

I'm not sure how I found myself driving up to Plas Gwyn with him, wearing my rather muddy jeans and a T-shirt printed with a picture of Angel in Fang Mode – except, perhaps, that he turned out to be a big *Buffy* fan too, and we had such an interesting conversation that when he pulled up I only vaguely remembered how we'd got there.

There were strange people, vehicles and equipment all over the place, as though a nest of mechanical ants had been stirred with a cattle prod. Most of the inhabitants of St Ceridwen's had been drawn up by some kind of osmosis too, and were clustered on the other side of the ha-ha together with a herd of curious heifers.

Nia was very pleased to see me since Rhodri had gone to pieces from nerves and she needed some support; and actually Gabe was right, it *was* quite interesting seeing them shoot the thing out of sequence and in little bites.

After a couple of hours Gabe vanished to rendezvous with the helicopter and we went to brew tea and calm Rhodri down in Nia's studio. I don't know why he was in such a fuss, since they'd already shot the conversation between them, so all he had to do now was look up when he heard the helicopter and then walk forward and shake hands with Gabe after it had landed.

A woman popped her head in and said, 'Get into position please, Mr Gwyn-Whatmire!' and we went out into the courtyard.

'Here he comes,' Rhodri said, as the faint beating of a helicopter became audible, and ran a distracted hand through his hair.

'Don't do that, it's all sticking up now,' Nia ordered, stretching up to smooth it down. 'Right, don't touch it again, just go straight to the spot and stand there looking vaguely intelligent!'

I think she's missed her vocation.

'Good luck,' I said, and we quickly ran back to the workshop, where we waited, brewing more tea on Nia's little stove.

Eventually the helicopter took off and vanished, and then Gabe and Rhodri came walking across the courtyard chatting, so we figured it was all over.

'How did it go, Gabe?' Nia asked as we emerged like troglodytes, blinking in the spring sunshine.

'Oh – good, I think.'

'We seemed to be doing it for hours,' Rhodri said.

'Yes, but it will all edit down to just an opening sequence. That's it now until the team arrives for the project itself, and of course we will be coming back and filming the changes just like with the earlier projects. Gardens take years to evolve – this one won't be any different.'

'Look at the time!' I suddenly exclaimed. 'I haven't done a bit of work yet, *and* Rosie's coming back from Ma's any minute. I'd better go.'

Gabe insisted on running me home again, since he said he'd persuaded me to come in the first place, and we arrived to find Rosie already unloading her stuff from the car. I hoped Gabe would drive away again, but he got out, obviously assuming he would be introduced.

'Rosie,' I said reluctantly, 'this is Gabe Weston.'

Rosie eyed him suspiciously. 'Hi,' she said unenthusiastically, and his eyes crinkled up at the corners in the way he has when he's amused.

'Nice to meet you,' he said gravely. 'I've heard a lot about you.'

Clearly considering the social niceties had been addressed, Rosie turned a severe gaze on me. 'Where've you been, Mum?'

'Just up watching the filming at Plas Gwyn. I wasn't expecting you until later, darling.'

'I left early. That Mona Wevill came out and tried to be friendly,' she added, 'but I told her I knew what she'd done to your Mermaid and I thought she was despicable, and she went bright red and went back in.'

'Good for you,' Gabe said. 'But I think the rose will recover, with a bit of luck.'

'And manure,' I added gratefully.

'I'd better leave you to it and get back up to Plas Gwyn. I take it you won't be at the Druid's Rest tonight, Fran?'

'Mum and I are going to stay in,' Rosie said, quickly and jealously. 'We want to spend some time together.'

'Right. And you're off surfing tomorrow, I hear?'

'Yes, in Cornwall with my dad,' she said defiantly.

'Oh?' He looked from one of us to the other. 'I thought your dad was in Grand Cayman?'

'Oh, *Mal* isn't my dad, only a *step*,' she said airily. 'Excuse me!' And off she waltzed into the house with an armful of clothes.

Gabe looked at me, one eyebrow raised. 'You didn't tell me she wasn't your husband's child!'

'Well, why should I? And it's not like it's some huge secret, because everyone round here knows I had a previous relationship,' I said defensively, though my voice sounded strange and my heart was hammering so loud I thought he might hear it.

'Right,' he said. 'Well . . . I'd better get back.' And with a slightly frowning glance at me he strode off to his car, then paused and tossed over his shoulder, rather tersely, 'Maiden's Blush.'

'*What*?'

'An Alba. Pre-fifteenth century, a hardy pink.'

'Oh – Bullata!' I snapped, and strode into the house, slamming the door behind me. 'Rosie, where are you? I want to talk to you!'

Only of course she was unrepentant. I can see that she will brook no supposed competitors, now she has convinced herself that Mal and I will break up, leaving me free to marry Tom and make us one big, happy family.

Perhaps I told her too many fairy tales when she was growing up.

Something in the Water

Nia just called on her mobile, and apparently Rosie popped up to Plas Gwyn briefly yesterday to say hello – and I didn't even know she'd gone out!

Nia overheard her more or less tell Gabe that her father was an old flame and I'd taken up with him again now Mal had abandoned me! She said it was very artlessly done, but clearly Rosie *does* think that Gabe is some kind of threat to her dreams of a fairy-tale ending, which is not true, since there is *no* way I'm ever getting back with Tom!

Besides, the fairy-tale bit was when I met Mal and he swept me off my feet. Of course, he's spent the next ten years sweeping *around* my feet instead, but you can't have everything, and compulsive cleanliness is not the worst fault a husband could have (though, come to think of it, he's got one or two of those too).

The Wevills have spent the morning painting exactly half of our shared stone gatepost a dismal lilac, which rather reflects my current mood. When I asked Mal last night if they were still sending him a résumé of my movements, he said they never had done that, only told him any interesting bits of village news, to which I replied, 'Yes, and I really *am* Tilly the two-ton tooth fairy.'

'Are you?' he said vaguely, clearly not paying attention, but there were voices in the background so I expect he was at work.

Whether the Wevills are still sending him bulletins or not, he seems to have stopped being quite so jealous of my friendships, which is possibly an ominous sign rather than one of maturity. And he barely even *tries* to seem interested in news of Rosie, the hens, my roses or the events up at Plas Gwyn. In fact, the only thing he shows any interest in is the thorny subject of my weight loss.

Even when I told him Rosie was off to Cornwall with her boyfriend, to stay with Tom Collinge and surf, he just grunted, 'That's nice,' before reminding me again to put my driving licence on the list of things to take out with me. Presumably this is so I can drive his mother about, although I reminded him that I'm not good with strange cars, especially on unfamiliar roads.

The time we went to the south of France we nearly had a total marriage breakdown after he insisted I drove one leg of the journey and then criticised the way I did it. Then when we got there I spent two weeks looking like Elephant Woman due to an acute allergic reaction to the sun.

Colum turned out to be a stocky, spiky-haired young

man, not much taller than Rosie, who didn't say very much but smiled a lot. He was clearly the strong silent type since he somehow managed to efficiently pack her into his car and depart ten minutes after he got here.

Wish I knew how he did that.

Rosie asked me rather suspiciously what I was going to do while she was away, and I said work, work and more work – except for Sunday, when I had promised to go up and hide Easter eggs with Rhodri and Nia. Otherwise, I'm going to keep a low profile and hope Gabe has a trusting nature, so he believed what Rosie told him. A weak grasp of maths and a dodgy memory would also be desirable.

On Easter Sunday I was up at first light and, after tossing a handful of Happyhen into the coop, dashed up to Plas Gwyn to help hide the Easter eggs.

I was just grateful Nia hadn't insisted I wear a bunny costume, since anything to do with rabbits makes me think of *Con Air*: he really *should* have put the bunny back in the box.

There was no sign of Gabe even though his car was parked in the courtyard, but while I was doing one of my wider sweeps with my fast-emptying basket of eggs I came across him sitting in the middle of the maze like a minotaur after an earthquake, his chin resting on his knees.

I walked up to the edge and called, curiously, 'What are you doing?'

'Thinking,' he said shortly, his hazel eyes cold. 'I thought this was one place I would be alone!'

313

'Sorry,' I said, backing off. 'I was only going to put some eggs under the yew hedge, nowhere near the maze – Nia wouldn't like that. Weren't you supposed to be helping?'

'I didn't think you'd need me. I'll come back in time for the grand opening bit.'

'Right.' I took a couple of uncertain steps away – for all I knew of him his temperament might be as mercurial as the April weather, and I hoped so because otherwise I was very afraid that he might have started to put two and two together . . . 'Sorry I disturbed you.'

'Fran . . .'

I turned and found him still regarding me sombrely; then that slightly crooked smile dawned and he said, 'Celsiana!'

'Quatre Saisons,' I contributed uncertainly, thinking that Four Seasons pretty well summed up his moods. We seemed to be back in sunshine again, fighting a battle of flowers.

At this rate, I would shortly run out of old roses – I must scour my book and catalogue collection again.

True to his word Gabe did turn up in good time for the official opening, as did crews from both *Restoration Gardener* and BBC Wales, who filmed the proceedings and then rolled away again – but not before Dottie had stolen the show.

She had been invited to cut a symbolic ribbon tied between two trees, but when she failed to turn up it looked like Rhodri would have to do the honours –

until she appeared at the very last moment round the corner of the stable block, eating a chocolate Easter egg, which she must have found while riding through the grounds.

'Quick! You're on, Miss Gwyn-Whatmire!' Nia said, taking her elbow and pointing her in the right direction. 'See, over there – they're waiting for you to cut the ribbon!'

'Village fête, is it?' Dottie said vaguely. 'Should have warned me.' She thrust the half-eaten chocolate egg into the pocket of her Barbour jacket then, with a businesslike air, pulled out a folding hoof pick, strode over and sawed through the ribbon. 'I declare this fête open,' she said. 'What are you all waiting for? Off you all go!'

There was a smattering of applause. Dottie took the half-eaten Easter egg out of her pocket and began pulling wisps of hay off it.

Nia's sister, Sian, was hanging around Gabe, I noticed, probably in her official reporter guise. After a while they left together. She *is* very pretty in a hard way, but I think Nia is much more attractive, and, clearly, so does Rhodri. Nia said later that Sian had pretty well forced Gabe into offering to give her a lift down to the village where she'd left her car, but she'd put good money on it that that was as far as she got with him.

'I don't think Sian's his type,' she said rather meaningfully. 'He's got other things on his mind: he asked me earlier if this Tom Collinge Rosie had gone off to visit was the same man you used to go out with at college, the one who had dumped you at the end of term.'

315

'Oh my God – no wonder he was morose and pre-occupied earlier!' I said, a feeling of panic rising. 'What did you tell him?'

'Well, "yes", of course . . . but then I said he'd asked you to go back to him soon after you'd broken up.'

'Which is true,' I approved, with a sigh of relief. 'Well done, Nia! Quick thinking.'

'Fortunately, he didn't ask me whether you *had* gone back to him or not, so I didn't have to tell any lies.'

'So,' I said slowly, working it out, 'Gabe, Rosie and Tom think Tom's Rosie's dad; Mal and half the village suspect it's Rhodri; and I don't know for certain but am almost *sure* it's got to be Gabe.'

'Right,' agreed Nia, following this with an effort. 'Look, Fran, I'd better get back and help out – I'll talk to you later.'

There seemed to be children everywhere, all happy, since Nia had rather overdone the eggs, to the point where they could hardly take a step without falling over one.

I was sorely tempted to eat one myself, but the thought of thin-as-a-whippet Alphawoman Alison out there on Cayman with my husband seemed to be strengthening my willpower. I strengthened it even more by taking myself off home: there were more than enough helpers, what with Mrs Jones and her team showing the house, and even Dottie bellowing instructions at the people trying to park their cars, as though they were imbecile members of her pony club.

I only hoped she had remembered to stable Rollover

in his loose box and not Nia's workshop, or there would be hell to pay.

The start of week two of Atkins, and I can't face another chicken, let alone an egg. I *am* losing weight rapidly, but more because I've gone off all forms of protein and therefore am not eating much of anything apart from the odd leaf.

The latest copy of *S.O.N.W.* magazine came today, and Alphawoman seems to be popular. While they don't pay a huge amount, at least it's regular. There was a poem too, which I've copied out for the wall of my studio.

> Thorns of ugliness prick your eyes.
> In the garden of life
> See only the rose.

I'll do my best.

Gabe's car vanished again from outside Fairy Glen, so I assume he's gone back to London – though he didn't call and say goodbye.

Mind you, there's no reason why he should. None at all.

My Golden Showers and Mermaid are showing signs of renewed life already – that manure must have been exactly the tonic they needed!

I've just found a small card behind the door, half hidden under the mat, so I don't know how long it's been there. On it was written: 'I've gone. *Officinalis.*'

That's the Apothecary's rose, I think. Must ask the library van if the book about old roses I ordered has arrived yet.

'I'm back, my love,' Ma announced breezily on the phone.

'Hello, Ma, did you have a good time?'

'Lovely – so much to do and see.'

'What, the museums and art galleries?'

'Oh, no, there wasn't time for *that* kind of thing,' she said vaguely. 'We found a very good flea market, though. And I've brought you an Edam. I thought you could eat that on the peculiar diet you're on.'

'Yes, cheese is about the one thing I haven't gone off that I *can* eat,' I admitted. 'Are you coming over?'

'Saturday. Gabriel says we can exchange contracts any time I want to, so I thought I'd have a final sort-out of odds and ends.'

'I'd better borrow Nia's van and move any bits and pieces I want too, then,' I agreed.

'No rush. I'm sure he won't mind how long you leave them there.'

'He might need the room – he's bound to bring some things of his own.'

'I suppose so. How did the filming and the Plas Gwyn opening go, my love?'

'It was a roaring success. There seemed to be hundreds of people, and although most of them probably came to see Gabe Weston, they bought tickets and went on the Easter egg hunt and toured the house too. Nia said the collection boxes they'd dotted about for the garden restoration scheme were pretty full by the end of the day, but mostly with coppers.'

'I'm *so* glad. "Every mickle maks a muckle," as Lachlan would say.'

'I don't think he would,' I said doubtfully.

'Well, something like that. But do give my love to Nia and Rhodri, and I'll catch up on the rest of the news at the weekend. I must go, I'm tea dancing.'

Tea dancing? That sounds terribly staid for Ma!

Rosie's back from Cornwall in a strangely angry and touchy mood, and although she did say that she'd enjoyed the surfing and made a new friend (called Star, which sounds a bit hippie-child), she was tight-lipped on the subject of Tom.

Eventually I got out of her what was wrong, and – shock, horror! – it turns out that not only is Tom married, but his wife still lives with him and, until just before last Christmas, so did his lover!

Well, he *did* say in one of his emails that he'd recently ended a relationship, he just didn't mention that it was only one of many!

'Tom said they haven't *really* been married for years, just lived as friends, sharing the cottage, and he doesn't see anything wrong with that!' Rosie said primly. 'I said I thought it was indecent. Clara, his wife, is quite nice – Dutch. She cooks peculiar vegan food, though.'

She frowned and added, 'You know, Mum, now I've spent more time with Tom I can see that, although he's fun, he isn't really . . . well, next to Colum he just doesn't seem very *grown-up!*'

'No, he didn't sound in his emails as if he'd changed much,' I agreed.

'And he's so restless, Mum. Always wanting to go to pubs and parties. He can't sit still for a minute. And I've been thinking that, although I really like him, we don't actually have that much in common. I wanted us to be alike, but we're not.'

'I like him too, Rosie,' I said gently, 'and it's not his fault he isn't what you were looking for. But perhaps now you'll believe me when I say that it's highly unlikely that he's your dad.'

'I suppose so – but at least he was better than a nameless stranger I'm never going to find!'

'A father in the hand is worth two in the bush?' I suggested, and she gave me a watery smile and offered to make me a cocktail.

'No absinthe,' I said firmly.

Next day Rosie did her usual vanishing trick back to university with half my belongings and larder, leaving me with a seriously sandy washing machine. I'm not sure it's ever going to wash clothes again, but I may be able to use it to grind wheat.

Despite having hardly seen her I was actually quite glad to see her go this time, since part of me had an insane urge to tell her who her probable father was.

But then, of course, Rosie would have been round there like a shot, demanding to know the truth, and he'd probably have denied it until he'd got a paternity test result. And what if the whole thing got round the village – even into the papers?

What if they did the test and it *was* Tom after all, and Gabe thought we'd just been after a big pay-off?

Too many what-ifs. Just forget it, Fran, and keep it zipped!

I've got flu.

OK, I've got a heavy cold. I'm so sorry for myself I've abandoned Atkins and am eating and drinking all the wrong comfort foods, assisted by Ma. When she arrived for the weekend and set eyes on me she insisted that I needed feeding up, not starving, and brought me nourishing and fattening food and drink including the most *enormous* whole Edam.

News of my near-starvation quickly spread around the family circle, and Naomi, Joe's wife over in America, rang especially to tell me that the new version of the Atkins diet was much better than the ancient one I'd got, with more fruit and vegetables, and she is sending me a copy through Amazon.

Beth and Lachlan, who haven't seen me for about three years, assured me I looked absolutely fine, and I shouldn't bother about it. But then, *they* aren't married to a slim, fit and handsome man who was probably even now surrounded by bikini-clad and twig-thin women on a coral beach, one of them his ex-wife.

And speaking of Mal, he came in for an earful when he rang me and got Ma instead. She said I was wasting away, but she didn't tell him it would take me about ten years at my present rate to complete the job.

Ma nearly drove me crackers, bustling about like a

Romany version of Florence Nightingale, humming 'Tulips From Amsterdam' endlessly, and attempting to cheer me up by showing me the brochures for her round-the-world cruise.

How she thought the idea of her loose on the ocean waves for weeks, together with the madder and richer of her friends, would cheer me up, is beyond me.

Flu and over-anxious Ma both now gone, but weight increasing four times as fast as I lost it, so I have a figure to die *from*, not for. I feel really down. Carrie and Rhodri have been to see me a couple of times in an attempt to cheer me up, but they are both very busy – the restoration project starts in only a couple of weeks, just before I'm supposed to go out to Grand Cayman.

Oh my God – the Flying Pig lands in the Caribbean!

I've also missed the Walpurgis night ceremony up at the maze, which is a big shame because I was looking forward to watching it, but at least I managed to get Ma to post off a nice card and a cheque to Rosie for her birthday, which falls on the same day.

Nia came round to tell me how the ceremony went, but says she is looking forward to next year's, when the maze will be re-cut to its original size. She also said that Mrs Evans having to do the ritual walk using her Zimmer frame had rather held things up.

After the maze she'd gone alone up to the standing stones to perform some sort of personal Druid ceremony, and she left me a little glass bottle of what she *swears* is only dew, which I am to drink. I presume it's some sort of magic tonic.

After she'd gone, I tried it. I can't say I feel any different yet, but you never know, and I saved a drop or two to add to the hens' water, because Shania has been looking a bit peaky.

Tomorrow Fairy Glen officially becomes Gabe's and he's moving in, but I haven't got enough energy to care – or change the Flower Fairies bedding.

Have just assured Mal on the phone that I have lost most of my excess baggage and am nearly a shadow of my former self, and he said he looked forward to seeing the old Fran back again.

Bastard.

As soon as I put the phone down I went into the kitchen and wolfed down a whole bar of cooking chocolate, a packet of trifle sponges and a small frozen Black Forest gateau, which at least took a long time, since it was rock-hard to begin with and I had to suck it.

Carrie exchanged the copy of Atkins for a food combining book when she came round with some calorie-laden goodies to cheer me up. She said Gabe had been into Teapots to buy a big bag of doughnuts for the removal men to have with their tea, to the delight of her customers, and they'd had a nice chat before he went back.

It is a sad indictment of today's society that my friends have more dieting books on their shelves than anything else.

I've already started food combining. This sounds

possible: I can eat anything at all that I want, so long as I don't mix protein and carbohydrates at the same meal.

How hard can that be?

Great Expectations

Remembering that I still had a key to Fairy Glen, which I ought to hand back, I thought I might as well go the whole hog and give Gabe a house-warming present too. He was perhaps a bit terse last time we met, but I really should have been there to welcome him when he moved in.

The Flower Fairies linen on the little bed in the turret room is weighing on my conscience a bit too.

Laden with home-made goodies and a card with a Mermaid rose that I'd painted myself, I set out rather furtively at dusk, since not only did I want to avoid the Wevills' beady eyes, but by 'give' a present to Gabe I of course actually meant 'sneak up and leave it on the doorstep'. But I still think he's telepathic, for the front door swung open while I'd barely had time to admire the clipped box trees that now stood either side of it.

'They don't really go with the cottage, I know,' he said gravely, 'but I couldn't leave them in London. Perhaps Aled could add a touch of the grotesque to them next time they need clipping.'

'I wouldn't put it past him,' I replied, recovering from the surprise of his sudden appearance. He was wearing a loose natural linen shirt with the sleeves rolled up, jeans and bare feet. His hair looked as if he'd run his hands through it a few times, for several of the little silkworm cocoons had unravelled. All in all, he was a sight to make most women's knees go weak, let alone one with a shared history.

'Are you coming in?' he asked.

I stopped staring at his bare feet, which were rather beautiful in a Michelangelo's *David* kind of way, and remembered why I'd come. 'No, I've just brought you a house-warming present,' I said, thrusting the bottle and cake tin at him. 'And a card. But I don't want to disturb you, you must be busy.'

He looked surprised. 'A present? That *was* a kind thought, Fran!'

'It's nothing much,' I assured him, 'just a bottle of my elderflower champagne – be careful when you open it, it's *very* fizzy – and one of my legendary fruit-sinks-to-the-bottom cakes.'

'Whose bottom?'

'The bottom of the cake. It always does – I'm noted for it – but it tastes wonderful because I make it with butter, and dried fruit soaked for two days in dark rum. And the fruit is now on top, because I turned it over so I could ice it.'

'I think you'd better come in and show me this marvellous cake yourself,' he suggested, swinging the door wide and ushering me in.

'Well, I'll just put them down, then leave you to it.

'I can't *stay*,' I said, walking through to the kitchen.

'Not even to join me in a glass of champagne?'

I stopped dead. 'Oh, *no* – I've just remembered you don't like champagne! You said so at the pub.'

'Ah, but elderflower champagne is different – if it's good.'

'You've had it before?'

'Yes, my granny used to make it.'

I hovered uncertainly while he got out two unfamiliar glasses. Looking round, in fact, the whole cottage seemed to have acquired a slightly different air, though it was hard to put my finger on any changes.

'Let's see this cake, then. Your friend Carrie says you're a better cook than she is.'

'Does she? I'm not a better pastry cook, no one can beat her at that.'

He prised the lid off the tin and stared down at the cake with its rather wobbly blue 'Welcome To Your New Home' icing. I'd added one of the sugar roses I'd saved from my birthday cake too.

'You shouldn't have gone to all this trouble,' he said, lifting his head and smiling at me.

I don't know what it is, since he is nowhere near as handsome as Mal, but when he smiles like that he is *devastatingly* attractive. I felt as if the sun had come out just for me, and sat down on the nearest chair quite unintentionally.

'It was no trouble, because I make cakes all the time, unless I'm dieting.'

'So does that mean you can't eat a piece with me now?'

I considered. 'I *suppose* I could, because I'm food combining, and as long as I don't mix protein and carbohydrate I can eat anything. Cake's all carbo-hydrate.'

'You cut it then, and I'll pour the drinks.' With his back to me he added, 'Is it very odd to see a stranger here?'

'Not as bad as I thought it would be,' I confessed. 'Mainly because . . . well, I suppose I know you, you're not a total stranger. I've sort of got used to you being about.'

'That's nice,' he said, putting my glass down in front of me and taking the piece of cake I offered him. I'd carefully cut one with the entire word 'Home' on it, so it was a hefty slice. 'I've sort of got used to you being about too. I hope you're still going to come up to Plas Gwyn and help me plan out the rose garden?'

'Oh, I'm sure you don't need me for that,' I said, flattered.

'I do have a rough design,' he admitted, 'but I'd like to talk it through on the site with a fellow enthusiast. Please?'

'All right,' I said. I looked around the kitchen. 'It's odd, nothing much seems to have changed.'

'There are a lot more bookshelves in the other rooms, but otherwise there isn't a great deal of stuff. My gardening equipment is all out in that old shed, but I think I'll have to replace it before it falls down.'

'I hope you've moved into one of the bigger bedrooms too, now that you've bought the house. I'm sure Ma doesn't expect you to save the best one just

for her. Or my old room would be fine if you redec-
orated it.'

'Actually, I rather like the turret, especially now I've
got my own bed in there, even if it does take up most
of the floor space. The other was a bit short and narrow.
Nice bedlinen, though.'

I reddened. 'Was it? I expect I just used the first
clean set to come to hand.'

'I thought I might leave the girlie décor in your old
room. Don't you think Stella might like it if she comes
to stay?'

'Well, Rosie does, although she says it's over the top.
Is your daughter likely to come? Have you heard from
her again?'

'Yes, we've been exchanging more emails. She wants
to know all sorts of things about me from right back
before I met her mum, so I think she's catching up on
all the years we've missed. She liked the pictures of the
cottage, so I think she *will* come and see me, probably
in June when she's back staying with her grandparents
again.'

'I hope she does,' I said sympathetically.

'*Your* daughter, Rosie, is quite a character,' he
commented, rather admiringly. 'Did she enjoy surfing
with her father?'

'Er – yes,' I said, then swallowed the last mouthful
of champagne and rose hastily to my feet. 'Look, I
must go – I'm expecting a call from my husband.'

Gabe got up too. 'Right. And you still intend going
out to the Caribbean to see him?'

'Of course!' I said, surprised.

'So what Rosie said about you breaking up with him and marrying her real dad was just –'

'Wishful thinking,' I said quickly. 'She's never really got on with Mal, unfortunately. They're chalk and cheese. Mal can't wait to see me again.'

I think I was trying to convince myself as well as him, but I'm not sure the sincerity rang true enough for either of us.

'Petite Lisette,' he said at the door, but I was armed and ready for him.

'*Hemisphaerica.*'

He frowned. 'Haven't we had that one?'

'No, and it's growing wild up the glen, so it obviously does well round here. I hope you do too,' I added neatly, and walked off feeling quite pleased with myself.

I feel *wonderful* on food combining, and my head seems so clear too, so my work is going very well. I'm about to send enough Alphawoman strips off to the magazine to keep them going until I get back from Grand Cayman, my rose and hen calendar illustrations are mounting up, and I've had all kinds of ideas for cartoons.

Tom has sent me one or two more as well, but they are definitely getting odder, especially now I know about his weird domestic arrangements and can see them in a new light. I haven't acknowledged them.

The only downside to food combining is that I haven't lost a great deal of weight. Practically none, if I'm honest. Could this possibly be because I am combining chips, chocolate, butter and cream? I can even have chip butties, on white buttered bread – and I *do*, all the time.

I have been out and about a bit too: up to Plas Gwyn to talk over the rose garden with Gabe, and admire the stone bench Rhodri and Nia found at an architectural salvage yard, and down to the Druid's Rest to meet the three of them in the evening. Our trio seems to have just naturally become a quartet, but Gabe at least stops me feeling like a gooseberry, since Nia and Rhodri are definitely adrift on the sea of love.

How odd that we should love each other like brother and sisters all these years, and then for that to change into something more! And all they seem to talk about lately is Plas Gwyn . . . though, mind you, most of what Gabe and I say to each other concerns roses.

Mal has sent me the most enormous shopping list of things to take out with me.

I'm sure he must have been getting bulletins on my friendship with Gabe, but has not said anything about it – unless he has fallen out with the Wevills.

I certainly wasn't about to rock the boat by mentioning it, but I did ask him if he still wanted me to buy a special dress for the holiday, which I thought might kind of gauge how he was feeling towards me.

'Of course I do, darling. Get something pretty.'

'All right. And I've got your shopping list, but it's going to cost a fortune!'

'Then use the credit card. That's what it's for,' he said, slightly impatiently.

'Are you looking forward to seeing me, Mal? It's not long now, is it?'

There was an imperative female voice in the background. 'Look, something's come up and I've got to go. Talk to you later – 'bye!'

Somehow I felt unsettled rather than reassured by this conversation . . . and where on earth *did* I put the guilt card? Must search for it! Also for my sarong and flip-flops, which I haven't seen since last summer.

Eureka! I discovered the sarong behind the sack of Happyhen in the utility room. I must have rested a pile of clean laundry on top of it at some time and it slithered down behind.

The guilt card was in the cutlery drawer under the cake forks. I usually eat my cake fast, using both hands, which accounts for my not having seen it before.

Having now found the wherewithal to pay for it, I had another look at the truly horrendous list of things Mal wants me to take out. This includes all the copies of *Small Boats Monthly* that have arrived in his absence, three large bottles of his favourite mouthwash, aftershave and a small fortune's worth of toiletries, pills and potions from Boots the Chemists. I am also instructed to buy a huge bottle of duty-free sherry for Mrs M., whose only tipple this is, *en route*.

Must check my baggage allowance again. And will bottles of mouthwash explode in the hold? Or the aftershave?

* * *

'Well, my love, you'll never guess where I've been,' Ma said perkily down the phone.

'Probably not – tell me, it'll save time.' I propped myself against the wall, resigned to a long conversation.

'Visiting that village where you said the Wevills used to live!'

I stood up straighter. 'You *have*? Why?'

'To snoop. And do you know, they had poison-pen letters there, as well. And they stopped after the Wevills moved away.'

'They did? Good heavens, that looks a bit –'

'I told you it was them!' she interrupted triumphantly. 'Anyway, I thought I'd let you know.'

'But what are we going to do about it, Ma? I mean, presumably you haven't got any proof?'

'Only circumstantial, so *I've* sent an anonymous letter to the police, telling them. It's up to them now to make the right connections and put a stop to it.'

'Ma!' I protested, but I could see she'd thoroughly enjoyed her Miss Marple act.

'Is dear Gabriel settled in? When I last spoke to him on the phone he said how kind you'd been, taking him a cake and making him feel welcome. I'm coming down soon and he's going to show me his plans for extending the cottage a bit at the side, if he can get planning permission. Another bathroom and bedroom, I think, with a study underneath.'

'I thought he wasn't going to change anything!'

'Fran, of course he's going to update the cottage a bit, that's part of the reason I wanted to sell it! I'm sure he'll love the place, you'll see, and anything he does will only improve it. Now, what about you? Are you still intending to go out to see Mal?'

'Of course!' I said firmly. 'I can't wait.'

'Hmm,' she said, unconvinced. But then, she was never in favour of him going out there and leaving me in the first place. 'I worry about you, Frannie.'

'There's no need to worry about me. Honestly, everything's fine.'

'You've just started humming Bob Marley, my love,' she pointed out. '"No Woman, No Cry". Not a good sign in my book!'

I have spent the day in the nearest city and am *exhausted*.

I *hate* clothes shopping – that's partly why I make my own tops and wear jeans most of the time. And after all that there wasn't much that looked good on someone the approximate shape of a dumpling, so in the end I decided to make do with what I already have, i.e., the aged cotton trousers, loose shirts, ancient faded sundresses and flat sandals I wear for gardening.

But I did finally discover that special dress in a small but desperately expensive shop. It's in cream linen and magically makes me look taller and much thinner. You wouldn't believe the price! I had to use my newly discovered guilt card for the first time, which was fortunately stowed away in my bag for safety, and as I signed my name I felt like a thief and had this urge to shout, 'I confess, I have no money to pay for it!'

But then, I suppose Mal will be the one actually

paying for it in the end, and he did tell me to buy something smart.

It was addictive: on the way back to the car I bought a new swimsuit with control panels (I wish it could control my eating habits), and a pair of strappy sandals with high heels to go with my new linen dress. The guilt card took another hammering, and it just goes to show how easily I could get into the habit of spending money I haven't got. But at least the sandals will mean I won't look quite such a roly-poly little thing at the ceremony . . . so long as we're not standing on soft sand, that is.

I'm getting so jittery as the day I fly out rushes towards me. Part of me thinks Mal and I will fall into each other's arms and everything will be wonderful, but the other part is gibbering with nerves in the back room.

And desperate last-ditch measures are called for: it will *have* to be the cabbage soup diet . . .

I was woken at some unearthly hour of the night by loud hammering at my door, and staggered down thinking the worst, as you do when that kind of thing happens. Rosie? Ma? My heart was thumping with fear as I opened the door to find . . . *Tom.*

He beamed at me. 'Hi, Fran! I was passing and I couldn't resist dropping by. Can I come in?'

I goggled at him. 'Come in? No, you *can't* come in! Do you have any idea what time of night it is?'

He looked at his watch. 'Morning, just. Come on, Fran – I'd really like to talk to you,' he wheedled. 'Haven't you had all my notes and stuff? I can't stop thinking about you, and all the way up here –'

'Tom,' I interrupted, raising my voice, 'I'm a married woman – and you're a married man, come to that – and I'm not inviting you into my house at this time of the night, morning, whatever it is!'

He stared at me, brows knit. Then his face cleared. 'I see – Rosie must have told you Clara and I still live together. But it's an open marriage, and yours sounds pretty shaky, so how about we discuss getting together? You'd really like Clara! And don't you think we were always meant for each other, Fran?' he asked winningly, reaching out for me.

'For goodness' sake, Tom!' I exclaimed, stepping back. '*Will* you go away? I don't know why you think my marriage is on the rocks, but it's fine, absolutely fine. I'm very happy and I have absolutely no intention of having any sort of relationship with anyone else, including you!'

'But –'

'But *nothing*, Tom! Obviously you haven't read what I've written to you, or listened to what I've just said. There is nothing going on between us. I wish you well – but I wish you well in Cornwall or somewhere other than here. Got it?'

He seemed taken aback, all the blond sunniness extinguished. Then he ventured hopefully, 'So, I could just come in for a cuppa and a quiet chat like an old friend then, instead?'

'Absolutely not. Now, good night!'

'Shame!' he said with a sudden grin. 'You look very fetching in that robe.'

I tugged the lapels a bit closer together.

'Well, let me know if you change your mind or things don't work out. You might find yourself out there in the Caribbean thinking of me.'

'I don't think so, Tom!'

Unabashed by my rejection, he turned and gave me a sort of half-salute as he walked down the drive, and being still half-woman, half-zombie I waved back, which is not a good idea if you haven't found the belt of your dressing gown yet. And *especially* not if Gabe Weston is just passing in his big flashy car, slows down and cops an eyeful before you pull yourself – and your dressing gown – together.

Quick as thought I stepped back and slammed the door shut, leaning on it, heart thudding.

That must have looked *really* dodgy. I'd have to explain to him what happened and –

But hold on – *nothing* happened! And why should I try to explain something that I didn't do when, even if I did, it is none of his business?

'Because you don't want him to think you're a complete slut?' a little voice in my head said helpfully just as I was on the point of finally falling asleep again.

I was meeting the others at the pub tonight, but when I arrived Nia said Gabe had already been in but had had to go out somewhere. He'd also seemed in one of his darker moods.

It couldn't be because of last night, could it? I mean, why should he care? And how dare he jump to the wrong conclusions without even asking me what happened?

At least Rhodri and Nia believed me – but then, they are *true* friends. Nia is looking after the hens and roses in my absence, which I feel guilty about, since she is working so hard both at her pottery and helping Rhodri, but there isn't anyone else. Carrie is not a hen person.

It's been several days now, and I haven't seen Gabe at all. I think he's avoiding me, and *I'm* certainly not going looking for him. It's strange how I miss talking to him, though . . . *and* I'd found some more old roses to toss at him.

Still, I have more pressing problems: although I *have* managed to lose half a stone from sheer desperation (and I wouldn't recommend the cabbage soup diet to anyone who has friends and wants to keep them), that only makes me more or less what I was when Mal went away.

I just hope that after all this time he won't remember, or be so pleased to see me that he doesn't notice. On the other hand, he may have seen so much of Alison that he's started to think it's normal to have all your bones sticking out and boobs like two fried eggs.

I've done my best with what I've got, anyway: I'm buffed, defuzzed and exfoliated. Carrie has trimmed my hair to just below shoulder length, and camomile shampoo has taken the winter's dinginess out of it, but unfortunately *not* the pinkness, though with all these fluorescent wash-in colours people use these days, it doesn't stand out like it used to do. My eyelashes and eyebrows are freshly tinted and I've been soaking my hands in bowls of washing-up liquid to try to get half the garden out of them.

That's it: this is as good as it's going to get.

I'm almost organised . . . I think.

I've decided to travel in a pale blue Gap T-shirt and matching sweatshirt with jeans, and a light jacket. I can peel layers off when I get on the plane.

I've stuffed my comfortably shabby summer clothes into a huge yellow suitcase with a wonky wheel (one of Ma's cast-offs), added my expensive linen dress, wrapped carefully in tissue paper, and found my dark glasses. I wish now I'd washed the sarong instead of just shaking the dust off, since it smells of Happyhen, but I suppose I can do it when I get there.

There is no way I am putting potentially exploding minty mouthwash in with my lovely new dress, it will have to go in my hand luggage.

Rosie phoned me in a last-minute panic about my going, and to cheer her (and me) I told her some interesting snippets about Grand Cayman that I'd gleaned, like the average dress size in the Caribbean being a sixteen. I hope that's USA size sixteen.

'And there's a botanical garden that looks lovely, with blue iguanas,' I said. 'I'm really looking forward to seeing that.'

Rosie said she loved all wildlife except Mal, though on second thoughts he was tame to the point of comatose, so didn't count, but seemed a little comforted by the time she rang off.

I do wish I'd studied the information earlier, though, because I've suddenly realised just how hot it is going to be on Grand Cayman, and I don't think even my summer clothes are going to do. And also I don't cope with heat terribly well, being allergic to the sun and practically all suncreams.

But it's too late to worry about any of that now – tomorrow's the day.

I rang around to say my goodbyes, which took longer than I expected, so that it was late when I took my car out to fill with petrol for the drive to Manchester airport tomorrow.

As I was driving back the radio started to go slower and slower, and the windscreen wipers and the headlights started to fade – and by the time I rolled to a stop in my drive the poor little thing was as dead as a dodo.

Perfect timing.

I knew Rhodri or Nia would have driven me to the airport, but I didn't want to ask them when they are working so hard (and hopefully playing hard too), so I had to ring round and find a taxi to take me early in the morning instead. It's going to cost a fortune, so thank goodness I didn't change *all* my money into US dollars!

As you can imagine, I couldn't sleep for worrying about whether the taxi would turn up or not, and even when it did I must have checked that I had my tickets and passport five times before we were even out of the village.

It was quite a cool night, unless I was chilly from nerves, so I was glad of the sweatshirt under my light jacket. I could simply carry my outer layers when I got there, and my sandals and sunglasses were in my hand luggage, together with the damned mouthwash and aftershave – and I was *sure* the bag was overweight.

I dolorously droned out that song about leavin' on a jet plane as the taxi drove through the endless dark, deserted roads, and after a while the taxi driver turned the radio on, loud.

I was convinced I'd forgotten something vital, like saying goodbye to the hens.

Paradise Falls

Thirteen things <u>not</u> to do on a long-haul flight:

1) Do not drink too much alcohol just because it's free.

2) Do not get depressed (see 1).

3) Do not eat the airline food, it mutates in your intestines.

4a) Do not sit in front of small children (they kick the back of your seat).

4b) *Definitely* don't sit in front of toddlers, who are inclined to vomit down the back of your neck.

5) Do not sit behind someone very tall, who will recline their seat so far back their head is in your lap and you can't use your tray. If you ask them to sit up, they flex their tattoos at you and pretend they can't speak English.

6) Do not accidentally lock yourself in the loo to remove toddler vomit (see 4b) and have to shout for help: the whole compartment

will be watching you like a floor show when you come out, and may even applaud.

7) Do not forget to take a change of clothes in your hand luggage (see 4b and 6).

8) Do not forget to take refreshing wet wipes (see 4b, 6 and 7).

9) Do not worry about the future (see 1 and 2), because it's going to happen whether you worry or not.

10) Do not forget the name of the apartments you will be staying at, thus delaying for half an hour the rest of the queue at the sticky Styx of customs as you attempt to convince them you are an innocent tourist.

11) Do not attempt to explain the presence of half a gallon of mouthwash, a bottle of sherry, a rancid T-shirt and a hundredweight of assorted men's toiletries in your hand luggage.

12) Do not ignore any of the above points or you may arrive jet-lagged, constipated, hungover, depressed, smelly, and so hot you are about to spontaneously ignite like a gum tree because you're having to wear the thick sweatshirt you set out from home in.

13) Do not try to work out whether you have lost or gained a day of your life, just concentrate on blocking all memory of this flight out of your memory *for ever*.

I oozed out on to the airport concourse in Grand

Cayman like a wet and odoriferous dishcloth in need of a good wring out, dragging the suitcase with which I had been reunited after a nail-biting wait by the luggage carousel. Had I been able to remember where my suitcase keys were I might have abandoned all modesty and ripped off my sweatshirt then and there in favour of something much cooler.

I felt dizzy from jet lag and panic at the thought of seeing Mal again. I was most definitely *not* the slender sylph he was expecting and I could only hope that he'd be so happy to see me again that he wouldn't care if I was just a *little* overweight.

I'd already put this theory to Tanya, the young woman who'd sat next to me on the plane.

'I'm sure your husband is *dying* to see you and you'll have a lovely time,' she'd assured me sympathetically. Then she urged me to drink lots of water to prevent dehydration, which I did, although I also continued drinking the gin, of which they must have had an endless supply, unless they were distilling it in the galley.

I could see Tanya now, cool and elegant in tie-waist linen trousers and a sleeveless top, heading off with her husband, who was on Grand Cayman designing a house for a rich client. She'd said we would be bound to keep running into each other on such a small island and pressed on me as a parting gift one of her bottles of expensive sun lotion, which she assured me I wouldn't be allergic to.

There was no sign of Mal, but everyone else seemed to be heading out towards the front doors so I followed after them slowly, dragging my enormous suitcase, bulging carry-on bag and duty-free carrier with me. I was starting to have *very* dark thoughts about butt of malmsey-style, double domestic drowning incidences, one in minty mouthwash, the other in sherry – but that was probably the more homicidal aftereffects of the gin.

I spotted Mal standing outside in the shade, perfectly bronzed and with his dark, glistening hair clinging like satin to his beautifully shaped head. He wore a crisp blue shirt unmarked by any unseemly hint of perspiration, and ironed cream chinos.

He didn't notice me immediately since he was talking to his mother – or to be more accurate she seemed to be haranguing him on some subject. She looked like a wizened sparrow next to him, her skinny frame decorously covered in drab floral cotton and the green lining of her sunhat casting an unearthly pallor across the sagging folds of her face. It rather beggared belief that the one had ever sprung from the other.

I trudged towards them like the last survivor of an expedition, an unwelcome one they'd already claimed the life insurance for, and when they caught sight of me they abruptly stopped talking and stared.

'My God, it's the summer pudding!' Mal exclaimed, unforgivably.

'Well, Frances,' Mrs Morgan said, 'you look rather hot and bothered, I must say.'

'Hello, Mrs Morgan; hello, Mal,' I said, with a slight, betraying quiver in my voice, for there seemed to be a complete dearth of bunting, flags and loud hurrahs about my advent. The cherished dream in which, our passion freshly rekindled, we renewed our vows under the palm trees before returning to the marital nest like a pair of homing doves shrivelled and turned to ash on the spot and was blown away by a hot breeze that smelled of coconuts and fruit cake.

Mrs M. poked Mal with the handle of a furled black umbrella, and he finally advanced and kissed me gingerly on the cheek, then recoiled. I could hardly blame him, for he is *so* fastidious and I was hardly in the chilled and plumply perfect condition in which I had set out from the refrigerator of North Wales.

'Ugh! You smell rank!'

'Do I? I hoped it had gone off a bit. I'm sorry, darling – a baby threw up on me and the smell sort of lingers. I'm dying to shower and change into something cooler, it's so hot!'

'And *I* am urgently in need of a rest, so perhaps now that you have *finally* arrived we can go back to the apartment?' Mrs M. said.

'Of course, Mother. And *this* isn't hot, Fran,' Mal said, picking up the case and leading the way towards the car park, leaving me with the carry-on bags and duty frees. 'This is quite cool for Cayman. You'll soon acclimatise.'

Personally, I thought I had more chance of stewing in my own juice until perfectly braised, but all my breath was taken with trying to keep up without dropping anything breakable. By the time we got to the car the sweatshirt was soaked through and I longed to remove it, toss it in the rubbish and never see it again. My jeans felt like thermal corsets.

Mal's hire car was a monster: some big four-wheel-drive thing that he had to hoist his mother into. She sat regally in the back while we loaded my luggage in, and then I got in the front, since he said the air conditioning would hopefully take the worst of the smell away.

This was not quite how I had envisaged the start to my second honeymoon.

'Where are we going?' I asked. 'Only I couldn't remember for the customs people, and I thought they weren't going to let me in for a while there.'

'It's an apartment block by the sea, on the edge of town. Paradise Falls.'

'It certainly seems to have,' I muttered limply. All my pores were so far open I felt like a loofah.

'That's the name of the apartments, not the area. I've hired a car for you from tomorrow,' he added casually.

'Tomorrow?' I echoed, staring at his dark and competent profile. Relaxed and, aside from a faint wrinkling of his patrician nostrils, seemingly happy.

'Yes, of course. How else would you get around? It's the only way to show Mother the island and do the shopping and so on, because I'll be working most of the time. You did bring your driving licence, didn't you?'

'What?' I was starting to go light-headed and gritty-eyed; was this jet lag or a hangover? Or both? 'Oh, yes, I think so . . . Mal, the car's not as big as this one, is it?' I enquired timidly.

I've only ever really driven one car, the little Beetle

currently rusting mournfully on the drive at home.

'No, it's quite small, but air-conditioned. Automatic. They're mostly automatic.'

'But I've never driven an automatic, Mal!'

'Nothing to it. You'll soon pick it up.'

'I feel a bit nervous about it,' I ventured. 'I'm twitchy enough at home in my own car!'

'You'll soon get used to it,' he said impatiently. 'I don't know what the fuss is about! They drive on the left here too, and in all the residential areas the speed limit is only twenty-five miles per hour.'

He pointed things out to me in an instructional sort of way as he drove – not the sights, but a sort of orienteering programme: the supermarket, the way to the hospital, the road to the centre of George Town . . . I hoped he wasn't going to test me on them later, because they all passed me by in a glaze of exhaustion.

'Here we are,' Mal said, turning down a rough road and pulling up on coral sand outside a low white block of apartments. I couldn't see any falls, paradise or otherwise.

Inside, it was all open plan, with tiled floors and ceiling fans. Through the windows lay an improbable vista of wooden decking, coconut palms and a swimming pool, and beyond that a coral beach and wide expanse of turquoise sea.

It was just like an advert; when Mal opened the sliding doors to the deck I expected lithe, tanned young men to rush up and offer me their Bounty bars, but the only thing to rush in was a great rolling wave of hot scented air.

I was still standing by the door surrounded by baggage, like a wilted lettuce in urgent need of a bit of TLC, when Mal said solicitously, 'You must be tired.'

'Gosh, yes,' I began, then realised he wasn't talking to me.

'The flight out took it out of Mother, Fran: she's still taking it easy.'

'I'll just rest for a little while,' she agreed. 'I will see you later, Frances.'

Mrs M. did look pretty whacked, and I was glad to see her vanish into her room like a genie returning to its bottle. I uncharitably wished I had a stopper.

'*At last we are alone together!*' I whispered melodramatically to Mal once our bedroom door had swung silently shut behind us, because, truth to tell, I was feeling a bit strange and shy after our separation, and he wasn't exactly looking user-friendly.

But I don't think he can have heard me, since he just said, 'That's my bed near the window, Fran, and the shower's through that door. I'll leave you to unpack. Oh, and you needn't bother about the cooking tonight because I've got cold food in,' he added, and vanished without even one tender word.

Then I finally registered his last sentence: I needn't bother about the *cooking*? I *was* cooking!

I found I was mournfully singing 'Don't You Want Me, Baby?' Then I caught sight of myself in the long mirrored doors of the wardrobe and decided that even the most loving husband could have been excused a quick getaway: it was definitely another 'Thriller' zombie moment.

Removing my clothes and showering with some exotic-smelling gel (a strange choice for Mal, I thought) was blissful – except I couldn't get dry afterwards. My pores seemed to be permanently jammed into the 'open' position.

I put the coolest of my old sundresses on, then picked at cold meats and salad in a haze of exhaustion before crashing out on my designated twin bed ... but not before reviving just enough under the cooling whirr of the ceiling fan to kiss Mal good night.

He accepted the kiss rather unenthusiastically, then fended me off with the news that, in deference to his mother's presence and prejudices, we were not going to cohabit in any meaningful sense!

'I wasn't intending running through the first ten pages of the *Kama Sutra* tonight anyway,' I said tartly. 'I just wanted a hug! Is that too much to ask after we've been apart for so long? Haven't you missed me, Mal?'

'Yes, but one thing leads to another, and I just feel ... well, we should abstain. Until she's gone home,' he added, not looking noticeably eager to sweep me into his manly embrace. Then his mobile phone went off and he dashed out.

Maybe this was all a nightmare, and I would wake up any minute to find myself still at home, with time to cancel my ticket?

Next morning Mal woke me up at some hideously early hour.

'I've had breakfast,' he informed me, as though he had performed some amazing feat. 'I let you sleep on, but now you'll have to get up so I can drop you at Coconut Rentals on the way to work to pick up the hire car.'

'Today?' I wailed pathetically, scrabbling in my open suitcase for something cool enough, even though I knew there was nothing remotely suitable in there. It would have to be last night's faded and shabby cotton sundress again. 'Now? I've still got jet lag, Mal, and I don't know my way about yet!'

'It's a small island and they'll give you a map,' he said callously, easing me out into the living room by sheer willpower. 'You can't get lost.'

I can get lost in our *village*.

I made some coffee, hoping it would wake me up a bit, while Mal got himself perfectly organised for work. I opened and closed all the cupboard doors while I drank it, to check out what was in there. The fridge was an enormous thing with an ice dispenser that I would have liked to have taken home with me. Or climbed into.

'I've left you some instructions under that piece of coral on the counter,' Mal said. 'And I've hired you a mobile phone while you are out here in case I need to call you, and you can also use it for *brief* trans-atlantic calls.'

Just as well Nia had explained the newly discovered delights of her mobile phone to me! I expect they all work much the same way.

Mal was still holding forth, neatly ticking his mental list off item by item: 'The maid's not in until Monday. You need to wash up and clear any food spills immediately or we'll get ants and cockroaches in. Turn all the ceiling fans off and open the doors and windows when you get back – we only close them and use the fans at night, electricity is expensive. We don't need the air conditioning at all. Here's your door key. I'll be back about five thirty, probably, but I usually have a swim before dinner. Oh, and leave Mother to sleep – she hasn't got back into her usual routine yet.'

I noticed the washing-up from his breakfast was still sitting in the sink, presumably awaiting my attentions, but since I'd also found the dishwasher I shoved it all in there and closed the door.

Mal was running late and simply dumped me at the car rental place and drove off, just remembering to kiss me at the last minute. There had been last night's phone call too: they must be working him very hard.

The car was small and also – oh, happy, happy day! – air-conditioned, but my legs trembled with tiredness as I sat there in the driver's seat feeling totally disorientated.

The lady behind the desk kindly came out and explained the workings in the most soothing accent in the world. 'And just tuck your left foot back out of the way and pretend you haven't got one,' she added as a parting piece of advice. This was easier said than done, but after making a few circuits round the car park, I gingerly set off back to Paradise Falls.

Remembering the twenty-five-mile-an-hour speed limit in built-up areas I crawled along and a small string of cars appeared behind me like an entourage.

It seemed very slow, and when I peered at the dial again I realised that the speedometer was in kilometres. I was doing twenty-five *kilometres* an hour instead of twenty-five *miles*. Was that good or bad? I clenched the wheel hard in both hands as if the car might make a bolt for it at any moment, but we seemed to be practically at a standstill.

'Past the airport, turn left,' I muttered to myself, trying to remember the way. There was the big supermarket . . . so this morning we'd come out of a turning nearly opposite . . .

'My God, but I'm brilliant!' With a triumphant rendition of 'Sisters Are Doing It for Themselves', I pulled up outside Paradise Falls.

Inside, all was quiet, so I cautiously popped my head into Mrs M.'s room to see if she'd died; but she hadn't, just sleeping the sleep of the righteous. She looked about three hundred and ninety and as frail as a bundle of dry twigs wrapped in thin leather.

I found a bottle of a soft drink called Ting in the fridge, added plenty of ice from the crusher and then retrieved Mal's instructions from under the lump of coral. The bumper bundle included helpful hints like directions for using the washing machine, a shopping list, what he thought we should have for dinner that night . . . well, you get the picture. He might as well have hung a banner out front saying: 'Welcome, new housekeeper/dogsbody', and so far there hadn't been any hint of 'Welcome, lover!' to sweeten it.

I was starting to feel angry; and if I'm expected to work all through my supposed holiday, then I'm going to use Mal's guilt card to get some cool, pretty clothes, and some big clips to get my hot hair up off my neck too.

I took my drink and a bundle of tourist brochures, and went and lay on a recliner in the shade, remembering Tanya's parting gift and anointing myself with expensive unguent first.

I dozed for an hour or so, then woke to find a tall, handsome young gardener swiping at the vegetation with the most enormous blade, which he called his cutlass – and I wasn't about to argue with him. He engaged me in soft-voiced conversation as he languidly tidied and removed fallen coconuts.

'Don't you go sitting under the trees,' he warned me. 'Coconuts drop on your head, you know about it.'

He was right: every so often you do hear crashes and dull thuds as they hit the decking or sand, which makes you wonder about all those holiday brochures where bronzed women are lying in hammocks strung between palm trees. There's probably a special hospital department for concussed tourists.

Between the decking and the beach lay a strip of white sand, edged with conch shells and large, brain-like lumps of coral, which the gardener raked into a neat pattern. It seemed so much easier than lawn-mowing.

Mrs M. finally emerged in time to eat a cold lunch of last night's leftovers washed down with copious amounts of hot tea, but I am now a Ting-driven thing – I love its refreshing, grapefruit taste.

After that I left her sitting bolt upright on a wooden chair in the shade with a virgin Booker winner while I explored the beach. I just couldn't resist it, though I had sense enough to borrow Mrs M.'s umbrella against the hot sun. I must get one; it's a good idea even if I look ridiculous.

The sea inside the reef was as warm and salty as fish soup, with sea grass lining the bottom, but dotted with rather sharp coral. I had a swim in the pool instead, which was surprisingly cold, then lay in the shade again lethargically, still feeling horribly hot but relaxed. Limp as a Dali clock, even.

Mentally I was still functioning at about fifty per cent below normal, and although I hoped I might be semi-human by next morning I wasn't holding my breath: it was so hot my brains just seemed to be running right out of my ears, and my temper was on a much shorter fuse than usual.

I decided to ignore Mal's instructions: there was enough food and drink to see any normal crowd of sixty or so people through a couple of days, and I would live to shop another day.

'I need a cool dress, and there are some great-sounding shops in the malls off Seven Mile Beach,' I murmured, studying the brochures again.

Mrs M., who to all intents and purposes had appeared dead, opened one beady eye. '*And* a fancy needlework shop,' she contributed, so clearly she wouldn't be entirely averse to a bit of retail therapy.

'Hadn't you better start dinner, Frances? I expect Maldwyn will be home soon.'

Ting-Driven Thing

Last night it became clear to me that Mr Hyde has gained the upper hand since Mal came out here.

When he arrived home to discover that I hadn't done the supermarket shopping, cooked a wonderful dinner, sorted the laundry, passed on some instructions to the gardener, or any of the other things he left on his list . . . well, he wasn't pleased, let's put it like that. I'm not sure he remembers the difference between the status of a wife and an unsatisfactory employee any more. Is his love conditional on how I look and behave? I'm beginning to wonder. And he may still appear to be the Mal I fell in love with, but a stranger is looking out of his eyes.

When he also found he had run out of rum (a new drinking habit, this one) he threw a minor tantrum, though there was enough alcohol in the house already to satisfy even a hardened drinker, even leaving aside his mother's enormous bottle of duty-free tipple. (Mrs M. has signed the pledge, but it had an exclusion clause in regard to sherry.)

When I pointed out that I had been too tired and

hot to run around after him the very first day I got here, he said that *he* had had to work in that heat right from the moment he arrived on Grand Cayman.

'Yes, but you *came* here to work, and I supposedly came for a holiday!' I snapped, and Mrs M. said acidly that she hoped her presence hadn't increased my heavy burden, and personally *she* had always found her wifely duties to be a joy.

'Some of them are more joyful than others,' I said tartly, and started slapping out the cold meats and salad, but Mrs M. barely picked at hers.

Mal finally asked her if she wasn't hungry.

'I can't seem to face cold cuts again, Maldwyn. But it's all right, I don't expect Frances to produce a hot meal just for *me*,' she said, martyred.

'You said earlier you never had any appetite in the heat,' I pointed out, 'but if you want something hot there's a pizza in the freezer I could cook for you.'

She shuddered. 'Oh, no, thank you – I think that's teenage food. I'll just have a cup of tea and a biscuit later.'

Mal cast me a look of deep reproach, as though I were trying to starve his mother to death, though presumably they managed to survive before my arrival. I mean, someone bought the pizzas and the other fast food in the freezer; they didn't grow in there on their own like some strange fungus.

'If I've got to cook every day in this heat I'll probably expire!' I protested. 'It's ridiculous!'

'I'm sure I can manage to do all the cooking,' Mrs M. said nobly. 'Perhaps if Fran wouldn't mind just taking me to the supermarket tomorrow and helping me carry out the heavier bags?'

'I won't hear of it, Mother! You know the doctor said you should have a complete rest. No strain or exertion at all.'

Of course, then I had to say *I'd* do it: if her wonky heart conks out just as she's hefting a casserole out of the oven, or she drops a pan of scalding custard on her foot because of her rheumaticy little paws, it would all be my fault. But I most definitely am not a happy bunny. What's more, the skin round my eyes has gone prickly, the first sign of my sun allergy, though only a bit. I've taken an antihistamine pill, so hopefully between that and Tanya's cream I will not turn into a complete Elephant Woman like the time we went to the south of France.

After I'd cleared up dinner and put the dishwasher on, I retired outside on to the dark patio with the sound of waves on the coral beach and the odd thud of a coconut, and called Ma on the mobile.

'Hi, Ma, it's me!'

'Frannie? Did you have a good trip?'

'No, it was horrible, but it's lovely here, only very, very hot.'

'I hope Mal is looking after you.'

'Of course, Ma,' I lied. 'He's hired a little car for me so we can go and look at all the sights.'

I didn't add that the first one seemed destined to be the supermarket.

She grunted. 'And his mother? *I* wouldn't have thrust myself in between a husband and wife when they've been apart as long as you and Mal have!'

'No . . . but she is going home in a week, and then we'll be alone.'

'Apart from his ex-wife, you mean!'

'Apparently Alison is off the island on business for a couple of weeks – Mrs M. told me.'

In the band of light from the window I saw one of the shells on the deck get up and start walking sideways. As if this was a signal, suddenly all round my feet there seemed to be soft dragging noises, and the air was filled with clicks, taps and rattles . . .

'I – I'll have to go, Ma,' I said nervously. 'I need another early night to try and get back on an even keel. My body doesn't know whether it's day or night yet.'

'Well, you take care of yourself, and relax. Don't try to do too much in that heat.'

Some chance, I thought, switching the phone off, and I ran back inside.

Mrs M. was sitting in front of the TV knitting something sweaty while she watched an old British sitcom. Mal was at the dining table tapping away at his laptop in a concentrated sort of way, and hardly noticed when I said I was going to bed.

It seems to me that if I want any kind of happy hols then I had better take steps to encourage the return of Dr Jekyll. Maybe Appleton premium rum is the antidote.

This morning I woke before Mal, feeling nearly normal, and decided to try to reprise my former role as part-time Stepford Wife – the one who boils his egg and makes his toast and tea while he showers – even though I am now out of the habit.

I actually got the smile of approval when he came in, fragrant and freshly shaved, and we breakfasted together quite pleasantly since his egg, by some fluke, was just right and I hadn't burned the toast. I told him I was off to the supermarket this morning.

'And the liquor store,' he reminded me. 'It's in the same building. You can use your credit card for the shopping. What are you going to do this afternoon?'

'I haven't decided yet, though possibly the turtle farm,' I said off the top of my head. It was one of the few attractions on the shopping mall side of George Town, but I didn't mention my intention of hitting the dress shops in search of something cooler to wear.

'I don't think Mother will want to see the turtles,' he said dubiously. 'She'd prefer the botanic park.'

'So would I, but I thought it would be better to do it on a day when we don't have to go shopping too. I wonder if they've got any roses.'

'You and your roses!' he said fairly affectionately, then kissed me goodbye and left, looking ten times cooler than I felt. I settled down with coffee and the map of the island.

Even I couldn't miss the supermarket, it was so close, but the turtle farm was right the other side of George Town. There was a road to it around the coast that would take me past Seven Mile Beach, where all the malls were.

I would see how wilted I felt after the shopping.

Although Mal had opened all the doors and windows the second he got up, letting the cool air out and the warm in, it wasn't yet unbearably hot.

Mrs M. loved the supermarket, and we were in there all morning. I got most of the things on Mal's list, plus fresh fruit and vegetables, but I kept adding stuff to the trolley, like Reese's Peanut Butter Cups, strangely flavoured ice creams, a packet of sugar cane pieces and loads of Ting.

After all, there was no point in dieting now Mal had *seen* me, so I might as well enjoy my holiday as much as I could in the circumstances.

Mrs M.'s purchases were more in the tea-towel-and-household-fragrances line, though she collected armfuls of American magazines from a stand near the checkout.

Just as well Mal had told me to pay for everything with the guilt card – the total was horrendous. Still, most of it was stuff on his list or for his mother, so he can't complain.

I loaded the shopping and Mrs M. into the car and then popped into that den of iniquity, the liquor store. It was blessedly cool, but I couldn't linger since I was conscious of my melting frozen goods and Ma-in-law in the hot car outside.

Quickly I collected the expensive French wines and the premium rum on Mal's requisition order and took them to the till, passing an attractive display of boxed rum cakes, apparently a local speciality, in various flavours.

On the counter was a plate of pieces for tasting . . . melt-in-the-mouth nuggets of deliciousness. (Maybe I should be writing advertising slogans?) I came out with a chocolate one, though had they not been hideously expensive I'd have had one of each flavour. It was quite a small cake – I hadn't gone *quite* mad – but maybe I could get one of the bigger ones later?

I managed to jam the bottles into the car around Mrs M., seated regally in the back, and set out for home, the taste of heaven on my tongue . . . which for some reason made me think of Gabe.

But that rum cake is really something, even better than chocolate – and we all know what *that's* better than . . . and there I went, thinking of Gabe again. Why *him*? Why not my husband?

When we got back, Mrs M. went to freshen up while I carried everything in and stowed it away, the doors and windows firmly shut and the ceiling fans on. I hoped Mrs M. wouldn't rat on me to Mal, but when she came back she didn't seem to notice, just sat gloating over her new tea towel, home fragrance and magazine collection, which she spread all over the coffee table. At least she was happy. Let's hope she stays that way when I present her with a sandwich and fresh fruit for lunch.

'This satellite television *sounds* all right, all those channels,' I said, flicking from one to another, looking for something to listen to while I finished making lunch, which is one advantage of having an open-plan living area, 'only they seem to repeat the same things over and over again until everyone in the universe must have seen them millions of times.'

'Then they shouldn't watch so much television,' Mrs M. said severely, diverting her gaze from *Stitch-Up Monthly*, or whatever exciting periodical had been her choice. Then she added suddenly, 'Stop!'

I stared at her in surprise, my finger hovering over the remote.

'It's *Restoration Gardener*, my favourite programme!' she said reverently as the familiar title came up.

'Is it? Did Mal tell you that he's doing the gardens at Plas Gwyn, Rhodri Gwyn-Whatmire's house?' I said, hastily slapping a plate of sandwiches on the corner of the table and sitting down in a wicker armchair. 'They're doing it now – I'm going to miss most of it.'

'I'll look out for that one. Gabriel Weston's *such* a nice man,' she said as that familiar face appeared on the screen, smiling warmly.

Clearly she never reads any gossip magazines.

'Did Mal tell you he's also bought Fairy Glen from Ma?'

'So ridiculous, keeping two houses on at her age!' she said disapprovingly. 'I hope she got a good price for it.'

'Yes, she's using it to go on a round-the-world cruise.'

'Ridiculous!' she said again, but absently, for her attention was now riveted on the screen . . . as was mine.

Suddenly I felt *overwhelmingly* homesick, which was silly – I haven't been here five minutes.

Mrs M. declined to visit the turtle farm, but seemed happy to be left on the sofa with her magazines and TV, so I boldly went where I hadn't been before.

It was a pleasant drive round the coast past pretty, brightly painted houses and the tourist bustle of George Town harbour, before joining the Seven Mile Beach road. It was edged with shopping plazas and there was much more traffic – including an open-topped Jeep full of young men in shades verging from pinky-tan to hot chocolate, like a delectable selection box. Every one a winner.

The air conditioning cooled me to a comfortable temperature, but getting out at the turtle farm was like opening an oven door, and I'd have got back in except that I wanted to be able to tell Mal where I'd been.

But the huge turtles desolately circling their tanks, or trying clumsily to climb out, were strangely fascinating, though terribly sad. I thought how stale the water must taste to them after the open sea and how boring their captive lives. I know they have a huge turtle release programme at the farm, but even so . . .

I remained sombre until I stopped at my chosen shopping plaza on the way back and indulged in some retail therapy. I found a little dress shop called The Mermaid's Cave and went *berserk*.

Three light, cool dresses, a batik sarong and an umbrella shaped like a giant pink water lily later (let's hope there are no matching giant frogs on the island), I emerged, blinking, into the strong sunshine. The guilt card had taken another beating, and my spending had acquired an unreal Monopoly-money feel to it. It was just numbers.

My skin was still a bit tight and itchy round my eyes

with the rash, but it didn't seem to be getting worse. I bought aloe vera gel in a pharmacy to cool it down, and butterfly clips to get my hot, heavy hair off my neck.

Back home Mrs M. was asleep on a lounger in the shade, my copy of *Skint Old Northern Woman* magazine on the deck next to her. Bet that made a change from knitting patterns! I just hope she doesn't realise the comic strip and some of the cartoons are mine.

I had a cooling swim in the pool, and then began preparing one of Mal's favourite meals, laying the table and opening a bottle of wine, even though I wasn't sure if it would breathe, or just pant in the heat.

Right before he got back I went and put on one of my new dresses and let my hair loose again, and I didn't look half bad, if I said it myself! The soft, sugared-almond shades of the silk dress were flattering, and my face hadn't swollen or gone red to any great extent – just a bit round the eyes. And aloe vera's wonderfully soothing, the pharmacist was right.

I applied a little perfume and make-up, because it's amazing the difference a bit of slap can make, especially when your eyebrows and eyelashes seem to have bleached themselves out of existence overnight, though at least my eyelash tint didn't turn green in the pool, which was one of my biggest fears.

I'm *not* going to think any more about Gabriel – he's part of the past. This is *now*, and I want my handsome, loving husband back, the one I married. He's in there somewhere.

Mal arrived home with a present for me, and when I saw the little jeweller's box my heart started racing a bit, thinking it was a ring.

'Oh, *earrings*,' I said, opening it. 'I mean, how *lovely*! Thank you, Mal. Are they Colombian emeralds?' Ungratefully, I wished I had a microscope so I could get a really good look at them.

'Yes, from the shop in George Town.'

Mrs M. came over to look, and sniffed. 'I thought it might be a ring. If she's a married woman, she should wear one.'

'Oh, Fran doesn't like rings.'

I stared at him. What *could* he mean? I don't wear one because he hasn't given me one!

However, the gift set the tone for a happy evening, and Mal got right into the spirit of the thing as soon as he smelled the dinner cooking, even shutting the doors and windows and putting the air conditioning on – major concessions.

It was the first time I'd actually felt really comfortable since I'd arrived. As I cooled down I seemed to feel myself turning back into a different person: one who could think.

He opened a second bottle of wine with dinner and got very mellow, kissing the back of my neck while I was cooking and his mother was out of the room.

Mrs M. had a nip of sherry, acquired a spot of colour

in each cheek and forgot to complain about the food; but afterwards she sat determinedly between us on the sofa, knitting for chastity, so eventually I said I was going to bed.

Mrs M. immediately put her knitting away and said she would also go.

'I could do with an early night too,' Mal agreed, but I heard his phone ring as I closed the door and got into bed – yet another late-night call! They do seem to expect their employees to be on tap twenty-four hours a day out here. Still, I hoped he would soon follow me.

He hadn't turned the air conditioning off, and the room was cool and comfortable. I could stay awake and . . .

I awoke briefly in the middle of the night and could hear Mal's breathing, fast asleep in his own bed.

Maybe he didn't want to wake me when he found me asleep? No, he would have done if he'd wanted to, he's not *that* unselfish!

So perhaps he's taking his promise to his mother more seriously than I thought? And his phone call must have gone on a bit too.

The air conditioning was off again, but though the fan whirred and the room was still pleasantly cool it took me ages to go back to sleep.

The strange rattling noises at the window didn't help.

I woke up again feeling slightly happier – until I looked

in a mirror. Although my swollen eyelids are improving, the rash has left sore red rings round them. Sometimes when things are almost healed they actually look much worse than before. Or perhaps I'm allergic to Mal as well as the sun.

I got up and made his breakfast, expecting him to be softened and affectionate like he was last night – even sympathetic about the allergy rash. But either he had a severe hangover or Mr Hyde had taken over again, because he seemed if anything rather morose and reproachful, as though I had swung one over on him, though I am not sure how.

'Your face looks dreadful this morning,' he told me, as if I might not have noticed. 'Can't you put something on it?'

'I have, and although it looks worse it's actually almost better. But I'm going to keep under an umbrella when I'm out from now on.'

'A yashmak would be more to the point,' he said cruelly, inspecting his breakfast. 'You've burned the toast.'

'Mal,' I said, remembering something, 'last night I woke up and there was this strange rattling noise at the window to the balcony. Did you hear it?'

'No, but I know what it was. Go outside and look up – they'll probably still be there.'

Puzzled, I went out on the deck, and do you know what had been making the noise? Crabs!

There they were, huge spidery crabs hanging under the eaves, tired after a night of trying to claw their way through the mosquito doors into my bedroom!

Who would have thought it? I mean, I've only just got used to perfectly innocent-looking shells suddenly getting up and wandering about, but this is something else: definitely not the behaviour you *expect* of crabs.

Later, they had mysteriously vanished.

Postcards From the Edge

The next few days settled into a sort of pattern of sightseeing, shopping and housekeeping, though in between I think Mrs M. and I have now watched every *Restoration Gardener* programme at least once.

Unfortunately, she's taken to getting up early every morning and joining us for breakfast, so our only tête-à-tête has become a threesome-reel. She has the sensitivity of a rhinoceros.

Clearly Mal has been living a rich bachelor life, and he's carrying on doing it pretty much as though we weren't here: going off sailing with his new friends, or for a drink after work. And when he does come straight home he changes, has a refreshing swim and then lies on a lounger looking like a tanned and sophisticated escapee from San Tropez, waiting for a drink to be brought out to him and his dinner to be ready.

It's a nice life if you can get it. Or maybe a core of selfishness is every man's Heart of Darkness because, let's face it, Mal's behaviour since I arrived has been so self-absorbed he's practically vanishing up his own exhaust pipe.

He was the one who was so keen for me to come out here – but I'm starting to think he really *did* just want me to entertain his mother and do the house-keeping!

Dear Ma,

Today we went to Hell, which looks exactly like the picture on the front of this card, and was as hot as its namesake. My sun allergy started up, but is now going again. I've been using aloe vera gel, which is wonderfully cooling and takes away the irritation.

Mal is very busy, Mrs M. as you might well expect . . .

Had Mal not wanted to take his mother about I'm sure he wouldn't have been seen out with me, though, actually, now the allergy is in decline phase I don't look *that* horrific. I feel pretty dizzy most of the time, though, but that's mostly the heat.

Mal keeps telling me I'll soon acclimatise like he has (though he's had four months to get used to it), but it hasn't happened yet, and I've come to the conclusion he is some kind of lizard. I think Alphawoman, a.k.a. Blobwoman, is about to discover she has inadvertently married Lizardman, the frill-necked monster terrorising the city: in the shade he's Svelte-Executive Man . . . but let him recharge his batteries on a hot sun lounger and see him change!

'Oh my God, Lizardman is climbing up the building!'
'This is a job for Blobwoman – and here she comes!'

Squirt! Splat!

'She's spraying him with liquid chocolate!'

Slither!

'He can't keep his grip . . . he's falling right into the nets!'

'Blobwoman, you're our hero! Oh, she's vanished. Ms Alphawoman, did you see her go . . . ?'

Housekeeping under these circumstances is not easy, and I have ceased to feel guilty about the clothes – I deserve them! I also deserve the consolation of delicious rum cakes and this wonderful liqueur I've discovered called Mudslide. They're warming the cockles of my heart in a way Mal most certainly is not.

He has taken us out for meals in expensive restaurants a couple of times in the evening, but I found that very boring – what is the point in eating French cuisine on Grand Cayman? Why not local food? Sometimes on the way back we see land crabs on the road, waving their claws threateningly at us. Once there was a cat dining off a squished one, but I can't say I felt sorry for it in the least. I seem to have gone off crabs.

Dear Nia,

This is Seven Mile Beach, though actually it isn't seven miles at all, and I've seen more palm trees in Blackpool, so there isn't much shade about either. It's hot as hell on Cayman but beautiful as Paradise, especially where we are staying – pool, deck, coral beach, palm trees, turquoise sea . . . the works. *I* am not so beautiful due to the red suede rings around my eyes where the allergy was, but they're fading!

Dear Beth and Lachlan,

This is a view of George Town harbour, which is very lively, especially when the cruise ships are in. On Saturday we went round the museum, where I got this great straw hat made by a lady on the island. It's about the only thing to buy I've found that is. The museum is fascinating – a whole slice of island history . . .

I got chatting to one of the ladies in the museum shop while I was trying on hats, and somehow we ended up talking about roses. She said lots of people still had old-fashioned yellow and pink roses in their gardens, which had always done well on the island, and although people tried the new varieties, Cayman didn't really suit them.

Cayman doesn't really suit *me*, either, but I can understand why people try to transplant here, because I think I am falling in love with the place.

Dear Carrie,

You would absolutely adore the botanical park – the gardens are beautiful! There is a lily pond with a cool, shady arbour overlooking it, and lots of roses. Apparently Sir Thomas Lipton and Seven Sisters have traditionally flourished here – must try and find them when I get back home, to remind me. This is the best part of the holiday so far!

A dear little blue iguana, like a miniature dinosaur, walked majestically across one of the paths too. It's made me look more kindly on Mrs M., who is nearly extinct herself.

Dear Rhodri,

Drove up the coast to see these blowholes today, and my ma-in-law poked me in the back with her umbrella and nearly sent me headfirst in there! Don't think this was an attempt on my life, though, just trying to catch my attention. I am the chauffeur and so not really supposed to be enjoying myself. I bought a chilled coconut with a straw in it from a nearby roadside stand, which was delicious, but when the man chopped it open afterwards for me to eat, it didn't taste particularly of anything.

Well, I'm *almost* sure she didn't mean to push me in – and with my stomach I'd probably have got wedged like a cork in a bottle anyway. But it was a tricky moment, slipping about on the sharp, wet rocks.

Dear Rosie,

We've just spent a couple of hours wandering round the shops in George Town, and I'm writing this sitting at a lovely open-fronted restaurant waiting for Mal to come and join us for lunch.

This afternoon we're going to visit the pirates' graves and caves, this being one of the few things we haven't seen yet. The apartment is lovely, and this morning there was a huge cruise ship moored on the horizon, like an improbable mirage.

Apart from the housekeeping, I have now fallen into a routine of going on expeditions to see the sights every day, and since there aren't that many of them I've already pretty well covered the island. Everywhere is starting to look pleasantly familiar, and I've spotted lots of roses in people's gardens.

Sometimes Mrs M. comes with me, though she often seems content to stay at the apartment instead. On Sunday she insisted on going to a church service, but I don't think she really enjoyed it: when she got back she said she thought religious observance should be quiet and serious, not joyful, and God would be their judge, bless her Calvinistic little soul.

Today being Monday, the maid came, which gave her someone other than me to criticise. But actually they got on well in a godly, fire-and-brimstone way, and Mrs M. not only showed her the way to clean windows with crumpled newspaper, but also exhibited the glories of her tea-towel collection, a sign of great favour.

I hardly seem to be seeing anything of Mal, he's working such long hours – and then going off doing his own thing half the time! And it's not as though he's really pleasant to me when he *is* around.

I'm starting to feel I'm married to a stranger. I don't

really think I want to be left alone with him when Mrs M. leaves, and he won't talk about what we are going to do – or even whether he has booked those few days off like he said he would so we could be together. He just says we'll discuss it after his mother has gone home.

And the final blow was when I just casually mentioned wedding vow renewal ceremonies, and he looked so absolutely aghast that I'm convinced the thought never entered his head and the printout was an accident!

Later I asked him why he was so insistent I buy a special dress for the holiday, and he said I always looked a mess, and since he's expecting his friend Justin to drop by for dinner one night, it would be good if he could actually feel proud of me for once!

Mr Hyde again, you see.

I actually visited the botanic park for the third time today, but on my own, since Mrs M. wanted to stay at home. Whatever she says about watching too much television, she is now addicted to it, so I was free to do what I liked.

I'd already walked the nature trail last time, so I headed straight for the roses and then the little pavilion overlooking the lily pond, where I lay down on one of the reclining chairs in the shade.

A gardener was wading about the deep pond in waist-high waders, tending the lilies, and it was a lovely scene. Despite all the worries, the heat and Mal's horrible attitude, I had a feeling that I would never forget Grand Cayman: it has its own magic.

One day I will look back at my time on the island and only remember the sunny hours – and God knows, there are enough of those!

Today Mrs M. decreed that she would like to see all the expensive shopping outlets at Kirk Freeport out of interest in the base pursuits of Mammon (i.e., the tourists off the huge cruise ships).

Really, though, I expect she was just keen to look at the designer shops, though it's not my cup of tea. I was never going to be able to afford any of it, and in any case, the only person who knows whether you've shelled out a fortune for a Cartier watch or are wearing a cheap copy is yourself. The Mickey Mouse one that Nia gave me as a joke fortieth birthday present seems to be working just fine.

Even Mrs M. was flagging by the time we got to the huge Colombian emeralds showroom where my earrings came from. It was cool and dark, and had a by-now-familiar expensive smell. Perhaps it's the tang of money?

All my pores immediately snapped shut, which was a welcome relief, so I stood there just inside the doorway like a half-melted tallow candle, letting my eyes adjust and thinking how I never wanted to go out into the brash heat of day again. Mal's mother determinedly marched up and down between the showcases, loudly uttering disparaging remarks about the quality and prices, and I pretended I wasn't with her.

When I spotted Mal's friend Justin, I had to look

twice to be quite sure because he looked so very odd – but then, the lighting in there was poor.

He saw me at more or less the same time and his glance flicked in a startled way over my rolling figure – though it lingered on the cleavage exposed by one of my new, more flattering dresses – and came back to my still slightly sore and reddened face.

'*Frannie?*' he said, and Mrs M. looked up sharply, her bird-bright eyes going from one to the other of us.

'Yes, it's me! How are you, Justin? I didn't expect to run into you here!'

'Well, you know.' He shrugged. 'I chartered a yacht for a couple of months and I've been around the islands. Mal's invited me for dinner tonight, didn't he tell you?'

'No – he did mention that you might be coming at some point, just not *when*.'

Mrs M. had shuffled up sideways like a parrot on a perch, and was observing us with extreme curiosity.

'Mrs Morgan, you remember Justin?' I said.

'Is that *really* you, Justin?' she said incredulously. 'Well, I'd never have known you!'

'How are you? Enjoying your holiday, both of you?'

'I didn't come expecting to enjoy myself,' Mrs M. told him severely. 'I came from *duty*.'

'Right,' he agreed. 'Fran, how do you like Cayman?' He looked me directly in the face this time, rather than down the cleavage. 'You seem to have caught the sun.'

'Oh, that's not sunburn, it's allergy,' Mrs M. told him. 'And it's getting better – you should have seen it the first few days! Frances has only got to look at a sunbeam and she comes out in the most peculiar rash.'

'The sun doesn't suit me, unfortunately.'

'You'd get on much better in the heat if you lost some weight,' my dear mother-in-law said tartly.

'You *have* got a bit plumper,' Justin agreed, as though I might not have noticed. 'Not that a bit of extra weight doesn't suit you,' he added hastily, his eyes straying to my neckline again. 'There used to be nothing of you!'

Mrs M. invited him to go along with us to meet Mal for lunch, but he said he had something else arranged, though he didn't say what.

'Mal, we've just seen Justin,' I began, the moment we got to the restaurant.

'And he was surprised to see how heavy Frances has become,' Mrs M. added, with her usual complete lack of tact.

'Oh? Did he tell you he was coming to dinner tonight? He might be around for a few days too, so perhaps he could take you out and about a bit, Fran, while I'm busy,' he suggested generously – and this from a man who used to go green-eyed if he thought I was even *looking* at someone else!

'I'd rather take myself out and about,' I said coldly, because not only was this really special holiday not turning out the way I'd hoped, but my Great Expectations were in danger of turning into Apocalypse Now.

Someone was singing 'Things Can Only Get Better' in my head, and I must have been humming along, because Mrs M. gave me a repressive look.

'When is Alison coming back, did you say,

Maldwyn?' she asked. 'Only I thought I caught sight of her earlier today in the distance.'

'She's still away, as far as I'm aware,' Mal said with an uneasy glance at me. 'Must have just been someone who looked a bit like her.'

'No, my long vision is good, as you know. I am almost certain – and if she *is* back you must tell her that I can't see her,' Mrs M. said. 'I'm not at all happy with the situation.'

She's not happy? How does she think I feel – especially now I know how small the island is!

'I will if I run into her – but I probably won't,' he said casually, but with another betraying glance at me – and I suddenly wondered if Alison had ever been off the island at all. Or just lying low.

'Mal, I really need to talk to you – *alone*,' I said pointedly.

He looked at his watch. 'Well, it'll have to be later, Fran, I've got a meeting. Now, what are you two doing this afternoon?'

'The food shopping for dinner this evening, of course, seeing I've only just found out. I don't suppose you want cold cuts?' I said sourly.

The Bartered Bride

I can't believe that with the temperature hotter than summer ever gets at home, I'm cooking a full roast chicken dinner in a strange kitchen – and without even the benefit of the ceiling fans, since all the doors and windows are open.

Mal came home from work early today, but the whispered argument we had in the bedroom has not cleared the air any. He's still insisting that Alison *has* been off the island and he's no idea if she's back yet, but I'm not sure I believe this horrible new Mal about *anything*.

Marriage used to seem to me like a chess game, all advancing and retreating with the occasional checkmate; sometimes you even had to sacrifice the odd pawn, since you needed to keep your eye on the bigger picture.

Now suddenly I feel that I'm taking part in a Thomas Hardy novel instead, and although the scenery is delightful the odds are so stacked against me I might as well abandon hope now.

Jude the obscure is lying in the sizzling sun out on

the deck with a long cold drink, while his little bag-of-bones-and-acid mother sits knitting some sort of steel-grey straitjacket under a palm tree. It's probably a present for me, though I haven't forgotten the opportune poke in the back at the blowhole that nearly brought an abrupt end to my holiday, so maybe it's Mrs M. who should be in the straitjacket?

The only chickens the supermarket had were cook-from-frozen ones, which rather flies in the face of everything I've ever been taught about cooking poultry.

By the time it had been roasting for an hour or two the temperature in the kitchen area was reaching meltdown, and so was I. Opening the huge fridge I tried to get in, only of course it was full of food and drink so I just pressed myself against it for a few wonderful moments.

My legs have turned to jelly, my head is swimming and I'm about to pass out. This is ridiculous – I'm putting the ceiling fans on.

Mal, coming in for more cold beer, found me in a wilted condition and said he expected I would feel the heat more, being overweight, while it does not seem to bother dear Mother in the least.

'No, but she's not slaving in a hot kitchen, is she?' I pointed out, and added menacingly that if he switched the fans off I would kill him. How I wished I were driving round the island in my little car with its efficient air conditioning and the radio tuned into a jolly local station!

The ready-stuffed chicken, solid as a lead bullet, is roasting away as instructed, so we will see if dear Mother's metabolism can cope with Salmonella Surprise later. The packet of bread sauce I sneaked out in my luggage has been decanted into a bowl, though of course Mrs M. will know it's not home-made the minute she tastes it. But then it will be too late for her to go all stiff-lipped and insist on doing it herself from scratch, 'with her bad heart'.

Come to that, the oven is big enough to cook *her* in, trussed and with an orange in her mouth, if my homicidal impulses should rise even further. I never knew I had them before, but now the heat just makes my brains run out of my ears and my temper rise . . .

This gave me a wonderful new cartoon idea, which I jotted down quickly before I forgot. I haven't finished a single drawing since I got here, mainly because I feel so hideously hot, sweaty and uncomfortable all the time, except when I am in the pool. I wonder if I could get an underwater sketchpad? But anyway, I can work up all the ideas when I get home.

And forget what people say about the sun making you feel sexy: the one night Mal left the air conditioning on was the only time I felt truly interested, *or* Mal, come to that. I simply don't believe any longer that he's abstaining from respect for his mother's wishes, so perhaps a combination of my excess weight and Elephant Woman appearance has had something to do with it.

Justin is joining us shortly for Salmonella Surprise and rum cake. It couldn't happen to a better person,

Mrs M. apart. No, that was mean: Justin has never done me any harm, apart from the gleam in his eye and roving hand, easily dealt with. And I may not have *that* problem any more – he hadn't seen me for ages, so my appearance obviously came as a *very* large surprise.

Having reached a point where everything was cooking under its own steam and almost ready, I went to change, and when I got back found Justin had arrived and everyone had come indoors. Dusk is mosquito time, and until it gets properly dark even Mal doesn't sit outside.

The Colombian emerald shop had been poorly lit, and although I'd thought Justin looked a little odd, seeing him now I was stunned: what was left of his hair was dyed a strange shade of green and sticking up at the front like a cockatoo crest, and it clashed horridly with his red Hawaiian shirt.

Aloha.

The chicken was very peculiar, but fortunately Justin had brought lots of bubbly to wash it down with, and after that no one much noticed. Even Mrs M. allowed Justin to persuade her to try a glass. Mind you, it didn't stop her giving me a very suspicious look after her first taste of bread sauce, and later I found her peering into the pedal bin; but I'd already been across to the trash can with the empty packet and other incriminating evidence, double-bagged.

Then she apologised to Justin about the lack of 'a real dessert', but I don't think there could be anything more delicious than chocolate rum cake ... except maybe the banana one.

Afterwards, while I stacked the dishwasher, Mal and Justin retired to the now-dark deck to drink and talk boats and money, while Mrs M. snored gently in front of the TV. I was dripping with sweat again by the time I'd finished, so went to have a cool shower and put on a fresh dress, even though I knew it would be limp in five minutes.

Through the reopened bedroom doors wafted the lazy sound of the two men talking, and my attention was arrested by hearing Justin say, 'Why on earth did you let Fran get so fat? She was such a slim little thing last time I saw her!'

'I didn't let her – in fact I've done everything I can think of to get her to lose weight! I mean, she's still *pretty*, but I have a real thing about fat.'

'Gross,' agreed Justin. 'And that allergy doesn't help.'

'Believe it or not, it's miles better than it was. I was ashamed to own her.'

'Well, *I'm* not taking her off your hands, looking like that,' Justin said lazily. 'She's your problem.'

'Thanks for reminding me,' Mal said, and then their voices faded as they moved away.

I just sat on the bed and cried silently. Is this how men usually talk when they think they are alone, even about their wives? And what did Justin mean, 'take her off your hands'?

The tears stung the pink and tender skin around my eyes, and I felt despondent and so depressed. I wanted to run home to my mother; but then something stiffened my spine and I thought, no, this is something I would have to sort out myself.

And really, there's no escaping the conclusion that if your husband *acts* as though he doesn't love you, *talks* as though he doesn't love you and *looks* as though he doesn't love you . . . then probably he *doesn't* love you.

It was to hell with the hostess bit after that, and I got absolutely slammed on Mudslide, the wonderful liqueur that fulfils all cravings and soothes the worried breast. Also numbs the worried head after a while too.

I don't remember Justin's departure, or really anything else much after that, and this morning I had the hangover from hell and a dark cloud of depression hanging over me, so I didn't exactly spring out of bed at dawn and start cooking breakfast.

Let them eat cake.

When I finally emerged, Mrs M. looked as if she regretted having agreed to share a roof with the Scarlet Woman, and the only thing she seemed to be communing with was the TV.

Being a Saturday, I knew Mal would do exactly what he felt like doing all day, regardless of the rest of us: lying outside reading, swimming, walking along the beach, or popping out to unnamed business in his monster machine. So, in a spirit of rebellion, I took a leaf out of his book and pleased myself: I had a nice swim, lots of long, cold, non-alcoholic drinks, a snooze on the bed with the ceiling fan turned on, lunched on rum cake and then drew rather dark-edged cartoons in the shadiest corner of the deck.

If anyone ate anything cooked that day it wasn't done by me.

Later, when Mal had gone off on one of his mysterious and now suspicious solo drives, I went down and sat on the beach under my large pink water-lily umbrella and called Nia, mobile to mobile.

'Nia, it's me!'

'Fran? Is everything all right?'

'No, not really – but don't tell anyone, especially Ma. I don't want to worry her. Mal's been a total pig since I've been out here, and I have a strong suspicion he's been seeing a lot of Alison. He told me she was off the island, but Mrs M. is sure she's seen her.'

'Can't you have it out with him?'

'Not with Mrs M. about – it's impossible! I'll have to wait until she goes home. How are things with you?'

'Fine. I'm up at Plas Gwyn now, in my studio. You'd be amazed at how the rose garden is taking shape, *and* all the rest of it – and the filming doesn't go on all the time, so that's not too intrusive, either.'

'How are the hens?'

'They're OK – and, actually, Gabe offered to do them. I hope you don't mind, Fran. He's been looking after your roses too.'

'I – well, no, I don't *really* mind,' I said slowly.

'To be truthful, I'm practically living up here with Rhodri now, so it was very convenient when he offered,' she confessed.

'Nia!'

'Don't get excited. I don't see how it can possibly work out, long term.'

'Don't be such a pessimist – of course it will!'

'We'll see,' she said cautiously.

'Nia, did Gabe mention that night when he saw me with Tom?'

'Not a word, and –' She broke off and said more faintly, 'Hi, Gabe!'

'He's there now? Don't –'

'I've got Fran on the phone – do you want to say anything to her?' I heard her ask.

'Hello, Fran,' said that familiar deep, warm voice, and for some reason my eyes filled with tears and my legs went trembly. 'Your Mermaid and Golden Showers are going to make a full recovery, but I don't think I'd ever realised quite how stupid hens were before.'

I thanked him for looking after everything for me, and then told him about the roses I'd seen out here. 'I don't know about Sir Thomas Lipton, but I'm pretty sure Seven Sisters is old enough for the Regency garden.'

I'd quite forgotten that I was clocking up an enormous phone bill until Nia reminded him where I was calling from. 'Champney's Pink Cluster,' he said quickly before she grabbed the phone back.

Strangely comforted, I found I was humming 'I Will Survive' – and so, apparently, will my savaged roses.

I should have tried the self-centered male route before, since I'm suddenly being treated with much more respect.

Mind you, Mrs M. seems to think I'm suffering from some sort of delusional state brought on by sunstroke, though actually I'm feeling much, much better apart from trying to fend off the dark cloud of depression. I can feel it hovering, but I'm not giving in: I'm a rebel with a cause – my sanity.

No one's mentioning the lack of hot dinners, they just seem grateful for anything; nor does Mal complain that I keep turning the fans and air conditioning on, though of course he follows me round switching them off again when he's here.

Mrs M. announced that she had now seen everything on the island, and would spend the last days of her holiday around the apartment, so I take myself off to my favourite spots as the fancy takes me, especially the botanic park, where I can sit in the pavilion by the pond and feel peaceful.

Strangely enough, I seem to have lost a little weight without trying. Perhaps it's simply melted off – or maybe it's because my appetite is not great in such heat. Whatever the reason, I must be looking better, since Mal has ceased to avert his eyes from me with that look of fastidious distaste, and indeed has started to be quite kind in his way. But he'll have to be a damn sight kinder before I forgive him for what I overheard him say to Justin – *and* I want the truth about Alison.

Once his mother has gone home and we are alone at last I need to tell him just how strangely he's been behaving these last few months, but the thought is making me feel very nervous. *Can* we clear the air, put everything behind us and recreate our love? Or are we way beyond that?

I'm probably sending out inadvertent subliminal

messages by my constant humming of songs like 'Where Did Our Love Go?' and 'Band of Gold'.

Not that I've ever *had* a band of gold.

Lost in Space

Mrs M.'s plane left in the early evening, and we both went to the airport to see her off. She turned unexpectedly gracious as we parted, allowing me to kiss her cheek, and saying that she wished me well, as though I were embarking on some new venture. Perhaps I am.

'You'll look after Frances, won't you, Maldwyn?'

'Of course, Mother,' he assured her, putting an affectionate arm around me, but she gave him a severe look and he dropped it again.

Once she'd vanished through the gate he said abruptly, 'Come on, let's go home, we need to talk.'

This sounded ominous, but then the air certainly needed clearing, and the sooner it was over the better.

When we got back darkness had fallen and Mal said he would shower and change and then join me out on the deck.

'Don't you want anything to eat?' I asked.

'No, I'm not hungry,' he said shortly, and vanished into the bedroom. He was in there for ages.

I sat sipping Ting, since I felt I needed a clear head.

Beyond the deck the moon silvered the sea and the lights of a huge moored cruise ship seemed to hang improbably somewhere between sky and water. A coconut dropped off a tree and bounced nearby with a loud clunk, and I hastily moved my chair further away.

Mal finally emerged and sat a little way off, where I couldn't quite make out his expression clearly.

'Well, five more days, with just you and me,' I ventured, trying to ease into what I wanted to say to him, which was more along the 'Why have you changed?' and 'Is something going on?' lines; but he wasn't playing by my rules.

'No,' he said flatly. 'Actually, there *is* no more you and me. Things have changed. You aren't the girl I thought you were, and I don't think you ever really loved me. I was just a meal ticket and a good home, like Alison told me when we married.'

'She – she did? You've discussed me with her? And how *can* you say I never loved you? How can you say such horrible things?'

'Because since I came out here I can see things clearly – and our marriage was a mistake practically from the start.'

'But – but you said this holiday would be a new start, a second honeymoon! And we needed time to get over our loss. Remember all the things you said when I was in hospital?'

'That was then, this is now, Fran!' he said impatiently. 'And I want a divorce.'

'A – divorce?'

'Alison and I intend getting married again, and we hope to make our home out here. My contract's been extended for two years.'

I stared at him, stunned and shaking. Even though I knew things hadn't been right between us lately, it was still a shock. And was this the man who once said to me, 'You've been hurt, but you can depend on me, Fran – I'll look after you'?

'I've been in contact with my solicitor back home. I hope you're going to be civilised about this, Fran.'

There was a silence between us, though the insect life chirped, squeaked and chirruped in the background as usual.

'Civilised?' I echoed eventually. 'And if you'd already made your mind up you wanted a divorce, why did you let me come out here and string me along, all this time?'

'Alison thought that under the circumstances I had to let you and Mother come out here. It was all arranged.'

'Big of her! But how *could* you? And all those times you've gone off in your car, not saying where ... I suppose you were seeing her!'

'I'm not discussing it. But I'm not going to be ungenerous if you play ball, Fran – I'm making arrangements to transfer the ownership of the house into your name.'

'My name? But the mortgage is *huge*, isn't it?'

'Pretty high, especially since I took those two loans out on it for the car and the boat.'

'But you sold those and paid them back!'

'No, actually I decided to pay my credit cards off

with the money instead,' he said. 'But I could have sold the house outright, since it's in my name, and you will still make quite a profit when you sell it. Justin wanted to buy it as an investment, but if you'd played your cards right he would have let you live there rent free! Well, he's always fancied you, and it seemed like a good solution, only when he saw you again . . .' He shrugged.

I stared at him. 'Is that what you were talking about when I overheard you the night he came round for dinner, saying I was fat and gross, and discussing me as if I was a commodity that had gone down in value?'

'You can scarcely blame me for agreeing that you'd let yourself go and were hardly the woman I married any more!'

'Why *should* I be the woman you married? I mean, I wasn't cryogenically frozen on my wedding day, was I? And *was* there a bargain, Mal? Were you thinking you could just pass me on to him like a – a used toy?'

He looked uncomfortable. 'No, of course not, but you've always seemed to like him – and it's not as though you haven't been seeing other men while I've been here, is it? I know all about you and this Gabe Weston, *and* that Tom Collinge has been seen at the house in the middle of the night! For all I know you're still carrying on with Rhodri too. Alison says she'd be surprised if that baby you lost was actually mine at all!'

'Then she's a slut who judges other people by her own moral standards! How dare she say that about me when she's been carrying on with my husband behind my back for months? You're both just trying to justify the way you've behaved, and I think you're *despicable*!'

'Well, it doesn't really matter what you think now, does it?' he said quietly. 'I think I've made you a pretty generous offer in the circumstances, and you're going to have to accept it. I'm staying out here, so even if you take me through the courts and get maintenance I'm not going to pay it – and there's no way they can make me. You can get a decent job and pay the mortgage, or sell the house to Justin and move out – it's up to you.'

In the ensuing silence a coconut dropped onto the sand with a dull thud.

Mal got up. 'I'm going to stay with Alison tonight, and then we're spending a few days on Cayman Brac. You've had the sort of exotic holiday most people only dream of, and you can stay here until you leave. I won't be back until you've gone.'

I was too stunned to respond, and he started ticking items off one of his neat mental lists: 'You can arrange to drop the car at the airport, but I'll return the phone. Leave the key in the house and slam the door when you go . . . There, that's it, I think.'

I found my voice again at last. 'That's – *it*? Ten years and a lost child, and that's it, Mal Morgan?'

'I'm sorry it had to end like this,' he said coldly, and walked off into the apartment.

Forget Thomas Hardy, this felt much more like *The First Wives Club*.

I'm marooned . . . all alone on a desert island with no Man Friday – *or* Saturday, Sunday or any other day of the week.

It's now suddenly become plain to me, all the things that I ignored or didn't want to see, dropping into place. The signs are clear that he actually started the process of leaving me more than a year ago: all those 'friendly' meetings with Alison, the sudden enthusiasm for 'women who could do it all', his dissatisfaction with me . . . Yep, all as clear as crystal now.

I must have been a complete ostrich.

Mal might have meant what he said to me about second honeymoons and new beginnings when under the influence of guilt and compunction at the hospital, but clearly, once he met up with Alison again out here, my dream holiday became just a game of charades I didn't know we were playing.

Have you ever seen that old horror movie where there's this big, black, mysterious cloud sitting on top of a mountain, and the ski lift keeps taking people up until they vanish into it, where unspeakable and unnamed things are done to them? Well, I felt I was on that ski lift, a one-way ride that I couldn't stop.

The sound of the surf whispering sweet nothings on the beach began to be drowned out by rustlings, clickings and soft dragging noises as the creatures of the night got going – and I remembered the spidery crabs and rushed back inside.

Once I'd closed all the doors I turned the air conditioning on full blast and headed to the kitchen for a drink – which was when I spotted Mal's final list of instructions under the lump of coral on the counter, wrapped around a small wad of banknotes.

It more or less repeated what he'd said to me about

the car and phone just before he went, then added that he'd left me some cash to keep me going for the rest of the holiday, the equivalent of a hundred pounds in USA dollars. This isn't exactly munificent considering the price of everything out here.

I'd have liked to have ripped his money up into shreds and put it back under the coral, but it looks like I'm going to need every penny I can get: I think I have to fill the car up with petrol again before I return it, and I might want to eat and drink in the next week, unlikely though it seems just now. And isn't there some sort of exit tax I'll have to pay when I leave the island?

The house felt very empty. I switched on the TV for some background noise and it was another old British comedy series, which was sort of comforting, as was the big glass of cold Mudslide over crushed ice: manna from Cayman heaven.

Do you know what was *really* rankling? That barbed comment about my never having really loved him, I'd just married him as a meal ticket for life! That is *so* untrue. We were in love, and the me he fell in love with was the scatty, arty, hopeless-at-getting-rich Fran. It's the only one of me there is.

I've *never* spent any of his money on myself – except, come to think of it, with the guilt card recently . . .

The guilt card!

Making a dive for my handbag I found it still nestled in my purse. Had he forgotten I'd got it? Or just assumed I wouldn't use it any more?

I sat in front of the burbling TV holding the rectangle of plastic and thinking things over while I downed most of the rest of the bottle of Mudslide. I worked through the hysterical broken-hearted sobbing bit, including another weep over my poor lost baby, whom he'd never wanted anyway, and moving on to a sodden state of searing anger that he could string me along like this and then dump me the moment it suited him.

Mal Morgan owed me something, and if he thought he could make it up with money then I'd just have to become a Material Girl until he remembered to cancel the card.

Anger and depression are now slugging it out between them. May the best mood win.

I haven't called anyone to tell them what's happened – I just can't face it yet. It all seems so unreal, especially being alone here on Grand Cayman.

All I've bought to eat and drink for the rest of my stay is Mudslide, Ting and rum cake in various flavours. I'm going to eat myself to death, one way Dorothy Parker seems never to have thought of. The big black cloud has got me, and my whole existence is pointless, but I need to kill myself *very* slowly, since Rosie will need me for a while yet.

I'm feeling slightly revived today, after reading a magazine article that hit just the right chord: all about what horror writer Cass Leigh would like to do to the book reviewers who rubbish her novels. I simply can't believe her appalling inventiveness and my eyes are still stretched so wide I'm not sure I'll ever be able to close them again – *especially* at night! And maybe 'pulling their intestines out through their ears with eyebrow tweezers while forcing them to listen to loud Bee Gees music played backwards' was going too far even for the most horrible reviewer?

Still, visualising it all happening to Mal was terribly cathartic, and I revived enough to go on a huge spending spree, clocking up a frightening amount on the guilt card.

Mal should just be grateful I didn't visit the expensive tourist outlets at Kirk Freeport. Most of my purchases were gifts for the family and friends, including lots of miniature boxed rum cakes. Oh, and a lovely leather holdall from De Bag Man for me, and another visit to The Mermaid's Cave in search of a gift for Ma.

I bought her a big sarong, which she will probably wear as a shawl, or tied around her waist over her skirt, or something. No, on second thoughts, she'll probably turn it into a turban.

I love their unusual clothes, though I don't know what the effect of bright floaty cotton batik and tie-dye silk will be like in Wales. But I did also get cool cotton trousers and T-shirts and stuff, handy for gardening – if I've still *got* a garden after the dust settles, that is.

I don't know what is going to happen to the cottage, except that I can't afford the mortgage. The studio is mine, though, bought by my own money. Could I move it somewhere if I have to leave? And what about my roses? I *can't* leave them . . . but I can't take them, either, they are too big and too well-established, though

I could put one or two of the newer, still small ones in large tubs just in case.

I must try not to panic. I'll work something out when I get home.

On my last day I paid one more visit to my favourite spot, the pavilion overlooking the water lily pond at the botanic park, and afterwards sat with an iced drink at the open-air café in the courtyard behind the information centre, feeling calmly widowed.

Then I went back and tried all the permutations possible to fit my belongings into the suitcase, had a last swim and walk along the beach – then finally phoned Nia, to tell her what had happened.

'Mal's *left* you?' she repeated incredulously. 'He's gone back to his *ex-wife*?'

I could hear male voices exclaiming in the background, and realised she wasn't alone. But, then, everyone is going to know Mal's left me soon enough; it's such a small village that anything that happens is round the place like wildfire.

'Who's that I can hear in the background, Nia?'

'Rhodri and Gabe,' she said apologetically. 'Sorry, I was just so shocked I couldn't help myself.'

'It's OK, it'll get around fast enough.' I poured out all that had been happening.

'So you've been alone the last few days? Why didn't you call me before?'

'Oh, I don't know – shock, I suppose. Do you know what *really* rankles, Nia? Alison is the same age as Mal, so I've been left for an Older Woman!'

'You sound really down,' she said worriedly. 'I wish you weren't so far away.'

'So do I, but I'll see you when I get home tomorrow . . . or will it be today when I arrive? Or the day *after* tomorrow?'

'Whenever,' Nia said. 'I've got it down on my calendar that you arrive tomorrow our time, and I'm going to come and pick you up.'

'No, don't – I'll get a taxi back. I've used the credit card for everything I've needed this week, but I'm leaving that behind, and I intend using every last penny Mal gave me by the time I get home. If I can still call it home. What *am* I going to do, Nia?'

'Not panic, that's the first thing. We'll make a plan of action when you get back.'

'I want my studio and my roses, even if they won't be mine for much longer.'

There was a voice in the background again.

'Gabe says your roses are doing well, the hens are fine, and he can't wait to show you how the Regency garden is doing. The filming's almost finished.'

'I wish I was home now,' I said wistfully, 'without the endless flight, and the hassle of catching the connection up to Manchester.'

'Last hurdles,' she said. 'Try not to worry too much. And one bit of good news: the Wevills have been arrested and –'

'What? Nia, can you hear me?' I demanded, jerked to attention. 'Did you say the Wevills have been *arrested*?'

But the battery had died a death, and by the time

it recharged it would be too late over there to phone her ... it would have to wait until I got home.

Everything would have to wait until I got home, back through the looking-glass into the real world.

Homecoming Queen

I left the apartment behind me with mixed feelings. It was a lovely spot, a hothouse paradise, but now I had to go home and face up to reality – alone.

Remembering the fiasco of my outward flight I pondered two survival strategies for the journey back. One was staying sober, refusing all alcohol and most of the food, existing only on water and *very* thin air; the second was to drink even more than last time in the hope that I would pass into a drunken stupor for several hours.

I plumped for the second, fearing it would otherwise turn into one endless Groundhog Day of a flight, and discovered that, providing you stay pleasant and quiet, the stewardesses just keep them coming.

When the shopping brochure came round I impulse-bought two tinned racoons, and had I not left the chopped-up remains of my guilt card bobbing about in Mal's bottle of Appleton premium rum back at the apartment I could have done even more captive shopping.

Remembering that water helps prevent DVT, I drank

lots of that too. Self-induced DVT is another method Dorothy Parker missed, but I don't think she'd have fancied it; eating myself to death seems a much better option.

Having drunk and slept my way back to Britain I found my co-ordination was a bit shot by the time I arrived at Gatwick, and it was a miracle I managed the transfer on to the Manchester flight . . . on which they also served drinks. You could go around the world in eighty whiskies and I almost had.

But it was just as well, because when we arrived at Manchester everything looked grey and cold, just the way I felt inside, and a great big northern front of depression was sweeping across me.

Yawning and shivery, I weaved my way out on to the airport concourse, a drunk pushing an obstinate, equally inebriated trolley, wishing I hadn't told Nia not to meet me.

A voice calling my name stopped me in my tracks, and not just me – heads were turning.

'Fran!'

'*Gabe*?' Maybe I was hallucinating? I zigzagged nearer, but he looked real enough. '*Gabe!*'

Letting go of the trolley I clutched him instead, and found myself in a warm, strong bearhug.

'But why are you here? Everything's all right, isn't it? Nia isn't –'

'No, everything's fine, don't worry,' he said soothingly. 'I just felt like coming to meet you.'

'You did?' I gazed up at him and tears came to my eyes, for this endless day had left me so exhausted I could have fallen on anybody's neck and wept . . . though admittedly he would have been first choice. 'That's *so* kind, Gabe!'

'Oh, well, I thought you could use a lift, and so did Nia. My car's right outside in the short-stay car park, but we could have a sandwich or something first, if you're hungry. Aeroplane food is so disgusting, isn't it?'

'Yes, but I seem to have lost my appetite temporarily,' I said. 'I don't know why, but it's a pity, because I can eat anything I want. *Anything*,' I told him earnestly.

'Of course you can,' he assured me. His face seemed to be receding and then looming forward in a very strange way.

'Are you shrinking or expanding, Gabe?' I asked him.

'I think you're very tired,' he said sympathetically. 'It always makes everything look strange. And what on earth have you been drinking?'

'Whisky, whisky . . . more whisky,' I said. 'Gin makes you sad.'

'Very true. I think you may feel pretty sad in the morning as it is. Is this *all* your luggage? What's the matter with the trolley?'

'It's drunk.'

I let him take charge of it, and after kicking the back wheels briskly a couple of times it gave in and meekly rolled forward just like anyone else's.

I was wearing a straw hat and a tropical dress with my jacket over it, and when we went outside I was freezing, which sobered me up a bit, I can tell you.

'I'm really, really grateful,' I said as we sped off towards North Wales and the haven that was mine . . . temporarily. Soon perhaps to be on the market, my roses sold into strange hands.

'I've got to go back and short – *sort* – things out . . . decide where to go and what to do and . . .' I gave a great yawn. 'Excuse me!' Waves of sleep seemed to be pounding me down in my warm seat. My *very* warm seat . . .

'My bum's on fire,' I said drowsily.

'That's all right, the seat's heated,' he said sooth-ingly. 'Don't worry about it – don't worry about anything now: tomorrow is another day. Why not have a nap?'

And I must have done, because that was about all I remember until we were nearly home. I came to as we rattled over the hump-backed bridge into the village and turned into our lane.

'No,' I said suddenly, waking fully as he slowed outside my house. 'No, Gabe, I don't want to go back home tonight. I want my own room in Fairy Glen.'

'But, Fran –' he protested reasonably.

'No! I don't want to be here alone tonight,' I insisted. 'If you don't take me, I'll come and hammer on your door until you let me in!'

'Well, we certainly can't sit out *here* all night!' he muttered, and drove on.

'Go and put the kettle on while I bring your luggage in,' he said, opening the door of Fairy Glen for me. 'You can have hot cocoa and go straight to bed.'

'I don't want a hot drink, I want whisky,' I said mutinously.

'I think you've had enough whisky. I've installed a shower over the bath, though, if you want to get under that.' He looked at me judiciously. 'It might do you good.'

Suddenly a shower was the one thing I longed for most, and I took his advice. When I came out, he'd put my luggage in my old familiar room and was waiting with the steaming mug of cocoa.

'I borrowed this,' I said, holding the dressing gown up with both hands to stop it trailing on the floor.

'Looks better on you than me,' he said, smiling. 'Here's your cocoa – and then straight to bed, I think. You're going to feel like hell in the morning.'

'I've felt like hell for days,' I muttered, looking at the contents of my mug in disgust.

'Try not to worry too much, Fran,' he said gently. 'I'm sure it will all work out in the end.'

Suddenly I wanted to wrap myself in his comforting arms again, but I don't think it was personal, he was just the nearest big warm male.

In my room I opened the window and tipped the cocoa out, then found the bag with the Mudslide rations in it and filled the mug to the brim – anything to stop the cold, shivering desolation I was feeling. But even though I was exhausted my mind wouldn't let me go to sleep, and after a while I heard Gabe come upstairs and go into the turret room.

When the soft sound of his movements had ceased I walked silently down the landing and climbed into bed next to him, and his arms came out as though he'd expected me.

He did try and resist – he got as far as, 'Fran, I really don't think this is a good idea . . .' before I made it impossible for him to say anything else.

My body clock jerked me wide awake in the darkest, earliest, cruellest hours of the next morning, disorientated and scared – until my eyes adjusted to the light from the landing and outlined an unmistakable nose and familiar knotted-silk hair on the pillow next to me.

Déjà vu – only no camper van this time, just the circular shape of the turret at Fairy Glen.

There was no blinding flash of illumination to show me the chain of events that led me from leaving Cayman yesterday, or whenever it was, to now. I did remember how pleased I was to see him at the airport, and after that I expect one thing just naturally led to another.

But shouldn't he have seen how tired and distressed and – well, frankly, *drunk* – I was, and not taken advantage of me?

OK, OK, it's coming back to me and I'll rephrase that to 'he should have fought me off'.

I eased out of bed. He was sort of half hanging off the other side, and I hoped he wouldn't be suddenly precipitated on to the floor so I'd actually have to talk to him.

He muttered a bit, turned over (fortunately the right way) and with a deep sigh was fathoms deep again.

Light-headed, I tiptoed out of the room and into my old one, where I scrambled into my clothes, found my handbag and sandals, and then let myself out into the lane.

Walking through the darkness home I felt disembodied, as though it was all some nightmare. The house was chilly and unwelcoming and I trailed through it straight to my bed, where I didn't so much fall asleep as suddenly pass out with flying colours.

I resurfaced around six, feeling parched and with a headache trying to split my head in half like a coconut, but if there had been any of the milk of human kindness left in there it had gone rancid. I hated the world and everyone in it, but especially myself.

After drinking about six gallons of water I was just about to climb back into bed in the hope of another few hours of oblivion (please, *please* let last night's recollections be just a nightmare), when there was a thunderous knocking at my door.

It went on, and on, and on . . . and finally I grabbed my dressing gown and staggered down to open it, more to stop the hammering echoing through my skull than anything.

On the doorstep stood Gabe, and even through half-slitted eyes and a thick fog of hangover I could see he was in an almighty rage. His eyes were practically shooting off green sparks and he looked like Thor about to annihilate me with a well-deserved thunderbolt. Actually, it would have been a merciful release.

Brushing past me, he strode in and dumped my luggage on the floor none too gently, then turned and surveyed me.

'I can't *believe* I let you do that to me again!' he said furiously.

I stared at him dumbly.

'What is it with you? I'm OK for a bit of quick comfort on the rebound, but you can't bear to wake up to the reality? I should have known better when I saw you chucking your lover out in the middle of the night!'

And out he slammed again, practically grinding his teeth.

Might As Well Live

'You *what*?' Nia said, when she popped round at lunchtime to see how I was. She stared incredulously at me with her dark, bright eyes. 'Are you *quite* mad? I don't mean *sleeping* with him – I get the "in need of comfort" idea, and there are sparks between you two anyway – but what possessed you to get up and leave without a word in the middle of the night?'

'I just felt totally confused and disorientated and sort of *frightened* when I woke up. I think it's because nothing's real,' I explained. 'It came over me in the Caribbean, as if there's a plate-glass wall between me and the world. I had it even worse just after I lost the baby, but I thought it was anaemia. Do you ever feel like that?'

'No, you must be still short of iron or something – and you look like hell. Couldn't Gabe see you weren't yourself last night?'

'It wasn't his fault,' I confessed. 'He was really sweet when he picked me up at the airport, and I – well, I don't know – I just thought I would feel better in my old room at Fairy Glen. Only when I was there my mind kept going round and round in circles, and I felt so desolate and alone that in the end I couldn't bear it. So I – I went and climbed into bed with him. I still can't believe I *did* that!'

'Neither can I!' she replied, staring at me. 'And did you get what you were looking for?'

'I can't really remember,' I said evasively. 'I'm so very tired, Nia. So tired, and everything is going round and round and round again.' My words seemed to have started to slur into slow motion and my eyelids were trying to close.

'That's jet lag and booze,' she said unsympathetically. 'And haven't you had enough yet? What *is* that stuff you're drinking?'

'Mudslide. Lovely stuff – last bottle. Last bottle *ever*,' I said sadly, tipping it to see how much was in it, which was precious little. 'Prosh . . . Prospero's island – n'more rough magic for *me*.'

'Just as well, you can't afford to turn into a lush.'

'Don't be cross, Nia. I'm so very tired . . . tired of everything. I want to sleep and sleep and sleep . . .'

Nia eyed me resignedly. 'You go back to bed. Come round to Teapots at nine tomorrow when you're back in your right mind and we'll talk it all over with Carrie. Meanwhile, I'm going to go back to Plas Gwyn and have this out with Gabe, getting my friends drunk and exploiting them!'

'He didn't get me drunk, I'm quite capable of doing that myself,' I pointed out with dignity.

'Evidently.'

'And I think *I* exploited *him*.'

'It takes two to tango, Fran,' she said severely.

I remembered to give her the tinned racoon before she left, though I advised her not to take the lid off. Mine was still captive.

'Once you let them out it's never the same again,' I told her, but she did and unceremoniously stuffed it into her pocket. I could tell she liked it, even though she's not a fluffy-toy person.

'Speaking of letting things out, have you done the hens? It didn't sound like Gabe hung around long enough to this morning!'

'No, he didn't, but I remembered when I woke up and fed them. There were two eggs.'

'Then eat them, they'll do you good,' she ordered.

When she left she took every last aspirin and paracetamol in the house with her, even though I quoted Dorothy Parker and told her about my new take on suicide.

When I resurfaced in the late afternoon I felt like hell – but, strangely, not like drinking any more alcohol ... *ever*. My head was splitting, but since Nia had confiscated every headache remedy in the house I just had to suffer, until I thankfully remembered the first-aid kit in the bottom of my suitcase.

After that, I drank a couple of pints of water and set about loading my holiday clothes into the washing machine, unpacking and putting everything away. Mal's shirts always used to look so happy going round and round in the tumble dryer, as if they were waving at me ...

I brewed coffee, but I still wasn't hungry. If my appetite doesn't come back, eating myself to death might be a bit of a non-starter, and even if I hadn't suddenly gone off alcohol I certainly wouldn't fancy drinking myself to death, because there's something so pathetic about a drunk.

But when I took a good hard look at myself in the bathroom mirror I was pretty pathetic anyway. Gabe must have been either desperate or have strange taste in women, because some evil genie has trapped me inside the roly-poly, dumpling figure of someone else: a sad, pallid, puffy, exhausted little fortysomething that's been taken down, dusted and then put back on the shelf.

Hello, whoever you are – you can have your body back now.

Then I remembered that I really *am* that dumped, roly-poly fortysomething: woe is me.

In the shower my skin was so dry it felt like blotting paper and I worried I might just swell up and crumble, clogging the entire village's sewerage system. Afterwards I anointed myself all over with tons of cocoa butter and then gingerly applied hypoallergenic face cream and cool witch hazel eye gel to my poor war zone of a complexion – though funnily enough it's starting to become fresher-looking after its inadvertent skin peel.

The sun and sea had made my hair the consistency of bleached pink candyfloss, but nothing that a gallon of conditioner wouldn't cure. And at least now the allergy rash has gone you can see where my hair stops and my face begins.

Rosie called me, and although I didn't intend telling her what had happened yet – unloading on your children is *so* unfair – it all somehow came pouring out.

Of course she immediately wanted to rush home and drive me crackers, like she usually does. 'I thought he was being a total pig lately – but to leave you for his ex-wife! I mean, I've seen her pictures, and she isn't half as pretty as you, Mum!'

'Thank you, darling, but she is half the size – and Mal doesn't seem to find me attractive any more.'

'No, because he's weird! Every other man does. Tom says you're twice as pretty as when you were a student.'

'When did he say that?'

'Yesterday – email. What are you going to do, Mum? I mean, where do you stand about the house and everything?'

'I don't know. I'm going to talk it all over with Nia and Carrie tomorrow. I'm not qualified for any kind of job that would pay enough to afford the huge mortgage on this place, so I think I'll to have to sell it even though I hate to leave my roses and the studio, and I love St Ceridwen's Well.'

'You bought the studio *and* the roses,' she reminded me.

'I know, but I don't think I can take them with me. Never mind, we'll worry about it later.'

'And you're not really, really upset and depressed?'

'No, of course not!' I said brightly, and sang a snatch of 'I Will Survive' to reassure her. 'How's Colum?'

'Fine,' she said, and then clammed up as she usually

does. I don't know why she won't say anything about her boyfriends; he seemed very nice.

'By the way,' she added, 'my friend Star – you know, the one I met surfing? – well, she's coming to stay with me next week, and I thought I'd bring her up for the weekend if that's OK with you. Then she's off back to Cornwall again.'

'But won't you have to take some time off from university?'

'I don't have much on Mondays. It'll be OK.' She paused. 'I don't suppose you've seen that gardener man since you got back, have you?'

'You mean Gabe Weston? I . . . yes, actually, he picked me up from the airport, which was kind of him. And he's been doing the hens and watering the roses while I was away. Nia and Rhodri have – well, they're living together,' I explained.

'Oh, I saw that one coming on last time I was home,' she said. 'There was something about the way they kept looking at each other. Like you and Gabe Weston flirting right in front of me.'

'Rosie! I did *not* flirt with him!' I protested.

'Oh, no? Well, that's what it sounded and looked like to me!'

'You're imagining things,' I said with dignity. 'I'm not interested in men and I'm going to live a single life from now on. Why did you want to know if I'd seen him?'

'Just interested in our local celebrity, that's all,' she said. 'Did you know Granny shopped the Wevills to the police?'

'Well, yes, but I forgot to ask Nia what's happening. I *thought* she said they'd been arrested.'

'They have, and charged with the poison-pen letters. I expect you'll find out all about it tomorrow and you can give me the dirty details!'

'You don't know where Granny is, do you? Only there was no reply when I phoned to tell her I was back.'

'A mini-cruise on the Rhine, or the Rhône, or some-where,' she said promptly. 'A last-minute bargain, she said. And she's got her round-the-world one all planned out and booked now. Wish I was going too!'

She rang off reluctantly, but really, I'm not about to do anything stupid however miserable I am.

I sort of half hoped, half feared that Gabe would come round again for a rematch, but he didn't, and feeling sad, lonely and empty I finally opened my tinned racoon just for something to cuddle and took it back to bed, where I cried myself to sleep.

I woke early next morning feeling *much* better – which was just as well, since there were two letters with Caribbean stamps on the mat.

One was in Mal's handwriting, but I'd have known it was from him anyway, because on the back he'd added: 'Save the stamp!'

Hello? He asks me for a divorce with one breath, and wants me to save my used stamps for him with the next?

Dear Fran,

This should get there about the same time as you do. Hope you got back all right and the Caribbean holiday made up a bit for the shock. I know you will be feeling more reasonable by now, and have realised that things between us just weren't working out. Hadn't been for a long, long time.

My solicitor will be sending you some forms to sign. If we are in agreement, the cottage, and the equity in it, will be transferred to your name, and there's no reason the divorce shouldn't go through fast. You might want to reconsider Justin's offer for the cottage – it's a good one.

Finally, would you please pack up any personal possessions and I will arrange to have them removed to Mother's house? The metal box containing my stamp collection needs to be parcelled up and sent out to me by some kind of insured special delivery – they will advise you of the best way at the post office.

Mal

As if that wasn't enough, Brideshead Revisited had also penned a friendly little note.

Dear Fran,

I thought I'd just like to tell you how sorry I am that it didn't work out between you and Mal, but from what he's told me you must have realised that things weren't going well for a year or two. He's a great guy, and I know how much you relied on his support, but a man appreciates an independent woman when he gets to a certain age. This time round I'm sure it will work – we have so many interests in common now.

No hard feelings?

Alison Morgan

That bit about his 'supporting' me makes me sound like a clinging vine, and reminded me of how he'd more or less implied on Cayman that I'd only married him for what I could get.

I was a few minutes late arriving at Teapots, since I'd had someone out to look at my poor dead-as-a-dodo little car, though it turned out it simply needed a wire to the battery replacing. I could see he thought the new wire was the most valuable bit of the whole vehicle.

Nia had already filled Carrie in on what had been happening – including some of the embarrassing bits I might have left out myself, like what Gabe said to me next morning when he was really angry.

'You do seem to have a habit of using him for comfort when you're dumped,' Nia said.

'You can't call *twice* a habit,' I protested. 'And the first time I slept with him I thought I still loved Tom, and this time . . .' I examined my inner workings and made a discovery. 'This time I woke up confused because I *didn't* love Mal! And although Gabe had been really nice to me I supposed he didn't want to reject me after Mal just had.'

'You and Gabe have got something going,' Nia said.

'Maybe you don't realise it, but when your eyes meet you stare at each other for ages. It's quite embarrassing – and he looks at you all the time. He was even flirting with you on the phone to Cayman; I heard him.'

'He didn't say a thing, except about roses and the hens,' I pointed out, going pink. 'You're imagining it.'

'No, I'm not, and it's not what he *said*, it was the way he said it.'

'Well, it doesn't matter now, because his opinion of me is clearly that I will sleep with anyone – he jumped to conclusions about Tom, didn't he?'

'Fran, he's jealous! I think you are going to have to apologise to him, because he's been going around like a bear with a sore head since you got back. In fact, Carrie and I think it might just be confession time, don't you?'

'Confession time? You mean *everything*? Rosie?'

'Yes. Tell him you're sorry you walked out on him the other night, and you wished you'd stayed till morning this time, and that Tom was trying to get into your house, not being let out – and explain about Rosie perhaps being his child.'

'Nia, I couldn't possibly!' I said, appalled.

'But just think how good it would be not to have secrets any more!' Carrie suggested. 'Nothing to hide. And he's such a nice man – don't you think you owe it to him?'

'Well, there is that, I suppose,' I admitted. 'Maybe you're both right – I'll think about it. After all, it doesn't matter if Mal finds out about it now, does it? There's just Rosie to consider, but I'm not sure how she would take it . . . She didn't really seem to like him.'

'She's never liked any man who showed interest in you,' observed Nia.

I sighed. 'All I ever wanted was a quiet life in the country, doing my designs and cartoons, loving Mal, looking after Rosie, my hens and my roses – where did I go wrong?'

'Nia's told me about the cottage, and that you might have to sell it,' Carrie said. 'It's such a shame.'

'I will have to sell it – there's no way I can afford to keep it, especially since no maintenance is likely to be forthcoming. I don't earn enough to cover it.'

'If you do, then I've got a suggestion which is better than nothing – we've *both* got suggestions,' Carrie said.

'Yes, I'm living up at Plas Gwyn now,' Nia said, slightly self-consciously, 'so you could rent my little cottage from me.'

'And I'm tired of being cooped up over the café, and since our gardens back on to each other I thought I could buy your house and put a door through the wall into mine.'

'But, Carrie, it's worth quite a bit and –'

'Oh, I've got money,' she said nonchalantly. 'And just think, you could still use the studio and see to your roses, and even, if you needed a place to live, have my flat over the shop!'

I didn't know what to say, but my eyes were swimming.

'Have a madeleine,' urged Carrie, pushing a plate of comfort food towards me. 'Or a chocolate brownie.'

'No, thanks, not just now – I'm not hungry,' I said,

and they both stared at me as though I'd turned green and grown another head. 'It's just . . . hard to take in! A complete rescue package – if you're both sure?'

'Of course we're sure – unless you get a *better* offer,' Carrie said.

'Don't be silly,' I said severely. 'If you mean Gabe, that was a one-off.'

'Mal's friend Justin?'

'In his dreams!'

'What were you saying about trying to commit suicide by gluttony last night?' Nia demanded suddenly.

I shrugged. 'When Mal dropped his bombshell and went off, that Dorothy Parker poem about suicide popped into my head – you know, the one that lists all the different methods, and then concludes that you might as well live?'

'Yes, because all the alternatives have a nasty catch to them. But you weren't seriously thinking of suicide, were you, Fran?'

'No, not really. Not in the short term, anyway.'

'The short term? What on earth do you mean?' asked Carrie.

'Well, since the only things I really wanted to eat and drink out there were rum cake, Mudslide and sugary soft drinks, I thought eating myself to death might be quite fun.'

'But you must have eaten something beside cake!' demanded Nia.

'Not really, but it's OK, I've given up any idea of

eating myself to death on purpose. I'll probably just do that naturally when my appetite comes back.'

'Have you eaten anything this morning?' she asked.

'Come on, Nia! Do I look starving? There's enough fat on me to keep me going for six months.'

'No there isn't – you've actually lost weight. And that's not the point, anyway – you still need to eat properly. I think you're run down.'

'How can I be run down when I'm the size of a medium minke whale?'

'It's not size, it's content. Vitamins and minerals and stuff.'

'All right, I'll buy some multivitamins next time I'm in town.'

'And I'll do a special rite, to speed up the inner healing process and give you strength,' Nia said, a faraway look in her eyes.

'What sort of rite?' I asked uneasily. 'This *is* just Druidry you're up to, isn't it?'

'Of course, I told you! What did you think I was doing? Black magic?'

'No . . . it's just that I happened to see you once, burying something up at the stones,' I confessed.

She looked slightly embarrassed. 'An elderly member of my circle's last wish was to be laid to rest up there, so I did.'

'You buried a *Druid* in the stone circle?'

'Just ashes,' she said defensively. 'Why not? But don't worry, all my sacrifices are inanimate.'

'You know, I think I've just thought of a sacrifice on the altar of revenge,' I said, a brainwave illuminating the inside of my head like a flashbulb. 'Mal's going to make it. He's asked me to send him his stamp collection, and that's *exactly* what I'm going to do.'

Stamped Out

Nia and Carrie wanted me to go right up to Plas Gwyn and talk to Gabe then and there, but I needed to think about it a bit first.

Besides, I had some urgent business to do this morning: drive to the nearest post office and buy loads of stamps, a stick of glue and glossy postcards of St Ceridwen's Holy Well.

After that, all I had to do was crack the six-figure number on the safe box Mal kept his stamp collection in, which was easy when you knew him as well as I did. Using the simplest of number codes for the word 'Cayman' I hit pay dirt first time and his treasures lay in my hands.

I spent the next couple of hours very pleasantly, addressing the postcards out to Mal in the Caribbean, and gluing his collection of stamps on to each one in pretty patterns. Of course, I also added the correct postage, too, so they should get to him OK. They were a very colourful lot, and practically filled the little village postbox.

I felt like a wicked child sticking fireworks in a dustbin.

*   *   *

Next morning I set out for Plas Gwyn, assuming I would find Gabe up there somewhere, and on impulse turned off the drive and headed for the maze.

I'd found him sitting there once before – and I struck lucky again. The heart of the labyrinth seems to be his favourite place for brooding.

'Gabe?' I said tentatively, but since he didn't look up I slowly started to walk around the pathway like a reluctant sacrificial victim.

It seemed twice as big now the outer edges had been re-cut, but of course you can't get lost in a turf maze, even if you do have to go to and fro a bit.

'Gabriel!' I said more sharply, finally reaching the middle, and he looked up sombrely. 'Gabe, can we talk?'

'*I* certainly can, but you seem to specialise more in silent departure at dead of night,' he said rather bitterly.

'I know, and I want to apologise for my behaviour the other night.'

'Which bit?'

'You *know* which bit!'

'No, I don't. Are you apologising for sleeping with me, or leaving in the middle of the night?'

'Neither,' I snapped. 'I don't know why I even bother trying to explain – and that nasty crack you made about throwing my lovers out in the middle of the night was *totally* unjustified!'

'I saw him, don't forget, Fran.'

'You saw me telling him to go away – the doorstep was as far as he got! You just automatically drew the wrong conclusions.'

'Maybe, but your own daughter told me you were getting back together,' he pointed out.

'Yes, and I told you that was just wishful thinking on her part – not that it's any of your business anyway!' I was beginning to wish I'd never embarked on all this.

'You can't deny that the other night was my business,' he said darkly, 'even if I *was* just the consolation prize.'

'Well, I'm sorry if it rankles, but I wasn't in a fit state to think straight when I woke up, that's why I left. It was totally different from last time!'

'Was it? Last time you went back to your boyfriend, Tom, didn't you? Is that what you intend doing this time too?'

'No.' I sat down on the grass next to him. 'Gabriel, I *didn't* go back to Tom last time.'

'Nia said –'

'Nia said he'd asked me to go back to him, but she didn't say I *had*. I didn't. I came here to St Ceridwen's alone, instead.'

He turned and looked at me, but I didn't meet his eyes. 'I probably should have told you this right at the start, when you first recognised me ... but knowing about the paternity claims and the gossip mags, I just couldn't. It's ... there's something I *really* have to tell you.'

'It's Rosie, isn't it? She's mine,' he interrupted, to my complete astonishment.

I stared at him, dumbfounded, the wind taken right out of my sails. 'She *might* be,' I admitted. 'Or she might be Tom's, I don't know. I always suspected she

427

was yours, but short of a DNA test there's no way to be certain.'

'Oh, I was certain almost the moment I set eyes on her,' he said positively.

'How on earth could you be? She doesn't look like you in the least!'

'No, but she *does* look like photos of my mother as a girl.'

'She – she does? And you didn't say anything?' I demanded indignantly.

'*I* thought that *you* thought she was Tom's, and I didn't see any sense in rocking the boat – especially if you might get back with him.'

'There's no way I'd ever think of getting back with Tom,' I said hotly. 'And even Rosie's gone off the idea now she knows he's still got a wife!'

'He has?' He sat up and looked at me intently, his eyes sincere. 'Fran, when I saw Rosie and realised she was mine, I felt really bad that you'd never been able to tell me about her. And I wished I'd known. *Another* daughter I've missed seeing grow up,' he added bitterly.

I was feeling rather anticlimactic. 'To think that you knew all this time, when I've been going frantic worrying that you would find out. Or Mal – or the *press*.'

'There's no reason why anyone should find out unless we tell them, Fran.'

'Are you absolutely *sure* she's yours?'

'Positive. I've had the photos out several times, and she's my mother's image as a girl. I think she's got a bit of my nose too, don't you?' He turned his impressive profile towards me.

'No, of course she hasn't,' I said scathingly. 'She's got a neat little nose!'

'Are you saying mine's huge?'

'Yours is fine for a man,' I allowed graciously.

'Thanks. Your ma thinks Rosie's got a look of me.'

'*Ma* does?' I exclaimed. 'Good grief, does *Ma* know? Who else knows?'

'No one. Your ma guessed. She said she could see there was something between us from the first time she saw us together,' he added pensively, 'and then Rosie has mannerisms that are just like mine.'

'Well, of all the secretive old . . . ! She could have told me that you knew!'

'I asked her not to. *Are* you going to tell Rosie? How do you think she'll take it?'

'I'll have to tell her now, but I don't think she'll believe me. Prepare yourself to be interrogated. And . . . you'll be nice to her, won't you, Gabe?' I asked painfully.

'Of course I will, Fran, what do you take me for?' he said, looking hurt. 'I'm delighted to have another daughter, and I hope she'll let me get to know her.'

'And what about Stella? Are you going to tell her that there's yet another skeleton in her dad's cupboard?'

'I haven't thought quite that far ahead yet,' he admitted. 'She might come and visit me soon. The term ends over there any minute, so she will probably fly back to be with her grandparents. If she does, I'll break it to her then.'

'Rosie's half-sister!' I marvelled. 'And she might not

mind too much, Gabe; after all, it was such a long time ago, before she was born.'

'I hope not. I don't want to find one daughter only to lose another. And, Fran,' he added gently, 'I'm sorry I was angry with you about the other night.'

'That's all right, I'm glad we've cleared the air,' I said, rising to my feet, and he rose with me, pulling me into his arms. The maze seemed to whirl around us dizzyingly – must have been delayed jet lag.

'Blush Noisette,' he said softly.

'La Belle Sultane,' I said. My knees seemed to be folding.

'Maybe you should think twice before running from my bed in the middle of the night next time?' he suggested in my ear.

'What makes you think there will *be* a next time?' I said indignantly.

'I feel it in my bones.'

'Then you feel it wrong.' I pulled away and said politely, 'Excuse me.'

'I'm not blocking your way,' he pointed out, looking amused.

'Yes, you are, I have to walk back on the path.'

'You mean you won't cross the lines?' He stood aside with an incredulous grin, and watched me tread my intricate course round the maze until I emerged by the yews.

'Come up and see what we've been doing on Thursday when the crew have all gone,' he called.

'I might,' I said, walking away.

But first of all I have to think out how on earth I

am to tell Rosie about Gabe, when I don't think she even likes him!

And I wonder what Gabe's daughter is like?

I thought I'd go and talk things over with Nia, and was just heading for her workshop when I came across a tableau in the courtyard that stopped me in my tracks. For a minute I thought the cameras had returned and were using the place as the backdrop to a soap.

A medium-sized, wiry man, whom I recognised as Nia's ex-husband, Paul, was just saying aggrievedly, 'But I'm asking you to come back to me, Nia! Emma's left me – she went off to France with some man she knew before. It was all a mistake and I should never have let you go.'

'Well, you did,' Nia said shortly, 'and now I'm gone for good.'

Rhodri, who had been standing by looking rather anxious, now put his arm round her and said, 'That's right, she belongs here, now.'

'And *you* would be . . . ?' enquired Paul nastily.

'Rhodri Gwyn-Whatmire – and you're on my property.'

Paul turned on Nia. 'I see how it is. You've decided on the soft option – finding a man with money this time?'

'Oh, don't be silly. I've worked my butt off with hard physical labour the last few months, and Rhodri hasn't got any money, just a pile of stones and a lot of ambition.'

'So you won't come back to me, then?' Paul said almost incredulously, as though he had only to walk up and ask, and all the infidelity, the betrayal and the divorce would be wiped out with a great, smiling 'of course!'.

'No, she won't,' Rhodri said pugnaciously. 'She's with me now.'

I remembered that *Flash Gordon* was still Rhodri's favourite film, and felt the dialogue was taking a turn for the worse.

'It doesn't matter whether I'm with anyone else or not, I still wouldn't come back to you, Paul,' Nia said. 'You've wasted your time coming.'

'If that's the way it is, then,' he said, looking from one to the other of them uncertainly.

Rhodri tightened his grip on his prize and Paul muttered something, turned on his heel and stalked off.

'I feel I should applaud,' I said, and they finally looked round and noticed me. 'The dialogue was a bit melodramatic, but it was well acted.'

'The cheek of the man, thinking he could just walk up here and claim me back like a mislaid belonging,' Nia fumed. 'As though I were just sitting here waiting for him. Well, I didn't! I got a life, instead.'

'Yes, with me,' Rhodri agreed enthusiastically. 'Let's get married!'

'God, no,' she said, 'I couldn't face being Nia Gwyn-Whatmire!'

'You could keep your own name,' I suggested.

'Whose side are you on?'

'Both.'

'Talking of weddings, where's Gabe?' Nia retaliated. 'Have you talked to him yet?'

'Why, is something going on between you and Gabe, Fran?' Rhodri asked intelligently.

Nia gave him a look. 'Of course there is, you big idiot – they're meant for each other!'

'Hold on, Nia! I've just discovered my marriage is on the rocks, so you might let me come up for breath first before pairing me off again!'

'They *do* both like roses,' Rhodri admitted.

'Among other things,' she agreed. 'Didn't you hear or see *anything* when they were together up here? They flirt all the time under the pretence of talking about roses – it's embarrassing.'

'No, of course he didn't, because there wasn't anything to notice,' I said hastily.

'*And* he did it on the phone when you called from Cayman!'

'He was just trying to cheer me up by talking about gardening.'

'Admit it, Fran, you started falling out of love with Mal nearly a year ago when he began turning weird, and fell back in love with Gabe the minute he re-appeared on the scene.'

'*Back*?' Rhodri asked, puzzled.

'I was never in love with him in the first place – it was nothing, a one-night stand.'

'*What*?' Rhodri said, his light-blue eyes startled.

Nia patted his arm. 'Don't worry about it, Rhodri, I'll explain later. Fran, are you going to come to the pub tonight? I think you ought to get out, not sit at home brooding about everything.'

'So long as I don't have to drink any alcohol,' I said. 'I think my entire system is poisoned.'

I heard Rhodri's voice raised on a questioning note as I left, but whether it was about me or about the possibility of nuptial bliss is anyone's guess.

At home, a removal van was packing up the contents of the Wevills' house, but of the poison-penners there was no sign, and hadn't been since my return.

Gone, but not forgotten, for they had left a legacy of false rumour that would echo down through the years and never quite die. As we all know, there is no smoke without fire.

Double Trouble

Whatever explanations Nia gave to Rhodri caused him to cast puzzled but affectionate looks in my direction all evening, so I'm not sure he's got the hang of the situation yet. That makes two of us.

Gabe was at the pub too, his mood set to Fair bordering on Sunny, despite having to sneak in the back way to avoid a last lingering coachload of adoring fans.

Afterwards he insisted on walking me home, and we were almost there before he stopped dead and said, very seriously, 'Fran, I've been thinking about you – about us – all afternoon.'

'You have?'

'Of course I have. And I've come to the conclusion that, since you're now an unattached female and I'm an unattached male, and we strike sparks whenever we get together, we should just start again from the beginning.'

'Start what again?' I asked cautiously.

'A romance, a relationship – whatever you want to call it. But take it slowly this time and see where it goes.' He took my hand. 'You know: I walk you back from the pub like this for a week or two and kiss you good night. One day you invite me in for coffee; then I take you home to see my roses . . . And one fine morning – hey presto! – I wake up and you're still there. Transplanted and bedded down. Sown, mulched and rooted.'

'You say the most romantic things,' I said breathlessly – because, actually, it works for me.

'So what do you say?'

From what I could see of him in the poorly lit lane he looked serious enough.

'A cautious yes . . . though things could come unstuck when Rosie and Stella find out the truth.'

'We'll take it as it comes. We have to live *our* lives, Fran, because they'll be off living theirs soon enough. So – here's a fairly chaste, first-night kiss.'

If *that* was chaste, I'm a vestal virgin.

It's been a week of cautious discovery – and recovery. I'd heard from Mal's solicitor and accepted his terms, so the house would soon be mine, and I'd turned down an offer from Justin. I wasn't interested in how much he was willing to pay: I wanted Carrie to have the house.

Ma came back and phoned me, unrepentant that she'd been keeping secrets with Gabe behind my back; and Rosie had her friend staying with her, though she hadn't mentioned bringing her up again for the weekend, so I presumed she wasn't after all.

But that Friday night, as I sat in the back parlour

of the Druid's Rest with Nia, Rhodri and Gabe, in they walked – and it wasn't just *our* table who went deathly quiet and stared, either.

The two girls were like the positive and negative of the same photograph: Rosie fair and Star dark; but otherwise they might have been identical twins.

They made their way across the silent room until they reached our table, and Rosie said, 'Hello, Mum.'

'Hello, Dad,' Star said to Gabe – and then the penny dropped. Star – Stella – Cornwall – oh my God!

'Haven't you both got something you'd like to tell us about?' they asked, more or less in unison, and I groped blindly for Gabe's hand and gripped it tightly as we stared at our little Midwich cuckoos, come home to roost.

Rhodri, looking profoundly baffled, got up and kissed Rosie. 'Rosie, great to see you, and –'

'My sister, Stella,' she introduced her. 'Half-sister, really, and she likes to be called Star.'

'Er, right,' he said uncertainly. 'Hello, Star.'

'This is Uncle Roddy and that's Mum's friend Nia, who's living with Uncle Roddy –' began Rosie.

'*Really*, Rosie!' I said indignantly.

'That, of course, is my mother, Fran –'

'And this is Gabe Weston, alternatively known as Adam the gardener, my father – *and* yours,' Star said sweetly.

'We've been rumbled,' Gabe said to me.

'Did you have to choose quite such a public spot for the revelations, Rosie?' I said bitterly. 'Why didn't you go the whole hog and hire a town crier or take an announcement out in the paper?'

437

'We're not ashamed to be sisters – in fact, we like it,' she said, and they smiled a smile of such similarity that it was quite unnerving. God knows, it had been bad enough having only *one* of Rosie.

'We wanted everything out in the open,' Star said, and they finally sat down, to my relief.

'I don't understand how you met.' Gabe was staring at them with wary fascination.

'I went surfing when I was at the Gramps' in Cornwall, and met Rosie there,' Stella said. 'Only I call myself Star mostly. Everyone said we were so alike it was uncanny, and we really got on – better than sisters – and, well, we talked, and then when I had to go back to the USA to finish school we've been texting and emailing.'

'And you were asking me all those questions about when I was younger,' Gabe exclaimed.

'Yes, and Rosie's mum had told her all about this gardener she'd met, and so we just worked it out.'

'So Gabe is Rosie's father and Star's?' Rhodri said, his brow furrowed.

'Duh!' Nia said. 'Hand the man a coconut.'

'Well, it's all a bit confusing,' he confessed. 'So . . . if Fran and Gabe get married eventually, when her divorce comes through, they'll all be one big fam – *Ouch*!'

Nia's elbow had connected with his ribcage.

Rosie and Star bent identical severe gazes at Gabe. 'That depends. Rosie and I both have to get to know Dad. I was only a little girl last time I saw him, and Rosie's hardly met him.'

'You were such a plump little thing last time I saw

you!' marvelled Gabe, and Star gave him a dirty look. 'I can't believe you two look so alike now.'

'Puppy fat,' Star said. 'I outgrew it.'

'Look, this has been quite a shock,' Gabe said. 'A nice one, but a shock. So why don't we all go back to Fairy Glen and talk things over? Get to know each other a bit? I've got some family photo albums there too. What do you both say?'

They looked at each other, then nodded.

'Well, OK,' Star agreed. 'But I'm staying with Rosie tonight.'

'That's all right, Mum, isn't it?' Rosie demanded.

'Yes – yes of course!' I said hastily.

'Good luck!' Nia mouthed to me as we left.

I thought we would need it.

I thought so even more when we got near enough to see a familiar estate car parked outside the cottage. Then the door swung open and Ma stood in the doorway, resplendent in layers of lurid paisley print and high-heeled mules with pink feather pom-poms on the front.

'Darlings!' she said when we were all inside and barely begun on the who's who bit, and took us all into a sort of group hug. And even when she declared slightly cheesily, and with tears in her eyes, 'One big happy family at last!' there wasn't a dry eye in the house.

Gabe's were watering more because he was laughing, and so, after a minute, were mine.

'If you only knew the heart-searchings we've had about how we were to tell you two girls the truth!' I gasped. 'And then you walk into the pub bold as brass together as if you'd known each other all your lives.'

'Well, that's just how we feel,' Rosie said.

'Now I have *two* granddaughters,' Ma said complacently, and I didn't point out that actually Stella is no relation to her at all.

'You, Fran,' she directed me, 'go to your house with Gabriel and bring back some elderflower champagne. This is a celebration! And food – bring food. While you're gone, I want my new granddaughter to tell me all about herself.'

As we walked down the dark lane we both heaved a sort of sigh, and I said, 'Well, that's not how I'd have *chosen* to do it, but at least it's all out in the open.'

'Do you think it's all going to work out, Fran?' he asked.

'I don't think everything's going to be a bed of roses instantly; we're all going to take some time to get used to each other and settle down to the idea that . . . well, that we're a sort of extended family.'

'We could be a *contracted* family,' he suggested, putting an arm round me. 'If you marry me when your divorce comes through, that is.'

'I don't think that is the opposite of an extended family,' I said critically. 'And it's too soon. Remember *slowly*?'

'Oh, *sod* slowly,' he said and, pulling me close, kissed me long and hard.

The champagne was a trifle delayed . . .

Epilogue: Heaven-Scent

Of course it all had to come out in the press (I suspect Nia's sister, Sian, of having something to do with it), and 'SECRET LOVE-CHILD SCANDAL OF TV GARDENER!' was possibly my least favourite headline. But on the whole there really wasn't that much scandal to rake up: Rosie'd been born before he was married to his first wife, and she was only secret because I never knew who Gabe was. Our engagement made a neat and tidy ending to the story – love restored, and sealed with a rose diamond – and of course he promised me a rose garden too. How could I resist?

Media interest in the story soon died down, but I've had to accept that Gabe will never be able to walk from one end of St Ceridwen's Well to the other during the holiday season without being accosted by drooling female fans.

Luckily, most of the locals see him as the jewel in the crown of the area's growing prosperity and clam up when asked for directions to where he lives, so Fairy Glen remains for the most part quietly dreaming in its little backwater.

But then, once the new series of *Restoration Gardener* is aired he may lose some of his celebrity status to Dottie, who he says can be seen in practically every shot, generally brandishing a riding crop and telling the cameraman to 'Clear orf!'

By high summer it was clear that Rhodri and Nia were making a rip-roaring success of Plas Gwyn – *and* of their relationship. They've had more coach-party bookings than they can handle, so goodness knows what it will be like after they feature in the autumn TV series!

Nia's lovely pottery pieces, especially the delicate porcelain jewellery, sell like hot cakes, as do my cards and calendars in the gift shop. And, speaking of hot cakes, Carrie has opened a tea shop up there now, Teapot2, where you can buy perennial favourites such as 'Mades of Honour', 'Furry Cakes' and 'Ginger Parking' to your heart's content.

Before the extension to Fairy Glen was built, the cottage was bursting at the seams whenever Rosie, Stella, Ma and the dogs were all visiting at once. And until we all shook down into the normal give and take of family life things were sometimes difficult; but, then, I never was a romantic who expected everything to go right all the time.

Just as well.

When I look back on my life, it's been like a maze, a rose maze, where all the paths bring me back to Gabe, however I twist and turn. Now both I and the garden around me are settled, seeded and well dibbled, and an air of heavy expectancy hangs on the hot August air.

I work with the door and windows of my little Caribbean-style studio open and the faint chatter of the two girls can be heard in between the joyful ditties of suicidal despair they are playing.

Every so often one of the hens strays over the threshold, moaning quietly (usually Shania, she's very sociable). The fragrance of the old roses in tubs outside hangs heaven-scent on the air, and the heavy drone of fat bees adds the base notes to a symphony of bliss.

Gabe's been away filming but he will be home soon and I can feel little shivers of excitement running up and down my spine just at the thought of seeing him again.

I tell you, if any serpent dares to raise its ugly head in *my* new Eden, the Apple of Contentment is going to be rammed right down its throat faster than you can say Cox's Pippin.

Read on for an extract from Trisha Ashley's
Chocolate Wishes

Prologue

Mortal Ruin

When the normally innocuous radio station she always listened to while she was working suddenly started pumping out Mortal Ruin's first big hit, 'Dead as My Love', Chloe Lyon was in the kitchen area of her small flat, carefully brushing a thick coating of richly scented dark criollo couverture chocolate into moulds, to make the last batch of hollow angels before Christmas.

That seemed pretty appropriate, because a hollow angel was what Raffy Sinclair had proved himself to be, but it meant that it was a couple of minutes before she had a hand free to·reach across and snap down the off button. By then they'd moved on to Eric Clapton's 'Tears in Heaven', so it was becoming obvious that the guest on *Desert Island Discs* (she'd missed the start) had much happier memories of 1992 than Chloe did. In fact, she'd take a bet on the next song being Whitney Houston and 'I Will Always Love You', and that really *would* finish her off.

But the music carried on playing in her head even after the radio was silenced and it was already too late to suppress the memories. The dark, viciously searing tide of anger and pain at Raffy's betrayal was rushing in as sharply as if it had all happened yesterday and she was once again that love-struck nineteen-year-old, thinking she'd found a kind of magic more potent than any of her grandfather's chants, charms and incantations.

She'd loved that Clapton song, though Raffy'd teased her that it was mawkish. But then, as well as being keen on Nirvana, he'd had a worrying penchant for Megadeath and older bands like Iron Maiden, Judas Priest and Black Sabbath, all of which influenced the lyrics he wrote for his own band, Mortal Ruin. This obsession with the dark side was part of the reason why she'd never mentioned her grandfather to him – he might have been *too* interested had he known about her connection with Gregory Warlock.

But actually, there had simply not been enough time to explore their family and backgrounds, since they'd met and fallen in love at the start of her first university term and those few weeks spent intently engrossed in each other encompassed the whole span of their relationship.

It wasn't surprising that *she'd* loved *him* at first sight – he was tall and handsome, with long black curling hair, a pale, translucent skin and eyes the greeny-blue of the Caribbean Sea in a holiday brochure – but he'd seemed as transfixed as she was . . . And anyway, the Tarot cards, when she consulted them, had told her that change was coming and she would meet her soul mate, so she'd naturally assumed he was the one.

Big mistake.

She hadn't believed it was the end, even after that final argument on the last night of term, when he'd told her he and the other three Mortal Ruin band members had decided to gamble their futures on a recording contract and he'd asked her to go with him, rather than head home for the holidays as she'd intended. She hadn't explained why she absolutely *had* to go home either, though she might have done if she hadn't been so angry – or if he had been capable of talking about anything other than Mortal Ruin by that point.

If only she'd known she wouldn't be going back for the next term . . . If only they hadn't had that final, bitter argument, so she never even gave him her home address . . . There was a whole series of ifs, but they probably wouldn't have made any difference in the end, because he turned out to be *so* not the man she'd thought he was.

A hollow angel: dark and handsome on the outside, an emotional void within. A Lucifer echoing with false promises.

Of course, she hadn't known that then. Looking after Jake, her baby half-brother, while waiting for her mother to come back from her latest fling, she'd had plenty of time to worry about what would happen when Raffy finally got her letter. She'd sent it via her former roommate, Rachel, to hand to him when he came to his senses and went back to look for her. Because, despite their last argument, she'd been quite sure of his love and that somehow they would find a way of being together, of working things out. He'd told her he loved her often enough . . .

Even in her darkest moments she'd believed that, right up to the day she received the note from Rachel, telling her that Raffy had returned briefly at the start of the new term and she had given him the letter, but after reading it he'd simply crumpled it up and shoved it in his pocket without comment.

She hadn't needed the tear-stained confession on the next page to know how easily and quickly he had replaced her, or how little she meant to him. Out of sight, out of mind.

It was not so easy for her to forget him, when his music seemed to be out there everywhere, assailing her at unexpected moments, but eventually her searing anger had cauterised the wounds and given her a certain measure of immunity.

So why now was she sitting at the kitchen table weeping hot, scalding tears?

Saltwater and chocolate are *never* a good combination.

Chapter One

There Must Be an Angel

You know those routines most people have, the ones they fall into automatically when they wake up? Well, until a few years ago, my morning rota had 'read Tarot cards' neatly sandwiched between 'brush teeth' and 'breakfast'.

It was just the way I was brought up, and nothing to do with magic – or not the sort my grandfather practises, where the effects of his rites are so hit-and-miss that most positive results are probably sheer coincidence, like the way the sales of my Chocolate Wishes went stratospheric right after he gave me part of an ancient Mayan charm to say over the melting pot. Fluke . . . I thought. I have to confess that I've never been entirely sure.

But really, apart from the novelty value of the concept, my success was probably more the result of my having finally perfected both my technique and the quality of my moulded chocolate, mostly by trial, error and experimentation – and the really good thing about working with chocolate is that you can eat your mistakes.

What originally sparked the whole thing off was coming

across a two-part metal Easter egg mould at a jumble sale when my half-brother, Jake, was a small boy. I made lots of little chocolate eggs and put messages inside them from the Easter Bunny, then hid them all over the flat and court-yard for him and his friends to find.

And while I was making them I started thinking about fortune cookies, which are fun, but not really that good to eat. And from there it was just a short bunny hop to creating a line of hollow chocolate shapes containing 'Wishes' as an after-dinner novelty and selling them in boxes of six or twelve.

The 'Wishes' are encouraging thoughts or suggestions, inspired by the Angel card readings that have replaced my earlier devotion to the Tarot, and I'm positive that each person will automatically pick the appropriate Chocolate Wish from the box – their own guardian angel will see to that!

It was all very amateur at first, but now the Wishes come in printed sheets and the boxes are also specially made to hold and protect the chocolates in transit, because most of my orders come through the internet, via my website, or by word of mouth.

Nowadays I favour mainly criollo couverture chocolate, the best and most expensive kind, which not only tastes delicious but has a superior gloss and good 'snap'. I temper it in the machine Jake christened the Bath and then, with an outsize pastry brush, coat specially made polycarbon moulds in the shape of angels or winged hearts until I have a thick enough shell. When they're cold, I 'glue' the two halves together with a little more chocolate – but before I do that, I put in the 'Wish'.

And I am so much happier since I began to read the Angel cards instead of the Tarot! They never seemed to come out right when I read them for myself and I often wonder if my future would have been different if I hadn't always looked for signs and portents before I did anything. Do we make our own futures, or do our futures make us?

Granny, who was of gypsy descent and taught me how to read the cards in the first place, said they only showed what *might* be the future, should the present course be held to; but I'm not so sure. She would have approved of the Angel cards, though, which is more than my grandfather (whom Jake and I call Grumps, for obvious reasons) and Zillah, who is Granny's cousin, do.

But I truly believe in angels and have done from being a small child when Granny, who despite her Tarot reading was deeply religious, assured me that the winged figure I glimpsed one night really *was* a celestial visitor, rather than a figment of my imagination. (And my friend Poppy saw it too, I do have a witness!)

Why an angel should appear to an unbaptised and ungodly child of sin is anyone's guess, unless it was my own personal guardian angel making an early appearance in my life, to counter Grumps' influence and set my feet on the right path. But if so, she hasn't visited me since in that form, though sometimes I can hear the soft susurration of wings and feel a comforting presence that is almost, but not quite, visible. And the Angel cards . . . maybe she guided me to those too?

Granny died when I was twelve, but she too did her best to counter Grumps' influence, flatly forbidding any kind of baptismal ceremony involving his coven, or involvement in its rites until I had reached the age where I could make a considered decision for myself – a resounding 'No way!' She had already done the same for my mother, though unfortunately without instilling in her any alternative moral code.

That February morning, when I shuffled the pack of silky smooth Angel cards and laid them out on the kitchen table, they predicted change, but at least they also assured me that everything would work out all right in the end, which was a great improvement on coming face to face with the Hanging Man or Death over the breakfast cereal and trying to interpret the reading as something a little less doom-laden than the initial impression.

Rituals completed, I went to wake Jake up, which took quite some effort since, at eighteen, he could sleep for Britain. I made sure he ate something before he set off for sixth form college, dressed all in black, from dyed hair to big, metal-studded boots, a cheery sight for his teachers on a Monday morning.

When he'd gone – with a cheeky 'Goodbye, Mum!' just to wind me up – I checked my emails for incoming Chocolate Wishes orders and printed them out, before going through to the main part of the house to see what Grumps was up to. Our flat was over the garages, so the door led onto the upper landing, and was rarely shut, unless Jake was playing loud music.

In the kitchen Zillah was sitting at the table over the remnants of her breakfast, drinking loose-leaf Yorkshire tea and smoking a thin, lumpy, roll-up cigarette. As usual, she was dressed in a bunchy skirt, two layers of cardigans with the bottom one worn back to front, a huge flowered pinny over the whole ensemble and her hair tied up in a clashing scarf, turban-fashion. Grumps says she was bitten by Carmen Miranda in her youth and after I Googled the name, I suspect he is right. Today's dangly red earrings made her look as if she had hooked a pair of cherries over each ear, so the fruit motif was definitely there.

She looked up – small, dark, with skin not so much wrinkled as folded around her black, bird-bright eyes – and smiled, revealing several glinting gold teeth. 'Read your tea leaves?' she offered hospitably.

'No, thanks, Zillah, not just now. I'm running late, it took me ages to get Jake up and on his way. But I've brought you another jar of my chocolate and ginger spread, because yesterday you said you'd almost run out.'

'Extra sweet?'

'Extra sweet,' I agreed, putting the jar down on the table.

It's really just a ganache of grated cacao and boiled double cream, with a little finely chopped preserved ginger added for zing. It doesn't keep long, though the way Zillah lards it onto her toast means it doesn't have to.

Zillah turned up on the doorstep the day after Granny died. She'd read the news in the cards and come to burn her cousin's caravan – metaphorically speaking, anyway, because she'd had to make do with burning Granny's clothes and personal possessions on the garden bonfire instead.

Grumps seemed unsurprised by Zillah's sudden appearance, as if he'd been expecting her, which maybe he had, and his purported magical skills aren't a *complete* figment of his imagination. She'd never given any suggestion of remaining with us permanently, yet here she still was several years later, cooking, cleaning and caring for us, in her slapdash way.

She handed me the fresh cup of tea she'd just poured out, put two Jammie Dodger biscuits on the saucer and said, 'Take this in to the Wizard of Oz then, will you, love?'

'Grumps is up to something, isn't he?' I asked, accepting

the cup, because although he is taciturn and secretive at the best of times, I could still tell. I only hoped he wasn't about to try some great summoning ceremony with his coven, because on past form all they were likely to call up was double pneumonia.

Zillah tapped the side of her nose with the fingers holding her cigarette and a thin snake of ash fell into her empty cup. I hoped it wouldn't muddle her future.

In the study Grumps was indeed sitting at his desk over a grimoire open at a particularly juicy spell, which he was probably considering trying out when the weather improved. (The coven practised their rites in an oak grove, skyclad, and none of them was getting any younger.)

His long, silver hair was parted in the middle and a circlet held it off a face notable for a pair of piercing grey eyes and a hawk-like nose. His midnight-blue velvet robe was rubbed on the elbows, so that he bore more resemblance to a down-at-heel John Dee than a Gandalf, but it was a look that went down well with the readers of the beyond Dennis Wheatley novels he wrote as Gregory Warlock. Sales had been in the doldrums for many years, apart from a small band of devotees, but they were suddenly having a renewed vogue and his entire backlist was about to be reprinted in their original, very lurid covers.

Grumps is one of those annoying people who need very little sleep, so that by the time I pop in to see him in the mornings, he usually has achieved quite a heap of hand-written manuscript. There are often lots of letters too, because he corresponds with equally nutty people all over the globe, and since his handwriting is appalling I take everything away and type it up on my computer.

When I was younger there was a time when I thought

10

Grumps was a complete charlatan. You can imagine what it was like growing up in a small town like Merchester, with a relative who both looked and proclaimed himself with every utterance to be totally, barking mad. For example, his eccentric clothing, the ghastly novels and his definitive book on the magical significance of ley lines. (Leys are straight lines that link landmarks and sites of historical and magical importance.) Add to all that the rumours of secret and risqué rites in remote woodland, and you will begin to see my point.

Yet as I grew older I came to realise that he believed completely in what and who he was and then it ceased to bother me any more: if he wasn't embarrassed by it, then neither was I.

Now I picked my way towards the desk through a sea of unfurled maps that covered the carpet, each crisscrossed with red and blue lines showing both established and possible new ley lines. The crackling noise as I inadvertently trod on one drew Grumps' attention to my presence.

'Ah, Chloe – I believe I have found the solution to my financial problems,' he announced in his plummy, public-school-educated voice, looking distinctly pleased with himself. He is distantly related to lots of terribly grand people, none of whom has spoken to him since he chose his bride from a fortune-telling booth at the end of a Lancashire pier, at a time when one simply didn't *do* that kind of thing.

'Oh, good,' I said encouragingly, putting his tea down on the one empty spot among the clutter on his desk.

'Yes, it came to me and I acted upon it, once the clouds of confusion sent by Another to conceal it from my knowledge were suddenly dispelled.'

Grumps has a private income, but he'd settled Mum's huge debts six years before, after her last, permanent, vanishing trick. Besides, his investments weren't paying out in the way they used to and even the recent four-book contract his agent had secured wouldn't be enough to cover the bills and still enable him to purchase rare books and artefacts in the manner he seemed to think was his birthright. Even now his desk was littered with auction catalogues sporting bright Post-it notes marking things that interested him.

'Great,' I said cautiously, because Grumps' good ideas, like his spells, have a marked tendency to backfire or fizzle to nothing. 'Did Zillah read the cards for you and spot something nice?'

'She did, and foresaw change.'

'She always does. You'd think we lived in a sort of psychic whirlpool.'

'Well, change there certainly *will* be, because I am selling the house and we are moving to Sticklepond.'

I'd started gathering up the loose sheets of paper inscribed in a sloping hand, which were the latest chapter of *Satan's Child*. Now I stopped and stared at him. 'We're moving? But how can that help?' Then the penny dropped. 'Oh, I *see*. You mean you and Zillah are downsizing to a small cottage? That's a good idea, because now that sales of Chocolate Wishes have taken off in a big way through the internet, I can easily afford to make a home for Jake on my own.'

'No, no,' he said impatiently, 'I am not downsizing – the opposite, in fact – and there will be room for us all. An estate agent recently approached me with an advantageous offer for this house from someone who has taken a fancy to it, just at the very moment when I happened upon an advertisement for the Old Smithy in Sticklepond, which a friend had sent me, and which had somehow got mixed up among some other papers. It became apparent to me that this was a *sign*, and I therefore moved quickly.'

He pushed the grimoire aside and handed me a leaflet that had been underneath. It pictured a low, barn-like building, set longways onto the road, with a small ancient cottage at one side and a larger Victorian house at the other, like mismatched bookends.

'It's Miss Frinton's Doll Museum!' I said, recognising it instantly, because it's not only just up the road from Marked Pages, the second-hand bookshop run by my friend Felix, but almost opposite the pub where I meet up with him and Poppy two or three times a week.

'It *was*, though of course not for some time – it has lain empty. I knew it was for sale prior to this, of course, I just hadn't realised its significance.' He indicated the larger house with a bony finger adorned with a substantial and oddly designed silver ring. 'This is the main residence, where the Misses Frinton lived. There would be abundant room for my library and for Zillah to have her own sitting room, as she has here. The front room of the small cottage at the other end of the building was the doll's hospital – and I thought it would be ideal for your chocolate business, with enough room for you and Jake to live behind it, although it needs a little updating.'

'When estate agents say that, it usually means it's semi-derelict.' I wished there were photographs of the interior of the cottage as well as the house in the leaflet.

'Not derelict, just neglected. It used to be rented out, so there is a kitchen extension with a bathroom over it and two bedrooms. It is larger than your current accommodation.'

'It could hardly be smaller,' I said, though of course without Mum we had more space, especially since I'd packed up all her belongings and stacked the boxes in Grumps' attic on the first anniversary of her disappearance. But since Chocolate Wishes had taken off, I really needed a separate workshop.

'The cottage also has a walled garden behind it,' he added slyly, because he knew I longed for a garden of my own. Here we just had a gravelled courtyard and although I did grow lots of things in tubs and pots and in my tiny greenhouse, including herbs both for cooking and for Grumps' rites, salad vegetables, strawberries and a small fig tree, there were limitations ... especially for my cherished and constantly growing collection of scented geraniums, currently over-wintering on every available windowledge in the flat.

I was sold.

'The cottage is linked to the main house via the Smithy Barn, the former doll museum, and my intention is to open a museum of my own there,' Grumps explained, 'one dedicated to the study of witchcraft and paganism. I will be able to display my collection and increase my income, thus killing two birds with one stone.'

'Well, goodness knows, you have enough artefacts to stock *ten* museums, Grumps!' I exclaimed. 'But you surely wouldn't run it yourself? I can't see you selling tickets to a stream of visitors!'

'I fail to see why not,' he said testily. 'I will open only in the afternoons, from two till four, and can have my desk in one corner and let visitors roam freely, while I get on with my work. Zillah has said she will also take a hand.'

'But if you don't keep an eye on the visitors, half your collection will vanish!'

'Oh, I think not: I will put up placards pointing out that any thieves will be cursed. In fact, I might have it printed on the back of the tickets.'

'That should go down well,' I said drily.

'It will serve: they will ignore the warning at their peril. I shall have signed copies of my books for sale too, of course, both fiction and non-fiction.'

After my first surprise, the idea began to grow on me. 'Do you know, I think you might be right and it would be quite a money-spinner, because since that Shakespeare connection was discovered at Winter's End, hordes of tourists come to Sticklepond. At least one café and a couple of gift shops have opened in the village lately, and passing trade at Felix's bookshop is much better. There's a strong witchcraft history in the area too.'

'Precisely! And besides,' he added as a clincher, 'the Old Smithy is on the junction of two important ley lines; *that* was what was so cunningly obscured from my vision by the malevolence of Another. There may even be a third – I am working on it.'

'I expect the conjunction of the ley lines was a major selling point the estate agents managed to miss,' I said, ignoring the second mention of a mysterious and malevolent opponent, which was probably just a figment of his imagination.

He gave me a severe look over the top of his half-moon glasses. 'Its unique position imbues it with magical energy, my dear Chloe, and since the museum area is large, my coven may meet there with no diminution of power. Rheumatism has affected one or two of them,' he added more prosaically, 'and they have suggested we move to an indoor venue.'

'Yes, I can see that the museum would be ideal, provided you put up good, thick curtains,' I agreed absently, still turning over the whole idea of the move in my mind. 'What about Jake, though? He has to be able to get to sixth form college and he isn't going to want to move away from his friends, is he?'

Though now I came to think of it, a fresh start in a new village might be a good idea for my horribly lively brother. He's outgrown his childish pranks, but will still forever be 'that imp of Satan' to those inhabitants of Merchester who've been his victims.

'Jake may borrow my car and drive himself to school until he has taken his final examinations, and then of course he will be off to university,' Grumps said. 'He likes the old Saab for some reason. In the holidays, he can help me in the museum and I will pay him.'

Grumps seemed to have it all thought out.

I looked down again at the leaflet. A cottage of my own with a garden, separated from my grandfather by the width of a museum, and with room for my Chocolate Wishes business, sounded like bliss . . .

'So, have you actually seen the property and made an offer for it, Grumps?'

'Yes, of course – and the people who want to buy this house have also been to view it, though you were out at the time. I thought I would wait until everything was signed and sealed before I told you.'

'I certainly didn't see this coming!'

16

'If you *will* read Angel cards instead of the Tarot . . . Angel cards – pah!'

'They seem to work for me, Grumps.'

'Not, apparently, very well: Zillah saw the changes coming and she has already decided on her rooms in the new house.'

If Zillah knew and approved, then really, there was no more to be said: it looked like the Lyons were on the move.

A thought struck me. 'When Mum finally decides to stop playing dead and comes back, how will she find us?'

'Like a bad penny,' he said bleakly.

Chapter Two

Satan's Child

On the way back to the flat, with a lot to think about and a chapter of *Satan's Child* and three letters to type up, I found Zillah still in the kitchen stirring something savoury-smelling in a large pot. The cat, Tabitha, was draped around her neck like a black fur wrap, her tail practically in the stew.

Hygiene was possibly not Zillah's strong point but neither she nor Grumps (nor even Tabitha) ever seemed to suffer ill effects. Nor did Jake and I, come to that, because although I did some of our own cooking in the flat, we shared quite a lot of meals. We must all have been immune.

'Zillah, if you have time, maybe you had better read my cards,' I suggested. 'Grumps just told me that we're on the move.'

Zillah silently turned down the heat and put a lid on the pot, then fetched her Tarot pack and handed the cards to me to shuffle. Under my fingers they felt cool, snakily smooth and almost alive.

'You could read them yourself,' she grumbled as I gave them back, but she began to lay them out in a familiar pattern on the table. The cat, bored, disentwined herself and stalked off, holding up a tail like a bottlebrush that has seen better days.

'You know I've given up reading them, especially for myself, because there never seemed to be good news. I simply don't think I could bear it if I saw yet another dark stranger scheduled to enter my life bringing change, because it never turns out well,' I added gloomily.

It would have been really useful if the cards had ever given me some helpful hints about whether the changes would be good or bad too, especially regarding my ex-fiancé, David.

'It's all in the reading and how you interpret it, Chloe, you know that,' Zillah said. 'You don't have to make a self-fulfilling prophecy.'

While I puzzled over that one, she looked at the cards that showed what was currently going on in my life.

'Hmm . . . no surprises there, *or* in what will happen if you continue on your current course.' She turned over more cards and pondered.

'But my course *is* about to be changed, isn't it? Not only are we moving, but Jake will be off to university later this year.'

I'd had the maternal role for my half-brother thrust upon me and I'd done my best, torn between love and resentment, but although I adore Jake, I couldn't say I wasn't relishing the idea of being my own woman again.

That my own childhood had been a happy and secure one was entirely due to Granny but, though kindly and affectionate, Zillah seemed to have been born without a maternal gene

19

and could not take her place. That hadn't stopped Mum from thinking Zillah could quite easily assume Granny's role as mother substitute when she was off with her latest lover, though – but then, *she* didn't have the maternal gene either.

At least Zillah loved us in her own unique way, even if, like Grumps, she didn't find children terribly interesting until they were capable of holding a conversation.

'It doesn't say anything about Mum turning up again, does it?' I asked, following this train of thought. 'Only it would be just like her to walk back in, now there aren't any responsibilities for her to shoulder, what with Grumps having paid her bills and Jake an adult.'

My mother had spent less and less time at the flat until she had finally vanished altogether from a Caribbean cruise six years previously and was currently presumed by everyone except the family to be dead. *We* presumed her to be fornicating in sunnier climes, even if this time her absence had been inordinately prolonged. Her disappearance had coincided with David jilting me, too: cause and effect.

Zillah ignored me, turning over the cards showing what was happening with my relationships, which was not a lot apart from a platonic and fraternal one with my old friend Felix Hemmings, the bookseller of Sticklepond.

Through the thin spiral of smoke from her latest cigarette I automatically began to read the meanings upside down, and groaned. 'Oh, no, *please* don't tell me another man really *is* coming into my life? I can't bear it!'

'Maybe more than one person,' she said, frowning. 'Perhaps there's unfinished business with someone you knew before?'

'No way! Now I've realised I'm stuck in some endless

Groundhog Day cycle of love and rejection, I'm not even going to *look* at another man.'

'You can't call two failed relationships an endless cycle, Chloe.'

'Two? Have you forgotten Cal, or Simon or—' I stopped, unable to remember the faces, let alone the names, of some of my more fleeting boyfriends.

'I did not mention *men*, but in any case they were obviously unmemorable. And can we help ourselves if love strikes?' She thoughtfully fingered the card depicting a tower struck by lightning.

'We can if it strikes twice,' I snapped. 'But even if I'd been tempted to take any boyfriend seriously after David jilted me, they weren't prepared to take on Jake too. He's the ultimate love deterrent.'

I shuddered, recalling some of the hideous pranks my inventive half-brother had got up to over the years in order to get rid of my boyfriends. I was sure Grumps had had a hand in some of the more fiendish tricks.

'He *was*, but he's now an adult, and once he's at university he'll have other things to think about.'

'So he will . . . and it seems like only five minutes since *I* went off to university, too,' I said with a sad sigh, for that had been my one, abortive bid for independence, the year after Jake was born. It had been all too easy for Mum to absent herself for longer and longer periods, leaving me literally holding the baby, but I'd thought if she didn't have me to fall back on, then she would be forced to stay at home and behave like other mothers.

How wrong I was! I got back at the end of the first term to find she had dumped the baby in Zillah's unwilling hands, leaving me a scribbled note with no idea of when she would return. Jake was touchingly happy to see me, making me guilty that I had been so engrossed in my love affair with Raffy that I had hardly thought of him for weeks. Grumps and Zillah were also happy to have me back, in their way, but *I* was the one who could have done with a mother's tender care just then, rather than have to take on the role myself.

But surprisingly, in the end, Zillah proved to be a tower of strength when I most needed one . . .

I looked at the spread of cards again and asked hopefully, '*Can* the future be altered, Zillah?'

'People can change, and then the future also changes. Or perhaps the true future remains fixed, the other is merely a warning to put us on the right path to our fate.' Her gnarled hand reached out and flipped over the final cards. 'Your future has interesting possibilities.'

'What, you mean interesting in the Chinese curse sort of way?'

'Well, what are the angels telling you?' she asked acerbically.

'That change is coming, but it will all turn out right in the end.'

'Whatever "right" means, Chloe.' She swept the cards together, tapped them briskly three times and wrapped them up in a piece of dark silk.

Back in the flat I felt unsettled, which was hardly surprising when a positive Pandora's Box of painful recollections kept escaping from where I thought I'd had them safely locked away. Memories not only of my first love, Raffy, which even after so many years evoked feelings of loss and betrayal far too painful to dwell on again, but also of my ex-fiancé, David.

We met in Merchester's one upmarket wine bar and he

had seemed so different from any of my other, short-lived boyfriends. He was several years older, for a start, solid and dependable. Maybe I was looking for a father figure, having never had one? He was a partner in a firm of architects, so more than comfortably off, and even Jake's attempts to get rid of him (culminating in the plague of glowing green mice in David's flat – I have *no* idea how he worked that one) just made him go all quiet and forbearing. He said Jake would grow out of it – which he had, only not until David's presence in our lives was history.

And Jake *had* been the sticking point in the end. It was odd how I had remained completely blind to the fact that David was so jealous of my close relationship with my half-brother until that last day, only a couple of weeks before our wedding. I'd also assumed he understood that whenever my mother was away, Jake would stay with us after we were married, for the first few years at least. But as Zillah often says, men don't understand anything unless it is spelled out for them in very plain language.

'Jake could live with your grandfather and his house-keeper,' David had suggested when Jake was twelve and my mother had performed her latest vanishing trick.

I let the 'housekeeper' bit go, since although Zillah certainly wasn't that, her role in our lives defied definition. 'Hardly, David! Social Services aren't going to take kindly to a twelve-year-old living with a warlock, are they?'

'Now, Chloe, don't exaggerate, when you know that's just a *nom de plume* he adopts for his books. He may be a little eccentric, but the whole persona . . .' He smiled indulgently, his teeth very white against his tanned, handsome face. 'It's a publicity thing, isn't it?'

'No, it's how he *is*. I keep telling you.'

'You'll be saying your mother is a witch next, Chloe, and has simply flown off on her broomstick.'

'Oh, no, she never showed any inclinations that way and although Jake *is* interested in witchcraft, luckily it's only from a historical point of view. It's just a pity Granny isn't still around to help me bring him up, but he isn't a bad boy really, just lively.'

David shuddered.

'What? You *like* him, you said so!'

'Yes, of course I do, but that doesn't mean I want to live with him. And there's no reason why you should have to sacrifice your entire life to bringing up your half-brother, is there? Fostering might be the making of him.'

'*Fostering?* I can't believe you would even suggest that!' I stared at him with new eyes. 'Anyway, it's going to be only for a few weeks at most, until Mum comes back. The longest she's ever been away is three months.'

David's expression softened and he came and put his arms around me. 'Darling, you have to accept that she isn't coming back this time – she's dead. I know it's hard, but look at the facts.'

The facts, as Mum's friend Mags had reported them, were that Mum had simply vanished into thin air one night from the cruise ship taking them between Caribbean islands (a holiday won by Mags, who was ace at making up advertising slogans).

'Mags was lying and she isn't dead,' I explained. 'She's probably somewhere in Jamaica with a man, and when she gets tired of that, she'll come back again. She has a very low boredom threshold.'

'Look, darling, she was seen on the ship the evening after it left Jamaica, wasn't she?'

'Someone wearing one of her more flamboyant dresses and with dark hair was seen, but I suspect it was Mags.'

'But your mother's friend is blonde – and why on earth should she go to so much trouble anyway?'

'A wig? My mother often wore one when her hair looked ratty. And they were in the habit of covering up for each other.'

'Come on, Chloe! Look, it's been several weeks now, and I think, however hard it is, you'll have to accept that she had too much to drink – which you know was one of her failings – and went over the side in the small hours without anyone noticing. This time she *isn't* going to reappear as if nothing has happened. Which brings us back to what to do about Jake.'

'Nothing, because you're wrong. I expect she'll be back in time for our wedding, but if she isn't, then Jake can come and live with us, can't he? I mean, you always realised he would have to do that whenever Mum was away, didn't you?'

David was slow to answer, probably imagining the chaos one very lively boy could cause to his immaculately ordered life and minimalist white flat. I had already unintentionally caused enough of that while cooking chicken with a dark cacao *mole* sauce in his kitchen: chocolate *does* seem to get everywhere . . . And evidently he hadn't understood the strength of the bond between Jake and me.

'I'd like it to be just the two of us, for a while at least, darling,' he said eventually. 'You have to accept she's not coming back and that other, permanent arrangements need to be made. I mean, your grandfather's got a private income, hasn't he? He could send Jake to boarding school.'

'I don't think his private income would stretch that far

and anyway, Jake would hate it. He's always seen *me* as more of a mother figure than Mum. I'm the security in his life, and so it would simply be another betrayal. And his friends are all here in Merchester.'

'Then he'd hate being transposed to a city flat, wouldn't he?' David said quickly.

'Yes, but we did say we'd find a house in the country, one you could commute from. That could be somewhere round here, couldn't it?'

'I meant *much* later, when we want a family. I'd like to have you to myself for a bit. Anyway,' he added with a wry smile on his handsome face, 'I'm starting to think I'm allergic to the country because I come out in this damned rash every time I visit Merchester.'

'You can't really call Merchester country,' I objected, but it was true about the mysterious rash, because even now an angry redness was creeping up from the collar of his shirt.

I reminded myself to speak to Grumps about that . . . He and David had not really taken to each other, mainly because David spoke to him like an adult humouring a child: *big* mistake. He tended to take that tone with Jake too, and according to most of the locals, he'd never been any kind of child at all, but an imp of Satan.

'Look, Chloe, I really can't live with your brother. It isn't fair to ask me.' He ran his fingers through his ordered dark chestnut locks in a distracted way that showed me just how perturbed he was. He even loosened his silk tie – good grief!

'You'll have to find some other solution,' he announced with finality.

'I keep telling you Mum isn't dead!' I snapped, losing

patience. 'She bolts all the time, but she'll be back eventually: I've read the cards and I know I'm right. What's more, so has Zillah.'

But although they had told us that Mum was alive, they couldn't, of course, show us where she was or how long she would be gone.

'It's Jake or me,' he said quietly.

'But, David—'

'Do you love me?'

'Yes, of course,' I said, which I did, even if not with the searing passion of my first love. 'But—'

'Me, or Jake,' he repeated. 'I don't want to be hard-hearted, but it simply won't work having him to live with us – and I'm certainly not moving here, which I'm sure you were about to suggest next.'

'Well, yes, but it would be only until Mum comes back.'

He sighed long-sufferingly. 'Which she isn't going to do.'

He put on his jacket, which had been hanging neatly over the back of a chair in the chaotic kitchen area of the flat, where the paraphernalia of my budding Chocolate Wishes business covered every surface. In fact, there was a glossy smear of tempered couverture down one immaculate sleeve, which I decided not to point out.

'The wedding's in less than a fortnight, so you had better make your mind up fast, Chloe, hadn't you?'

'You can't really mean you'd end it all over this, David?'

'Yes, I do. Make other arrangements for Jake or you can call off the wedding.'

I still didn't really think he meant it and I might have tried to soften him up a little, but I was distracted at that moment by catching sight of the imp of Satan himself through the window. He seemed to be closing the bonnet

27

of David's car . . . But no, David was always careful to lock it, so how could Jake . . . ?

The door slammed behind David and he strode across the gravel and got into his sports car without, so far as I could see, a word or look at Jake, who was standing innocently by with his hands behind his back.

The engine roared into life and then coughed a bit, before the car sputtered off down the lane. It sounded pretty ropey; I'd be surprised if it got him home without breaking down.

It hadn't, either. He'd phoned me when he finally got back, incandescent with rage. 'That child did it – and that's the last straw, Chloe, I mean it. Make other arrangements for him, or this is the last you'll ever hear from me.'

So that was it, and though I was heartbroken, I was also relieved that I had discovered how jealous he was of my love for Jake before we got married. I'd already known he resented my closeness to my old friends Felix and Poppy, but thought he would get over that. Funny how you can be so blind, isn't it?

I called off the wedding, which was both expensive and difficult at that late stage, and, resigning myself to perpetual spinsterhood, settled back into my life as before.

Except that this time, Mum *didn't* come back. And the awful thing was, none of us missed her.